Th

the Prophet

By James Ward

Book four in the series: **Bob Steck's** *'adventures of a spymaster'*

This is a work of fiction, based on published historical media. Any resemblance to real characters or accounts is purely coincidental.

ISBN   0983959803

Printed in the United States of America

Scantum Press

www.scantumpress.com

This book is dedicated to the late **James B. Graves,** Southern gentleman and friend of the classics, professor, editor, and my mentor.

CHAPTER 1

Storm clouds gathered. First they streaked then covered the hazy South Carolina sunrise sky. Where two small creeks meet the Cooper River, several herons strutted nervously about the mud. High over-head gulls circled in the manner they always do when storms brew. On a nearby marsh bank a lone figure crouched, camera focused on the herons, contemplating how wildlife seems to perceive impending danger. The radio had blared its warning all night long. Hurricane Joseph would come ashore near Charleston today.

Just across the river from Charleston at Sullivan's Island, a man walked nervously, urgently along the shore. He was clearly not dressed for the terrain. Loafers on his feet slowed his progress along the bank of the river. As he passed a patch of tall grass and reeds, he suddenly crouched, as if reacting to some sound. Before he could turn, his assailant had him from behind. The man's eyes widened as gloved hands grabbed his chin and the back of his head. He swung his right arm back in a try at his attacker's groin, missing the mark just as his neck was deftly snapped. Falling on his back, rapidly losing consciousness, he tried to scream but nothing came out.

At the creeks a mile up the river, the muffled gurgle of a small boat's outboard engine broke the pre-storm silence. Four men in army fatigues sat upright waiting out the trip that had started hours before dawn. In the nose of the boat the leader, a lean and muscular man of about thirty, held a small weather radio to one ear and a cellular telephone to the other. After a moment, looking satisfied, he clicked off the phone and put the radio on the floor of the Zodiac. Turning his face toward the others, the first glow of daylight revealed his ruddy face, stern angular features and an ugly scar from mouth to earlobe. Steel blue eyes flashed confident resolve as he smiled, holding up his right hand in a "thumbs-up."

"Right on schedule," he told the others. "The storm will hit Charleston full force a little after nine a.m. The others are already in position. Everything's still condition green."

The herons flew, not able to handle both the pre-storm jitters and the noisy outboard motor. The lone figure on the bank crouched lower, taking cover in the tall grass. His telephoto lens caught a few more frames as the herons flew toward, then over the photographer.

At Sullivan's Island, a well-built middle-aged man with executive haircut, well trimmed salt-n-pepper beard and a golfer's tan finished his morning jog. Returning to his room at *The Gold Bug Bed 'n Breakfast*, he showered, dressed in fresh chinos, tennis shoes and golf shirt and went to breakfast. As he dug into grits, scrambled eggs and ham, his cell phone beeped. Fishing it out of his side pocket, he smiled, shrugged to the hostess and the other two guests, and excused himself. On the way out to the garden, he answered, "This is Roche." He listened intently while walking briskly toward a remote corner of the garden. The caller, a man named Blake, reported everything was going according to plan. Brandt and his men in the Zodiac were in position. Joe Battles and the others were in the warehouse.

"Fine, fine," Roche replied.

"I've got one hitch," he said in a low voice. "Where can I meet you to talk? ...Okay. Twenty minutes, at the bridge." No sense trusting that the cell frequency was clean, thought Roche as he returned to the breakfast room. Security must be job one.

"Would you be so kind, Missus Hildebrand, as to prepare my bill right away," Roche asked in his studied Southern drawl. "I've a long drive today, and I *must* get away from Charleston before the storm. Although," he added, wrapping a piece of his breakfast ham in a fresh hot biscuit and heading for the stairs to his room, "it sure is hard to pass up the rest of this fine breakfast."

"Why, Mister Roche," the innkeeper gushed, "I'm pleased that you find my cooking attractive." Missus Hildebrand, a widow of fifteen years, wished Mister Roche would find *her* attractive. Seeing the opportunity, Roche met her wistful eyes with a twinkle of his own.

"I find more than your cooking attractive ma'am. Maybe next time I'm in town we could..." His voice trailed off as he turned down the short corridor at the top of the stairs. Stuffing his things into his duffel, Roche cursed himself for leading her on. It would be better if he remained as anonymous as possible. It would be better if no one on Sullivan's Island remembered him.

At six forty-eight am, just as Roche drove onto State highway 703 heading out towards US Route 17 and the Cooper River bridge, a woman walking her dog at the Sullivan's Island waterfront discovered the "hitch" Roche had mentioned on the phone. Running to the Inn, she burst through the front door screaming. "There's a dead man on the shore!"

The Mount Pleasant police were notified, the dispatcher alerted, and car 3 diverted from breakfast at *Mary Sue's Donut Heaven*. Roche was turning south onto US 17 as the cruiser, lights flashing, sped by him. Roche drove south to a small turnout just before the road rose to form an entry to the Cooper River Bridge. A moment later, a Ford pickup carrying a camper body pulled in behind Roche's Buick. A lanky fifty-odd year old man in survivor boots, painter's pants and denim shirt left the truck and ambled up to Roche's open driver side window. Blake had to bend his tall frame a bit awkwardly to bring his weather beaten face to look Roche in the eye. "What hitch?" he asked pointedly.

"This guy I remembered from years back, at Langley."

"What guy?" Blake's deep-set eyes flashed warning.

"Just a guy I knew," drawled Roche. "He was an FBI special agent type. I remembered him from his work with one of the domestic teams at the Agency."

"What about him?"

"The S.O.B. was tailing me. He sat in his car all night just up the street from where I was staying. I noticed he was still there as I went out to jog. At the shore, I waited behind some rushes. When he came past me, I put him down. No weapons, no traces. I think the police already found his body."

Warning turned briefly to panic in Blake's eyes. "Why was he tailing you?"

"That's the hitch, man! You know I do a clean job of taking care of trouble. No worry that the police may find clues to operate on. But whoever sent him either knows or suspects something."

"So, what do you suggest we do, partner, abort?"

"No way!" said Roche emphatically. "We go on as planned. Just alert everyone to keep a close eye out for possible FBI surveillance."

Blake's eyes narrowed. "Don't blow this on me, Paul. If this operation screws up, I stand to lose a lot of money. You know I don't get mad but I do get even. Don't set yourself up as one I need to get even with!"

At seven-fifteen am the program on Roche's car radio was interrupted for a special report. The storm was going to hit downtown close to ten am, and high tide would be at ten-twenty am. The storm surge would flood much of Charleston, and some areas along the waterfront were already beginning to flood. Police and National Guard units were in place around the city. Anyone in the water front area who had not yet left was to evacuate immediately.

The radio announcer repeated her message as Roche pulled his Buick off the Charleston waterfront exit ramp from route US 17, doubled back under the bridge, and stopped just outside the loading door of a small warehouse. It was one of those old brick buildings common to the area. No windows, just the suggestion of former windows now filled with newer brick. The sign near the door in Navy blue-gray with black-stenciled lettering said "U.S. Government Property. No admittance to unauthorized personnel."

Roche pulled in beside Blake's truck, which was backed in to the loading dock. The warehouse guard, a forty-ish sailor with a big potbelly stood on the dock watching a crate being loaded into Blake's truck. He was sweating nervously. As Roche approached, he spun to challenge, then excused the move. "Oh, hi Mister Roche," he said. "Can we talk?"

The guard looked as if he was about to cry. Roche put on his most relaxed drawl and put his arm around the guard's sweaty neck and shoulder. "Sure, Battles. Let's go into your office and have a chat. This thing's going real well, thanks to you." After a few minutes of soothing conversation, Battles seemed more relaxed.

"I'm sorry I was getting rattled, Mister Roche. It's just that I'm the only one who'll be left behind after this is over."

"But that's the beauty of it, Ray. You get to be the hero that chased us out of here. You get to keep your job and retirement. You also get your share from us, deposited in that Cayman Island bank, which will *double* your retirement. Just hang in there a few more minutes and we're all a lot richer." Roche knew that he couldn't leave loose-cannons like Battles behind, but it wasn't yet time to deal with that issue.

The two men loading small wooden crates into Blake's truck finished their work. Battles paid them off, peeling out a hundred in cash for each of them, reminding them that they "were never here." From the looks of those guys, they would have it all spent in some bar or crack house by nightfall. As the men left, Roche called a quick conference.

"Where's Brandt and the others?" he asked.

"They were here about twenty minutes ago," offered Battles. "Brandt went with the men to be sure of their positions. The Zodiac is at the rear of the warehouse. Brandt should be back here any minute."

"Good," said Roche. "Blake, you get the cargo covered and pack the other stuff around it. I'll prepare Battles for effect like we planned."

It was now eight thirty-five am. The storm surge had pushed water up to the street in front of the warehouse, washing three inches deep along the curb. The wind was beginning to howl out of the darkening sky. Small branches fell in shallow water along the near-empty shorefront.

"Hey Blake, what's up?" Blake looked up from packing old furniture and blankets around the cargo and nodded without speaking. Brandt's steel blue eyes narrowed. His thin smile made his scarred face seem distorted. "My guys are all in place at the key points. Looks like the storm is right on schedule. This plan's coming together quite nicely, don't you think?"

"I dunno, grumbled Blake. Roche had to drop some snooper across the river, and the cops are prob'ly looking for him. I'll be glad when we're outta here."

"Piece o' cake," grinned Brandt, patting his M-16. "My team has the skids all greased up for you to slide right through."

Stepping lively through the water that now licked at the door stoop of the warehouse, Brandt hopped onto the loading dock and strode inside towards Ray Battles' security desk. Roche stood over Battles' slumped torso. Battles lay face down, blood trickling from a small gash in his skull. "Wow, you really made it look convincing, Roche. Is he out cold?"

"Sleeping like a baby," Roche replied. Are your men in place?"

"All set. This is gonna be easy."

Quickly the warehouse doors were secured. Blake started his truck and rolled slowly up the empty street towards the first police check-point, followed by Roche in the Buick. The check-point was manned by two Charleston police officers and two National Guard soldiers. Blake stopped on the signal of an officer. As Blake rolled his window down, she barked. "Where are you going, sir. The local streets are all closed."

"We heard the evacuation order, ma'am. My brother and I are movin' to higher ground." He gestured towards Roche in the car behind him. Roche smiled and nodded to the officer.

"What have you got in the back?" she asked, noting the way the truck sat a little heavy on its rear wheels. "We're supposed to patrol for looters."

"Just some furniture and stuff, all the food we could load, some family papers and photos." Blake tried to manage a smile, while fondling the Berretta in his side pocket.

"These guys are all right, sir," interrupted one of the soldiers. I saw them loading up at those condos over yonder when I got here."

"Okay," snapped the officer. "You better get up to the Interstate and out of Charleston right away. She handed Blake a card with a toll-free number printed on it. Call us after the storm has passed, we'll let you know when you can come home."

The soldiers flanked the truck, motioning Blake to move out. They waved Roche along behind him. As he drove off, Blake grinned. It was smart of him to put Brandt's guys at the check-points, he admitted.

When the full fury of Joseph hit Charleston ripping down trees, lifting roofs and shredding banners and awnings downtown, Blake and Roche were eighteen miles out of town on I-26. Brandt and his crew re-boarded their Zodiac at the height of the storm and pounded their way across the river to the north side, then up river until they came to an old pier.

After lashing the Zodiac to some pilings, they waded ashore and found shelter in a little draw behind some wildly waving brush to wait out the hurricane.

CHAPTER 2

It was eight o'clock pm in Dushanbe, Tajikistan. Darkness descended on this oriental city like a cloak. Soviet era electric lighting projects had once lit most of the city center, but now the poor economy forced an imposed darkness over a third of the downtown each night. The Al Kafajy trading company of Dubai, United Arab Emirates had located its Dushanbe offices in one of the overlapping areas at the very center of the city, so they always had electricity. It was the most expensive address in the city. Despite the hour, Chris Taylor sat at his desk studying a map of South Carolina. Noting the time, Chris squashed a half-smoked Turkish cigarette in his ashtray, punched a series of numbers onto his satellite PCS phone, and leaned back in his chair, feet on the desk. After a moment, a voice answered.

"This is Roche."

"Taylor here, where are you?"

"I'm in Orangeburg. We left Charleston right on time with the goods secure on board the truck." Roche sounded proud and calm. He was looking for praise.

"How close are you to the barn?" Taylor was all business.

"We'll be there in twenty minutes. Are you sure the meeting is arranged?"

"Don't worry, Roche, you're all set. My man will be there. Goodbye." Taylor clicked off. Picking at his cigarette pack for a fresh smoke, Taylor walked briskly down a small corridor and into the large, well appointed office of his boss, Mohammed Al Kafajy. Chris used this office frequently, since the boss rarely came to Dushanbe. After all, Tajikistan wasn't exactly main-street in the trading business. He sat down at his superior's PC (the only one in the offices, and one of only a few hundred in the whole country) and typed out a fax message to the home office in Dubai. *"Hurricane has passed. The family is safe and well."*

After sending the fax and receiving delivery confirmation from Dubai, Chris clicked off the fax program, browsed his email messages then placed the computer on password access stand-by. Leaving the office and walking the quarter mile to his flat, Chris took in the evening sights of the city. He paused at a *choikhona*, or tea stop at the corner of Shotemur Street and Pushkin Boulevard. He sipped the warm acrid brew while chatting with the tea vendor. Then he resumed his commute. The chilly night air was laced with the smells of cooking food, rotting garbage, open sewers and smoke from kerosene heaters. He passed open windows, hearing the sounds of mostly Russian state television programs along with an occasional satellite station from the West such as CNN – the sign of a wealthy household. He passed a cyber-café, where young Muslim men gathered to sin, drinking alcohol and surfing porno on the internet. He passed an intersection where mixed-breed Russian/Tajik prostitutes slipped from the shadows, chanting their come-on, hoping to score a trick. These were the signs of immoral invasion, the exported trash of Western culture, the reasons why Islamic fundamentalists issued *fatwa's* condemning the US and declaring *jihad* against the destroyers of their conservative morality.

Chris came to his building on Palat Utar Street. He nodded to his neighbor old Mister Najavi who sat on the stoop smoking. He walked up the three flights to his top floor flat. His woman servant greeted him from the kitchen while turning out his evening meal on a large plate. The meal consisted of a kind of Tajik stew made with lamb and some mysterious hot spices, served on saffron rice. There was fresh baked flat bread and a glass of cheap Russian vodka. A side dish of olives and cheese, yoghurt and fruit completed the repast, now laid out on a small dinner table. By Tajik standards, Chris' place was upper class. It boasted four rooms, both Asian and English toilets, and a small roof garden.

Chris sat to eat alone. He read a two week old *London Financial Times* while eating the rice and stew with a wooden spoon. The stew tasted good, but like most Tajik cooking, brought a chance of dysentery.

After dinner, the old woman cleaned up and left for the day. Chris poured another double measure of vodka and relaxed in a big overstuffed chair.

The first part of the plan had come together successfully. Several more complicated steps must also go without a hitch to get the information and the goods to their destination. The stakes were high, but so too, the rewards.

Chris Taylor's life had been a series of successes, but this would be the greatest. Mister Al Kafajy would probably make him a full partner when this was over. That would mean a twenty percent stake in a $1.5 billion gross volume trading company with offices in nineteen countries. Not bad for a thirty-five year old half Brit half Arab guy with meager education and no nobility in his blood on either side. For this he was willing to endure life in backwater mid-Asian towns with no amenities and lots of gastric distress.

Blake's truck lumbered up a dirt driveway, splashed through deep puddles of muddy water and rolled through open doors into a large red barn. Roche followed right behind him in the Buick. The storm had weakened considerably over land, but was now dropping about an inch of rain per hour on Orangeburg, in the middle of South Carolina. The door slid closed, pushed by two men in fatigues. Blake got out of the truck into the dim light of a few bare bulbs near abandoned horse stalls. Randy Pullin a lanky American sporting fatigues with Colonel's bars and an Australian bush hat stepped out of the shadows. 'Colonel' Randy was about six-foot three, leather faced, with dark, deep set eyes that would have made the Ayatollah Khomeini look like a school boy. "Hello Blake, Hey Roche, how did it go?"

Roche wanted to relate the "hitch" at Sullivan's Island, but a flash of warning in Blake's eyes stopped him. "Fine, it went fine," asserted Roche. "No problems." Blake nodded, eyes averted from "Colonel" Randy's piercing gaze.

"Have you heard from Brandt?" Roche posed the question quickly to break up any potential for deeper queries about the morning's events.

"Yeah, Brandt and his men will be here in a few minutes. They got up river and packed into a truck we left for them." Randy's eyes narrowed. "What about Battles?"

Roche understood the look. "I took care of that personally." Colonel Randy studied Roche. He figured Roche had killed him in spite of orders to the contrary. In truth, Roche had planned all along to kill Battles. Roche had made sure that Battles' knock on the head had put him to sleep permanently.

"So, everybody's clear of the area?" Roche seemed a bit nervous as he asked.

"Everyone that you know, or need to know," Colonel Randy replied. Randy always had double back-up plans. Roche figured that Colonel Randy probably had the two lumpers from the warehouse followed and neutralized. With their pockets full of money, they would get drunk or high then they would get dead. At least that's the way Roche would have done it.

Blake declared, "Let's get to work."

They unloaded the crates from Blake's truck. After personally checking the marking on the crate, Colonel Randy handed Roche and Blake each a passbook to separate bank accounts in their names at a Cayman Islands bank. Roche called the bank via cell phone to verify first his deposit, then Blake's by identifying himself with a password created when he had opened the accounts months ago. The bank verified the money was on deposit.

"Nice working with you again Randy, I'll see ya later," drawled Blake as he started his truck. Blake wouldn't feel good about this until he was safely a hundred miles away from this barn.

After Blake left, Roche made small talk with the men. He was waiting for Brandt to show up. Two of Brandt's men were Roche's personal friends. He had connected them with Colonel Randy's group over a year ago. Roche wanted to see the men paid off and safely out of sight.

This was the fourth time they had all worked together. He trusted Blake but couldn't muster the same feeling toward Colonel Randy or Brandt. These militia types were unpredictable to begin with, but Randy was crazy to boot. Roche and Colonel Randy had served together in Viet-Nam, sweating in the jungle, ducking Viet Cong bullets, toiling for freedom. They had been Special Operations officers, running a counter-intelligence unit that trained and managed South Vietnamese spies to infiltrate the V.C.

Their Vietnamese spies eventually betrayed them and they were taken prisoner, along with two others of their ops unit. One of those other officers was Bob Steck, now a senior operative for the CIA, the other was Brandt's father, Glenn. The men were treated worse than dogs in their V.C. prison camp, but the unspeakable cruelty of the guards only hardened their resolve to survive. During their seventh attempt at escape, Glenn Brandt was wounded. The V.C stripped him, hung him feet first from a tree limb then made the others watch as they disemboweled him alive. In his dreams Colonel Randy Pullin still saw this terrible scene and still heard the elder Brandt's screams of anguish. Randy came away from his Viet-Nam experience disillusioned by what he perceived as betrayal by his superiors and betrayal by the American people. On his return home Randy had refused several offers of good jobs. Brandt's wife died young, of drug addiction brought on by loneliness and despair. Randy adopted Brandt's son as his own. Disillusioned with the government that had abandoned him and his men, Pullin formed a militia group that lived and trained in a compound in the Rocky Mountains. The group soon attracted hundreds of similar minded men and their families. Word in the spy community was that for enough money, Colonel Randy would perform any task that called for military training, whether legal or not.

Roche's reward for his Viet Nam experience had been a career with the CIA. Twenty years of success had been cut cruelly short by one big mistake. The cold war was just about at an end when Roche's impeccable record had been tarnished forever by a big political mistake. By a series of unlikely circumstances, Roche wound up taking on the top man in the Israeli Mossad in a dispute over Palestinian top-secret information. A communiqué that Roche intercepted had directly proven the guilt of the Mossad officer in the assassination of a top Palestinian diplomat in Los Angeles. Roche vigorously pursued the Israeli. He had the goods on his man but, as his boss and old friend Bob Steck had pointed out, the truth is sometimes not compatible with career growth. Finally, he became an embarrassment to the Agency and to members of the Senate Intelligence Committee that staunchly supported Israel. Unjustly sacked, he had turned to a double life as owner of a small store in Norfolk, VA and as a mercenary for hire by anyone with the desire for a trained operative and the money to pay a market price for his services.

The headlights of a vehicle flashed through the barn window illuminating the half-darkness of the storm. Randy nodded to a man at the door. The man checked the source. "It's Brandt."

"Let 'em in." Two of the men rolled the door aside, and a rack-bodied crew cab Ford rolled to a stop inside the barn. Brandt and the men got out to stretch, dry off and change into street clothes.

"I guess Roche wanted to see that you guys were paid and out of here in one piece," quipped Colonel Randy. "Here's your pay, in cash as agreed."

The men took the money, exchanged high fives with Roche and packed into a rental car to drive away. Brandt stayed, going to work with Colonel Randy's men. They deflated the Zodiac and packed the truck for the long trip to Wyoming, careful to stash the crates safely under other gear. Colonel Randy's GMC Yukon and the truck rolled away Northwest towards Spartanburg.

Roche pointed the Buick back towards Charleston. He would pick up I-95 to Richmond, then I-64 to Norfolk, but not before checking on that "hitch" in Mount Pleasant, South Carolina.

CHAPTER 3

Bob Steck's red phone rang at six-fifty am, as he was on his way to Langley. There was almost never a red phone secure call during Bob's morning commute from his Virginia horse farm to his office at the CIA.

Slipping his BMW 750iL out of cruise control and drifting to the inside lane of George Washington Parkway, he answered the ring with a curt "Steck."

"Bob, there's been a strange event in Charleston, during the hurricane yesterday." The voice was his boss, Ryall Morgan. "Do you remember Alex Grayson, the FBI agent?"

How could Steck forget that weasel Alex Grayson? Grayson had tried to horn in on that messy Israeli thing, the one that resulted in Bob having to fire his number one operative and long-time friend, Paul Roche. "Yeah, I remember him."

"Grayson was found dead on the waterfront near Charleston, just before the storm hit."

Steck was tempted to make a crack, like "I'll write a memo to myself to grieve."

Morgan didn't wait for Steck to speak, but went on. "This needs to be addressed quickly and discreetly, Bob." Morgan was leading up to something.

Adjusting to Morgan's tone, Steck asked, "Addressed by whom? Certainly it should not be me Ryall in light of the circumstances."

"Bob, he was working under cover and hadn't filed any reports in days, but his boss thinks he might have been tailing Paul Roche."

Steck tensed. He knew that Roche had been so disillusioned after his firing that he had sought out some pretty unsavory company. The idea of making Roche 'disappear' had even been considered by top brass at the agency, an idea that Steck had blocked by a few well-placed political moves. Steck had investigated Roche personally. He had traced him to a gift shop in Norfolk, Virginia, had personally watched him for a few days then had him tailed for over a month. Nothing had been uncovered to dispute that Roche was a simple shopkeeper. Case closed, Right?

"Why would he be tailing Roche, Ryall? Still bent on harassment?"

"It's possible, but now Grayson's *dead*, Bob. Stop by my office when you get in. First thing, please."

Steck could tell by Morgan's tone that there was more to tell. "Yeah, sure, I'll see you in about thirty minutes." As Steck clicked off, he cursed. What had Paul Roche gotten into? Just the thought was condemning. After all, Steck himself had pronounced Paul 'clean,' in writing. This was not starting out to be a good day.

Steck called his secretary on his civilian cell-phone. "I may be late for the meeting with the Iran committee in the brown room. Please let them know. If you need me, I'll be in Ryall Morgan's office." Steck chaired the Iran Committee. His extensive experience in Iran, both before and after the revolution of the late '70's had helped to solidify his career. Add to that his intimate knowledge of Israel and the Palestinians, and it was plain to see that his success at the Agency had been assured. He would have a top job as long as he wanted to work and didn't screw up.

Steck's mind was full of questions and a sort of foreboding. He parked the BMW in his reserved space at the Agency. He made his customary stop at the coffee kiosk in the lobby, nodding to the attendant who had his crème donut and dark roast coffee ready. Nibbling on the sweet as he strode towards Morgan's office, he dribbled powdered sugar on the lapel of his grey Brooks Brothers suit. As Steck entered Morgan's three-room office suite, he made a feeble attempt to brush the powder from his jacket. All he did was spread it around, making the situation worse. Morgan's secretary, Marie, chuckled, holding up a hand to stop him.

She snatched a packet from her desk drawer, opened it and swished the stuff away with a moist towelette. She giggled then patted him on the shoulder.

"There," she said, "you're all set for business, Bob. Go right in, He's waiting for you."

Ryall Morgan was a career bureaucrat. He had started as a glorified clerk in the Russia section in 1963, mentored by a Senator who was Ryall's father's golf buddy. At first, his only value to the Agency was his mastery of the Russian language in all its regional variations. But Ryall quickly showed himself to be a good student of the politics of bureaucracy. Tutored by his father, who was a multi-millionaire deeply involved in international trade, Ryall quickly rose through the ranks at Langley until he was a section chief. Then a career defining moment came when he helped break the Aldrich Ames case. Now an assistant director, Ryall's career was at the apogee. He was known as a personable yet dedicated man whose great strength was in his ability to perceive his own weaknesses, admit them and appeal to those with offsetting strengths to team with him in achieving any goal before them. A conservative man in his personal life, happily married with 3 children, Ryall Morgan was considered to be incorruptible. Steck liked his boss.

Morgan looked up as Steck entered. He motioned to the side chair by his desk. Peering over half-lens glasses, he shoved a thin sheave of papers towards the edge of his desk, to the spot where Steck's elbow would have landed.

"Morning," he slurred, "read this."

Steck half spoke, half nodded a "Good morning Ryall," gathered up the loose papers and sat back to read.

The top page announced, "Security level secret plus F6, eyes only." As Bob read the introduction, the words in red "Navy is missing (intentionally blank) materiel" leapt off the page. He tensed, sat up straight and read intently.

Ten minutes later, he finished reading the document. Agitated, Steck waived the paper at Morgan in a gesture of frustration. "What materiel?' he asked. Steck knew that when the words "intentionally blank" appeared in this kind of document it meant something big, something very secret. Something that by security classification standards could only be taken from a short-list of abominable things: State secrets, battle plans, advanced weapons blueprints or maybe WMD.

Morgan shrugged. "I don't know, yet. This just got to me."

"Well, who wrote it? How do we find out more? My Gawd, Ryall, If Roche has turned on us he can do a *lot* of damage."

"Joe Bergen wrote it. I've never seen anything he published proven wrong. You and I will be on center stage at NSA in Beltsville today at 2:00pm. Cancel your agenda for the day, Bob and prepare all the background you can get on Roche. Be back here at noon with a brief to present to NSA. We can ride over in my car."

Steck nodded, already heading for the door. Fifteen minutes later, Steck and seven staffers were busy sifting documents and computer files. By 10:30am, they had a fifty page dossier on Roche covering his entire career at the agency. By eleven, the dossier had been reduced to a ten page brief. Instructing his administrative assistant, Mary to hold all messages for the afternoon, passing on only those from a short list he had hastily dictated, Steck trotted the hundred yards to Morgan's office. Over cold sandwiches, they reviewed and edited the material. Satisfied that they were ready for their inter-agency meeting, Morgan and Steck double-timed it to the garage, got into Morgan's big Buick, and began the drive to Beltsville, Maryland.

Colonel Randy strode through the parade ground at his Wyoming training camp, busy talking into his cell phone. His booming, raspy voice always sounded angry. This morning it was even louder and angrier, a sign of impatience.

"Dammit Major, you're hours behind schedule, you sound half drunk and now you say you're having car trouble. Why the hell do you think I sound upset?"

Brandt bristled at the reprimand and his steel blue eyes narrowed. "I'll be there on time, Colonel. You can count on it."

"That's more like it, Colonel Randy said sternly. No excuses, just performance of your duty son."

Brandt steered the black Suburban back onto Interstate 90 just west of Butte, Montana after some timely help from a trucker at a rest area, who was kind enough to lend him tools and advice to fix the engine. The girl he had picked up 300 miles ago was passed out drunk in the back seat. He muttered a curse that he would now have to drive all night to make up for time lost fooling around with her at the rest area. He repeated the curse louder because by the time he was getting to his intended business, the whiskey had already overtaken her. She lay in a heap, snoring loudly.

Brandt squinted into the rear view mirror to check on the crate behind the back seat. Re-packed in new wood, the precious cargo was now marked "fine English bone china." Brandt swigged black coffee from a large thermo-jug. He set the cruise control to 80, intent on finishing the drive to Coeur d'Alene, Idaho by daybreak.

Chris Taylor sipped acrid Tajik coffee at 4:30 am, speaking softly on the phone with one of his agents in Calgary, Canada where it was 4:00 pm. "Meet a dark blue Ford Explorer at the Kootenay Hotel in Creston, just over the border. Just get the crate to our Vancouver office," he said. "We'll have a manifest drafted that includes it as part of a full container shipment to Dubai. When you're sure it's loaded, call me."

Taylor hung up without any good-bye. He shuffled about his apartment, packing a change of clothes, business papers, cigarettes and a few magazines for the flight to Paris.

Leaving a note in Russian for the housekeeper, he locked the apartment and lugged his bag down the dingy brown staircase. The front door creaked loudly as he opened it towards the street. No sense trying to be quiet when everyone in the building was already preparing breakfast to eat or food to carry for the long Tajik workday. The company Mercedes diesel was parked at the curb. Taylor greeted Alimand, the driver, and got into the back seat. He lit a cigarette for the ride to the airport. Recounting in his mind the present operation and thinking ahead to a successful conclusion, Chris whistled softly to himself. He reckoned the excrement would just be hitting the fan in Washington.

CHAPTER 4

The briefing at Beltsville confirmed that Ryall Morgan and Bob Steck were really in the crap. All that was known so far was that part of a very secret stash was missing. The stash, explained the assistant director of Naval Intelligence, was materiel seized as part of the freezing of Iraqi assets ordered by the first President Bush in the early 1990's. The Navy had not yet found out what part of the stash at the Charleston warehouse was actually missing. The dead FBI agent, Grayson had been on official business that the FBI would only talk about at a meeting already scheduled for the next morning at the Intelligence Director's office. Steck was startled when told that Ryall Morgan would be a presenter at that meeting. It meant his boss was privy to more than he had shared with Steck.

Steck's briefing about Paul Roche got a somber response from the assemblage. When added to reports from the Mount Pleasant police that he was a definite suspect in Grayson's murder, it became absolutely clear that Roche was mixed up in something awful, something treasonous. The FBI was already working to get the Mount Pleasant Police removed from the case. Ryall Morgan assigned Steck to the investigation. Since it was on US soil, Steck would have to be accompanied by FBI agents who would officially run the effort.

Morgan and Steck parted that evening at the Langley parking area. "I figure we've got a couple of days at best to nail this thing," said Ryall as he looked Steck in the eye. "You know what it will mean for the agency if this Roche thing gets out of hand." He worried that it already was. "Roche is the key. You have to get him alive, and quickly. Bring him to the old Oceana Naval base and lock him down. I'll have an interrogation team waiting there for you. I'll be there myself tomorrow night."

"I can't get anywhere with some FBI goon riding herd on me," complained Steck.

"Use the FBI's quick reaction resources to your advantage, Bob. I don't have time to give you the details of their operational posture on this, but you'll learn when you get to Charlottesville." Morgan's tone was serious, eyes narrow, ruddy face tense. "I'll see you tomorrow night at Oceana."

Steck jogged inside to his office, called his wife, used the shower and changed his clothes. Black leather flight jacket, golf shirt, jeans and Reeboks would serve better than the Brooks Brothers suit, silk tie and British Walkers donned at home this morning. Packing his leather sport bag with electronics, his Mauser and ammo, Steck made a few quick internal calls and left some secure email for his secretary. Leaving his BMW in the garage, he signed out an agency car and ten thousand in cash. Next stop would be in Charlottesville where he would meet and brief an FBI team that was already waiting for him.

Ralph Baker poured coffee from a fresh pot he had just brewed in his farmhouse kitchen near Coeur d'Alene Idaho. The stuff tasted good as he took a big gulp, washing away the sleep from his body. It was still dark outside, three am.

Ralph was a veteran of the first Gulf war and had been decorated for valor after saving some soldiers from a burning building set fire by SCUD missile fragments in Saudi Arabia. One of those he had saved that night was his brother, Ricky. Years later, when Ricky died of "gulf sickness" after having been ignored by the US government and denied medical help from the Veteran's Administration, Ralph sought out the company of others who believed their government had done them wrong. Today's would be his eighth "secret errand" for Colonel Randy since associating with the militia group *Free Nation* three years ago. It was a struggle for Ralph to keep up the mortgage payments on the family farm and to maintain his wife and four children. He made good use of the thousand dollars he was paid for each "errand."

Ralph had sent his wife and children to Boise the day before. Visiting her parents for a few days was the only real break Ralph's wife ever got from the farm chores. There was no need to worry her with knowledge of what he did for the militia. She didn't even know he was involved with them.

The usual errand would be to pick up a package in Canada, where he went often in his work as a John Deere salesman. His frequent trips through the Porthill border station had given Ralph the opportunity to befriend the customs and immigration officers. One of the US immigration guys, Rob Carstair, had relatives in Coeur d'Alene. The friendship had extended so that Rob brought his wife and children to visit the Bakers once in awhile. Ralph knew Rob's shifts, and so knew what times to cross when he had a package for *Free Nation* among the sales files and give-away toy tractors piled in the back of his Explorer.

This time he would carry a package in the other direction, to Canada where he would meet one of Colonel Randy's friends for the drop in Creston, British Colombia. This was more risky. Even though he went to Canada often enough to be familiar, Ralph did not have any well-established personal relationships on the Canadian side.

Ralph spent the next hour rushing through his morning chores. He had just finished feeding the dairy cows in his main barn when lights from a vehicle traveling up the farm's long driveway flashed through the barn window.

"Hey Baker," shouted Brandt, leaving the Suburban and striding toward Baker. "Got any Java?"

Baker didn't like Brandt, with his strident manner and intense attitude. Those steely eyes and that big scar on Brandt's face sent chills down Ralph's spine. "Sure, Brandt, there's a pot in the kitchen."

The two men drank Baker's now stale coffee at the farm kitchen table while Brandt went over the details of the drop to be accomplished at *The Kootenay Hotel* in Creston, British Columbia. Brandt poured himself another cup, gulping the contents, then helped himself to large white foam cup from a stack on the kitchen counter and poured another one. "For my passenger," he mumbled, picking up a lid and snapping it into place.

Baker seemed surprised, peering out the window expecting to see someone in the Suburban. No sign of anyone.

Outside, as Baker and Brandt wrestled the small crate from the Suburban to the Explorer, Baker saw the girl suddenly rise from sleep to a bolt-upright position in the back seat. She seemed in a fog, looking about in bewilderment. "One for the road," chuckled Brandt, making a gesture toward the girl.

Baker half-smiled, then finished heaping small boxes and files to make the crate look as if it belonged there. He recited his orders for Brandt again "The drop will be tomorrow morning at eight-thirty in the Kootenay Hotel. I'll meet the man in the coffee shop. He will be carrying a yellow notebook."

Brandt nodded. "Just be sure you're there," he instructed. If you don't show by nine, the contact will leave." He focused his steel blue eyes on Baker's face. "If you bring this crate back, Colonel Randy will not be pleased." Brandt flipped an envelope onto the dashboard of the Explorer. "There's a thousand in there. There will be another thousand when the mission is completed."

Baker wondered why this run was considered worth twice the usual amount, but thought better of asking.

Brandt got behind the wheel of the Suburban. He spoke softly to the girl, who nodded, slipped out the back door and into the front passenger seat. She took the coffee and settled back, sipping slowly. Neither one looked at Baker as Brandt sped off down the dusty driveway.

Half an hour later, the Suburban was parked at the rear of the *La Quinta Inn,* just off the junction of I-90 and state route 95. Brandt and the girl were having the rest of breakfast in their room.

Toward noon, Baker packed his overnight bag in the back seat of the Explorer, stuffed a sandwich and some Cokes in the center console, and started the hundred and fifty mile drive to Creston. His plan was to cross the border during Rob Carstair's three to eleven pm shift at the US border station, then on to Creston for the overnight.

Steck walked stiffly from his car to the front door of a small middle-class house in Charlottesville. Although his fifty-five year old frame was fit and muscular, the years showed when he drove long hours without getting out of the car to stretch.

Inside, Steck shared what he knew with the three FBI agents he found there. They responded with all the information they had from the Mount Pleasant Police plus a bit from their own investigation, barely underway. Steck learned three new pieces of information. First, that there was a second murder victim, a Navy security guard at the warehouse. Second, the FBI had several agents on the ground, combing through every neighborhood in the Mount Pleasant and Charleston areas, seeking clues to either the murders or the robbery. Third, the team had been tracking Roche for months because of links uncovered between his shop in Norfolk and a suspicious trading company in the UAE.

The chief investigator for the FBI was Morton Lindsley, a thirty-year career man who had accumulated many honors over the years for his ability to solve complex cases quickly and quietly. A tall man with angular features and a perpetual suntan, he spoke in the slow and easy lingo of a southern gentleman. The other two attending this briefing were young FBI case officers. Susan Deet was the kind of woman feared by most men. Her speech was quick and succinct, rattling off facts and slicing arguments to pieces with a shrill voice that gave expression to a mind like a steel trap. Steck heard New York in her accent. Not pretty but attractive, she had close cut dirty blonde hair, athletic figure and butch clothes. Her hands were way too big for the rest of her. He judged her to be twenty-eight or so. The other was a pale kid just out of college with nondescript features, a typical white male nobody in jeans and a tee. He looked a bit puny. He was the kind who could easily vanish in a room with three people in it. He didn't say much, but what he offered was thoughtful. It was clear he idolized Lindsley who seemed to regard the lad with benign tolerance. Steck was to learn that this young man, Greg Liss, had graduated first in his class at Dartmouth and had scored higher than anyone ever on the FBI screening tests. Steck decided to reserve judgment until he had a chance to work with this trio. One thing was sure. They were ready to do anything to avenge their fallen brother and team member Grayson.

In two hours of intense briefing Steck gave them all he knew about Paul Roche and they told him about Grayson. The more he heard the more anxious Steck became.

Grayson had been part of a secret terrorist tracking group set up by the FBI after 911, called JUMP. This was one of several units that the government had mandated to go after the terrorists. The team had been successful in thwarting eight different terrorist attacks upon the United States and three upon the president. So secret was their work that the public, especially the media knew nothing of their existence, never mind their accomplishments. The team had every possible resource at their disposal: Secret Service, FBI, NSA, CIA, Department of Homeland Security and The Pentagon. They were housed at the Office of Naval Intelligence, with direct contact to a key member of the White House staff.

The JUMP team consisted of Lindsley, Deet, Liss, six other agents, a small clerical staff and for the moment Bob Steck. Increased traffic on communications lines that included suspected terrorists, the UAE trading company, Paul Roche and a shadowy man whose name might be Blake had prompted Lindsley to assign Grayson to tail Roche.

Steck had tried his best not to show his gut reaction to the mention of Blake's name. He wanted to hear more before getting that deep into this. The old master Lindsley caught it, also deciding not to go further until he needed to.

They decided to head straight to Norfolk. They would try to take Roche before dawn.

CHAPTER 5

Paul Roche returned to Mount Pleasant the day after the storm, to check on the investigation into Grayson's murder. He wanted to know whether to disappear or return to life in Norfolk running his shop.

As he drove up to the *The Gold Bug Bread 'n Breakfast* he became convinced that disappearance was the best move. The place was crawling with cops. Roche was surprised that the FBI had not yet called the locals off the case. He figured that might give him a day or so to make his next moves. He hoped the reason Grayson had been tailing him was personal. That way, the FBI would be late arriving at his door. He sped off toward Virginia.

Roche arrived at his modest house in Norfolk just off Indian River Road at midnight. Though dog tired from the drive, he quickly packed some things into the trunk of the Buick, took extra cartridge clips and ammo for his Beretta and started the short drive to Hampton Roads Airport, where a charter plane piloted by an old friend was waiting. As he came to the intersection at Military Highway, two vehicles caught his eye. One was a plain Ford Victoria with the look of an unmarked police car. The other was a black Suburban with some white numbers on the bumper, definitely FBI. Bold as ever, Roche circled and tailed them. His nerves tightened when he saw that Bob Steck was driving the Ford. Steck's involvement in this meant the feds were much too hot on his trail. He knew he now had none of the head start he needed. Turning the Buick at a crossover, he raised his friend the charter pilot on his cell phone and advised him to have the plane warmed up for immediate take-off. Twenty-five minutes later, while the JUMP team rifled through his home and his shop, Roche took off from Hampton Roads Airport for a destination he had yet to figure out.

———————

Mohammed Al Kafajy and some of his retinue sat at lunch in a private dining area just off the lobby of the Hotel des Chaumes near the Champs Elysee in Paris. He was a distinguished looking man of about sixty-five, with chiseled dark features and dark, deep set Middle Eastern eyes. His hair and beard were grey, his head topped with a traditional Arab Keffiya headdress. His six-foot frame was portly but solid. Light gray silk designer suit, Bally shoes and belt, and an Italian silk tie completed the look. His puffy right hand sported a bold diamond ring with a center stone as big as a sugar cube. A matching ring with rubies adorned his left hand. He had the air of a Saudi Prince rather than a merchant from the Emirates.

Lunch with "the boss" was usually a three-hour affair, partly business and partly pleasure. Al Kafajy's family was usually close by, his wife and five children sitting near daddy. The rest of the dozen or so guests were there to have an "audience" about one or another business deal. Shrewd as they come, Al Kafajy had built a trading empire that spanned the globe. He was worth more than a billion dollars.

Chris Taylor always felt somewhat inadequate at these extravaganzas. He sometimes stammered when addressed by the intimidating Al Kafajy and he hated himself for it. But his record of performance and his loyalty had earned him a place of ultimate trust with the boss. Accordingly, he sat high in the pecking order at table between Missus Al Kafajy and one of the children, a snooty little twelve-year old brat named Basil.

At three fifteen pm Al Kafajy dismissed most of the diners, including the family. Some minor business matters were disposed. Then all but Chris cleared out. The boss took an apple from a big bowl of fruit and pushed the bowl toward Chris. "So, how is our most interesting "import" moving along, Christian?" Al Kafajy seemed to take some bizarre pleasure in calling Chris by his full first name. He sometimes wondered how his mother, a Christian Arab, had allowed it.

She must have known that Chris would be the target of jokes among Arab family and friends.

"Quite well, sir. The goods themselves are on their way to Canada to our Vancouver office for trans-shipment to Dubai." Chris was still unsure of what the boss would do with his newly acquired trinkets. He had been told by Al Kafajy himself that there was something of great religious significance involved.

"But have they left the United States?" Al Kafajy produced a razor sharp knife with a jeweled pearl handle from inside his vest. He began casually peeling the apple.

"I should have confirmation early tomorrow that they are safely in Canada." Chris was sure that his voice sounded uncertain of that. The boss either didn't notice or ignored it. "Will I be delivering the goods to you personally?" he asked, selecting an apple for himself.

"No, no, no," the boss answered. "I give thanks to Allah for all things, but I am first a merchant and a trader. There is much money to be made in the sale of our prize."

"I see," Chris said. He didn't, really.

"I'll feel much better when it arrives in Dubai," Al Kafajy mused. "Your success in this endeavor will get you a very big promotion," he said. Stabbing a piece of apple and waving it in the air he added, "Ah, Christian, what a beautiful auction we are going to have!"

Ralph Baker pulled-in to the parking lot behind the US border station at Porthill, Idaho at four pm. He had made routine sales calls at Sandpoint and Bonners Ferry along the way, just in case there was anybody watching. Make it appear to be business as usual.

Ralph ambled in to the employee's lunch area through the back door of the border station. He was greeted by one of the Customs agents on break. He recognized him as Rob Carstairs' friend. "Mister Baker, isn't it?"

"That's me," Ralph replied with a smile and a handshake. "How're you doing today?"

"Oh, I'm just great, but I'd rather be hunting in such great weather," the agent replied. "Have a seat and help yourself to some of our lousy coffee. Carstairs will be taking his break in about fifteen minutes. I'll let him know you're here." The man took a long sip of coffee and a bite of sandwich, then produced a key on a chain from his pocket and passed through a steel security door to the front part of the station.

Ralph had just poured his second cup when his old friend joined him for cordial conversation. "So, where are you headed this time, Ralph?"

"Just the usual business stop at *Jerry's Tractor Depot*, up in Creston," replied Ralph. "He sells a lot of John Deere product. I'll head back home tomorrow."

The two men exchanged jokes and family greetings, then Ralph said goodbye and drove the short distance to the Canadian side. Ralph cursed under his breath, as he was stopped by an agent that he didn't recognize. Most of the agents knew Ralph and just waved him through. This one was new, so he might be a problem. Quickly, Ralph hit a pre-entered number on his cell phone and rolled down his window. The agent checked Ralph's papers, then he mumbled, "Wait here a minute, sir," and stepped in to the gate kiosk to pull up Ralph's information on his computer. Knowing the drill, Ralph figured the next step would be a routine search of the car. Bad luck to get a rookie agent, he thought.

Ralph had a plan for such an event. He pushed the send button as the agent made his way to Ralph's driver's door window. "I see that you cross here often, Mister Baker. Is this a business trip?"

Ralph said into the phone, "Hold on a minute," and looked up to meet the agent's eyes trying not to seem anxious. He pressed the speaker button. "Yes, sir," he replied. "I go through here a couple of times a month. I don't remember you, though. Are you new here?"

The agent paused as if catching something suspicious in Ralph's tone of voice. "Yes, I'm new. What do you have in the back?" he asked with a gesture to the rear of the Explorer.

"Just my sales literature and toy tractor giveaways," said Ralph carefully. "It's all on the papers. Look, I'm late for a meeting in Creston. Could we do this the next time, perhaps?"

The agent's training was kicking in and he stiffened a bit. "This will only take a few minutes, sir."

Inwardly desperate, Ralph put on his best business smile and said affably, "Maybe you could talk with agent Carstairs here, on my cell phone."

Carstairs had heard the entire conversation through Ralph's phone. Ralph handed the phone to the somewhat apprehensive Canadian agent. "This is agent Robert Carstairs of U.S. Immigration," he said. "Ralph Baker is okay. I can vouch for him. Look over here and I'll wave to you."

Surprised, the Canadian looked over toward the U.S. Station, across and down the street. He saw a uniformed agent waving, cell phone held to one ear. "Are you the agent Carstairs that taught the anti-terrorism course at the Seminar last month?"

"That's me," he replied, "You must be Larrivee." Hearing that, Ralph relaxed, seeing the name tag *B. Larrivee* on the breast pocket of the Canadian's uniform.

For a moment that seemed like eternity, the Canadian agent considered the information before him. Finally he said, "Okay Mister Baker, you can get to your meeting. But the next time you come through, expect to spend some time here."

"Thank you kindly Mister Larrivee," said Ralph. "I'll be back next week and I'll be ready to stay for as long as it takes."

As Ralph Baker drove away, he thanked his friend profusely for helping him get to his appointment on time. Switching off the cell phone a mile or so into Canada, Ralph pulled the car to the side of the road and let the repressed sweat and shakes run through his body. After a few minutes, he opened a can of Coke, took a long draught and resumed his drive to Creston, British Columbia.

CHAPTER 6

Ryall Morgan stood at the large projection screen in SECURE MEETING ROOM #3 housed in a long single story cement block building at the former Oceana Naval Base in Virginia. He was briefing the JUMP team about events in Charleston on the day of the hurricane. Steck was sullen, but attentive. Missing Paul Roche by what appeared to be only minutes weighed heavily on his mind. Steck knew Paul well enough to believe him capable of eluding the feds' best efforts for days. Roche knew how lead a merry chase-to-nowhere better than anyone Steck ever trained. The trick would be for the teacher to find the pupil. He knew he could do it, he just didn't know how much precious time it would cost the team, or how finding Roche would help in the primary investigation. This meeting was allowing Roche's trail to get colder.

Morgan was recounting the facts known thus far. There were for the moment two separate incidents under investigation. One was Grayson's murder at Sullivan's Island, top suspect Paul Roche. The other was an apparent murder and a theft at the Navy warehouse. There was a suspicion, not yet confirmed, that Roche was somehow involved in that crime as well.

Ryall's meeting at the director's office was recounted. Meeting minutes hastily recorded on Morgan's laptop were projected for all to read as Ryall moved methodically through his personal notes. The missing crate was identified as having contained some "artifacts" from the seventh century. There was gold, mostly in jewelry and coin, a "figurine" made of plaster and an ancient book written in Arabic on papyrus. Estimated value of the gold and jewelry was eighty thousand dollars. The value of the book and the figurine were unknown, but had been entered into the inventory of Iraqi goods made by the FBI at the time of seizure as "estimated value under ten thousand dollars." The curious thing was that adjacent crates contained millions of dollars in gold bars, but were untouched by the robbers.

One by one, Morgan displayed photos of the contents that the FBI had taken to inventory the seized items. When he came to the last picture, showing the book and the figurine, Greg Liss came to attention, whistled softly and uttered, "Oh, dear."

"Whatcha got, Greg?" drawled Lindsley.

Liss didn't answer. He just got up and went closer to the screen, staring in awe and amazement. After a long time, he held out his hand as if to touch the image of the plaster figurine of a human hand, laid out in the picture next to the ancient Arabic book. The paint on the figure was faded and cracked, clearly very old. It was a casting of someone's right hand, rather delicate, the fingers touching the thumb in the manner of blessing or greeting customary to Muslim men. Greg's fingers touched the screen, startling him as if awakened from a trance of fascination. He slowly turned to face the group.

Steck turned up the lights, while Morgan turned off the projector.

Greg Liss was in a cold sweat. His face was pale, his eyes wide. "Tha-that could be *The Hand of Mohammed*," he half stammered.

Ryall Morgan stared at the young agent intently. "You mean the prophet of Islam, *that* Mohammed?"

"Yes, *that* Mohammed," replied Liss. "When I was at Dartmouth, we studied ancient myths and religions under the great professor William Wigglesworth. Doctor Wigglesworth is an expert in historical analysis. His life's work has centered around investigation and verification or exposure of Para-religious myths, such as the so called Shroud of Turin, the Holy Grail, the Greek pagan gods, the…"

"I get the picture, Greg," interrupted Lindsley, waving his hand in a gesture to move along. He leaned across the table, eyes fixed on Greg Liss. "What about this plaster hand?

Greg sat, drew a deep breath and began speaking as if he were the taking on the role of teacher. "Well, the teachings of Mohammed are followed by nearly a quarter of the world's population, but no direct links to his corpse have ever been made public. Islam teaches that Mohammed was taken bodily to heaven. In his efforts to find whether Mohammed's body was in fact rotting in the earth just like any man's, Doctor Wigglesworth uncovered an ancient text that mentioned the existence of a plaster casting made from the prophet's own right hand, left as a legacy to his true followers. According to this legend, Mohammed had decreed that only one figure be made from the cast, which he himself painted to look like his own hand. After that was accomplished, Mohammed himself reportedly broke the mould."

The room was silent for a long moment, while the team absorbed Greg's story. "So," said Morgan in a measured tone, "how do we verify all this?"

"Simple," declared Susan Deet. "Start by contacting Wigglesworth."

"That's not going to be easy," Liss remarked, "Doctor Wigglesworth left teaching at Dartmouth two years ago, retaining only a lecture chair at the college, along with a residence for his wife. He has become obsessed with this *hand* thing. He's determined to either find it or disprove its existence once and for all. It has become his life's work.

"So where is he?" asked Steck.

"He's somewhere in the middle-east. The last I heard, he was in Yemen, living in the desert and traveling from place to place along the old caravan trade routes, looking for clues." Liss held his hands palms up, eyebrows raised. "I don't know how to find him."

"Okay," offered Lindsley laconically, "so we're not going to just ring him up on a cell phone, eh?"

"Let's call Dartmouth College," suggested Deet. "We can get to interview family, friends, people who know this professor. Someone's got to be in touch with him."

Steck's patience was growing short. "I think we should split up, one team going after Roche, who is real, and the other team working on this imaginary *Hand of Mohammed* theory. Whatever was stolen, it looks like the heist was accomplished by a well organized bunch that included Paul Roche, one of the best agents I've ever known, whose services do not come cheap. Even not knowing more, I consider that reason enough not to let him get away. And then there's the crate, which is being taken God knows where. The whole track on this is going to get cold, fast. By sitting in this room all day, we're allowing just that to happen!" Steck ended with a gesture of supplication to Ryall Morgan.

Ryall made eye contact that showed he agreed with Steck, but decided to defer to Lindsley, who looked like he had something to say. Lindsley caught the gesture in Morgan's eyes, acknowledged it, leaning forward to engage Steck by looking him straight in the eye. "Well, it seems, Mister Steck that you might be forgettin' that a member of our team and colleague of five years has been killed. I assure you sir that we are just as anxious as you are to find his killer. I do hope you will assist us in this matter." Steck slumped, mildly exasperated. Satisfied that he had effectively delivered his admonishment, Lindsley continued in even tones. "Notwithstanding that the JUMP team has an urgent agenda, as Mister Bob here has correctly observed, I believe Greg should take a couple of minor staff and spend the next two or three days chasing this *Hand of Mohammed* theory. Greg, you will have a full report in my hands not later than three days hence. Steck, Deet and I will continue the search for this Roche fellow and the whereabouts of the Navy's missing crate."

Steck caught Ryall's warning glance. He understood that it was in the best interest of the investigation not to take on Mort Lindsley over some stupid turf issue. "Understood," he replied tersely.

Ralph Baker delivered the crate to his contact at the *Kootenay Hotel* precisely at 8:30 am, finished his business in Creston and started the drive home. Crossing the border at Porthill, he sped toward home, satisfied that he had done his part in whatever deal Colonel Randy was up to and planning how he would spend the money he had earned. After fantasizing about taking his wife to Vegas, he decided the two thousand would have to go towards catching up payments for the mortgage on the farm.

About ten miles from Coeur d'Alene, Baker dialed up Brandt on his cell phone.

"This is Brandt," said a raspy voice at the other end.

"Baker," Ralph replied. I made the delivery and I'm back, about ten minutes from home.

"I'll meet you at the end of your driveway in ten." Brandt clicked off and poked the girl, who rolled out the other side of the bed. He motioned her to get her stuff. She protested that she wanted to shower. "Just pee and dress," he said sternly. "We go in five minutes."

Ralph waited at the entrance of his driveway, reading junk mail he had collected from the rusty rural route mailbox with faded black letters that spelled BAK_R. He made a mental note to fix it or get a new one.

The Suburban rumbled to a stop in a cloud of reddish dust, just behind Ralph's Explorer. Brandt got out, taking the keys and locking the doors with the remote. He figured the girl was stupid enough to believe the child locks would keep her inside, even though the driver's door could be opened from inside. He carried an envelope.

"That's my money?" asked Ralph, uneasy as ever in Brandt's presence.

"Only if I don't see a crate in there," smiled Brandt. He walked past Baker, opened the tailgate and rifled through the stuff in the back of the Explorer. Not finding the crate, Brandt stepped away from the SUV to a spot where he had both Baker and the Suburban in plain view, flipped his phone open and selected Colonel Randy's cell phone.

"Brandt?"

"Yes sir. Am I authorized to proceed?"

"Yup, Pay the man. The goods are safe and on their way." Colonel Randy's voice was relaxed. "Complete your mission, son."

With blue steel eyes flashing and the trace of a smile, Brandt snapped, "Yes sir." He stowed the phone and walked slowly toward Baker, proffering the envelope. As Baker reached for it, Brandt pulled it away. "What if we split this?" teased Brandt. "I think I need some extra cash for the ride home."

Ralph Baker, angry and scared, blurted out. "You sonovabitch Brandt, That's my money. I earned it. Give it to me!"

"Or what?" taunted Brandt. "You gonna beat me up?"

Raging, Ralph lunged at Brandt, grabbing at the envelope. Brandt's combat training snapped on. He moved aside deftly, bringing a strong right arm up to punch Baker's head just above the left ear. Ralph slumped to the dirt in a limp heap. Brandt strode over to Baker's hunched form and placed a boot on his face. "Like I said, I think we should split this money."

Ralph Baker did not move.

"That's better," growled Brandt. "Get up!"

Ralph Baker still did not move. Brandt reached down and grabbed Baker by the shirt, rolling him over. "C'mon Baker, get up!"

Baker's head rolled to the side, revealing a large gash at his left temple, blood streaming down his face. Instinctively, Brandt felt for a pulse.

No pulse. Brandt's face flashed alarm, as he realized Baker was dead. Then he heard the front door of the Suburban slam. Dropping Baker, he set off at a full run after the fleeing girl. She wasn't so stupid after all.

Brandt threw open the driver's door of the Suburban and reached for the glove box to retrieve his sidearm. The glove box was open and the gun was gone. He cursed and shouted after the girl, who had now run into a field of tall dead grass. Suddenly, she turned and dropped to one knee, raised the weapon, clicked off the safety and pulled off a careful shot at the charging Brandt.

"Crap!" shouted Brandt half to himself, as he recognized in the fleeing girl a trained adversary. His body slammed onto the ground as the bullet whizzed just over his head. He knew that he would not survive another exposure to her line of sight. He drew a knife out of his boot and began to slip through the grass in a flanking move.

At once, she was standing nearly over him, the gun pointed at his groin. "Get up!" she shouted. "Get up or I'll neuter you right here!"

He lunged at her leg with the knife, but she was too quick for him, spinning on the other foot, rotating to a spread-eagled stance, still holding the gun true to its intended target.

"Throw the knife over there!" she shouted, gesturing with her eyes to the left.

Brandt saw his chance. In one deft motion before her eyes re-focused on him, Brandt let fly the knife. It slammed to the hilt in her gut. She grunted, fired two shots wild, and fell. In a rage Brandt was on her, beating her face bloody. He grabbed the gun and leveled it at her head. "Okay, who ever you are, you are going to tell me who you really are, or I will kill you."

Groggy and clutching the knife wound with one hand, she rose up in a furious move to strike at him. Brandt pulled the trigger. The bullet went through her head. Now he would never know who she was.

Brandt cursed himself. He loaded her body into the Suburban, cleaned up the field as best he could by digging up the bloody soil and loading it too, then ran the Suburban back and forth over the field to mask the effects of the struggle in the grass. He pulled the vehicle out to the road again. He had retrieved the money and was about to deal with Baker's body when he perceived the dust of a vehicle at some distance down the straight country road. Slamming into gear, he sped off in the opposite direction.

Paul Roche drove out the entrance road to the Lazy Daze dude ranch near Emporia, Kansas in an old Chevy pickup he had just bought from the ranch manager, Jim Buel. After a stop for fuel in Tennessee, his pilot friend had dropped in to the dirt strip used by the Lazy Daze for VIP guests. Roche had known Buel from an assignment in Eastern Europe some years back. He hoped Buel knew how to keep quiet, but was not confident of it. Buel owed Roche for keeping mum about some difficulties in Buel's past when asked by several would-be employers for a reference.

Roche now had two days growth of beard, some western clothes and a good pair of western boots, along with a dog-eared leather valise replacing his Samsonite.

Stopping by a small crossroads post office, Roche mailed a package containing money and ID along with his clothes to a private mailbox in Salt Lake City. A few hours later, he parked the truck in the long-term lot at Kansas City airport. Presenting a Canadian passport with the name of Terry Jansen, he boarded a flight for Calgary. On the plane, he ordered a scotch and soda, feeling good about his prospects for a clean escape. Every change of ID and appearance from here on would widen his margin of safety. He relaxed, reading a paper novel purchased at the airport stand.

CHAPTER 7

In his motel room just off the VA Beach expressway, Bob Steck sat at the small desk crammed between the TV and a coat closet that barely held one coat. Government rate motels weren't very elegant in this military town. He was sipping free lobby coffee and munching some kind of fake cake out of the vending machine in the hallway. Bob tapped out notes on his laptop, organizing his files about Paul Roche. Morton Lindsley had flown to Charleston immediately after the meeting at Oceana. Morgan was back at Langley. Greg Liss was off to hunt for the professor. In the past few hours, Susan Deet had proven her value as an agent in Steck's eyes. She had quickly picked up Roche's trail, working with the local police to find Paul's Buick at the Hampton Roads Airport. She set up a stakeout using two local FBI agents who waited for whomever Roche would have arranged to pick-up and dispose of the car. Shortly after mid-day, it paid off. She was now interviewing the pilot of a small plane that had landed at noontime. Having tied his plane down, he approached the Buick. He was carrying Roche's car key.

The phone rang, snapping Steck out of his concentration on the keyboard.

"Steck." He answered.

"Hey, Mister Bob," drawled Lindsley. "I got a strange report from our folks in Charleston. Just before the storm hit, some wildlife photographer took pictures of an Army zodiac with four soldiers in it, coming right up the Cooper River. These guys were in combat fatigues and armed. We checked with the Army and the Marines, and they did not have any training or other mission going on at that time. Anyway, I had them send me the photos. Maybe you can have a look, on the secure link we gave you this morning?"

"Sure, Mort, I'm on it." Steck was already logging in to a secure internet site. Two passwords, then an encrypted message from the USB memory stick retrieved from his jacket pocket. After one more password, he found the link and double clicked on the photo file.

"Okay, Mort. I've got it open." Steck saw photos of marsh banks, herons contrasted against a threatening sky and a zodiac with four figures in it. "I'll play with the photos for a bit and see what I can make of it."

"Call me if you get any ideas or leads, Bob. I hear Susie Deet's got some good stuff for you to follow-up."

"That's right," Steck replied. "She's pretty good."

"I knew you'd like her work. Call me, y'hear?" Lindsley clicked off.

Steck sat back, rubbed a bit of tiredness from his eyes, then finished up his notes and closed the file. He ordered a sandwich and a beer from room service then called Deet on her cell phone. "You got anything, Deet?"

"Yes, I do," she replied. "Roche was dropped on a ranch near Emporia, Kansas just before dawn. I've got two agents out there now."

"He'll be gone from there by now," Steck mused. "Try to find out when he left, what he wore, what he carried and what means of transport he used."

"It's already done, chief." Her sarcasm pricked him. "Our man is in an old pickup, dressed and accessorized like a cowboy. The guy that runs the ranch is a Mister Jim Buel. He knows more than he's telling. Our people are going to continue with an intensive interview for a while."

"Roger that." Steck had tensed. "I know Buel. I want to talk with him in person. Get us to Emporia right away."

"Okay, boss, Norfolk airport in thirty minutes. Meet me at the South end of the general aviation terminal." Deet clicked off.

Steck packed hastily, wrapped the sandwich, left the beer. At three-thirty pm they were airborne in an agency Learjet, streaming towards a landing strip in Lawrence,

Kansas. A helicopter would collect them there for the short run to the Lazy Daze ranch.

The Learjet had soda on board, no beer. Steck shared half the sandwich with Susan. After some chat time with Deet and praise for her work that day, Steck remembered the photos. He opened the file on his laptop and found one shot that was straight on the faces of the men in the boat. He zoomed in, hoping the photographer had used a high resolution setting so the faces of the men might be made out. It turned out the photographer was good.

"Son-of-a-gun!" he exclaimed, seeing what appeared, except for the scar, to be the chiseled, stern face of his old comrade-in-arms, Glenn Brandt. "Brandt's kid!" he exclaimed. Quickly, Steck connected the dots. Randy Pullin had to be involved in this.

Half an hour later, Steck and Deet sent email to the rest of the team. Steck reclined his seat, closed his eyes, and began running scenarios through his mind. Awful memories kept intruding on his thoughts.

Chris Taylor went to bed at two am in his Paris hotel room. It had been a good day. The crate would be arriving at the Vancouver warehouse in an hour or so. It had been arranged to load the crate into a gasketed fiberglass transit box that would serve as an outer water proof container stacked so it could be accessed during the voyage. The small container ship would leave the harbor on the evening tide bound for Durban, South Africa, with a stop in Santiago, Chile. His men on board that ship would secretly open the container on board, remove the crate, and get it ashore in Santiago for air shipment to the Cairo free zone, then to Dubai.

Mister Al Kafajy had sent a bottle of Dom Perignon to Chris' room. A strict Moslem and non-drinker himself, Al Kafajy took strange satisfaction in catering to the decadence of his minions from western cultures. Chris poured the dregs of the Dom Perignon equally between the two glasses on his bedside table. He nudged the woman lying beside him, also a gift from the boss. "Wake up," he commanded. "The night is just beginning."

Paul Roche cleared Canada Immigration under his assumed identity, Terry Jansen. He took a short taxi ride from Calgary International Airport to Moraine Lake Lodge on McKnight Boulevard. He checked in under the name of George Leland and prepaid his room in cash, telling the clerk he would get up in the night to get on the road again. After a short nap, he strolled to the Sampan Restaurant, nearby. Turning on his charm, he convinced the waitress, a mousy-looking half-Asian bleach blonde in gingham to seat him by a window that gave him clear view of those coming and going. After a meal of seafood and tea, he used the public phone to ring up Naval Reference, Ltd. He asked for Albert Gray. Gray answered after a few moments, "Gray Here."

"Hello Albert," Roche said, as if they spoke daily.

"Roche?" answered Albert, incredulous. "What do you want?" Albert figured Roche was calling to collect on a debt. While at a convention in Washington a year ago, Albert had a minor run-in with the police about a certain girl he was found with during a drug bust at a sleazy motel. Roche got him released before arraignment, through some lawyer friends and intercession with the cops. A few thousand later, covering Roche's "expenses" Albert had gratefully declared that he owed Roche. He knew that was a mistake. Now Roche was probably going to ask him for some favor that would involve a trip to Virginia.

"I'm at the Sampan, across the way from you," Roche asserted.

Gray was suddenly frightened. Roche was here in Calgary? This could not be good. He summoned all his bravado. "So Roche, what's up?"

"I need you to do me a small favor, Albert."

Hours later, in Gray's minivan the two men drove south along route 2, through rugged back country, then east on route 3 toward Lethbridge. Along the way, they reminisced about working together in Kuwait shortly after the Gulf War.

"Things were simpler at the agency then," mused Gray. "You knew who the enemy was, at least." Albert was outwardly relaxed, but inwardly tense. He was always tense around Roche. His mind dwelt on the ease with which Roche simply disposed of anybody in his way, as long as the mission got done. He worried what kind of trouble Roche might be in. It was serious enough that Roche needed to sneak into the states without going through a border station. Albert knew he couldn't ask without putting himself in danger.

As they passed by Lethbridge, Roche changed to a more serious tone. "So, this friend of yours knows the back country well, eh?"

"Sure he does, Paul. He's Blackfoot, just like me. You will call him Little Cloud, though that's not his real name. You will travel on ATV's. He'll take you to the border through the woods and point you toward a pond on the Montana side. You will be met there and brought to Interstate 15, where a trucker will give you a ride to Great Falls. No names, no questions. From there you're on your own."

"These guys on the level?" asked Roche.

"Yup," Albert said simply then added, "As long as you are." He paused, hoping that would sink in. Then he added, "They're just trying to make some money for the winter, Paul. There aren't many opportunities for that out here. Play it cool and everything will work out. Try to screw them and your body will be lunch for some wild bear."

They rode on in silence, through the area called Whiskey Gap, then a further fifteen miles east. The road, if you could call it a road, split. Albert took a fork that was worse than a logging road. After thirty minutes of bump and grind, they pulled off the road into a clearing where two men on ATV's waited, engines off.

Nobody shook hands. Albert said something to Little Cloud in Indian, handing over a wad of cash. Little Cloud grinned, sizing up Roche with a piercing look. He started the motor on his ATV and motioned for Roche to get on behind him. Roche told him that he wanted to drive his own bike. Little Cloud just grinned again and said "Out of the question." Roche got on then turned to say something to Albert. All he saw was tail light beams bouncing through the dust as the minivan sped away. Roche was about to get off, when the ATV lurched forward, taking off down the bumpy road at a fast speed. Roche had to hold on to keep from being tossed. He cursed loudly. Little Cloud kept grinning. The second bike was following thirty yards behind. It carried a younger man who was clearly there to protect Little Cloud. The young buck had some sort of high-powered rifle slung across his back, leather strap tight to his barrel chest. Roche figured he probably had a sidearm too.

The road became a trail, then after a while the trail became a path. It was still dark, so Roche had no idea where they were. It seemed like they were constantly climbing, then dropping, with occasional runs along a creek bed. After what seemed like hours, Little Cloud stopped his ATV in a small clearing. The trailing rider stayed behind, keeping an eye on the scene, his headlight glaring in Roche's eyes.

"Piss break," muttered Little Cloud, stepping off the trail. Roche followed suit. He was real uncomfortable, not just from the ride, but uneasy about his lack of control over the situation.

Returning to the vehicle, Little Cloud reached into a side bag and took out two bottles of water, tossing one to Roche. The water was tepid, but still quenched thirst in the cool night air. Little Cloud offered Roche some jerky, but Roche declined. The stuff looked rank and smelled worse.

They resumed their journey, traveling down a long draw, to a wooded spot above a small pond.

The sky was turning pre-dawn blue-gray. Roche could see the pond clearly. This was where Albert had foretold he would have to go on foot. The older man spoke, plainly and slowly. "Go to the right of the pond. There is a footpath. Go to the south end of the pond, where there is a small brook that leaves the pond. Two men will meet you. Tell the men you are from Little Cloud. They will take you to the highway."

Roche had no choice but to follow those instructions. He wanted this to be over. "Okay," he replied. A few steps down the path, he turned to wave. The two men stood stony-faced, watching Roche intently to be sure he followed orders.

Roche figured this must be the border. Actually, they were already six miles into the United States. The Blackfoot had their own sense of "borders."

Tired and haggard looking, the mock cowboy Roche emerged into the further custody of Indians, who proceeded in the same manner as Little Cloud, winding through back country for two hours. The sun was up, chasing the chill night air away when they stopped below the crest of a hill.

"Walk" ordered the leader, motioning toward the east and the sun. Roche was apprehensive. "Go," ordered the man. Roche started up the trial to the top of the hill. He heard traffic sounds from the other side. Cresting the ridge, he spotted a big semi rig stopped in the break-down lane. The driver waved to him. Roche scurried down to the highway and got in the cab, as the driver stoked up his big diesel.

"Hi. My name is Terry Jansen." Roche offered his hand to the driver.

"No names." The driver declared, heading off down the highway.

———

Steck and Deet spent precious hours interrogating Buel at the Lazy Daze ranch. Buel was an old hand at playing the game. He would give them just enough information to hold off arrest, all the while buying time for Roche to smudge his trail. After getting all they could, including the information about the pickup truck, Deet took off in search of the vehicle while Steck stayed with Buel.

As soon as they were alone, Steck barked at Buel. "Now it's time to cut the crap! You're not in this too deep yet, but if you don't come clean with me, it's going to get real unpleasant."

Buel tried to give Steck a look of indifference, but Steck caught the caution in his eyes. "No baloney, Buel," Steck flashed warning. "Roche has crossed some serious lines and you're going to be right in the same soup if I don't get all you know right now!"

Buel gave Steck a long stare. Then he studied the floor as if trying to decide something. The bravado that seemed so easy to Buel in front of Deet seemed to be draining out of the man. Finally he blurted "Look Bob, you know Roche. People who get in his way often disappear. I like my life here. It's the best deal I've ever had. I don't want to risk losing it. All I can tell you is he showed up bought some cowboy clothes and an old pickup and then left."

"Look at me!" ordered Steck. "Roche is mixed up in murder, espionage and maybe even international terrorism. There are people we both know that seem to be involved along with him. You know I won't go into the details, Buel, but this is really big league stuff. If you are involved, you're in deep mucky, dude and you better tell me all you know before it is used against you in front of a judge."

"I told you what I know, Bob." Buel seemed tired, almost whipped. His eyes were on the verge of tears."

Steck waited a long moment. "I'm not sure yet, but I think Brandt's kid is involved. So is Randy Pullin. Buel cringed, putting hands to his ears. "I don't want to know!" he wailed.

Steck waited until Buel had dropped his hands limply to his lap. Tuning his trained senses, Steck eyed Buel carefully. "It's possible that Blake is in this too."

Buel's whole countenance changed to fear. Steck knew the fright in Buel's eyes was genuine.

Greg Liss boarded a Southwest Airlines flight from Baltimore to Manchester New Hampshire in the early afternoon. He would rent a car, drive up Interstate 93 to Interstate 89. That would put him into Hanover, New Hampshire at the Dartmouth University campus by nightfall. Fortune was with him. Driving from Norfolk to Baltimore, he had contacted Doctor Wiggelsworth's wife Margaret by cell phone. She remembered Greg and she was anxious to see him again. She invited him to come for a visit. She insisted he stay at her home over-night, knowing that if her husband had been home he would insist on extending that courtesy to a former star student. He arrived at the Dartmouth campus around six-thirty pm.

Greg parked his rental in the shade of one of the hundred year old maple trees that lined the large quadrangle. This was a magic time in New England, when tiny wisps of yellow and red begin to invade the still vivid green canopy of the great hardwood trees. Only a portent of the explosion of color that would follow in a month or so, the flashes of color in early September were a signal to get out that extra sweater and start yearning for a crisp apple from the new harvest. Greg took a deep breath, a fond sigh in remembrance of his undergraduate days in this place. Late afternoon sunlight turned to early evening shadows as he strapped on his hastily stuffed back pack and strolled across the big field, alive with students and townsfolk out for a walk. The senses and sounds of campus life penetrated his being as he walked. Lots of wonderful memories flooded in, happy carefree times. Meandering, he nodded to faculty members whom he remembered.

One older gentleman with a weathered, chiseled face and distinctive white beard stopped him with a gesture. "Now, let me see," mused the old gent, Mister …Liss, is it?"

Greg was surprised at being recognized. "Why, yes. You must be Professor Greene? Natural Sciences, if I recall." They chatted for a few minutes, each self-satisfied that he had remembered the other. Seeing the sun getting lower, Greg decided to end the conversation. "Could you direct me to Doctor Wigglesworth's residence, Professor?" Greg knew perfectly well that the Wigglesworth home was at the northwest corner of the campus, just a few hundred yards directly in front of him.

"Why yes, Mister Liss, I could," the older man replied, thoughtfully stroking his beard. He slowly gestured in the direction of a large white Victorian directly ahead. He called after Greg, who had already begun to move along, "But I'm afraid you'll find that old Wiggie's out of town."

"Thank you Professor Greene," Called Greg as he turned back toward the gentleman and waved. "I'm here as the guest of Missus Wigglesworth. I hope to see you again before I go." Greg knew he would be long gone before Professor Greene's day began next morning.

As Greg walked the rest of the way across campus, something reminded him of Carole Hinson. Maybe it was the hairstyle of the brunette co-ed passing buy at that moment. Maybe it was her perfume. Whatever the queue, a flood of memories, both exquisitely pleasant and excruciatingly painful came on him all at once in an unexpected jumble.

Carole was Greg's first and only love. They had been classmates. Both studied hard and excelled in their studies. Both wanted a career in federal service. Both wanted the other carnally and intellectually. But Carole wanted more. While Greg was content to build his life around her, Carole's thirst for relationship with others, including other men quickly overwhelmed the romance. Finally, she threw him over for a young officer in her native Canada. She tried to remain his friend, but he couldn't bear it. She went off to become an officer in the Canadian Security Intelligence Service (CSIS) and Greg lost track of her, except for one brief encounter at a joint security meeting in Toronto about a year ago. It was a terrible experience for Greg. She had greeted him cheerfully with a hug and a kiss on the cheek, then for the rest of the day clung to her escort, a big burly guy in a business suit. That evening, he ran across them along with another couple at a disco, where she seemed to be putting on a deliberate display of lewdness for Greg's benefit. It was the worst memory of the young man's life.

Greg suddenly realized that he was now sitting on a park bench, crouched in a near-fetal position. He shook off the clouds in his mind as best he could and resumed his path to the Wigglesworth home. He would drown those memories in the work at hand.

CHAPTER 8

Brandt had eleven hours to think what he would say to Colonel Randy. He drove along Interstate 90 at a moderate pace, aware that even a routine traffic violation could ruin him. It would fix his position relative to the crime scene that by now had surely been declared by the local police at Coeur d' Alene, Idaho. If it really went badly, the body in the back of the truck would cook his goose for sure. Nevertheless, each mile of separation from the scene of Ralph Baker's demise gave him a bit more confidence.

In the middle of the night just short of Billings, Montana, near a place called Yegen, Brandt pulled the Suburban off the highway and made his way to a public park he new about that ran along the Yellowstone river. Finding an obscure road that was little more than a path, he put the truck into four wheel drive and rumbled to a secluded spot, dousing the headlights. Donning a small headlamp, he dragged the girl's body out of the rear access door, stashing it for the moment behind some large rocks at the bottom of a little draw. With an entrenching tool from the survival kit in the Suburban, Brandt scratched out a shallow grave from the hardpan. He mopped sweat from his brow in spite of the cold night air, as he finished the burial. Using far too much time for comfort he carefully made the area look as undisturbed as possible. Brandt slowly retraced his path to the park road, taking care not to race the engine and using the waning moonlight to pick his way along without headlights.

It was nearly dawn when he got back to the highway. Instead of getting back on the interstate, he rolled to an area of fast food and truck stops. After a hearty breakfast and a truck stop shower, he ran the Suburban through a car wash, taking care to clean out the back and dispose of some blood stained blankets in a dumpster behind a Taco Bell.

Back on the highway, Brandt cruised along a hundred mile arc around the Crow Reservation, past Little Big Horn, to the Wyoming border. Reaching the small community of Buffalo about nine am, Brandt stopped at a local tire store and paid cash for a new set of tires for the Suburban. Hopefully the woman's grave would not be found any time soon, but if it was, fresh tire tracks lifted as evidence would not connect to his vehicle.

Brandt turned onto route sixteen towards Bighorn National Forest. He turned off at a dirt road that meandered beyond government property. Waving to a couple of outpost guards, Brandt piloted the big black SUV to a turn-around at the end of the road amidst a slew of no trespassing signs at the gate to *Free Nation*'s main base.

"Welcome back, Major!" snapped the guard at the gate as he saluted Brandt.

"Hey, morning Jim," Brandt smiled as he retrieved the proffered gate pass, stuffing it into his fatigues. He still had no clue what he was going to tell Colonel Randy.

After successfully wrenching Roche's "new" identity out of Buel, Steck figured he had to shake Susan Deet for a couple of days. He knew where he had to go. He wanted to speak with a couple of folks in Wyoming, man to man.

Just prior to boarding the company plane for a quick trip to Wyoming Steck raised Deet on her cell phone.

"Susan, your man is traveling under the alias Terry Jansen. He most likely took a flight from the K.C. Airport. You should find the truck abandoned there. Get with the airlines and see if our man took a commercial flight. My best guess is that he will try to get out of the country."

"I'm on it," Deet declared. "What are you up to?"

"I'm going to contact the guy we saw in that picture. I know where to find him. I'll be taking the plane for a day. I guess you can take a commercial flight back if you need to. In order to get results I must approach him alone. We know one another so I hope I can get some information without raising suspicion." Steck shivered at the thought. Actually he had no clue whether he could pull it off.

"I'll have a make on Terry Jansen by this evening. Call me when you touch down in … where did you say you were going?" Deet was using that self-assured case officer's demeanor, trying to get information that she sensed Steck was reluctant to give her. Inwardly she seethed. This guy was taking her airplane!

"I'll let you know." Steck clicked off.

Minutes later, the jet roared above the clouds on a flight plan for Sheridan County Airport, Wyoming.

Greg Liss was in luck. Not only was he well received and fed a hearty New England boiled dinner by a gracious Missus Wigglesworth, but she was expecting to hear from the good professor by satellite telephone during the evening and offered to include Greg.

"I'm so glad you came to visit, Mister Liss," remarked Missus Wigglesworth. She was serving sherry in the library of the big house. "Isn't it odd that you should come on the very day I'm to receive my first call from William in over a month?" She stirred her coffee with what had obviously once been a delicate hand, now gnarled by arthritis. She was short and very thin, with weathered skin that revealed her lifelong love of the outdoors. Her features were angular and strong, yet serene. Greg guessed her to be about seventy years old. She dressed simply but elegantly in clothes reminiscent of those in her photo on the mantle over the fireplace. Greg figured the photo was late nineteen forties, of a beautiful young woman in dressage standing beside a Morgan horse. It was clear that the infirmities of age now dominated her life, except for her eyes. Missus Wigglesworth's eyes were bright and twinkling, full of life and ideas, just like those in that old photo.

"Yes, it's fortunate, and so kind of you to share some of your and the Doctor's time on the satellite phone." Greg decided he would be brief with the Professor and then leave the room to allow privacy for husband and wife to converse.

Later she led Greg down a dark paneled hallway. They sat at opposite ends of a long dining room table. A pudgy combination part time companion, maid and cook served the meal. She was obviously a student on some campus work program. As he ate heartily, Greg tried to find out what the Professor's wife knew about *The Hand of Mohammed.*

"I'm afraid I don't pay much attention to his work," she declared, "except I admit, to feign interest while he tells me all about it. I do know that this 'hand' is one of the things he's been looking for throughout his whole career, but even William thinks it is probably fictitious."

Greg decided to drift the conversation in a direction that would build relationship with the lady in case she became useful later. "So, what does the wife of a traveling professor do while her husband is out and about?"

"Gardening, Mister Liss. Gardening is my passion and orchids are my pride. Later on I'll show you my greenhouse and my award-winning *orchidae*. I've collected eighteen HCC (Highly Commendable Certificate) awards from the American Orchid Society, the Royal Horticultural Society and even the HOC which is the Hawaii Orchid Society. My own creation, *Odontioda Galaxy 'harlequin' ACC/AOS* has made a sum of money over the years."

As she droned on about her obsession and success with orchids, Greg tried to mimic her "feigned interest."

At eight-thirty the phone rang as scheduled. Doctor Wigglesworth's raspy voice rattled over the remarkably clear satellite line. After some greetings and exchange of affection marred by Missus Wigglesworth's seeming inability to deal with the characteristic transmission delay, she turned the phone over to Greg.

Greg stared at a photo of Doctor Wigglesworth along with some of his co-workers at a dig. It gave him a better sense of the man on the other end of the line.

"Well Liss, I always like to hear from former students, especially one as brilliant as you. I hear you are with the government now which in my opinion is a perfect waste of time for a man of your intellect!" Doctor Wigglesworth always spoke his mind, which is why Greg held him in such high esteem.

Coming right to the point, Greg said "Sir, I have an urgent need to speak with you in person. Where can we meet?"

"Meet!? Out of the question! I'm at the archeological dig of an old caravanserai in the middle of the blasted Yemeni desert!"

Greg would have to chance a more direct comment. "Doctor Wigglesworth," he half stammered, "I have possibly located an item that I know you have been seeking for some time. One we discussed many times in class as being either fact or fancy."

After a pause, Wigglesworth blurted "The *hand*? Are you telling me you've found it?"

"Yes sir, I believe that to be the case." Greg was taking a really big chance, painfully aware that he was not on a secure line.

The Professor blustered. "PREPOSTEROUS!" he shouted. "If I can't find the thing, how does a wet behind the ears Washington bureaucrat?"

"That is all I'm going to say on this line, sir. Will you meet me? I will come to you anywhere in the world." Greg waited tensely, giving the old man time to absorb the news.

In the long pause that ensued, Wigglesworth reasoned that a smart kid like Liss would not trick him, nor would he demand a meeting unless he had found something worth looking into. He finally decided it would be worth a meeting.

"I'll be in Amman, Jordan two weeks hence. I can meet you at the Intercontinental hotel."

"No good, sir. This needs to happen within the next two or three days." Greg hoped that the Professor would hear the urgency in his voice.

"But how can we do it?" Wigglesworth was incredulous.

"I have your location. Stay there for the next three days. I will contact you. Please do not speak of this to anyone. Please do not speak about it further on this line." Greg knew the JUMP team tekkies in Virginia would have Wiggie's satphone located by now. "Good night, sir." Greg handed the phone to Missus Wigglesworth and disappeared into the next room, closing the door behind him.

Half an hour later, Greg had completed his excuses and thanks to Missus Wigglesworth and was driving back to Manchester, speaking constantly on his secure mobile phone with JUMP headquarters and with Lindsley.

Chris Taylor spent the morning strolling through the Tuilleries, now resplendent with late summer blooms of bright red, orange, white and purple. The warm fresh air and modest breeze meandering out of a sunny sky helped wipe away his slight hangover. Around noontime he opened a small attaché and set up his laptop on a wide bench to browse his email. It was a great day in a great place and he was not going to waste it indoors.

His man aboard the ship had left a message that they were now past Los Angeles on the way down the coast, and would be out of signal distance for two days. The message stated that all was well thus far. Contacts in Santiago were waiting, having received instructions for their task. They would receive the crate and re-consign it to the Microwave Company of Egypt, via airfreight. Mister Al Kafajy's controlling interest in the Egyptian company was not motivated by profit. The company was a miserable performer. His sole interest was to have a place in the Cairo free trade zone that could trans-ship goods like the ones in the crate without much red tape.

Chris made a few electronic trades and took care of his correspondence for the day. He closed his laptop and sat back to enjoy the sights and sounds of summer in Paris. The only thing lacking at the moment was a sandwich and a glass of Beaujolais. No matter, he would take care of that shortly at some sidewalk café.

Chris had nearly nodded off, when a female voice rose above the background of chatting students, nannies and other Parisians out for a midday walk.

"Monsieur Taylor?"

Chris didn't move, but peered at her through his Ray-ban glasses. A rather attractive young lady in a hotel uniform stood at a distance, leaning and peering at him as if over a tall counter. "Chris Taylor?"

Chris sat up and gestured with a hand. "Come closer Mademoiselle, I won't bite. I promise."

She straightened up seeming a bit embarrassed but came no closer. "Excuse me, sir. Are you Mister Chris Taylor?"

"May I ask who would like to know?" Chris took off the glasses and winked. Her look of embarrassment turned to a scowl.

She held up a note. "The gentleman who wrote this note would like to know." she said almost scolding him.

Chris reached for the note, but she withdrew it. "First please identify yourself!"

"I am Chris Taylor," he said simply. His eyes were now fixed on the note.

"May I see some identification?" she said, assuming a tone not unlike the French police.

Chris was clearly agitated now. Fumbling in his attaché he produced his passport, turned the page and held it up. "See, it even has my picture," he said sarcastically.

Without a word, she handed him the note with a look of disdain and turned to walk purposefully back in the direction of the row of hotels across the boulevard.

The note was in Mohammed Al Kafajy's hand. *"Come to my suite at one pm. Change of plans."*

Chris checked his watch. It was already twelve-forty. He packed his stuff into the attaché and headed for the hotel, hoping there would be food in the boss's suite.

Susan Deet had no trouble locating the pickup or finding which flight "Terry Jansen" had taken. She contacted Canadian immigration authorities and also some friends in CSIS. By evening she was certain the Roche was in Calgary, but had melted away, probably under another alias. Faced with a cold trail, stuck in Kansas City without her airplane and having lost Steck, she paced her motel room totally frustrated.

She knew better than to try raising Steck. He had given clear direction about that. As much as his actions upset her, she knew better than to potentially put Steck at risk by attempting some blind contact. She brooded over a sandwich in the motel restaurant. It faintly resembled ham and cheese. With no bar in the motel, she had to wash it down with acrid coffee. Finally she could bear it no longer. Deet returned to her room where she retrieved her secure mobile phone and took it to her rental car. From the privacy of the car she called Mort Lindsley.

Lindsley was disappointed that Roche's trail had gone blank for now. He asked Susan to think hard about how to pick up the trail and to use any JUMP team assets to do so. He filled her in on Greg Liss and the Dartmouth professor. When she told him about Steck's side trip, he flipped out.

"Mister Bob is really tryin' my patience. Why did you let him go adventuring alone to a place that is clearly FBI jurisdiction?"

Susan cringed. She knew the boss was right, but it hurt to admit it to herself never mind to him. "He just took the blasted airplane then didn't let me know until it was too late to stop him." She pleaded.

"I know it's not your fault, Susie," Drawled Lindsley. I'm gonna take this up with Ryall Morgan. Mister Bob Steck is rubbin' me the wrong way."

"I'll second that!" Deet added.

CHAPTER 9

Steck bought some western duds in Sheridan; boots, Levis, and a burgundy sailcloth shirt with pointed flaps on the dual breast pockets. He topped it off with a wide belt and a silver buckle festooned with turquoise. He stopped short of the Stetson. The altogether too new clothes made him look the part of a casual tourist, but definitely one from "back east."

Randy Pullin was surprised to receive the call from Steck. It was one of those "just happened to be in the neighborhood" calls from an old war buddy. Colonel Randy didn't seem suspicious at all. He invited Steck to drop by the compound to chat about old times. He seemed eager to see his old buddy and to show off his accomplishments. "You still with 'The Company' Bob?" he queried, figuring that was the only way Steck could have tracked him down.

"Yup, officially I'm still with them, but it's getting close to the time I can take my pension," declared Steck. "I'm working off accumulated vacation time."

"I'll bet you get a lot of that," replied Pullin.

Steck caught the implication in Randy's voice. Pullin always had a dim view of any civilian that worked for the government. He thought they were a bunch of parasitic no-accounts sucking the blood of the US taxpayer. Steck decided to play into that. "Yeah, I take lots of vacation," he lied.

"Well, just drive out here and present yourself to the gate guard. I'll make sure he is expecting you. Is Amy with you? Can you stay a few days?"

Steck feigned that Amy was at a horse show in Maryland and was probably going to join him in California in a few days.

As soon as Randy hung up, he called the head of the post guard detail. "There's a CIA agent coming to stay with us for maybe a couple of days, name of Bob Steck. I want him welcomed and accommodated, but keep a keen eye on him. Put him in the guest cottage and turn on all the surveillance gear. It'll be a good test of our security system."

Colonel Randy's radar was up, not only because there was a CIA agent visiting, but because of his all too recent job with Paul Roche. He worried that Steck had picked up the trail then dismissed the thought. Even Steck would not be that quick to get on to such a well planned escapade. Still, he felt uneasy about Steck's impromptu visit to the compound after all these years.

Steck called Susan Deet, who reported what she had found including the fact that the trail on Roche had gone cold. Bob was not surprised, in fact he expected it. Roche was an old hand at covering his tracks, something essential to longevity in agents.

Deet let him know that Lindsley was rankled, and that Steck needed to call Ryall Morgan. The tone of her voice let him know that she was not happy with her circumstances either.

"Look, Susie," Steck declared. "I'm going deep into an organization that we know is involved in this case. I'm the only one that can pull it off, *if* I can pull it off and you know I have to do it alone to avoid suspicion on the part of these Para-military nut cases. Please try to cut me a bit of slack here, will you?"

She was not to be dismissed by some spook agent. "You took my damned airplane, Bob!"

"Don't worry, Susan. I'll bring it back safe and sound. The pilot has orders to pick you up in KC day after tomorrow in the evening. He will leave Sheridan at two pm day after tomorrow with or without me."

"Do you think I'm gonna hang around here waiting for you?" She was raising her voice in frustration.

"Just stay with me on this, Susie. If it goes right we can pick up a new trail. If it doesn't, we can get back on Roche." Steck wouldn't admit that if it didn't go well he might be Pullin's prisoner.

His next call was to Ryall Morgan. Morgan was sipping scotch in his study. It was a good time of day to speak with the boss because he mellowed in the evening. Not this time.

"Where are you, Bob?" Morgan knew quite well where Steck was. It was a signal to go easy.

"I think you know," was the bland reply.

"Steck, you've managed to get Lindsley all riled up. I expect you to be more sensitive to turf issues."

"Turf or no turf, Ryall, I've got a chance to pick up the trail on that crate, or on Roche, or both and I'm not going to miss that opportunity. You know that if Susie was with me, I would have no shot."

Morgan simmered down then he filled Steck in on Greg Liss' story. "I need you back here. Your knowledge of Arabia and the Persian Gulf will help us to get in and communicate with Doctor Wigglesworth. Get out of there as quickly as you can."

"Saudi Arabia is one thing, Ryall. Yemen is quite another. I believe the only guys that can help with Yemen would be Task Force Orange. I suggest you get hold of the Pentagon and ask their help. They're the only chance for you to get an American in and out of Yemen with his head." There was a pause while both men thought about that.

"Greg Liss wants to go himself," offered Morgan.

"You got any turf issues with that?" Steck immediately regretted the remark. At any rate, he sure didn't want to have to baby sit a green kid like Liss in a quagmire like Yemen. He hoped Morgan would have more sense than to set him up like that.

"Just get whatever you can and get back here pronto, Bob." Morgan clicked off.

———————

Steck rented a car in Sheridan, and drove out early in the morning. He presented himself at the guard shack near the main gate to *Free Nation* around nine-thirty a.m.

"We've been expecting you Mister Steck," the guard wore fatigues, a gray beret and spit polished boots. On his shiny black belt was a .45 Caliber sidearm. He gave Steck directions to the headquarters building. "You have exactly three minutes to get there before we come after you. You will be met by a captain in a purple beret." Steck gave him a puzzled look. "In case you get lost. We wouldn't want you to wander into a live fire area, sir."

Steck knew better. He figured they had been given orders to keep him under wraps. "Have a good-day sir!" The guard snapped a smart salute and waved Steck in. Steck marveled at the high level of training and organization everywhere he looked. This was no tinhorn outfit. Discipline was tight and everyone seemed well equipped. Exactly three minutes later he was greeted by a young Captain and whisked into the guest quarters. It was a small cottage with white siding and black shutters. Inside it was clean and neat, sporting two bedrooms, a modern kitchen, a dining room, living room with a stone fireplace, and a bath. The place had a woman's touch, all tastefully decorated in rustic western style.

"Make yourself at home, Mister Steck," said the Captain. "Colonel Randy will send for you at ten hundred." There's food in the kitchen and linen for your use. He handed Steck an index card with a number on it. "Call this number if you need anything." He gestured towards an antique telephone. The officer started to leave then he paused by the door. "I suggest you stay inside. There's a lot of traffic today on post." He snapped a salute, turned and went out, closing the door tightly behind him.

Steck waited a few seconds then tried the door to see if he was locked in. He was not. He quickly searched the place for evidence of electronic surveillance. "Phew!" he exclaimed to himself, impressed by the array of electronic bugs he found, wondering about the ones he did not find. At the refrigerator, he opened a coke and took a long draught.

Returning to the living room, he pulled a straight chair to the largest window and sat, watching the activity outside.

The post was alive with vehicles ranging from converted Jeep Wranglers to heavy trucks. Paved roads and even sidewalks gave the impression of a small western town. Work crews were busy maintaining the streets. At his extreme right, Steck could see an electric utility truck and crew hanging a string of lights by the entrance to a PX that looked like a small version of Wal-Mart. To his left, off the big main square was a long low building he surmised was an elementary school by the sounds and spectacle of children at supervised play on the grounds. In the distance, he heard the shouts of a drill sergeant. He figured there must be a parade ground nearby.

The headquarters building, just across the big square was another surprise. It was a large two storey brick building with lots of windows. A steady stream of both men and women flowed in and out of the building. Many of them were in civilian clothes, but many sported the odd looking military full dress that had first impressed Steck at the guard shack by the main gate. It seemed a cross between US and European, with a grey and red beret that had a stripe of green galun around the brim. As he saw more of it Steck thought of tin-horn African third rate military dress. He thought it best not to advertise that observation while he was here.

Steck sat quietly by his window and concentrated on burning a mental image of all he could see and hear.

At one minute before ten, the Captain strode up to the front door of Steck's cottage and knocked loudly. Steck swung the door, facing the man. "The Colonel will see you now sir," the Captain snapped a salute.

Paul Roche had checked in to a resort hotel in Salt Lake City after a five hundred mile straight run in an old Ford Taurus he bought out of a farmer's front yard in Great Falls, Montana. The car ran okay, but it smelled of cow manure. He was glad to get to a city he knew well, where he could change identity again and maybe complete his "fade" from the police trail. Since he had a passport that worked okay through Canada immigration, he decided to remain "Terry Jansen" for today. After a shower and a couple hours sleep, he ate a hearty breakfast and went shopping. Paying cash for a business suit and casual accessories, he stopped at the hotel barber shop and got his three day beard shaved off, along with a brush cut, something he had not had in years. The new Mister Jansen looked every bit the modern business traveler.

Roche had his best set of contacts in the US around Salt Lake City. A couple of calls from the prepaid cell phone he had bought on the road got him a new set of Chevy wheels and rid of the smelly Taurus.

By afternoon, Roche was relaxed enough to rent clubs and play a round of golf on the hotel's reasonably good course. His plan was working fine. He had tapped a bank account that he had long held in SLC, deciding not to risk a transfer from the Caymans yet. In the evening, he would keep an appointment with a guy who could supply him with his final change of identity, including a British passport with all the trimmings. This trip was costing him a lot, but safety and security came first. It was just part of the cost of doing business Roche style.

Ryall Morgan had just left the office of Colonel Radcliffe at the Pentagon. It was the first official meeting for these two men since having served together teaching a top secret class of special agents just after the September 11th tragedy. The class brought top members of the clandestine services, military and FBI together to map strategies in what was to become the "war on terror." Out of that had come several new operating entities including Mort Lindsley's FBI JUMP Team domestically and Task Force Orange in the military. One of those new "entities" was also Ryall

Morgan's group, headed by Bob Steck. Contrary to Washington banalities, Ryall's group purposely didn't have a name. The ones with names have a way of finding their way into the press, a great way to lose cover.

Steck's observation had been right. After a briefing by Bill Radcliffe, Morgan knew for sure that he would need help from a group like Task Force Orange to get someone in and hopefully out of Yemen in a hurry. He marveled at the apparent ease with which old professor Wigglesworth and his archeological team moved in and out of that horrid place.

The problem was that Radcliffe's team was fully deployed. The eight men he had in Yemen at the moment were chasing a hot lead obtained from the interrogation of Sheik Khalid Muhammed. Radcliffe made it clear that he wasn't about to drop the trail of top Al Qaeda operatives to find some college professor out digging in the desert. He also opined that any American who thought he could get away with digging all over a rat hole like Yemen must be a perfect idiot.

Realizing that he was not going to get the resources he wanted from Radcliffe, Morgan stopped short of telling the Colonel about *TheHand of Mohammed.* The fewer involved in this the better, for the moment.

On the way back to his office at Langley, Ryall Morgan spoke with Mort Lindsley on the phone. "Mort, I can't get Pentagon resources that would get your man Liss in and out of Yemen safely."

"Well, Mister Morgan, I tell you what," began Mort. "I can get him in or out of any place in the world with a few pokes from the State department." Not waiting for Ryall's response, he drawled on. "I guess my boys will have to figure it out themselves." As he said this Mort sat back and smiled, waiting for Ryall to react.

"Negative!" snapped Morgan. The last thing he needed was meddling from the State Department. "Come up to my office at four-thirty. I'll see what else I can arrange."

Brandt sat on his bunk at the head of about forty bunks and lockers in the bachelor officers quarters (BOQ,) a long, low barracks style wood-shingled building amidst several others near the parade ground. It had the typical spotless floors and walls, toilets at one end and a vacant day officer's desk at the other. The events at Coeur d'Alene Idaho were buzzing through his mind. He stared into space, his face taught, trying to organize bits of information. Some were vivid, some were obscure.

The scuffle that led to the unfortunate "accidental" death of Ralph Baker was something he thought he could explain or excuse to Colonel Randy with just a slight spin on the truth. His involvement with the girl, her startling reaction to Baker's demise and Brandt's killing of her in self defense was a gigantic problem.

The trip back to the post had been handled just like any military assignment, cool and professional. Now in the quiet of his quarters, Brandt trembled like a kid who had been caught stealing chickens and would have to face his parents.

Colonel Randy trusted Brandt to carry out any mission, anywhere in the world, with absolute adherence to discipline and training. It was a trust not given easily, but rather earned over a long period of flawless performance of duty. Now Brandt would have to report to his mentor his total breakdown of discipline and disregard for the importance of the mission entrusted to him. It was as if he was about to take his knife and pierce the heart of the only person who's love and trust he ever craved.

The violence was just his military training in automatic mode, he reasoned with himself. Every man has to have a woman companion once in a while, he postured. After all, he had covered his tracks well and would probably never be connected to this incident. Did he really have to tell Colonel Randy the whole story? Maybe he could just omit the part about the girl. The agonizing answer was that he could not. That would be dishonest to Colonel Randy, something Brandt knew he could not live with.

Finally, he put on a clean set of fatigues, donned his beret, and slowly jogged up to the headquarters building to face the music.

Susan Deet had wrapped up and filed a report on the pursuit of Paul Roche. She thought of checking out of her hotel and going up to Sheridan, Wyoming to find the airplane and re-join Steck. Instead, she decided to kick back and get some tanning time.

Susan donned a fairly modest two piece bathing suit, sunglasses and a sun hat. Taking her laptop and a book to read, she went to the ground level and took a chaise by the hotel pool. She connected via secure WiFi and was now exchanging email with Greg Liss, who was back at Jump Team headquarters near Washington.

Greg was trying to enlist her aid to convince Mort Lindsley to let him go to Yemen and conduct a de-briefing of Doctor Wigglesworth about the "Hand of Mohammed." Lindsley had just told Liss that the mission to Yemen would be honchoed by the CIA because it was outside the United States and the FBI had not been invited by the "host" country. Whether Greg would be part of the mission was still to be determined.

Deet was tempted to get unprofessional about the obvious breach of the same type of turf protocol by Bob Steck, but thought better of putting it in an email. She was still wrestling with the emotional sting but savvy enough not to let it screw up her next performance review.

As if persuaded by that argument, she wrote to Greg "better to honor the chain of command, accept your orders and keep the boss happy."

Paul Roche returned to his hotel room in Salt Lake City just after ten o'clock pm. He now had all the things he needed to get to his final destination for the next few months. Soon he would be living quietly and quite well in a villa high in the hills just outside of Mexico City, under the name and identity of Hugh Coles, a British author of romance novels.

Hugh Coles' *persona* had been practiced for years by Roche but never used except to create some superficial social contacts that could some day serve to verify his identity. Among his many assumed personae, Roche had held this one in reserve for a difficult occasion like the present one. The 'Hugh' character that Paul had practiced for so long in front of his hall mirror in Norfolk, Virginia was a wealthy refugee from the British upper Class. He never really had to work for a living, but kept busy writing un-published novels. Hugh bore a classical British education (which was close to the truth, for Roche had studied the classics via internet links to prestigious British schools) and he even belonged to a couple of British men's clubs, although no one at those clubs would remember meeting him. Roche had cleverly donated several sizeable amounts to their charities, just so he could accumulate correspondence on the clubs' letter head, in appreciation of his generous support.

Now 'Hugh Coles' stood before the bathroom mirror in his hotel room, adjusting his hair and eyebrow color to add more gray, then fitting a paste-on moustache of short bristly gray lip-hair. "Rather handsome, aren't you Mister Coles," he exclaimed to the mirror in a very British accent.

After completing his transformation task, Roche decided to use the last minutes on his prepaid cell phone to call Buel. He was interested in how hot or cold his trail might have become in the past day or two.

Buel had just finished his chores at the ranch and sat to watch TV. A bit after nine pm the phone rang. "This is Buel," he answered in his customary way. The unmistakable voice of Paul Roche chilled him.

"Has any one been around looking for me, Buel?"

Buel foolishly lowered his voice as if that would help foil any bug on the line. "Damn right, they have!" he forced a shouting whisper. "You got me in a heap of trouble. Bob Steck and some woman came-a-calling and put pressure on me. I didn't tell them anything, I swear!" Buel was sweating. He reminded himself not to tell Roche that he knew Blake was involved. That would surely get him killed.

Roche was not happy and he let Buel know it. Then he decided to throw some flak. "Are they buggin this line, Buel?"

"No. That is, I don't know!" stammered Buel.

"Just don't tell them anything about my ranch here in Calgary, you hear?"

"Of course I won't, Paul. You know me, I wouldn't..." his voice trailed off.

"Be sure now." Roche clicked off. He went to the sink, drew about six inches of water and doused the phone to wipe out the call memory. When he was sure the phone would no longer work, he flushed it down the toilet and began packing.

CHAPTER 10

Steck spent three hours of intense conversation with his old friend-turned-criminal, Randy Pullin. At times during those few hours, he felt as if his life was in danger. At other times he felt sympathy and admiration for Pullin and his organization.

Colonel Randy started out by showing Bob the strength of his operation. Long dismissed as a few nuts living in the wilderness by the FBI and CIA types who were supposed to be keeping an eye on him, Randy had built a military organization that many third world governments would be proud to call their army.

Randy's organization boasted over Three thousand five hundred men trained in some ways as well as any U.S. Marine. More than two thousand of them lived at the post. He had quarters for their families and a school system inspired by the famous Calvert curriculum. The schools had turned out kids who were on full boat scholarship at major universities, including magna cum laude graduates of Harvard. He had accumulated military hardware from all over the world. This included Leopard and T-82 tanks; self propelled howitzers, rocket launchers, MANPADS (Stinger) missiles, and even his own brand of UAV (Unmanned Aerial Vehicle) that boasted GPS and multi-spectral sensors. This small airplane carried advanced imaging cameras as well as a tiny rocket designed and built at the post. Randy boasted that the UAV's rockets could take out a coffee can from five miles away with a ninety-nine percent kill rate.

Steck was flabbergasted to think that a Para-military group could "sneak" tanks and howitzers into the U.S and then get them into the mountains of Wyoming without detection. He was confounded to imagine how in the world *Free Nation* could possibly use this kind of hardware except to play soldier on this patch of ground. Randy admitted that the heavy stuff was only useful for training. But he hinted that the value of a soldier for hire was enhanced by familiarity with the materiel of their clients.

The most amazing impression on Steck was the gung-ho atmosphere and absolute dedication and loyalty to Colonel Randy that he sensed in every person on the post. The officers and men all seemed to be US or European military types, a few Asians too, who had combat training as their background and constant personal improvement as their goal.

When he asked the obvious question – "How do you finance all of this?" Steck had been disarmed by the reply. Colonel Randy had looked him straight in the face and declared, "Our resources are for hire anywhere in the world for nearly any mission at the right price. We have our code of ethics, which obviously doesn't match yours, Bob, but is rigorously adhered to by all hands. I don't tolerate killing unless it is part of a military mission or in self-defense, and I won't engineer a coup on sovereign governments. Every thing else is fair game."

"Is it really that simple?" Steck queried, incredulous.

"Yes, Bob. It is really that simple," was the straight-up reply.

Rattled by Pullin's cold candor, Bob decided to go right back at him with the question he needed answered. He had no idea whether the next few minutes would seal his fate. "Randy," he started, "There was a recent event in Charleston, during Hurricane Joseph. Do you know the one I mean?"

Randy turned away, staring at the wall. "Why should I?"

Steck unbuttoned his shirt pocket and removed the folded photo of Brandt and his men in the Zodiac. "I have a photo taken by a wildlife photographer." He proffered the grainy blown-up print that clearly showed Brandt's face. "There's just no way that face is anyone else but Glenn Brandt's kid. I know you have him here with you."

Randy Pullin stared at the photo for a moment then fixed his deep set dark eyed stare on Steck. "So how do you connect one dot?"

"There are other dots Randy, too many other dots." Their eyes stayed locked for way too long a time. Steck continued, "I'm not going to connect them unless I have to, Randy. There was something taken from a Navy warehouse that morning that I need to retrieve. If I get it back the dots don't need to be connected."

Colonel Randy broke eye contact. He paced the room for about a minute in deep thought. In silence he dropped his big frame into a big leather office chair behind his massive desk. Steck sunk into a leather couch along the opposite wall.

The silence was palpable. Steck decided to break it. "It's your choice, Randy. So far this is just between you and me."

Pullin stared at the ceiling for a moment more. Steck figured he was either a dead man or about to make a break-through.

Finally, Randy pulled himself upright, looking the part of an officer and a gentleman. He fumbled with a letter opener that looked too much like a dagger for Steck's comfort. "My men and some of your former compadres liberated a certain crate full of antiques that belongs to some guy in the Middle East. It would have been a real clean operation if a certain psychopath who has no connection with my organization hadn't indulged his penchant for bloodletting."

"That would be Paul Roche," Steck asserted.

"Yup, that would be Roche." Pullin was learning that Steck in fact had many dots to connect. "I should have known better than to accept an assignment that involved Roche."

"Who wants the crate, and where is it now?" Steck continued calmly.

Pullin seemed his usual casual self, but Steck perceived he was choosing his words carefully. "I don't know where it is, except that by now it's probably out of the country."

"Does Roche have it?" Steck was fishing.

"I said out of the country, Bob." Steck took that to mean that Randy was unaware of Paul Roche's whereabouts. He didn't think Randy would try to protect Roche. So far Randy was cooperating. Steck had no idea how far he could go without getting himself detained or worse.

"Okay, Randy. What country and who has it?"

Randy's eyes widened and fluttered. "Canada." He said simply.

"And who has it?" Bob persisted.

Pullin's mind raced. So this was not about Paul Roche murdering a Navy guard, he thought. Steck is fixated on finding that crate. Why is he so driven by the crate? "See here, Steck, it's only a few trinkets, for goodness sake why all the fuss?"

"All I can tell you is that the contents of that crate could ignite a flipping holy war if they get into the wrong hands." Steck was getting perturbed. "Look, Randy this is no child's game of soldier or spy or thief. I'll bet you got paid a lot of money to obtain that crate full of 'trinkets' as you call them."

"Roger that," Randy replied, "A heap of money." He got Steck's point. "So, it's not just some antiques sought after by some Arab Sheik with a big ego and a bigger bank account?"

"Tell me who has the crate," Steck repeated. Bob cautioned himself. He had asked the wrong question. He figured he only had one, maybe two more chances to get more information.

"Truthfully, I don't know," was the terse reply.

Steck waited a moment, carefully forming his last question. "Randy, this is very important. I'm not going to threaten you. I just need to know. Who paid you to get this crate?"

"I've gone way too far here, Bob." Pullin was collecting his thoughts carefully as well. "Do I have your word that this goes no further, that *Free Nation* is never implicated, and it ends here?" He was asking a lot and he knew it.

"I'm not in a position to make deals, Randy." Bob wanted to tread lightly. "I can assure you that in honor of our friendship and what we have been through together, I will do my utmost to shield you, but that's all I can offer."

Pullin knew that was the best he was going to get from Bob Steck. After some time, he set his face in a manner Bob had never seen through all their relationship. There was softness in Randy's countenance that Steck would never have thought possible from the big man. Pullin leaned back in his chair, hands knotted behind the back of his neck.

"This organization has done a lot of good for a lot of people, Bob. I took people in who were getting crapped on by the American people, the pinko politicians and even by the military they were willing to give their life for. If we had time, I would walk you over to our veteran's home, where there are dozens of guys who could never live a normal life anywhere but here. They come without legs, without arms with PTSD and mostly destitute because our illustrious government doesn't think they're sick. We've mended broken families and raised their children to be good soldiers. We've raised and educated more than nineteen hundred Amerasian children over the years, most of whom now have productive lives in the outside world. This has been my life's work and I'm proud I did it. Now that screwball Roche has managed to mess it up." He paused, waiting to see what effect he might be having on Steck.

"None of what's happened ever gave you the right to break the law." If he was going to be killed here, Steck figured it would have to be now.

Randy looked crestfallen. "Of course you're right," he said softly.

A loud knock at the door broke the awkward silence that followed. Colonel Randy stood up as his orderly entered, with Brandt right behind him.

Randy's face reset to hard-nuts military. "Bob Steck, this is Major Glenn Brandt, Jr. Major Brandt, this is Bob Steck, an old buddy of your father's and my workmate in 'Nam."

Brandt came to attention and snapped a salute. "At ease, Major," said Pullin with almost fatherly pride. Brandt came to a military 'at ease' then offered his hand to Steck.

"Uncanny," Steck said, looking him over as he shook Brandt's hand. You are your father's twin, a generation removed.

"That's what they say sir," Brandt replied, "except I'm not worthy of his name."

"From the look of you I think he would be proud," Steck offered.

In the moments that followed this feigned cordiality, Steck fixed a tough stare on Colonel Randy.

"Can this wait?" Pullin asked Brandt.

"No, Sir!" came the reply.

Colonel Randy began to make excuses and to move Steck toward the door. Bob took the opportunity to get off the post with his skin.

At the door of Pullin's office, Steck shook his hand. Then he half whispered, "I still need to know what I know you know. Who has it?"

Randy shook his head. "Not now, Bob. I'll be in touch."

Steck handed him a card. "Call me. Call the cell phone on the card. I have hours, not days to get on with this."

The two men shared a manly embrace. Then Steck left the building. He jogged across the square at the double, collected his stuff and got into his car, heading for the main gate. As he approached the gate, the guard on duty was conversing on his hand-held tactical radio. He held up a hand and Bob slowed the car, rolling the window down as he stopped. The guard came along side the car. "The Colonel expresses his regards, sir. He says take care and he'll be in touch."

Speeding away from the main gate to *Free Nation* Steck breathed a sigh of relief. It was now one pm He decided he could drop the car and meet the airplane in time to get back to Kansas City before day's end. He hoped Randy would realize it was in his best interest to co-operate in retrieval of the crate before it left Canada.

He phoned Ryall Morgan's office.

When told by his secretary it was Steck on the line, Morgan picked up immediately. "What have you got, Bob?"

"The crate is in Canada. I figure from the geography that it's probably on the way to Vancouver."

"Who in blazes has it? Morgan sounded anxious.

"I don't know yet, but I'm hoping to have it later today. I'll explain when I get to Langley tomorrow morning."

He then called Susan Deet. She had just returned to her room with a better tan. It was all she had to show for the day, so far.

"Susie, I'm on the way back to your location. I have some new information about the package. I think it's in Canada headed for Vancouver. Can you line up with anyone there?"

"I sure can," was her immediate response. She knew Greg Liss had a former girl friend at CSIS. She would start there.

"We need to get shipping records, both air and sea out of Vancouver. We need to get coverage by the Canadians or send our own people to close the loop on this. I hope we can get to it before it leaves. Can you get on this while I'm on the way to pick you up?"

"I'm on it," was her reply. They clicked off then Susan rang up Greg Liss.

CHAPTER 11

Greg Liss had just entered Mort Lindsley's office when his pager went off. His self-chosen mission for the day was to make himself enough of a pest to Lindsley that the boss would grant his wish to leave immediately for Yemen to de-brief Doctor Wigglesworth about *The Hand of the Prophet.*

When he saw that the return number was Susan Deet's field phone, he informed Lindsley, who dialed her back and put it on his office speaker phone.

"Hello there Miss Susie," drawled Lindsley, "I'm here with Greg. What do you have for us?"

Susan skipped conversational amenity. "This is urgent. The crate is in Canada, headed for Vancouver. It will probably be shipped by air or ocean from there to who knows where. I called to see if Greg's old girlfriend is still connected to CSIS. Maybe she could get some help from the Canadians to find the thing before it leaves their country."

Greg nodded to Lindsley that he still had 'contact' with Carole. His heart beat faster at Susan's reference to her. It could be an opportunity for another chance with Carole. "I could find her." He said brightly.

Mort sensed the rise in Greg. "Whoa there," he said, taking on a fatherly stance, "Let's all think this through for a minute. We can't go stompin' all over the Canadians without briefing them about this situation. It's technically out of the FBI's jurisdiction. We need to get input from Ryall Morgan and lots of others before we get CSIS involved."

Greg slumped in his chair, sullen at the prospect of losing the opportunity to contact Carole.

"We don't have time for that, Mort!" Susan Deet blurted. "The crate is probably in or near Vancouver right now. It'll be gone out of Canada before you can get permission from anyone to go look for it."

Mort secretly loved the youthful vigor of his charges. In a way, it did make sense to do as Susan suggested. He could ask forgiveness of the higher-ups later. "What do you hear from Mister Bob Steck?" he queried.

"I just got off the phone with him. That's how I got the information," Susan replied. "He's on the way back to pick me up. Unless you divert us, we plan to come back to Washington tonight."

Mort paused, thinking over the information he had just received. "Tell you what Miss Susie," he started, "You and Steck come right over to Ryall Morgan's office at Langley as soon as you get in. Greg and I will be there. We can get our heads together and plan some quick moves. In the meantime, Greg will get hold of his friend and see what we can accomplish unofficially with the help of CSIS."

Greg Liss happily nodded agreement.

"Susan, you did a great job," Mort added. "See you tonight."

Deet accepted the compliment. It was at least something to show for what she had earlier reckoned to be a wasted day. Not that Steck had redeemed himself with her, but it was a start. She clicked off and finished packing.

Mort dismissed Greg then he dialed up Ryall Morgan.

———————

Paul Roche (now Hugh Coles) emerged from the airport at Mexico City at dusk. The usual flight delays and hassles did not bother him in his new persona. Flying first class and drinking copious amounts of scotch made the hassles seem almost fun. He collected his suitcase, strolled to the curb and hailed a taxi. In perfect Brit-English he gave the driver an address, then sat back to enjoy a cigarette on the way to his new home.

Half an hour later, the taxi turned in at a long driveway that wound up a steep hill, ending in a courtyard with well-tended garden borders of bougainvillea and green shrubs. Shrouded in tall, well trimmed bushes was a footpath paved with terra-cotta tiles. It led to a modest sized *hacienda* of adobe and wood with the customary tile roof. Inside the large wooden front door was a hallway that divided three bedrooms from a kitchen-dining area. At the back of the building was a large living room with a cathedral ceiling. Adjoining the living room on the right was a study replete with library, large desk with modern electronics built-in and a small bar. French doors opened onto a patio.

Roche passed the two smaller bedrooms and entered the master bedroom at the rear of the house. Garish painted Mexican furniture included a king size bed and a massive double dresser that was connected to an equally massive armoire. A small coffee table sat between two love-seats near a sliding door that opened on to a tiny rock-walled courtyard. This courtyard had a wooden gate leading to the main patio. A connecting door led to the middle bedroom through a big bath and shower. Roche unpacked his small suitcase, stuffing the clothes into the dresser and armoire alongside the already large wardrobe he had pre-stationed here over the past years.

Stripping to his waist and kicking off his shoes, he trekked to the study and poured himself a large scotch. Stepping out to the patio, he surveyed the magnificent view from his "mountain top villa." Twinkling lights of small villages appeared here and there in the darkness of the hills as he faced north. To the south, the sea of lights was Mexico City and its surrounding area. He snapped on some outside lights then settled in to a chaise to sip scotch and survey his patio.

The patio was paved with tile and covered with a wooden pergola that held up a mélange of leafy vines to provide shade. To the right of the patio was a modest size swimming pool. The place was impeccably maintained, except for the pool, which was empty and dusty. As he surveyed his new digs, "Mister Hugh Coles" made a mental note to speak to the care takers first thing in the morning about getting the pool cleaned and filled.

With Bob Steck on his tail, he would not feel comfortable for a couple of days. Maybe he had just completed his last job, he mused. Oh well, he thought, it was probably time to quit pushing his luck. He had amassed enough money to sustain him for many years. Besides, being Hugh Coles would not be unpleasant.

Chris Taylor knocked at the door of his mentor's rooms. The door swung wide. A smiling woman in a business suit passed Chris in the doorway, relinquishing the door knob as she quietly left the room. He stepped back with a gentlemanly gesture.

"Good day, Christian!" proclaimed Mister Al Kafajy from his big overstuffed chair. "Have some lunch," he invited with a sweeping gesture.

"Th-thanks," stammered Chris. He hated it when he revealed how much the boss intimidated him.

The side-board in Al Kafajy's suite was laden with sandwiches and fresh fruit, lemonade, fruit punch and Coke. Several empty areas on the trays indicated that others had eaten lunch already. Chris opted for focaccia and Parma ham, along with some lemonade. As Chris collected the food, the boss continued.

"There have been some positive developments in the market for the contents of the crate, Christian. There will be several potential buyers meeting together with us in Amman just as soon as we can get the goods there."

"Sounds good," Chris mumbled through a mouthful of sandwich. He always enjoyed Amman, especially because he had a Jordanian girl friend who was ever pleased to see him.

After what Chris felt was too short a space of time, the boss's face turned all business. "Exactly when?" he asked loudly.

Chris thought for a moment, trying to figure the logistics. Finally, he declared, "Next Sunday noon, at the Intercontinental Hotel."

The boss smiled. "I know I can count on you, Chris. By the way, make it the Royal Amman Hotel. We must treat our guests well so they will be willing to spend more."

Colonel Randy was seething mad. Brandt had told him everything that happened on his mission to Idaho. On top of Steck's revelations about the crate and the realization that innocent people were getting killed because of this lousy crate of antiques, he now had to deal with abrogation of duty from the one he thought of as his son.

A few phone calls confirmed to Randy that there had been a mysterious accident at the Baker farm. Ralph Baker's wife had come home to find her husband dead beside their driveway. The coroner had found marks on Baker's body that were inconsistent with a simple accident or fall. Faced with that, the Coeur d'Alene police were cautiously treating it as a possible homicide while they conducted an investigation.

Everything Pullin had ever worked for could come crashing down on him if he wasn't careful. After long moments of angry reflection, he decided to get personally involved in the solution to this problem. Maybe Steck's visit could be turned into a positive event after all.

The meeting at Ryall Morgan's office went nearly until dawn. In the end, it had been decided to dispatch Steck and Greg Liss to Yemen. The trip would start with a charter flight to Jeddah, Saudi Arabia at nine am. They would be met there by some as yet to be designated "non-governmentals" (translate; soldiers of fortune) who would get them into and back out of Yemen undetected by the authorities. This was necessary due to the time it would have taken to get them in through regular channels, channels that barely existed anyway. Steck tried to object, yawning as he did to stave off the fatigue accumulated over the past four days. Morgan brushed it aside, reminding Steck of the time-urgency of their situation. It wouldn't be the first rest Bob had to get in an airplane.

Greg had tried to contact his old girl friend in Canada to no avail. Ryall Morgan got hold of the director of CSIS by secure phone. He was told that Carole was on a field assignment and was not expected to check in for another day or two. Morgan asked for a meeting between one of the JUMP team and CSIS in Vancouver first thing in the morning. It was soon arranged and Susan Deet was assigned the task.

Steck and Morgan spent a lot of time convincing Mort Lindsley that he shouldn't open an investigation into *Free Nation* just yet. Steck felt certain he could get more information applying to the case from Randy Pullin by keeping up informal discussions, than by interrogation. As a matter of fact, he knew that the moment Randy smelled trouble he would clam up and become an impediment rather than a helper.

After Lindsley had left Langley, Steck asked for a moment with Morgan. They settled in to coffee and donuts in Ryall's big office.

Steck said he was worried about a greenhorn like Greg Liss getting in and out of Yemen without knowledge of the Yemeni government. "It's a pretty big league move for a kid to make," he declared to Morgan.

"That's why I want you to be with him, Bob. I want you to let Liss get whatever information he can from the professor and then get him out of there with his skin. He's a smart kid. Maybe we could recruit him some day." Morgan sensed that Steck was not pleased at his assignment, so he added, "Shall I send someone else in your place?"

"No way," Declared Steck. "I'll bring him back." Inwardly, Steck had concerns that the kid might get both of them killed or worse. There was no chance he would share that feeling with the boss. "By the way, have you decided who will be our guardian angel on this trip?" He was asking who would get them in.

"I don't know yet," mused Morgan. "I have some calls in to some friends at INSA."

"Oh great," Steck grumbled. Steck was troubled by this and Morgan knew it. INSA is the Intelligence and National Security Alliance, a professional trade group that is reputed to represent rogues, mercenaries and soldiers of fortune as well as legitimate security intelligence workers.

"Don't worry Bob. I'll get the best I can. It's not like we have folks at the agency that can move around in that part of the world. So, we'll hire an expert. Someone will meet you in Jeddah."

Steck did not like the idea of going into the lion's den without knowing who was going to have his beck, or whether he would have his back covered at all.

––––––––

It was four-thirty a.m. when Steck checked in to a motel near Langley. He quietly opened the door to the modest room and stepped inside without turning on the lights. "Hi there mister world traveler," came a familiar though sleepy female voice from the king size bed. "We have to stop meeting this way."

"Roger that." Steck was so glad to hear Ameila's voice he almost laughed, then thought better of it, lest he be misunderstood.

"There's a suitcase full of clean clothes over by the closet," she said, yawning. "You better come to bed before I decide to just let you run to the airplane."

"Did I ever say I love having you as my wife?" Bob said tenderly as he climbed into bed beside her.

CHAPTER 12

The "charter" flight for Steck and Liss turned out to be a military hop to the Azores, followed by an executive charter in an aging Falcon Fifty registered to a company in France. As they waited to board the flight from Azores to Jeddah, Steck found a call back message from Randy Pullin on his cell phone. He returned the call in hopes of getting the location of the crate. What he heard was shocking. Pullin's operatives in Saudi Arabia were going to be his and Greg's guardian angels for the trip to Yemen.

At first Steck thought it might be a joke. If it was, then how did Pullin know about the planned operation? Steck checked his other messages, finding one from Ryall Morgan time stamped only a few minutes after Randy's message. Obviously Steck wished he had returned Morgan's call first. He decided to be frank with Pullin. "I don't think that it's the right time for your people to be in our employ, Randy."

"I'm sorry you feel that way, Bob," retorted colonel Randy. "It's just business, you know. My guys do this on a routine basis and they are simply the best for the job. They've got twelve missions behind them in just the last several weeks, same script, different guests."

Bob's instinct was to hang up and call Morgan, but before that he would try to get more out of Randy. "So Randy," he said in a changed tone, "have you located the crate yet?"

"Yeah, it's loaded on a ship going south. The ship's destination is South Africa."

"What's the name of the vessel?" Steck asked.

"No need to work that end of it, Bob," Randy sounded proud of himself, "your man Morgan has all the details."

"Morgan?" Steck was getting hot under the collar.

"Yes, Morgan. He's the guy that just hired me to get you into Yemen. He says he works with you."

Steck was flabbergasted. He took a moment to collect his thoughts. Forcing an even tone, he asked, "So who is going to meet us and when?"

Colonel Randy smiled so broadly that Steck could sense it over the phone. "You will be met at the airport by a driver holding a sign that says *Continental Oil Corp.* His name is Azziz. He works for me. Just go with him and everything will be fine."

"Got it," said Steck tersely. He clicked off, selected the secure line button and hit the recall for Morgan's number.

Randy Pullin sat back in his chair and chuckled. He knew what he had just pulled off was a coup for *Free Nation*. There was no better way he could think of to fix a problem like becoming part of the solution. It was a simple stroke of luck that a friend at INSA knew of *Free Nation's* capability to deliver goods, services and people to Yemen undetected. It was a greater stroke that his friend had recommended him for the job and that he was hired by that Morgan fellow before Steck got wind of it.

Morgan saw the call coming in from Steck, and opened with, "Hey Bob, I got a really good crew to angel you in Yemen."

"What were you thinking of, Ryall?" Steck was angry. Randy Pullin stole the bloody crate, so you hire him to protect us!?"

"Oh, so you already spoke to him," declared Morgan.

"I have." Steck decided to let silence do the talking.

"I know what you're thinking Bob, but these guys are the only ones with the credentials. We can't send the flipping US Military now, can we?" After seconds with no reply, he continued, "I asked people I trust who would have the best shot at keeping you guys safe and simply followed their advice. It's business, man."

More silence.

"Besides, Ryall continued, Pullin gave me new information about the crate. It's on a ship bound for Durban.

We have already contacted the South African authorities and they have agreed to impound the container when it arrives there. The ship makes a stop in Santiago on the way, so I've got a team headed there to watch for any movement of the container. The Coast Guard is checking on the whereabouts of that ship as we speak. With luck, it's still in US waters and we may get the crate back before you need to cross the border into Yemen."

More silence. Steck was busy stifling the urge to remind Morgan how bad this could become if the crate was not recovered. A report like the one Steck would have to file would terminate someone's career.

"Bob, Are you still there?"

"I'm still here. I'll call you before we leave Saudi."

"The place looks dusty," remarked Greg Liss as the Falcon Fifty swung toward Jeddah on its final approach to King Abdulaziz International Airport.

Bob nodded and smiled. He remembered one trip to Jeddah when there had been a sandstorm. It rumbled in from Mecca to the southeast of the city, over a rim of hills and out to the sea, burying everything in inches of sand. Mid-day had seemed like the middle of the night to the weary traveler Steck, holed up in a tourist hotel. On most occasions this city was quite orderly and clean. Dust was just part of what you had to endure.

Steck remembered that this was Greg Liss' first visit to an Islamic country. He inquired about Greg's luggage. "Do you have any booze in your luggage, any girly magazines?"

Greg gave him a puzzled look. He fished in his carry bag. "Just this issue of Playboy," he muttered pulling the magazine from the stash of papers in his bag.

"Give it to the pilot before we get off the plane," ordered Bob. "If you try to clear customs and they find that magazine, you could be arrested."

93

"Arrested for having a lousy magazine?" Greg looked incredulous.

"Yup, for a lousy magazine," replied Steck. "Those things and alcoholic drinks are against the law here. They don't fool around either. You could be detained for quite a while under their laws. You could even serve time. Believe me you don't want to serve time in a Saudi jail."

"Geez," Greg said. His eyes were wide.

Steck decided to treat this kid as a complete greenhorn until proven otherwise. "Just follow me, keep your mouth shut and don't look any girls in the eye."

The pilot accepted the magazine. Steck supposed he got lots of them this way. In the terminal, they passed through entry routinely, stating that they were on a four day business trip and would be staying at the Hilton. Emerging from the arrivals area, they spotted a man holding up a sign that read *Continental Oil welcomes Mister Steck party.* The driver was pure Saudi, in robes and Keffiya. The car was a big black Mercedes, just the thing for businessmen. Steck was relieved that they weren't met by some dudes in fatigues, as he had feared might be the case.

Arriving at the Hilton, the driver helped them get their bags to the bellman then called Bob aside. "You will be met for dinner tonight by Mister Grundstrom of Continental Oil Corp. Please pack your things for a brief trip early tomorrow to the desert."

When they got to their rooms, Bob suggested that a long nap would be in order. He knew that "early in the morning" could mean a midnight departure.

Chris Taylor's planned evening activities in Paris were no longer possible. At eight-thirty pm he was still doing business. He had been working the telephone ever since his meeting with the boss. Having committed to get the crate to Amman in four days turned out to be an error in judgment on his part. The logistics were not working in his favor. The ship had been loafing along the east coast of Mexico, and was now about fifteen miles off Lima on the Peruvian coast. There would be no time to wait for the ship's call at Santiago.

"Just get the crate off that ship at the drop point." he instructed his operative on board the ship. Chris lit a cigarette as he turned his phone back to standby. He had now completed the arrangements that were available to him. He did not have confidence that it would come off clean.

The crate was to be removed from its container within the hour. An ocean racing Donzi "cigarette" boat belonging to one of Chris Taylor's contacts had already left Callao and was headed due west. His men aboard the ship would toss the fiberglass tub containing the crate overboard. The boat would fall-in behind the ship to retrieve it, having confirmed their position by phone. This was not an unusual operation for the crew of the Donzi, since they made their living running drugs. The pickup was easy. The hard part was getting safely to shore through the chain of Peruvian patrol gunboats that routinely patrol the waters between the mainland and the Galapagos Islands.

Chris regretted the risks associated with this mission, now complicated by the need for many bribes as well as a bit of luck. Once on shore, his Lima trading contacts could take over, getting the crate re-consigned and shipped by air courier from Jorge Chavez International Airport to Cairo, then on to Amman, Jordan in a hurry.

Later that night, when he had just received word that the crate was safely aboard the Donzi and headed for port, there was a knock at the door of Taylor's hotel room. He cracked the door to see that the boss had sent his assistant, Ahmed to check on Taylor's progress. Sighing inwardly, Chris opened the door to the man and they exchanged the customary Muslim greeting. Ahmed was an older man, about the same age as the boss. He was tall, extremely strong, with a physical presence that could not be missed even in a crowded room. He wore a curled black moustache, now streaked with gray. His dark eyes were the most piercing that Chris could ever remember in a man. He wore a British-made gray worsted three piece suit, obviously a gift from the boss. Rumor was that he had served in the Iraqi army during the Iraq-Iran war. The story was that he had saved Al Kafajy's life in some awkward circumstance resulting from the trading company's dealings with the Shiites in southern Iraq. Ahmed and the boss had formed a lifelong bond after that. He was a mysterious man in many ways with an uncanny way of showing up wherever he was needed, even though he was never on the "guest list."

"A very good evening to you, Mister Chris," said Ahmed in his soft voice, close to a whisper, hardly the voice one would expect from his visage. He cracked a broad smile, revealing tobacco-stained teeth with gold caps at the front. "Mister Al Kafajy sends his compliments. He wishes to know how you have progressed with preparations for your intended meeting together with some customers in Amman four days hence."

Chris was annoyed that the boss hadn't just called him on the house phones. "You may tell him that the arrangements are complete and that air transport of the goods involved is now arranged. I expect that we shall be on plan for the meeting." Remembering to use customary language with Ahmed, he added, "if it be the will of Allah."

Ahmed held his smile, bowed and replied. "Indeed, may the will of Allah always be accomplished."

As Ahmed stepped backwards into the hallway, still bowing, Chris bowed in return. He closed the door, double locked it as if to preclude further interruption and began to pack his things for the trip to Amman.

Susan Deet could not believe her luck. After reviewing a phone tap tape of the conversation between Roche and Buel, she had enlisted the aid of some of Mort's friends at CSSI. They were trying to find their man on some imaginary ranch near Calgary, to no avail. But an FBI/CSSI search of hotel registers had picked up about twenty guests named "Terry Jansen" in the western half of the United States and Canada over the past few days. Normally it would take days to follow all those leads, except one was a giveaway. A hotel in Salt Lake City reported a guest named Terry Jansen whose reservation had been made through their affiliate in Calgary.

"That's why we pay you the big bucks Susie," Mort Lindsley chortled leaning back in his big office chair, "That's real nice investigative work."

Susan brushed the compliment aside saying, "It's just another piece of the puzzle. We don't have this guy in custody yet. Until we do, it's just a piece. We know that this particular Terry Jansen only stayed one night and seemed to leave no obvious trail when he checked out."

Mort knew that as a former agent, Roche would continue to take pains to cover his tracks, even if he felt safe. "Have we got any eye witnesses among the hotel staff, the local transportation folks, anything like that?"

"One of our agents interviewed the chamber maid that cleaned his room. She identified Roche from a file shot, but said that when he left the hotel he had a moustache, short hair and business clothes." Susan tossed a composite sketch across the desk. Mort picked it up and studied it carefully.

"Do you have anything else?" Mort queried.

"One more thing," Susan replied. "The Maid said he had greeted her in the hallway as he checked out. He spoke to her for a few minutes, in Spanish. She said he spoke Spanish with a *British* accent."

A quick phone conversation with Ryall Morgan confirmed that Roche was a master of disguise and character change. Ryall thought that a British character was within the realm of Roche's typical behavior. He also confirmed that Roche knew several languages, including Spanish. He asked for a copy of the composite.

"Mexico!" Susan leaned toward Lindsley to make the point. "I'll bet he's in Mexico!"

CHAPTER 13

Grundstrom rang Steck's room at six pm sharp. "Good day to you Mister Steck," he announced in business-like tone. "I trust you've had a good trip thus far? Meet me in the restaurant of the hotel at seven pm. We have a busy day ahead and I'm sure that you and Mister Liss will want to get to bed early."

"Sure thing," mumbled Steck. "See you at seven, then."

Grunstrom turned out to be a thirty-something former military officer, fit and trim. His light complexion, chiseled facial features and high-n-tight hair cut reeked of career Marine. Steck wondered how this guy would have become involved with the likes of Randy Pullin, but decided not to pry until he knew the man better.

Dinner went by quickly. The conversation was mostly about baseball and American TV shows, neither of which is readily available to Americans living in Saudi Arabia. Steck had to caution Liss twice about eating too much, citing the hard day ahead. Greg seemed to delight in the Middle Eastern food, which Bob envisioned might wind up splattered around a rocking helicopter.

Steck had been right about interpreting the words "early start." Grundstrom said he would fetch them about three am. He also let them know that this was not a mission with much appeal to the group he worked with. Three men would stay with Steck and Liss. Their time on the ground would be limited to one day maximum and they would return directly to the hotel, so as not to arouse suspicion among the hotel staff or others that might be observant. Grundstrom cautioned them to keep any political opinions to themselves until out of the country and to stay away from the hotel bar or any other "entertainments" while in Saudi Arabia. Greg Liss was fascinated by these admonitions. "Just act as if you were

at your maiden-aunt's house on best behavior," counseled
Steck.

Steck rose at one-thirty am, carefully packing for his
day in the desert. He would dress in jeans and a long sleeve
tee, rugged low shoes and wicking socks. He would carry a
jacket against the cold desert night. In its pockets he stuffed
some note paper, pens, a British passport, a miniature
satphone registered to Continental Oil and business cards that
identified him as a Geologist, all provided by Grundstrom.
He had counseled Greg Liss to take the same garb and
equipment.

He and Greg had prepared for the trip by careful
study of the terrain and history of the area they would enter.
This was really hostile territory in more ways than one. First,
it was rugged mountainous scrub, dotted with old volcanoes
and deep wadis with sheer rock-face walls. This moonscape
led east to desert sand hundreds of miles wide. Secondly, it
was now a hotbed of terrorist training camps and the domain
of several groups with close ties to Al Qaeda. Bin Laden's
ancestors came from the Wadi Doan which was only a
hundred miles or so from their destination Marib.

They would land in a small wadi cut into high hills
west of Marib, in the region that once held the grandeur of
the Kingdom of Sabba, known as Sheba in the Bible. Marib
had been the center of the frankincense trade at the time of
the Queen of Sheba. It was one of the most important
crossroads for trade between the Middle East and the Orient.
Spices and silk came west from India and Asia by camel, to
trade for gold and fine linens from the west, along with the
locally produced frankincense. The whole system was
enabled by the Marib dam, an earthen structure built in
fifteen-hundred B.C. that provided irrigation for vast forests
of gum obligatum trees, the source of frankincense.

By the sixth century A.D., when *The hand of
Mohammed* would have been cast, the dam was in ruins and

the desert sand had reclaimed the forest. No gum trees remained. Not far from the area, Mohammed had preached his new religion, one that would conquer most of the civilized world within only a hundred years.

Economic systems die slowly. Although only a scant vestige of the era of Sheba, the camel caravans still stopped in Marib at the time of Mohammed. Important wells still remained here, thus many caravanserais, or stopovers still remained in the region through the middle ages. The remains of some still stand as monuments to the former glory of Sheba. Doctor William Wigglesworth was digging around a site that held the mostly buried ruins of one such trading post, seventy miles east of Marib, in the desert.

At two-fifty am, Bob collected Greg Liss and they stepped outside the lobby into cold night air. As they donned their jackets, a crew cab pickup with the Continental Oil logo on the door rolled to a stop at the curb. From behind the wheel, Grundstrom hailed them. The two men climbed into the back passenger compartment. "Good morning, guys," Grundstrom said as though they were old friends, "there's coffee in the locker."

Steck opened the compartment in the back of the front seat and found two coffees and some flat bread. Before the coffee was finished, the truck rolled out onto the tarmac of a small airport and stopped beside a Learjet that already had engines running. The three of them ducked into the cabin and settled into wide seats. Grundstrom closed the door and the pilot began his taxi run. Within two minutes, they were airborne, climbing rapidly above the lights of the city, then veering south east.

As they flew this first leg of their journey towards Najran a small town near the Yemeni border, Steck made small talk with Grundstrom and studied him carefully. He learned that his host had served two tours in Iraq and one in Afghanistan.

"Tough duty," Steck remarked when he learned that ground missions near Kandahar had convinced Grundstrom not to re-enlist.

"Real tough," answered Grundstrom, "especially when you are ordered by morons to do the impossible with no resources. Here, it's different. I get what I need to do my job and the money's better."

Steck got the picture. He decided to leave it at that for the moment. Guys like this are easy recruits for nuts like Randy Pullin, he thought.

The six-hundred mile flight to Najran went by quickly. The jet landed at five am, just as dawn's first light began to displace the black desert night. The airstrip was only about as wide as the Learjet, which promptly wheeled around and took off, leaving the three men standing on scrub sand. There were no buildings, just a couple of Continental Oil vans parked beside the strip. After a quick transfer to a business helicopter with the same company logo on the door, they were airborne again. This time the pilot had a companion, a squat young fellow with a round baby face and an AK-47 across his lap. Greg's eyes widened at the sight of the assault rifle. Steck's glare stopped Liss from saying anything. Steck noticed that there was a locker marked *Lifevests* behind the cabin seats that by its size was probably full of light arms and ammo. He noticed that Grundstrom had retrieved a sidearm from his flight bag and was now wearing it.

The helicopter flew low, nearly following the nap of the earth, military style. Bob wondered if the craft had a military navigation system on board. If it didn't, he thought, this pilot's a magician.

As the one hundred-seventy mile trip to Marib was nearly complete, Grundstrom asked Bob and Greg if they wanted hand weapons "in case of snakes." Both accepted. Grundstrom opened the locker that Steck had spotted earlier and removed two Beretta 92FS side arms with belt holsters and three loaded fifteen round clips for each.

"You guys know how to use these?" Grunstrom queried.

"Affirmative," Steck answered. He exchanged looks with Greg, who held two thumbs up.

"Must be a lot of snakes in this place." asserted Greg with a grin.

"You get more respect from the locals with one of these on your belt," offered Grundstrom.

The helicopter flew low and fast over the Marib dam and slipped along a riverbed, turning right at the entrance to a small wadi. As the pilot eased the machine down, the ruins of a caravanserai appeared to the left. Steck could make out a campsite with several tents at one side of the ruins. About a dozen people were milling around the camp, while several Arabs worked a dig of moderate size.

The engines whined as if emitting a long sigh as the rotors slowed to idle. The pilot did not shut the engines down, but gave a wave to Grundstrom when the rotor wash had sunk to a safe level. He and baby face stayed in the helo while the three passengers covered their faces with the sleeves of their jackets against the dust and scampered clear of the rotors. They were met by a slender young woman in jeans, calf-high leather boots and a tee shirt. She was tall, red headed and quite attractive, with high cheek bones and angular features. She reminded Steck of a character from a Range Rover commercial. She looked strangely familiar to Greg.

"Are you Mister Liss?" she queried. Greg stepped forward and smiled, offering his hand. She dismissed his proffered hand with a wave, and turned toward the largest of the tents. The three men followed her inside.

Ten minutes later, Grundstrom emerged from the tent and waved to the helo pilot. Receiving the "all clear" the pilot shut down the engines.

Inside, the tent was cleared of all the workers and archaeological team. Doctor Wigglesworth insisted that the girl stay in the room. Steck resisted on impulse, questioning her need to know. Greg Liss was still troubled by the impression that he had met her before. "Professor, please ask the lady to wait outside," he said to Wigglesworth.

"Mister Liss," stated Wigglesworth emphatically, "there will be no discussion if she is not by my side. I trust her completely." Wigglesworth introduced her as Nancy Kinnear, a grad student at Dartmouth. Steck reckoned her to be Wigglesworth's protégé. Greg reasoned to himself that he probably remembered her from Dartmouth. He decided not to raise his concern to Steck. Nancy gave Steck a cold stare then stood at Wigglesworth's side.

Steck motioned to Grundstrom to go outside. He complied, but stayed at the door of the tent as if guarding the place. The meeting now consisted of Wigglesworth, his protégé, Liss and Steck.

Greg and Wigglesworth began debriefing about *The Hand of Mohammed.* Greg's electronic recorder was running, to be used for documenting later by the FBI. Steck listened intently as each of the facts Greg had asserted to the Jump Team was confirmed. While this was in progress, the girl served weak tea in small tumblers, along with some jellied candies covered with sesame seeds. She seemed bored with the conversation, probably having heard it all too many times before. When Greg produced a photo of the object, both her face and that of Doctor Wigglesworth froze in astonishment.

"By God, you were right!" exclaimed Wigglesworth after recovering from the initial shock. He sat at the table and fondled the photo, mumbling to himself about various features of 'the hand' while nodding affirmatively.

Nancy knelt at her mentor's side, staring at the photo. Steck made a mental note about the intensity of her gaze, the flush on her cheek and the tiny drop of drool she wiped from the corner of her mouth. Her demeanor went beyond satisfaction on behalf of her mentor, he thought.

The doctor launched into a sort of lecture about the significance of the object, noting that confirmation of its existence had been his life's work. He spoke about the legend of *The Hand of Mohammed*, and the bitter wars that had been fought through the ages over possession of the thing.

"Why fight wars over a simple figurine with only historical significance?" asked Steck.

"Because according to Islamic law, he who possesses it gains free passage anywhere in the Muslim world, forgiveness of any offenses at law and influence with the supreme leaders in matters of Islamic law," answered Wigglesworth.

Steck's mind fuddled for a moment, trying to take in the implications of the professor's statement. "So, any bad guy that gets hold of the thing is the next Bin Ladin."

"Vastly more powerful than Bin Laden, the old man said." Wigglesworth looked self-satisfied at having delivered the message, not seeming to grasp the implications. Steck felt his stomach churn.

Greg and Wigglesworth went to an easel and began sketching a timeline that showed the major historical events surrounding *The Hand.* Steck was fascinated at the Doctor's knowledge as well as Greg's contributions to the effort. As each sheet of paper became full of scribble and diagram, Liss shot an image with his digital camera then turned the page.

Of a sudden, Steck sensed movement behind him and turned towards the table, where Nancy was just snapping a picture of Greg's photo. "Hey! Stop that!" he shouted. Greg and Wigglesworth looked up, startled at the interruption of an interesting conversation. Grundstrom, hearing the commotion threw the tent door open and stood in its frame, sidearm drawn.

Steck held Nancy firmly by her right wrist. "Give me the camera!" he said firmly. She resisted. He flipped her right arm behind her back and applied pressure.

"You're hurting me!" she whined, trying to break the arm lock. She held the small Casio away from them.

"Let her go!" shouted Wigglesworth, striding toward them.

"Not until she gives me that camera," Steck replied.

Greg's training snapped in and he quickly relieved her of the camera. Wigglesworth seemed ready to get physical, but perhaps remembering his age thought better of it. Bob kept his grip on the girl's arm while Greg looked at the review screen of the digital camera, finding two images of his photo of *The Hand.*

Greg deleted the two photos, opened the camera, removed the memory card and slipped it into his jeans pocket. He frowned at the Girl. "Nancy, please don't do that."

Steck did not release his hold on her arm. "Why did you take that picture?" he said.

"Relax, Mister Steck," interrupted Wigglesworth. Seething, his neck had turned red. "It is standard operating procedure for archaeologists to document every shred of information. I am sure Nancy was just following her training, nothing more."

"Is that true, Nancy?" asked Steck taking a sardonic tone.

"Just let me go!" she growled.

Steck released his grip. Nancy spun around, giving Steck a defiant glare. She started for the door. Grundstrom blocked her.

"Put that gun away!" ordered Wigglesworth, "and stop this foolishness right now."

"Or what?" answered Grundstrom, holding a bead on Nancy.

"Or this meeting is over," stated Wigglesworth. He flashed a look of disdain at Greg Liss, who gestured frustration to his former professor.

Steck decided to let the incident go for now, and motioned Grundstrom to stand aside.

"I'll be in my tent." Nancy spat the words, marching out onto the desert sand.

Liss and the professor resumed their debriefing. Steck sat in attentive silence, while the two completed the timeline chart. They continued with a detailed discussion of each point on the timeline. Much new information came forth, including corroboration of the "safe passage" provision of *"The hand of Mohammed."* It was shown in an old volume that Wigglesworth produced about the Sinai desert in Egypt. In it, an historical account of Saint Catherine's Monastery at the foot of Mount Sinai showed the picture of a hand print. In order to stem the constant attacks by Moslems against the Christian monastery, the monks had allowed the building of a small mosque within the monastery walls. Mohammed himself had approved of this move, sending a letter to the monastery marked with his hand print. The monks thus armed any siege of St Catherine's by ambitious Moslem war lords could be diffused by showing the letter and image of the hand of their prophet to the would-be occupiers. Since that time, in the seventh century, St Catherine's has never been attacked. In return, the Christian monks to this day offer hospitality to any Moslem who wishes to worship at the small mosque.

"You may remember, Mister Steck, the visit to that monastery by Anwhar Sadat, during the Israeli occupation of Sinai that ended in 1980," remarked Doctor Wigglesworth. Steck realized that remark was aimed at his apparent age, in contrast to Greg's. "Sadat was only exercising his ancient right to safe passage, thereby also convincing the world of the monastery's 'vouchsafe' under the resumption of Egyptian rule."

By the end of the briefing, cordiality seemed to have been restored. Lunch had been served by an older Arab man, who delivered traditional middle-eastern food with much bowing and smiling, the gleam of his gold teeth accompanying each smile. Nancy had not returned. Steck checked with Grundstrom, who said he had not seen her leave her tent since the camera incident.

It was now late in the day, and despite Doctor Wigglesworth's insistence that they stay the night Steck was anxious to get going. They had the information needed and he wanted to report to the JUMP team. Steck thanked Wigglesworth with a hearty handshake and promised a generous contribution to his Archaeological foundation, courtesy of the American people.

Long shadows crept across the camp, cast by the rock walls of the wadi that encompassed the dig site. Steck and Liss emerged from the main tent. Bob reckoned it was about one hour to sunset. He spoke briefly to Grundstrom, who waved to the helo pilot and the baby faced guard that they would be leaving.

Steck jogged over to Nancy's tent, to say good-bye and hopefully mend her disposition. Greg trotted behind. Steck hailed her twice. Receiving no reply, he tossed the flap of the tent aside. She was gone.

Steck tensed, casting a look toward Grundstrom, who reacted at once to his view of the empty tent. They needed no further communication. Grundstrom whistled to the pilot, who was lazily going through his pre-flight checks. The pilot looked up to see Grundstrom waving his arm in a circular motion. That meant "hurry up, let's get out of here."

Steck shouted to Greg Liss and the two began trotting toward the 'copter. Nancy's absence, under the circumstances could only mean trouble.

"Bob, Look above us!" Greg squawked as they ran, "Up on the ridge!"

About twenty heavily armed men were picking their way down the rocky western slope from the ridge, using the glare of the late day sun for cover.

Steck saw 'baby face' standing beside the helicopter with binoculars to his face. He had spotted them too. "Unfriendlies!" he shouted above the engine noise, loud enough so that Steck and Liss could hear him. Professor Wigglesworth just stood in front of the main tent, bewildered.

Grundstrom had already taken up a position behind a large boulder about ten yards from the helicopter. Baby face tossed him an M40 sniper rifle from the aft locker in the helo. Grundstrom waited until Steck and Liss were near similar cover, then carefully sighted and pulled off two shots. Two of the invaders dropped, one careening about ten yards across the face of the wall as if hit by a truck, the other slumping over a large rock, part of his head blown away.

Even though they were still out of their weapons' effective range, several of the enemy began spraying bullets from their AK's. Most fell about seventy yards short.

Using their temporary range advantage Steck chose not to take cover, but kept running toward the helo. Liss followed. "No use using these Berettas," he hollered to Greg. Greg holstered his. As they got to the helo, Steck shouted to baby face. "Hey, have you got any more rifles? The whine of the rotor slowly winding up to speed drowned out the man's response.

Grundstrom fired again, a direct hit. Three bad guys down. So far, so good, thought Steck.

Steck counted the enemy twice. Thus verified, he signaled to Grundstrom, holding up first a single finger then seven. There were seventeen still moving.

Grundstrom gave him a thumbs-up. A moment later his M40 barked again and another man fell down the draw.

Baby face had retrieved two AK's from the locker. He tossed them to Steck and Liss then shouted, "Don't fire until they're closer! You'll waste ammo." He then retreated to the helicopter and scurried under the airframe, dropping an access panel to the ground. He stood up, shouted something to the pilot, then retrieved his AK and took up a position near the aircraft.

Grundstrom fired three more carefully sighted shots, missing one and dropping two. It would now be four against fourteen. The first of the enemy would be in range to fire at any moment.

The rotor was turning faster now, but the helicopter would not be ready to fly for another minute or two.

Steck and Liss cocked their rifles and waited.

CHAPTER 14

Chris Taylor sat at the big desk usually reserved for the boss at the Al Kafajy Trading Company office in Amman, Jordan. He was logged in to the PC network catching up on correspondence ignored during his brief stay in Paris. He had already conducted a brief meeting with the staff about coming events at the Amman office. They were busy sprucing up the place for the arrival of Mister Al Kafajy on Saturday. There would be no time off for anyone, excepting Friday prayers, until the boss left Amman.

He phoned his Amman girlfriend, Aliyah and made a date for dinner at her place. As he clicked off, he noticed an arriving email from the boss' right hand man, Ahmed. "Call on secure line" it said.

Chris locked the office door, picked up the telephone at the desk and dialed several long combinations of numbers from memory. Ahmed's whisper answered.

Chris skipped the customary niceties. "What do you have for me?"

"The gentleman we both know has learned that a photo has been taken of our prize," said Ahmed. "He wondered if you knew."

Chris was taken by surprise. "I did not know," he replied. "Where was this photo obtained?"

"It was obtained by one of our acquaintances in Yemen."

"Do you have it?" Chris tried to remain outwardly calm.

"The gentleman has a facsimile sent just now from Yemen. He asks if he should be concerned."

Chris tried to fathom the information. He wanted to ask who the bloody hell had such a thing, but needed to control his demeanor.

At length, Ahmed asked, "Are you still on the line?"

"Yes, I'm still on the line. Do you know where the photo originated?" He knew Ahmed was toying with him.

After a period of silence, Ahmed decided he had strung Chris out quite enough. "It was presented to an archaeologist who has sought our prize for many years, by some Americans keen to recover it. One of our friends took a picture of the picture."

"Please thank the gentleman for this information," Chris said in even tones. "Assure him that I will use the information wisely. Tell him that I will contact him as soon as I have located the source of this minor issue, and that I will deal with it." Then he added, "How do I contact our friend in Yemen?"

"The gentleman will see that you get that information," replied Ahmed. "May the results be pleasing to Allah," he stated. Ahmed clicked off.

Chris replaced the receiver on its cradle. He noticed his heart thumping and he felt quite warm. He sat for a few minutes until the rush cleared. No use revealing his state of alarm to the office staff. Moments later, the phone buzzed and the red light on its keyboard flashed, indicating a secure incoming call. The boss told him that the source was a young archaeologist named Nancy Kinnear. He supplied the dial-up sequence for her satphone.

"Do you have instructions?" asked Chris.

"Some other friends of ours are responding. They will insure that none of the visitors leave Yemen until our transaction is complete. Nevertheless, contact Miss Kinnear. She may have other information of use to you."

"Customers are already arriving in Amman, Christian," the boss warned. "We must take steps to assure they won't be disappointed."

Ryall Morgan was at his desk, going over the terrorist activity postings on his secure link to Home Land Security. The HLS briefing was available daily to those with a need to know. JUMP Team was high on that list. An item that caught his attention was the purposely random movement of several known Islamic terrorist leaders or their top assistants, all at once. The consensus of several agencies seemed be that they were converging on Amman, Jordan. This posting was linked to an intercepted message from a known Al Qaeda wannabe group in Indonesia to a brother cell in Somalia. The message was coined in the usual code, purporting to be merchant traffic, but when analyzed seemed to speak about an upcoming "event" in Amman.

Morgan scratched a few notes about this posting. He decided to ask the agency's bureau chief in Jordan what was known about an intended meeting. He would write up the results to present to Mort Lindsley and Susan Deet at two-thirty pm.

Morgan noticed that it was about noon, which meant about sundown in Yemen. He thought about Steck and Liss, probably sitting down to an Arab feast under the clear desert sky. He wondered what they had learned today. He tried to ring up the secure satphone that Randy Pullin's group had supplied to Steck. No answer. Morgan made a mental note to try again in an hour.

———————

Hugh Coles, formerly Paul Roche, sat on his favorite chair poolside, sipping strong coffee and chewing on a breakfast bun. He was getting comfortable in the assumption that he was safe in his new persona. Besides himself, there were only two people in the world who knew how to contact Paul Roche, and they would do it through a three tiered non-traceable contact chain, only in an emergency. He had worked for years setting this up, and at last felt free of the need to keep watch every waking moment for trouble.

He fumbled through a Mexico City newspaper, following the soccer news and browsing the previous day's results. The sun was high and the day had become quite warm, even at the usually temperate altitude of his house in the Mexican hills. Opting to read the balance of his paper later on, he stood, dropped off the bathrobe that covered his bathing suit clad torso and plunged into the newly filled crystal clear pool. Life was good.

At that moment, Hugh Coles had no way of knowing that tomorrow's newspaper would contain an innocent looking advert, one that would end his respite and threaten to suck him once again into the wicked vortex of his former life.

Susan Deet entered the conference room next to Mort Lindsley's office at ten 'til twopm. She greeted the other members of the JUMP team, mostly reference librarians and technicians. She had accomplished the task given her to track down Greg Liss' former girlfriend and had prepared some notes to use in today's meeting. The news would not be good for the lovelorn Mister Liss. At least she didn't have to face him with it today, since he was running around the desert with Bob Steck, she thought.

The meeting began precisely at two pm, when Ryall Morgan arrived. Lindsley recounted the information they had accumulated thus far about the missing crate. "We know it's on a ship bound for Durban. We will intercept it in Santiago. We've lost Paul Roche temporarily, but Susie will find him eventually." He paused to smile at her. "Steck and Liss are gettin' the background on that figurine, and we've gathered enough evidence to arrest Randy Pullin any time we want to. I'd say that's not bad for only a few days work." Satisfied that he had brought them up to date, he added, "What do you two have for today's meeting?"

Susan deferred to the senior Ryall Morgan. "I've got two items to report. First, I have not heard from Steck and Liss. There may be some trouble with the satellite phone Steck is carrying. It's dark in Yemen. They've had a whole day with the man they wanted to de-brief. I would guess we'll hear from them shortly." As he said that, he gestured to the satphone he had just placed on the table.

Second, there is some peculiar movement among some of the most influential bad guys. There could be some sort of meeting or even a terrorist operation coming down soon in Amman."

"What does that have to do with our operation?" Asked Lindsley, who had leaned back in his chair, slumping. He was peering at Morgan over the top of half-glasses.

"I just have a hunch that it may be connected to *The Hand of Mohammed*," replied Morgan. "Greg reported to us a while ago that there was some sort of archaeological meeting in Amman in a few days. He said the old professor plans to attend."

"I remember, Ryall. Again, what does that have to do with our mission?" Lindsley seemed perturbed.

"We know that the archaeological community has interest in *The Hand*, and that every Islamic fundamentalist on earth would love to have the thing, even if just to gain credibility. I just feel there could be a connection."

"I see," Lindsley mused. "Okay, let's keep tracking this Amman meeting, or operation, or whatever it is. Your guys gonna do it?" He meant CIA.

"Yes, I'm working it with our Jordanian bureau chief. I spoke with him at noontime today. He'll give us a report in the morning."

Lindsley paused, making a few notes. At length, he looked up. "Suzie?"

"I found some news about Greg's Canadian girlfriend," she began. "I used a big favor with a friend at CSIS." She shuffled some paper, sat up straighter and announced, "Did you know those CSIS buggers conduct ops in the States? I thought they were our buddies."

"Just as we do in Canada, when we have no alternative," quipped Morgan.

"Anyhow, Carole is one of their field agents, apparently one of the best. She is currently on a mission in Idaho, stalking some kind of traffickers, maybe drugs but I could not confirm that. She went missing two days ago, and the folks at CSIS are getting antsy about it. According to my source, she always checks in right on time. They're worried that something may have happened to her in the States, which of course could get embarrassing since they were not collaborating with us about her mission."

A thought trail was forming in Ryall Morgan's mind. It was not clear enough yet to speak about. He wondered if the movement of the crate to that end of Canada might be connected to Carole's assignment.

"Any luck finding Roche?" Lindsley sounded distracted, as if he was having the same thought that troubled Morgan.

"None yet, except I'm really convinced he is in Mexico," replied Susan. "I'm working on it," she added.

Morgan picked up the satphone and tried to contact Steck again. No luck.

After handling some mundane business for a few minutes, Lindsley seemed ready to adjourn the conference. Suddenly, Morgan's satphone buzzed.

"Steck?" said Morgan after clicking the receive button.

"Ryall Morgan?" The voice was Randy Pullin's.

"This is Morgan. What do you have for me?" Morgan gestured to the others and hit the mute button. "It's Pullin," he told the others then he hit the speaker button.

"There's some sort of cock-up going on at the landing site in Yemen," drawled Colonel Randy. Our helicopter pilot triggered a pre-programmed help message with a code that indicates people trouble, not mechanical issues."

"What else do you know?" Morgan's face was tense.

"All we know is there are unfriendlies and shots have been fired. There's another helicopter with heavy reinforcements on the way to them as we speak."

"When will the relief arrive?"

"About one hour." Randy sounded on edge.

"Keep us informed. I want a status every thirty minutes. Are there any other assets available in the vicinity?" Morgan's tone was elevated, the words coming fast.

"I'm working on it," snapped Randy, "Out!"

Morgan clicked the phone to standby.

"No one goes home until we have this under control," barked Lindsley. "We have to get them some help." The team spent the next thirty tension filled minutes confirming the fact that there was none available.

CHAPTER 15

At the first *ping* of a bullet off the side of the helicopter, the pilot lifted off. Grundstrom, Steck and Liss were too busy firing from their positions of cover to notice that the machine was airborne without them on board. Baby face clambered over to Grundstrom's position, bringing another AK-47 for his superior to use in place of the M40. Grundstrom gave him a thumb's up, but left the AK at his side. He needed the more accurate M40 for the moment.

In minutes the insurgents had taken cover and were rotating fire to cover their advance. Two of them continued to fire at the helicopter, which was a hundred yards off the deck. Steck felt the prop wash and looked up, startled to see the thing hovering over him. He started to shout at Grundstrom, but then realized that the helicopter was not leaving without them, rather was preparing to attack.

The pilot actuated a pod mounted machine gun. It deployed through the opening in the underbelly of the airframe where the access panel had been removed by baby face. The pilot slipped the aircraft from side to side to make him somewhat less of a sitting duck. He then spun it so the pod faced the enemy. Three short bursts erupted from the twelve barrels of the pod gun as the helicopter raked across the enemy's position from a hard angle. Several of the shooters fell in that hail of 40 caliber bullets. Grundstrom had dropped two more and Steck thought he had tagged one or two.

Steck scurried to another pile of rocks, flanking the enemy's position. He counted four bodies that were not moving and two that were writhing in pain, too badly injured to be effective. That made it four against eight. He shouted to Greg, who replied he was okay. Baby face and Grundstrom kept firing, which indicated they were all right as well. So far, so good, they signaled to one another.

The helicopter swept around to the opposite side of the fray, and fired again. As well as Steck could figure at least two more of the enemy dropped.

As the helicopter swung back to take a position away from the fight, it suddenly wobbled. The snapping sound of the rotor seemed strangely off key. Realizing his rotor was nicked, the pilot had no choice but to set the machine down real hard just behind the main tent. Steck heard the crunch of metal to rock. The rotor slowed. Chances were the helicopter was no longer flight worthy.

"Fall Back!" Grundstrom shouted as he slipped back towards the main tent. Greg Liss followed, taking cover from rock to rock. Baby face took off on the run across a short open area between him and the tent. Seeing a trail of bullets following the man, Steck stayed put and provided covering fire.

Through the melee, no one had noticed that Professor Wigglesworth was still standing frozen by fear near the entrance to the main tent. Greg was the first to discover it, so he ran full tilt to the old man, pushing him back into the tent. Greg felt a sting of heat in his backside as he entered the tent. The bullet passed clear through his flesh, leaving a trail of bloody ooze into his jeans.

"I'm hit!" Greg shouted. He was still able to shepherd the old man to a place of relative safety behind some file drawers.

Grundstrom and baby face had taken up new positions, firing to draw the enemy's fire away from Steck, who was now badly exposed and nearly cut off from the others by the enemy's advance.

Suddenly, a figure loomed over the rock that Steck was using for cover. The AK-47 in the enemy's hands was swinging toward Steck. He instinctively rolled to one side and came up firing. Riddled with bullets from Steck's weapon, the enemy fell at his feet. He heard sucking breath and choking, indicating that he had inflicted at least one chest wound. Steck poked the torso then rolled it over. A flash of red hair in the fading light made his eyes widen. He had just killed Nancy Kinnear.

"Fall back Bob!" shouted Grundstrom. "We have you covered."

"In a minute!" replied Steck. He searched the body of Kinnear, finding a photo of *The Hand of the Prophet* in her shirt. He muttered to himself. Searching further, he found the second camera she had apparently hidden in her pocket, a slim micro camera that must have been used to shoot before the Casio had been given over as a decoy. He wondered who else might have a copy of that photo. He whistled to Grundstrom then ran for refuge as covering fire was laid down for him.

The men took stock and set up positions from which they could hold off the enemy for a while. The last bit of daylight faded to black desert night, as they settled in to keep a stand-off.

The pilot was not hurt, but the Helicopter was trash. That meant they could not get out of the area, much less out of Yemen. Daylight would bring new perils. Meanwhile, they just hunkered down, exchanging occasional shots with their enemies. They reckoned that there were now only three or four fighters left to fire at them. Hearing some radio traffic on what they assumed to be cell phone walkie-talkies, they realized that their enemy would have reinforcements by dawn, if not before.

Greg's wound had somehow stopped bleeding, but he was in lots of discomfort. The professor was very quiet. Steck figured he was just so shocked by the events of the last half-hour that he would remain apoplectic for a while. Steck and Grunstrom began plotting how they might take out the rest of their enemy during the night. That would be crucial to their survival, even if it only bought them a few more hours of life.

Methodically, Grundstrom and Steck questioned Wigglesworth to determine how many others were scattered around the camp. They created a written list and then found each of the folks on it. Most had been cowering, unarmed. One Arab man, the one who had served lunch, had crept up on an insurgent and slit his throat.

After the non-combatants had all been accounted for, Steck and Grundstrom made a plan. They had four healthy armed men. As well as they could determine, the enemy had a maximum of four, maybe only three able to fight. Their last known positions, confirmed by the stealthy old Arab assassin were clustered at a position roughly sixty yards out in front of the main tent. Baby face produced a box of white flares and a flare gun from the helicopter. They decided to flank two men to an eight o'clock position and two to four o'clock about thirty yards out, then Greg, who was able to crawl but not to sit, would fire two flares. The old Arab would throw a rock straight out towards the enemy just before the flares were fired. Hopefully, they could elicit some movement from the enemy who would then be caught in a cross-fire.

"If that doesn't move them, what do we do next?" the pilot asked.

Steck and Grundstrom exchanged a knowing glance. "We charge them and hope we guessed their position correctly," said Grundstrom. Then he added, "Finish this man to man if you have to. Otherwise we're all dead men." Both Steck and Grundstrom knew that this would be only the first of many steps to survival. No use planning the next moves until this one was accomplished. They agreed to make their move in twenty minutes. That would make it about eight pm.

They lay still, waiting. Steck could hear the sound of machines in the distance. He figured the bad guys were moving more assets into position. A beam of light flickered from over the ridge behind them in the direction of the Marib Dam.

"They should wait until first light tomorrow," offered Grundstrom. Steck grunted, hoping he was right.

Chris Taylor was still at Al Kafajy Trading Company's Amman office. He had dismissed the rest of the staff at seven-thirty pm, directing them to stay available all night in case he needed to call them back to work. He had telephoned Aliyah to cancel their dinner date, but she insisted on bringing food to him at the office. She was due to arrive at eight o'clock, ten minutes from now.

Chris lit a cigarette, waiting for the Cairo office to answer his cell phone. After many rings, a perturbed voice answered in Arabic. "The office of Al Kafajy trading is closed for the day."

"This is Taylor."

"Oh! Mister Taylor! I did not know it was you, sir!" The voice spoke in English with attention. It was Mahmoud El Saeed, the office manager. "What can I do for you, sir?"

"I am interested in the shipment we discussed yesterday, incoming from Peru."

"Let me check on that. Just one moment please." El Saeed put the line on hold.

Chris picked a shred of tobacco from his lip then took a deep draught of smoke from his cigarette. He flicked the tip into the ash tray, absently studying the company's logo imprinted on the glass as he exhaled. El Saeed came back on the line. "The shipment was received in apparent good order this afternoon. It is consigned on a flight tonight at eleven o'clock to Amman."

"Very well, Thank you Mahmoud. Fax me the waybill number to the Amman office, please."

"You're most welcome, sir. I will fax it right away. I hope you enjoy your evening, sir"

"I will. Please give my regards to your wife and family, Mahmoud." The business-speak observed, Chris clicked off.

Lighting his next cigarette from the stub of the last, Chris tried again to ring the satphone of Nancy Kinnear. A man's voice answered in English. Chris tensed. "Is Miss Kinnear about?" He enquired cautiously.

"Who is calling please?" It was a soft male voice.

Chris hesitated. Finally he said, "An old student friend from Amman."

The man who had answered put his hand over the receiver and mumbled something unintelligible. After a pause, the voice said, "She is unable to come to the phone at the moment. She asks who is calling and would you please leave a message."

"No Message. I'll call again later." Chris clicked off. He tamped out the cigarette and began to form an impression of the tricky conversation just ended. He was interrupted by a knock at the door and the cheerful voice of his friend Aliyah.

Chris opened the front door and welcomed her with a warm embrace. She gestured to a big basket full of delicious smelling food on the door stoop. Chris scooped it and exclaimed, "It smells as if you have really prepared a feast."

CHAPTER 16

Steck and baby face managed to slip un-noticed through the darkness, taking up their eight o'clock position, while Grundstrom and the pilot were ready at four o'clock. When all was set, they were waiting in the darkness for Greg and the old man to start the operation. While waiting, he had felt the buzz of Kinnear's satphone in his pocket and had a brief dilemma over whether to answer and potentially betray his position. Finally, he answered almost in a whisper. The only piece of information he had gleaned from verbal sparring with the voice on the other end was that the call probably had originated in Amman. It was better than nothing, something to report to Morgan later, even if it turned out to be his last report before leaving this life.

At the appointed time, the old man threw his rock and Greg fired two white flares. Startled, the insurgents began to fire wildly. One stood up just as the flares dimmed. Grundstrom dropped him with a two shot burst.

The others began moving, trying to flank Grundstrom's position. Greg fired another flare. Steck and baby face knelt at the ready.

"Bingo," thought Steck as the bright flare caught the two remaining enemy with their backs exposed to him. "Take the one to the right," Whispered baby face. Steck nodded. Both men fired at once, bringing both of the enemy down.

After a few silent minutes, Steck decided to test whether any of the enemy could still function. He shouted to Grundstrom. "Is everyone okay?"

"Okay," came the reply.

"Greg?"

"Okay."

Steck stood up, lit his flashlight and began a purposely noisy retreat back toward the main tent, taking care to keep cover at hand. No shots and no movement were heard. When he and the others had reached the tent, he ordered Greg to put up more flares. "Keep them coming to light my way. I'm going to confirm the number of their dead."

Baby face joined him and together they found fourteen bodies in all, no survivors.

Back at the tent, they gathered to acknowledge their victory and to plan their next move. Wigglesworth produced a first aid kit. One of the archeological team was a doctor of sorts, a Brit who had forsaken his ill-paid job as a doctor in Britain for another one in archeology. He cleaned Greg's wound, declaring it just a nick in the flesh. Greg stated that the discomfort far exceeded the apparent triviality of his wound. He would not be sitting for long periods of time over the next few weeks.

Steck and Grundstrom took a short walk outside to talk in privacy. "You were pretty cool and very effective during that fracas," Steck offered.

"You were pretty good yourself," returned Grundstrom with a smile. "It's a pleasure to work with you."

"Well, the way I see it, this was probably only the opening round," said Steck. Grundstrom agreed.

"The way I see it," said Steck, "we have two main issues. The first is how to get out of this scum-hole before more unfrieldlies show up. The second is what to do with the professor and his team." He could still hear the noise to the other side of the wadi, and gestured in that direction.

Grundstrom acknowledged the noise with a gesture. "If that's our enemy, they won't come lightly armed this time. I figure they'll come at dawn. If they're night trained they'll arrive in less than an hour. As for the professor, remember it was one of his people that betrayed us. I say we leave him and his friends. They would be a liability in another fire fight, and it looks like they have some sort of relationship with whoever just tried to kill us."

Steck seemed momentarily attracted to that thought, but was keen to question Wigglesworth at length. He needed to understand why they had been attacked and by whom. Leaving the old man here could do more harm than help to the JUMP team's quest. "I need to interrogate the old buzzard."

"If we take him, it reduces our chances of ever getting out of Yemen to near zero," reasoned Grundstrom. "Without a helicopter, we have to negotiate a hundred and seventy miles of God-forsaken desert chock full of terrorists. We already have one injured guy that probably can't make the hike. To drag a freaking octogenarian along would be suicide."

After more talk, they decided to discuss it with the others and then risk voice contact with their respective organizations. As soon as they tele-communicated they would have to make a run to some new position.

Back at the tent, they gathered the pilot, baby face and Greg to discuss their options. The pilot was just opening his mouth to speak, when the camp lit up like Christmas. The noise of two helicopters was overhead. Steck and Grundstrom frowned. The pilot smiled. "I was about to tell you I got a distress signal off before I crashed," he shouted above the noise. "That's the sound of our machines!"

It turned out to be two helicopters in Saudi military markings. One was a twin rotor CH-47, the kind used to ferry troops. The other was a Cobra gunship.

Almost giddy about these new resources, Steck shouted to Grundstrom. "How the heck did you guys get these?"

"Never underestimate my boss," replied the grinning Gundstrom.

"You're right," Steck offered. "Randy Pullin is the most resourceful man I know."

Grundstrom gave Steck a quizzical look. "So you know the man?"

Steck nodded. "At this moment, I'm real glad to know the man!"

The two aircraft set down at the cleared area near the dig normally used as a makeshift helipad for supply runs. Since they now had the capacity, they offered to take the professor and his team of about a dozen with them. The professor refused at first.

"Were those guys that just attacked us your friends?" asked Steck.

"No, they were not," Was the reply.

"In that case you've got two choices professor. You stay and take your chances with those hostiles or you come with us. For the sake of your team, I think you better come with us." Steck was prepared to force this issue if he had to.

Wigglesworth discussed it with his team, and they decided to leave the dig. They hastily gathered some records and personal belongings then clambered on board the CH-47.

Ten minutes later, the two ships lifted off, with all safely on board. As they sped through the desert night, Steck grilled Professor Wigglesworth. He needed answers to many questions.

——————

Ryall Morgan's satphone buzzed at about four o'clock am. He bounded half asleep from the cot he had occupied in Lindsley's office and clicked both the answer and speaker buttons. Lindsley and Susan Deet both wiped sleep from their eyes, sitting up straight on their respective cots.

"Morgan, It's Pullin," the wide-awake voice announced. "We retrieved them all. One has a minor injury. Twenty-one of the bad guys are dead. The professor is in our custody in Jeddah."

"Good work, Colonel," Morgan blurted. "I knew I could count on you," he lied. Ryall stared at Lindsley who returned a 'go figure' gesture.

"Who is the injured one?" Morgan hoped it was not one of his men.

"Greg Liss," was the reply. "He'll be okay, just a scratch, I hear."

"Thanks. We'll talk later today." said Morgan.

"Just don't forget where to send the check." Randy said sardonically.

At five o'clock am, a silver Mercedes 500S wheeled into the customs holding area at Amman's international airport. In silk business suits, Chris Taylor and one of the Al Kafajy Trading company's staff emerged from the back and entered the customs office. They were armed with the necessary paperwork and also with two cartons of American cigarettes and a wad of cash to be used to grease the way for release of their incoming shipment. Ten minutes later, they left the airport with the crate containing their prize safely tucked in the trunk of the big auto. Chris could now breathe a bit easier, having come to the final part of his mission. He smoked a cigarette and read the Jordanian morning newspaper during the ride back to the office.

Chris would greet the boss and his entourage later in the day as they arrived on the mid-afternoon flight from Paris. Until then, he had some time to make last minute arrangements and hopefully to get some rest.

At seven o'clock, he held a staff meeting to go over the final preparations for the weekend 'conference' at the Royal Amman hotel. The fourteen room penthouse suite would be where Mister Al Kafajy and his family stayed. It would also be the site of the bidding, with a final sale to be arranged before the guests left the hotel on Monday. All thirty-four luxury suites in the hotel had been reserved by Al Kafajy Trading Company for Thursday through Monday. Four private dining rooms would be available 24 hours daily for the guests of Al Kafajy. No service of the hotel would be denied the honored guests at any time, and no guest would pay for anything they wanted, even in the large shopping mall that was part of the hotel property. A Mercedes and driver would be provided for each guest. Generous tips would be provided to the entire hotel staff. A meeting with hotel management assured that Al Kafajy's guests would be treated as royalty. Some of them would be royalty, after all.

The crate was opened and the *Hand of Mohammed* was removed, checked carefully by two experts in antiquities and deposited in a sack of fine gold cloth. Satisfied with the provenance of his prize, Chris took it with him in a leather brief chained to his wrist.

At nine-fifteen am, satisfied that all was ready, Chris decided to retire to his room at the Royal Amman. On the way, he telephoned Aliyah, explaining that he would be out of touch for the next five days but would call her Monday evening. He suggested they could take a vacation for a few days at a posh beach club in Dubai at the end of the next week. She sounded excited about that prospect. He arrived at the Royal Amman about ten am. At his room, Chris opened the door to the adjoining room and knocked. The connecting door was opened by a burly fellow named Tariq. He had served Mister Al Kafajy as a bodyguard for more than ten years. His mission today was to assure that nothing happened to either Chris or the parcel he was carrying. After thoroughly checking Chris' room, and supervising the deposition of the prize into the room safe, the tough guy assumed his guard duty position in the next room leaving the connecting door ajar. Chris ate some chocolate, part of the welcome basket that the hotel provided for all guests. Changing into jeans and a tee, he lay down to take a nap.

CHAPTER 17

At their hotel in Jeddah Bob Steck and Greg Liss had just finished a verbal de-briefing with the JUMP team via satphone. They had gained a lot of information from Doctor Wigglesworth about *The Hand of Mohammed*, its provenance throughout history and its significance for the current era of Islamist terrorism. Most of this had just confirmed the fears of the JUMP team. Their mission was now of the highest priority. The implication scenarios would be written and sent to the top national security advisors. A report would then be made to the President at his daily security briefing.

The open issues and subject of JUMP team's next assignment were first, identify Nancy Kinnear and second find out what organization had attacked the dig site in Yemen.

Wigglesworth had explained that Nancy was one of his students at Dartmouth. She had volunteered for a summer internship at a dig in Turkey seven years back. The professor had taken a liking to her, admiring her hard work and her keen mind. She had stayed on as an employee of the Wigglesworth team through digs in Turkey, Armenia, Somalia and Yemen. Along the way, she had accumulated two advanced degrees. She was a trusted member of the archeological community and had authored several original papers about Arab antiquities. The professor had no knowledge of her involvement with any national or terrorist groups. He seemed distraught about her death.

Steck was disturbed by Nancy's apparent skills in combat. Her band of twenty armed fighters could have been members of any one of several terrorist groups that had training camps in the Yemeni outback.

Steck made his feelings clear to Morgan, Lindsley and the others about Nancy. "She stole a photo of the figurine. We don't know whether she passed it on or to whom. I think we can assume she did pass it to someone she was working for. She was committed so strongly to her real employer that she accepted an order to take a team of mercenaries and to kill our whole team. Even if this had been successful it would blow her seven years cover with Wigglesworth and leave her with the prospect of killing the professor and the whole expedition to cover her actions. That tells me this was no casual operation and that we are up against an adversary that will not hesitate to kill on a grand scale to protect its operation."

"Greg, what do you think about this Nancy?" asked Lindsley.

Somehow at Lindsley's words, Greg's mind conjured the link to Nancy Kinnear that he had failed to recall. "Why I just remembered, she was in a framed photo with the professor and others that is beside the telephone in Doctor Wigglesworth's study."

"Should we send someone to interview Missus Wigglesworth?"

"Perhaps," offered Greg, "but I would like to do that myself."

"We don't have much time to do this, Greg." Lindsley exchanged a look with Ryall Morgan. "I'm going to send Susan today."

"Greg's flying back to Washington tonight," said Steck.

Greg flashed a look. It was the first he had heard of the flight. Steck motioned at Greg's bandaged backside and rolled his eyes. "Greg needs some time to recover from his wound."

"Will you come with him?" asked Lindsley.

"I think I should stay here until the archeological team is moved out of the kingdom." Steck asserted. They are not here legally. We need to make arrangements with our angels to get them to a place of safety. I'm thinking they could be dropped in Aden, where they can use their Yemeni visas."

"Good thinking, Bob." Ryall Morgan's tone sounded authoritative. "I think you should stay in the middle-east for now and run some issues to ground for us in Jordan. I sent you a communiqué about that today." He did not want to discuss his concerns about terrorist movements verbally, even on a supposedly secure satphone connection.

"I received it and have studied it," said Steck. "I agree that we need to stay close to that. Do I have other assets at my disposal?"

"Yes you do," Morgan stated. "The present angels will remain involved at your direction and discretion. You also have our bureau in Amman. Do you need their contact information?"

"Negative. They're all old friends."

"We're all glad that you are workin' this, Mister Bob," Drawled Lindsley. "My people have a file opened on Miss Kinnear. You'll get a complete report on that within a day."

"Thanks for that." Steck was finally feeling better about having the JUMP team as support.

"Is Susan still in the room?"

"I'm here, Bob." Susan Deet answered.

"Have you got any more information on the whereabouts of Roche?"

"Nothing definitive, except I am convinced he's in Mexico. Our people there are watching for any sign of him."

"I remembered a conversation many years ago with him about deep cover. I think he may be somewhere near Mexico City," Bob offered.

"Got it," Susan replied, "a pseudo-Brit living near Mexico City."

Steck sat back in his chair, the wheels spinning in his head. "My guess is he will be posing as a well healed bachelor, probably into golf."

"Thanks. We'll be on it twenty-four-seven."

"I also have the gut-feel that he knows a lot more about the present issue than we may think." Steck knew Paul Roche well enough to figure he would not be able to resist making some big score, if there was one to be made. It was pure speculation on his part, but worth keeping an eye out.

Hugh Coles had just finished his morning workout. Emerging from the shower, he sat to eat the breakfast his maid had prepared. Sipping coffee to wash down some toast and bacon, he checked the front page of the morning paper. His eyes stopped at a small window advert in the left bottom of the front page. It read *Seeking original 1963 Sunbeam Tiger in mint condition. Highest price offered.* He tossed the toast, drank the coffee down and went searching for his cell phone. When he found it, he dialed the number from the advert. A familiar voice answered.

"Good day to you sir," he said in his best slurry Brit accent. "I happen to possess a silver-grey version of the vehicle you have requested. I would be willing to sell it for the right price."

"When can I see it, and where?" asked the voice.

"Do you know the Palacio de Bellas Artes?"

"Why yes, that is a convenient place for me," the voice replied.

"Meet me in front, at three pm today?"

"Very well, sir." The voice clicked off.

Roche telephoned a taxi, dressed and shortly left for the meeting place. The voice on the telephone had been that of Alberto Montenero, a paid intermediary used on occasion by folks in the spy business. He was known and respected for the utmost discretion. The actual meeting would take place in a pre-arranged place about two blocks from the Palacio de Bellas Artes. It was a small café that catered to upper-crust émigrés. Alberto would not be the contact, nor did he know the meeting place. He would have made text contact only with a third party whose identity was known only to Roche.

Alberto's involvement was concluded with the text message. He would receive payment for his services via wire transfer from one account in the Caymans to another.

On the way, Roche's thoughts were at once troubled and intrigued. He was troubled at disruption of his new life just days after it had been established. He was intrigued that some new deal was in the offing, one that was important enough to cause contact to be made.

Susan Deet made it to the Dartmouth campus at sundown, after telephone conversation with the professor's wife. She was surprised to learn that Missus Wigglesworth had not heard from her husband. The gentle woman had agreed to an interview during the evening hours, sounding as gracious as Greg had reported in the brief Susan studied during the flight. Susan had dressed 'Ivy League' in a plaid skirt with white blouse buttoned high at the collar, knee-high socks and loafers. Deet feigned an interest in orchids, which prompted a tour of the solarium at the Wigglesworth residence. By the time tea was served, Missus Wigglesworth seemed relaxed and eager to be interviewed by such a nice young woman as Susan.

"Well, Missus Wigglesworth, I want to first tell you that Greg Liss has met with your husband and that they had a very good discussion."

"How nice," the old woman replied. "I do expect a call from my husband next week, when he gets to Amman. I'm sure he will have been glad to speak to Mister Liss."

"You know I am here on official business," Susan began. "Today, I need to complete a background check on Nancy Kinnear." She paused, watching keenly for any non-verbal response. Missus Wigglesworth's eyes narrowed, almost imperceptibly. She looked briefly to her lap and straightened her skirt. Her composure, if it slipped at all, was immediately regained. Smiling, her eyes met Susan's as she said gently, "Ah yes, my husband's protégé."

"She is his protégé?" Susan asked, as if declaring something new. "Given the number of degrees and published works she has accumulated, I would have supposed the more proper term to be colleague."

"Yes, of course," Missus Wigglesworth replied absently.

Susan decided to use silence for a moment to see of it elicited any further comment. The silence became a bit awkward. Finally the older woman leveled a friendly gaze at Susan.

"My dear," she said, "one of the great lessons I have learned in life is that relationships progress through many stages. Men, especially aging intellectuals like my husband who remain vital need to have relationships with attractive women who will challenge them in healthy ways. If they do not have such relationships they will naturally gravitate to either unhealthy relationships or vegetative ones."

"I see," said Susan, allowing another pause designed to keep the lady talking.

"No, you don't see," replied Missus Wigglesworth calmly. "I suspect you have not accumulated the life experience to fully appreciate my comments."

This time the pause caused Susan discomfort. Before she could conjure a counter-move, the older woman continued. "As you may have observed, my physical abilities have waned considerably." Susan's eyes betrayed agreement as they involuntarily fell to the gnarled hands resting in Missus Wigglesworth's lap.

"Please do not misconstrue what I am saying, Susan. My husband still loves me every bit as much as he did when we married and I love him with all my heart. We have had and still have a wonderful life together. Time was when my love of the outdoors and his love of digging up old things were quite compatible. We shared many years of closeness physically, intellectually and in our hearts. As we aged, we still shared the same love but the physical aspect became burdensome for me."

"I fail to see how this…." Susan began to say.

"Please don't interrupt." Missus Wigglesworth's gaze was still soft but her tone was determined. "I have something important to tell you, young lady." Susan sat back in her chair and uncrossed her legs, trying to correct the wrong move she had just made.

"No two people age in the same ways or at the same time," the older woman continued. "As my infirmity increased, my husband was at the peak of his personal power. Personal power will one day pass for every one, but while it is strong, a person needs to have ego-boosting activity to support their sense of that power. Nancy Kinnear became my surrogate, of sorts. She filled the void, so to speak, while our marriage relationship waited for my husband's personal power to play out its course."

Missus Wigglesworth leaned toward Susan and gestured with a wave of her hand. "Now don't be misled in thinking that there was physical intimacy between my husband and Nancy Kinnear. Nothing of the sort was even contemplated. I'm sure of it. Nancy had her young lovers for that. Now that my husband has matured and released much of his male ego, our relationship together has deepened in ways past telling. The sum of it is, Susan, that Nancy performed a very important role in my husband's life, a role that I always welcomed. That role is now waning and will soon be over."

Missus Wigglesworth sat back in silence for a moment then she added. "Did you understand me?"

"I understand that you are an extremely wise and prudent woman." Susan was sincere.

"You missed the best part." Missus Wigglesworth smiled. "I am a happy and contented woman."

Susan did not think it proper to reveal Nancy Kinnear's passing. The professor could handle that.

"Can you tell me anything else about Ms. Kinnear, such as her early life, her personal interests her hobbies?" Susan knew there was more to learn.

"Nancy was born in Canada. In Saskatoon, I believe. Her parents were wealthy. She told me they were in oil exploration and leasing. She graduated from a university in Toronto. Before she came to Dartmouth, she trained with the Canadian security service. She left that after a failed love affair." Missus Wigglesworth paused a while, seemingly deep in thought. "The only other thing I know about Nancy is that her family lost their fortune a few years back. It has been hard for her to maintain her wealthy lifestyle on the earnings from a few books plus the paltry money she earns at archaeological digs, but somehow she carries it off."

After a pause, Susan asked, "Is there anything else you want to tell me?"

"Yes. Nancy is not a happy person. That's a shame. She has a lot of potential, but she's not happy."

Susan thanked Missus Wigglesworth for the information and for her candor.

On the drive back to Manchester, Susan spent an hour on the secure phone talking with Mort Lindsley. At her hotel, she stayed up until four am writing a detailed report, which she emailed to Mort.

"You did a great job, Susie." Lindsley was sincere.

CHAPTER 18

Chris Taylor's brief nap was interrupted by a ringing telephone. He sat up, shook his head from side to side to chase away the fog, and answered. "This is Taylor."

"Allah is good." It was Ahmed. "The gentleman is now en-route to Amman. He should arrive at the appointed time. I trust you will meet him at the airport." It was a declaration, not a question.

"Yes, I will meet him." Chris wondered if that sounded petulant. He hoped it did.

"I wish to meet with you beforehand."

"Okay," said Chris, cursing in thought. "When will you arrive in Amman?"

"I am in the lobby," was the terse reply. "Stay in your room. I will be there directly." Ahmed clicked off.

"What an annoying man," thought Chris, as he quickly dressed in the formal suit he would wear for the rest of the day. He had just tied his silk cravat when Ahmed knocked at the door.

"As salaam alaikum," uttered Ahmed as he entered. He was dressed in traditional Arab garb. The big knife tucked into his sash had a polished silver handle encrusted with semi precious jewels. It seemed too big for Ahmed's squat frame.

"Alaikum asalaam," was the reply from the adjoining room. Chris remained quiet; realizing that Ahmed's greeting using the formal form was not intended for him, but rather for the guard who was Ahmed's Muslim brother.

Satisfied that Chris had not offended him, Ahmed acknowledged him with "Hello Chris."

Chris stood facing Ahmed, not offering him a seat. "I have much to do today, Ahmed. What did you want to talk about?"

"Did you contact that Kinnear woman?" Ahmed's piercing eyes upset Chris's inner calm.

"I tried but was not successful." Chris sensed some tacit move afoot.

"She is dead," said Ahmed, almost absently. He looked around the room as if trying to find a suitable chair.

In the silence that followed, Chris' mind raged, full of anger at this man who seemed so pleased to play head games with him. He waited until the urge to rant had subsided, deciding to withhold the fact that he had spoken with her apparent killer. In his best British nonchalance, he said, "Too bad. How did she die?"

"She was shot fighting the men from America who came to Yemen to find out about our prize. That is where she obtained the photo."

"Are the Americans dead also?" Chris felt his color rising.

"Unfortunately they are alive. It appears they escaped into Saudi Arabia. We do not know where, exactly."

Chris resisted the urge to fling a barrage of questions at Ahmed. Now that it was certain that American agents were on the trail, he would need to plan carefully and initiate some actions. "Thank you for the information, Ahmed," Chris said in even tones. "I have much to do," he said, urging Ahmed towards the door. What is your room number? I'll call you when the gentleman is settled."

"No need," Ahmed said icily as he closed the door behind him. "I will see you at dinner in Mister Al Kafajy's suite."

Chris shuffled in the closet and came out with a small suitcase. He left the room in the care of Tariq, moving almost at a trot down the hall. He stopped at a hotel room remote from his, produced a key from his pocket and entered, locking the door securely behind him. In the privacy of his second room, he unpacked the secure encoding machine and set up the satphone connection. Typing and sending several messages, he then made a voice call.

He lit a cigarette, waiting for an answer. "Who is this?" a drawling man's voice questioned.

"This is Chris Taylor. I need to arrange a secure conversation with Mister Roche right away."

"Hell, I don't even know where that rascal is holed-up." was the reply.

"Find him!" Chris half shouted. "I will call you at three am, your time."

"Negative. It will take a few days to contact him." The man sounded sincere enough.

"Then try someone else. I need to get some action today on an important matter."

"Maybe I could help."

Chris contemplated that for a moment. He quickly decided not to trust a hayseed with a limp to find and kill a bunch of U.S. agents.

"Not this time, Blake." He said.

"I'll do what I can, Mister Taylor. Call me at three and I'll have a plan."

Blake smiled as he clicked off the line. He dialed and waited. "Proctor," The voice answered.

"Mister Proctor, are you still plannin' to meet Roche in Mexico today?"

Ryall Morgan, Mort Lindsley and Susan Deet sat in Mort's office. The speaker phone was connected with Robert MacFergus, one of Morgan's friends and the head of CSIS in Ottawa. Susan read aloud her report about Nancy Kinnear. At Morgan's insistence, she had also drawn the connection to Carole Hinson, the CSIS agent that had gone missing in Idaho.

It took a while for MacFergus to absorb what he had just heard. The silence was palpable. Morgan held up a hand, silently asking Lindsley and Deet to let the silence remain.

MacFergus finally said, "Ryall, could you pick up the phone?"

Morgan and Lindsley exchanged looks. Deet lowered her eyes, studying the table. Lindsley motioned assent.

"Speaker's off, Bob," Ryall said, picking up the phone receiver and clicking the speaker button.

MacFergus spoke slowly, choosing his words with care. "Mort, this is quite sensitive. Can I have your absolute word that this conversation will go no further than necessary to solve your case?"

"Yes, Bob you have my word. Before it's over we may both have to rely on each other's confidence, if that's where you're going."

"I am, Ryall." MacFergus paused, as if trying to think of a reason not to continue. Finally he began. "Do you folks keep an eye on an organization called *Free Nation*?"

"We know them," Morgan replied.

"Well, we have a case open that involves that group. We suspect they have been moving goods illegally in and out of Canada through border crossings at Vermont, Idaho, Montana and Washington State. Five years ago, some antiquities from an archaeological dig in Turkey showed up in Montreal, consigned to a professor at Dartmouth University in New Hampshire. We were led to believe they may have been smuggled into Canada by *Free Nation*."

"Did the goods get delivered into the U.S?" Morgan asked.

"No, Ryall, they did not. We confiscated them and returned them to the Turkish government. After that incident, we assigned one of our operatives to infiltrate the archaeological organization responsible for the dig."

"Nancy Kinnear?" Morgan pointed out the obvious.

"Yes." MacFergus continued. "More recently, we assigned Carole Hinson to surveillance of *Free Nation*. Her assignment included infiltration, and of course required some travel in your country. She has been missing for a few days now. We have reason to believe she may have been witness to a murder by one of the members of *Free Nation* near

Coeur d'Alene, Idaho. At least that was her last reporting point. We fear she may have fallen victim to foul play. I have a report that we will offer to share with the local police at Coeur d'Alene, whom we believe are investigating the demise of a local farmer."

"I think this should involve the FBI, Bob. We would appreciate if you keep the local police out of this for now." Morgan waved off Lindsley, who had snapped to attention at the mention of his organization. Before MacFergus could go on, Morgan added, "I think we should conduct a joint investigation, but first I would like to request a detailed conference between our two organizations. At the moment we are in hot pursuit of another matter, but maybe next week we could get together, perhaps by videophone. Would that be okay?"

"Of course it would, Ryall and the sooner the better. One of our agents has been killed and another is missing. I don't want to let much time go by."

"My secretary will call you in the morning to set it up." Morgan said. "And thanks for your candor, Bob. It will not be forgotten and will not be compromised."

"Right-oh, Ryall," He replied. "I hope we can resolve this together." MacFergus hung up the phone. He sat for a few minutes making notes, hoping he had done the right thing.

Bob Steck landed at Amman about noontime. Thanks to Grundstrom, the archaeologists would be landing in Aden about the same time. Bob had engaged Grundstrom to deliver his charges then join him in Amman as soon as possible.

Steck was met by a limo service. The driver delivered him to the Intercontinental Hotel, where there would be rooms for both Steck and Grundstrom. Strolling across the lobby, Steck noticed that the Intercontinental had become rather seedy in appearance since his last stay. His room was also rather dingy. He made a mental note to seek a different place to stay next time.

After settling his stuff in the room, he went to the street level and took a taxi to the offices of Anwhar International, the front organization for the CIA's Amman bureau. After being vetted by the receptionist, he was led to a small conference room off the lobby. As she left the room, the receptionist locked the door with a key that she carried on a chain around her neck.

A few minutes later, a section of bookcase at the back of the room opened. Steck could see a bustling room beyond, full of folks working at computer work stations. Through the opening came a short and portly red-faced man in his middle fifties, sporting a great shock of gray hair that looked like an explosion in a bird nest. His bloodshot eyes seemed too large behind thick bone-rimmed trifocals. His open shirt looked like it had been worn daily for a month or so. This was Steck's old friend Charlie West.

The two men shot the breeze for a few minutes, laughing and catching up on family and friends of mutual acquaintance. Then Charlie led Bob to his private office to the rear of the clandestine work area. Steck briefed Charlie West explaining about the JUMP team. He spoke about its current mission. He voiced his concern about the reported movement of many influential Muslim figures towards Amman.

Charlie filled Bob in about the latest list of arrivals. Bob whistled softly as he read the names and titles on the list. They included some of the worst bad guy terrorists in person or representatives of their organizations, influential politicos and even some royalty. The common denominator was that they were all staying at the Royal Amman Hotel as guests of the Al Kafajy Trading Company.

Charlie produced a Jordanian lad of about twenty, who was a member of the service staff at the Royal Amman Hotel.

"This is Samir, one of my most trusted and loyal agents here in Amman," said Charlie proudly. He will work the next six days during the afternoon and evening at the hotel."

"I'm Pleased to know you, Samir," offered Steck as he extended his hand.

The young man took Bob's hand and made a small bow, saying "The pleasure is mine, Mister Steck."

"Samir will be wearing a wire during his work shift for the next few days," offered Charlie. "He has performed this service for us many times." He added, guessing Steck's un-asked question.

The three men went over the list of names carefully, along with file photos. They chose a few for Samir to monitor when possible. After Samir left the room, Bob asked "How many other agents will we have at the hotel?"

"Just Samir," answered Charlie. Noting Steck's incredulous look, Charlie explained. "Look Bob, we have a small operation here and a tight budget. That's the only asset I can give you right now. He's my best agent."

"And who is the next-best?" Bob asked.

"If you want more of my assets, get your boss to put some pressure on at Langley. From a personal standpoint, I'll be at your service night and day, but that's all I have to give, even to an old friend." Charlie was ever the consummate bureaucrat. "You know it takes a team of four to support one man on a wire. They will be here to help. If there's trouble, I have staff here at this address around the clock and we're only two blocks from the Royal Amman." As if to add punctuation to his remarks, Charlie shrugged and gestured with outstretched palms.

Steck knew he had pushed as far as he was able, so he smiled and slapped a high five to Charlie's outstretched hand. "Okay, old buddy. I still think we need more than one wire to watch this cast of characters. I'll take it up with Langley later today."

CHAPTER 19

After his attempt to contact Roche, Chris Taylor had supervised a photo shoot of *The Hand of Mohammed* at the Royal Amman Hotel. The photographer was famous for shooting objects d'art. She had been flown in from London, where she was employed at Christie's auction gallery. She was often used for this type of assignment because she had a reputation for utmost discretion.

After the shoot, Chris again locked the prize in his room safe. Now that he knew that American agents were trying to pick up the trail, he decided to engage two more armed guards to assist Tariq. He also set two men to watch the lobby area of the hotel and tied all five together with a network of small radios.

Muhammed Al Kafajy and his retinue of executives, lawyers, secretaries and body guards arrived in Amman on the Learjet he had rented for the flight from Paris. His own airplane, a larger Gulf Stream, was on a mission to Dubai, where it would collect one of the expected high bidders for *The Hand*.

Delayed by the business of tightening security for the prize, Chris now had to rush through the impossible Amman downtown mid afternoon traffic with his fleet of three large cars, himself riding in the lead Mercedes beside the driver. Fortunately, the Learjet was rolling to a stop on the tarmac just as the cars pulled to a stop on the apron.

On the way back to the Royal Amman Hotel, Chris briefed the boss about recent developments and the precautions he had taken as a result. Mister Al Kafajy first commended Taylor on his work thus far. He then directed that additional security be put in place for the personal protection of the bidders.

All possible surveillance of incoming travelers from Saudi Arabia was arranged by Al Kafajy himself in a cell phone call to one of his friends in Jordanian security.

The boss seemed in a very good mood. He chatted affably about who would be the top bidders and how much they might bid. He had decided to open the bidding at one hundred million. Chris now realized that this little "auction" would probably fetch close to half-a-billion dollars. When he mentioned that to the boss, he was answered with a hearty guffaw. "It will be more like half-a-billion *euros*, Christian!"

By Thursday evening, Steck had caught some sleep and enjoyed a hearty Middle Eastern meal of soup, lamb and vegetables, washed down with doogh, a yogurt drink he had learned to love while on assignment in Iran.

Grundstrom had arrived from Yemen, reporting successful delivery of the professor and his band of associates. Steck was glad to have him as a compadre for the next few days. When a guy saves your skin, you get to like him real fast.

"So, how did you get hooked-up with Randy Pullin?" Steck asked, as they sat together over coffee in his room.

"One night I was holed-up in a dusty hell-hole near Kandahar. We were taking small arms fire from the Taliban. I needed more men for my mission, but had been denied them. I was denied them by a jerk colonel who had plenty of men and equipment to give but was playing some stupid head-game with a peer officer. In the course of that fire fight, I lost six guys that didn't have to die, except for that colonel's stupidity. By morning, the few of us that were left had killed every last one of those buggers. If I had just six more men, I could've got them all without losing anybody. So, I decided right then not to re-enlist. I shopped around for a job that fit my skills, you know, like Blackwater and those types. Turns out they are run by folks just like that jerk colonel, guys who had been kicked out or passed over by the military. Kind of like the bottom of the barrel I was trying to get out of, if you know what I mean."

"I do indeed," Steck agreed, remembering some of that type from the Vietnam era.

"Well, then a friend put me on to Colonel Randy. He impressed me because he knew how to fit the assets to the task. I tried a couple of missions with *Free Nation* and the rest, as they say, is history. I've been with them for four years. One hundred and eighteen missions none failed."

"Pretty good record," Steck offered.

"Damn good record." was the reply. "The money's great, I run my own show and I expect to do this for quite a while."

"No problem that you're sometimes operating outside the law?" Steck had the thought that he might be able to recruit this guy someday.

Grundstrom gave him a queer look. "Operating outside the law? What is the law to me! I tried the law. The law ain't the truth, you know. Take you, for instance. You operate either just inside or just outside the law most of the time. A lot of the time you are way outside 'the law.' Do you think about 'the law' when you cross the line one way or the other? I don't think so. Me, I'm just like you spook guys. I operate under Gunny Grundstrom's law. That's the only one that ever got me anything."

"What about your country?" Steck was probing, for future reference.

Grundstrom leaned back in his chair. "I consider myself a patriot, if that's what you mean. I don't fall for some of the stuff that Colonel Randy preaches, but I can tell you one thing. That guy loves his country. Everybody in *Free Nation* thinks they are doing the right thing for the good old U.S of A. The way I look at it, we make up for the fumbles that guys like that colonel in Kandahar make every day. We carry the ball and we score. You got any problem with that?"

"None at all. You've already saved my neck once." Steck figured he would someday recruit this guy.

Grundstrom was inspecting his Beretta for cleanliness. "So, when do we go to this here party?"

"About seven pm. We will be in a room a few blocks from the Royal Amman Hotel listening to a guy on a wire. I'll brief you about the rest on the way there." Steck shook Grundstrom's hand. "Glad to have you aboard, Gunny."

At noon, Mexico City time, Hugh Coles strode into the appointed sidewalk café. He picked a table that had an un-obstructed view of the whole street and sat with his back to the outside wall of the café building. He ordered a bottle of tequila and a glass, lit a cigarette and unfurled his newspaper. Ten minutes later, a lanky man in jeans and a tee came strolling down the street from the direction of the Palacio de Bellas Artes. He looked the part of a hard-working outdoor type, with leather face, red-brown tanned arms and big rough hands. He wore a farmer's straw hat, the type you might see in west Texas.

Spotting his man, he ambled over to Coles' table and pulled up a chair.

"Hallo, friend," Coles said.

The man spat, leaning back on his stool. "Hey, Roche, how's it goin'?"

"The name's Coles. Hugh Coles. I don't know any gentleman named Roche"

"Oh yeah, I fergot. That's a purty good accent you got there."

Coles flashed a disdainful look.

"Can we talk here?" the man asked.

"If you can follow the rules," sneered Coles.

"Okay, Mister Coles." The man waved to the waiter. "Hey gar-son, brang me a glass, will ye?"

The waiter brought a glass, lemon and salt.

Pouring a shot for himself, then a fresh one for Coles, the man pushed Coles' newspaper aside. "I like to see a man's face when were talking," he said, staring straight into Coles' face. Coles downed his shot, returning the gaze.

"I got a two million dollar job for you, if you're interested," the man said. "Until this morning, I had different job for you, but that one only pays a hundred thousand. I figured you'd go for the big one anyway, so I got another guy to do the small one."

"Where?" asked Coles, flicking his cigarette on the table.

"What do you care? It's all expenses paid."

"What do I do?"

"You track and eliminate two guys."

"A million each, eh? Who are they, some kind of dignitaries?" For that kind of money it had to be.

"All I've been told is they're a couple of ordinary agents who happen to be on the wrong side of something very important to the man who contacted yours truly," the farmer replied.

"Do I know that man?"

"Yes, you do. It's the guy who paid for your last job."

That would be a fellow named Taylor from Tajikistan, Coles thought.

"When?" Coles seemed interested in hearing the farmer out.

"Yesterday wouldn't be soon enough for my client." The man snorted. "Seriously, that's the rub. If you want to do this you've got to fly tonight. There are only one or two days to get this done at most." He seemed suddenly to have lost a lot of that Texas ease.

"Like I said earlier, where?" Coles was staring at his glass.

"Amman, Jordan."

Coles stared a while longer into his glass. "Anything else?"

"Nope, that's the deal, short and simple." The man reached into his shirt and retrieved an envelope. Placing it on the table, he said, "First class ticket from Mexico City through Barcelona to Amman with an open return date leaves in three hours. Also, there's a prepaid room at the Intercontinental Hotel. The guy, Taylor will contact you in Amman."

Hugh Coles poured himself another shot of tequila and bolted it down. He picked up the envelope and stood up. "Still got the same cell phone number?"

"Yes I do."

"I'll call you in one hour. If I decide not to take the assignment, I'll mail this back to you."

"Got it," the man replied. "By the way, check your Caymans account. If you don't go you better return the deposit too."

Hugh Coles strolled to another café, sat and ordered coffee. He used his cell to check his Caymans account. A five hundred thousand dollar deposit had just been made. "One more job," he said to himself, "then I'm set for life."

Coles went to a department store and purchased clothes, a suitcase and necessities. He packed in the store then hailed a taxi to the airport. On the way, he called his maid, leaving instructions to keep the house in order while he took a holiday in Rio. Then he called the farmer and accepted the assignment. In a locker at the airport, he retrieved an Egyptian passport, business cards, a Visa card and other papers in the name of Jacob Breen, of the Cairo office of Hughes and Breen, investment advisors of London. Planning ahead always paid off.

He exchanged money from dollars to euros. He would exchange euros for dinars upon arrival in Jordan. "The first rule of self preservation as an agent: Never present a clear trail for your adversary to follow," he thought, walking toward the departure gate with his pocket full of euros.

Just before boarding he phoned a contact in Jordan and arranged for the purchase of a Beretta, clips and ammo to be delivered to him at the Intercontinental.

As the newly minted 'Jacob Breen' settled into his first class seat for the flight to Barcelona, he let out a sigh. He was on the road again, one last time.

CHAPTER 20

The evening festivities were lavish, to say the least. The great banquet hall had been decorated with banners of fine silk in varied brilliant colors. Some guests sat at great round tables, some at low tables with pillows for seating on the floor. In the middle of the hall, a large table held a giant ice sculpture of Arabian horses. Eight tons of sand had been deposited at one end of the hall against a giant mural of palm trees. Several real palm trees stood at one side of the desert scene, grouped around a pool with a fountain. The whole effect created the feeling of being in open desert.

All of the invited guests were dressed for a special occasion, many in traditional Arab garb. Several Pakistanis and a few Indians wore elaborate turbans. Three ayatollahs from Iran and one from Iraq were there with their entourages. All were treated to sumptuous food and the finest teas, coffees and exotic fruit juices. No alcohol was served in the dining area, but it was available for those who were less than strict Muslims in the bar and through room service.

Muhammed Al Kafajy was in his prime, mingling with the guests and playing gracious host. He tried in vain to get the few militants that dared to attend to mingle with the rest. They seemed quite uncomfortable amidst all the splendor of the Royal Amman Hotel. They were most uncomfortable with a few of the women who did not have their faces covered and were seated with the men. One, who was the self-proclaimed representative of Mullah Omar and several other Taliban, left the banquet hall in disgust, preferring to wait in the auditorium across the hall for the audio-visual presentation to begin.

Steck and Grundstrom sat in the CIA operations room along with Charlie West and some technicians. They had surveillance cameras hidden in the ceiling of the big hall, and one man with a wire was circulating through the crowd serving food. As their wired servant moved around the hall they were able to identify many of the guests. Charlie West worked furiously, making page after page of notes. At one point he muttered, "Man, one well placed bomb in that room could end the war on terror."

At the last minute, Al Kafajy changed the room location for the lecture. His aim was to accommodate a larger than expected crowd. That left West and his team with a dilemma. The two video cameras they had planted in the room adjacent to the banquet hall would only be recording darkness. Steck suggested they ask the wired agent to eavesdrop in the auditorium. Charlie felt uncomfortable about that because there had been no opportunity to set it up in a way that would protect his man. At length, they decided to risk it.

Charlie detailed one of his agents to get a secondary camera in place at the auditorium. To Steck's surprise, there was soon a small but terribly low resolution camera shooting stills and an occasional burst of video within the hall. Charlie West was an amazing guy, he thought.

The presentation in the auditorium started promptly after the last guest had been seated. Al Kafajy sat in the front row, while Chris Taylor made the presentation. First, Chris announced that there were several interested parties who could not make it to Jordan for the meeting or who wished to remain anonymous. They were to be patched in via satellite TV links. One of the guests objected. He wanted to know who he would be competing with. Chris assured him that the sale, when conducted, would be in a manner fair to all.

Chris then signaled and technicians dimmed the lights. Music from the Yemeni tradition rose to a background level. The massive TV screen lit up with scenes of Yemen, then flashed to a rolling script in Arabic and English on split screen. The script told the story of the use of the Prophet's hand print as surety and safe passage. It went on to describe the legend of how the Prophet himself had commissioned a plaster cast of his hand to be a remembrance to his followers, but also as the ultimate symbol of Muslim brotherhood. Its bearer would for ever be accorded royal treatment and safe passage and would be forgiven any and all offenses provided he was a believer; that is a true follower of Islam.

The screen changed to show a graphically stylized scene of the Prophet being taken to heaven then fluttered back to earth, finally focusing on an artist's conception of *The Hand of Mohammed.*

The screen went black. After a moment, vague light began to emerge from the center of the screen, revealing a severely out of focus depiction of the actual object. As the picture came into focus, gasps were heard among the audience. Once in focus, Chris queued a slide show of the photos taken earlier in the day. Reaction to each of these exquisite shots ranged from sighs to shouts. The final shot was of the hand laying aside the twenty-four carat gold sack created for it by the Al Kafajy Trading Company.

The screen held the picture of *The Hand of Mohammed* as the house lights were brought up. Chris then announced the terms of sale. Personal viewing of the object could be arranged over the next week to bidders that were prepared to make a good-faith deposit of one million dollars. Viewing would begin on Saturday, after the Muslim Sabbath and would take place at a local bank vault. Each bidder would have two opportunities to present their offers. After the first round the highest bid, if high enough to be acceptable to the seller, would be the winner. If the first round did not produce a successful transaction, a best and final bid round would ensue. Al Kafajy Trading Company reserved the right to reject all bids if in its sole opinion a satisfactory deal could not be made.

Chris paused then stated "The minimum opening bid level is One Hundred Million Euro dollars." He was pleased to hear only a few gasps about the opening bid price.

A question and answer period followed. Chris patiently answered every question, no matter how ridiculous.

While this session continued, the young Jordanian who carried the CIA wire lurked surreptitiously amongst the sound-breaking curtains along the side of the auditorium. Charlie West had finally dropped his pad and pencil, relying on the recording devices in his lab to provide material for analysis. Suddenly the sound track ended, preceded by the sound of a scuffle. Behind the curtain, the squat frame of Ahmed stood over the rapidly dying young Jordanian who had fallen to the floor, his throat neatly cut. Ahmed placed his knife back in its scabbard after wiping it on the young man's shirt. With a frown, he went to fetch the boss.

"I was afraid of that," Charlie West grunted. "I now have to face the task of informing this man's wife and child of his untimely demise. Worst part of the job," he grumbled.

CHAPTER 21

At eleven pm Chris Taylor sipped his third scotch at the bar in the Royal Amman Hotel. The evening had been a grand success. Thirteen prospective buyers had come forth after the presentation indicating that they would provide the one million euro deposit to become bidders for *The Hand of Mohammed.* The Al Kafajy Trading Company had now covered all its expenses, including the four day all expense paid buyer's party in Amman.

Muhammed Al Kafajy was so pleased he wrote a check for a hundred thousand to Chris and handed it over as they supervised the break-down of the audio-visual show. Chris accepted it graciously, but was disappointed that the boss had not spoken of the partnership he craved. Maybe that would be his reward for completion of the deal.

The only copy of the video presentation was entrusted to Chris with strict orders from the boss to destroy it. He patted the vest pocket that held both the check and the disk and chatted amiably with the bartender. Maybe a couple of more scotches would be in order. Tamping a cigarette in the ash tray at the bar, he ordered another single-malt then walked to the bank of telephones at the end of the bar. Picking up the house phone, he rang his room. After two rings, Tariq picked up. "Is everything okay, Tariq?" asked Chris.

"All is quiet," the big man replied.

"Very well, I'll be there around twelve. Help yourself to the snacks in the mini-bar. The key is under the telephone." Chris returned to the bar and sipped his drink. He decided he had earned a good drunk. This would be a six scotch night.

While Taylor sipped scotch at eleven pm in Amman, it was already eight o'clock am at the *Free Nation* compound in Wyoming.

Randy Pullin had endured a sleepless night. Yesterday he had dispatched a three man detail to the spot where Brandt said he had buried the body of the girl. Their orders were to dig it up and bring it to the compound where it could be safely reburied out of reach of any police that might be looking for it.

Late yesterday the sergeant in charge of the detail sent a message that when they arrived at the place, the body was not there. They found freshly turned soil that had not yet been rained on to tamp it down, evidence that the body had been very recently exhumed. The last rain in the area around Billings, Montana had been two days ago. Pullin had anxiously inquired if there was police crime scene tape at the site. "Negative," reported the sergeant. That meant that whoever dug up the body was not local police or even FBI. Who ever had the body was an agency that he needed to fear much more than the cops.

The detail had returned to the *Free Nation* compound late last night. Pullin called a briefing in his office for eight-fifteen a.m. Brandt arrived at eight sharp and was now sitting in the side chair at Colonel Randy's desk. Pullin paced the floor. He avoided eye contact with his protégé. No use losing his cool before the others arrived. Brandt, whose face had lost its usual high-color, looked like a beaten animal. The silence was difficult to endure for both men.

After the others arrived, Colonel Randy conducted a detailed inquiry into the conditions observed at the site. The men reported that the site was absolutely clean, no footprints, no tire marks, no tools or residue left at the scene. The team had worked in a spiral from the site out to the parking lot and beyond, looking for any shred of evidence that might be useful. Even the trash cans at the parking lot were empty. Returning to the gravesite and sifting the fresh earth, they had discovered one tiny shred of evidence. The sergeant produced a small plastic bag containing a cigarette butt and an empty matchbook. The cigarette was generic. The matchbook was a clue.

Colonel Randy dismissed the team. As soon as he and Brandt were alone, he began to launch into a tirade, but caught himself and paused for a long ten-count. Tirades would not solve this. Action might.

The matchbook was from The Fireside Steakhouse in Ottawa, Canada. As Colonel Randy read the name of the place aloud, Brandt looked up. "Canada?" he said.

"What does that mean to you?" Colonel Randy asked.

"The girl," Brandt mused. "The girl had a vague Canadian accent."

"Did she smoke?" Colonel Randy sat and reached for a notepad.

"I don't think so," Brandt replied, then after some thought, "no, she definitely did not smoke."

Pullin scribbled some notes, then sat back in his chair holding the pencil in his hand eraser down, he tapped it on the desk for emphasis as he spoke.

"Here's what I think." Pullin's gaze narrowed, piercing Brandt's consciousness. "I think the CSIS was investigating Ralph Baker, which led them to you. They detailed the girl to use your passions against you. When you fell for it, she became an inside agent that could gather enough information to close in on our transportation channels. I bet the Canadians had decided not to inform the American security people that they had an agent running around our country until they had enough hard evidence. Then the fracas with Baker made the deal too hot for the girl. She made a desperate play to either take you into custody or get out of there and you won. If I'm right then that matchbook was left by the CSIS team that took her body a couple of days ago."

Colonel Randy stood up and paced again, going over what he had just said. At length, he smiled as if satisfied he had it figured out. "If I'm right." He repeated.

Brandt brightened, as if Colonel Randy was now his accomplice instead of his interrogator. "But how did they find the girl's body?"

"Think about it, man!" Randy was trying to keep his cool. He was exasperated that Brandt's training was so incomplete. "She had probably reported confirmation of the link between Ralph Baker and Free Nation to her authorities from some road stop or motel. All she had to do was give you the slip for a few moments. Then CSIS, figuring that Baker's death was probably not accidental and now faced with a missing agent, would naturally come looking for her along the obvious routes between Coeur d'Alene, Idaho and this post! A bit of study and a road map would reveal there are only a few spots along the way where quick disposal of evidence could be accomplished."

Brandt felt awful. It was depressing that his actions were so transparent. "What should I have done?" he asked nearly allowing tears to flow.

"We can't use the results of 'could-haves' or 'should-haves' after the fact," Randy replied."

Colonel Randy thought for a moment, then added, "What you should have done is return here with the evidence. The lesson is to trust your superior officer, no matter what happens."

After he had dismissed Brandt, Randy Pullin sat for half-an-hour in silent thought. He wondered how long he had before the Canadians and the Americans would get their heads together. He needed a plan but had no idea what that could be.

Chris Taylor had just ordered his final drink for the night. He stared into the glass, pondering whether his plan to stop the American agents would materialize. Ahmed had reported his encounter with the waiter who was carrying a wire. Chris was upset that Ahmed had dealt with the issue with such a heavy hand. Now the Americans, if that was who was on the other end of the wire, would have cause to double their efforts.

Taylor lit a cigarette. Through smoke filled and scotch-dimmed eyes, he dialed his cell phone. While waiting for the international call to be put through, he chatted briefly with the bartender in an effort to determine how slurred his speech might be. It sounded okay to him.

"Mister Taylor?" the voice was the farmer's.

"Yes, it's Taylor. Did you make the arrangement we spoke about?"

"Yes sir, I did." The farmer replied. "The gentleman should arrive late tomorrow and be ready to work the following morning."

"That's fine. I appreciate the rapid response." Taylor decided to leave it at that, suddenly aware that he had pronounced it *reshponsh*."

As Chris Taylor clicked off and reached for his glass of scotch, he became aware of someone sitting next to him at the bar.

"Hello mister Chris." The voice was that of a man named Ali bin Akram Ajir, a customer. Chris had obtained some armaments for Ajir four years ago, contraband that had been surreptitiously shipped to Iran.

Chris tried to act sober, but knew it wouldn't work. "Ajir!" he said too loudly, extending his hand. "How have you been, my friend." Ajir was nobody's friend.

"Wonderful Mister Chris, I am very well." Ajir shook Taylor's hand energetically.

In his scotch fog, Chris motioned as if to buy Ajir a drink. He stopped himself after he spied the teacup in Ajir's left hand. That's the trouble with Moslems, Chris thought. You can't even buy them a drink.

Chris wanted to shake this guy and go to bed. He knew he was at a disadvantage being mostly drunk. Ajir kept up a lively conversation about trivial things for what seemed to Chris to be hours. Finally, after he had finished his drink,

Chris stood up to leave. Ajir was still yakking. Chris felt the room go into motion and had to steady himself by holding on to the bar.

After regaining his equilibrium, Chris spied the clock over the bar. It was just midnight. "Too late for me," Chris said, making far too grand a gesture toward the clock. "Nice to see you, Ajir," he lied.

Ajir was still talking a streak as Chris Taylor half stumbled across the lobby of the Royal Amman Hotel. "Thank goodness," Chris thought as he realized that Ajir had returned to the bar rather than following him into the elevator.

Taylor sensed something amiss as he got off the elevator and began navigating the corridor toward his room. The two guards that had been assigned to augment Tariq were not on duty at the door of Chris' room.

He opened the door to a horrible scene. Tariq lay dead in front of the room safe, blood oozing from a hole in his forehead. The other two men were on the floor of the adjoining room lifeless. They had been shot in the back of the head, execution style. The safe was open and *The Hand of Mohammed* was gone.

It took Chris Taylor only a few moments to sober up. The adrenaline of terror and fright replaced the fog of drunkenness with clarity of thought. He felt for pulse. All three had none. The blood was still fresh and flowing, so only a few minutes had elapsed after the terrible deed. It could even have happened while he was on the way up in the elevator. Chris ran to the end of the hall, bypassing the elevator and throwing open the door to the stairway. As he entered the landing, he heard scuffling on the stairway towards the lower floors of the hotel. They were still in the building!

Chris opened his cell phone as he bounded down the stairs and punched the key for the main number of the Royal Amman Hotel. He had plunged three floors when the clerk answered. "There has been a robbery and murder! he shouted into the phone. "The robbers are in the east stairwell. Can you lock it down?"

"No, sir" came the reply. "Fire laws prevent us from...."

"Then call security! Call the police." Chris clicked off, still bounding down the stairwell.

At the fifth floor, Chris paused to listen for sounds. There were none. He resumed his plunge, stepping wildly, taking the stairs two and three at a time. Ignoring the fact that he had no weapon, he burst into the lobby. There was no sign of the robbers. Two security guards rushed toward Chris. One drew a hand gun. Chris flailed his arms in frustration. Finally realizing that the prize was gone he collapsed to the floor.

CHAPTER 22

Paul Roche, alias Hugh Coles, Alias Jacob Breen landed in Amman just after two pm Amman time. He exchanged euros for dinars, collected his baggage and cleared passport control. Collecting his baggage, he took a taxi downtown, stopping at the shop of an acquaintance who supplied him with a paste-on full beard to complement his now nearly grown moustache. From his luggage he produced a Harris Tweed jacket and dark trousers. Satisfied that he looked the part of an émigré British lawyer, he presented himself at the Intercontinental Hotel.

In his room, he telephoned a blind number supplied by the farmer. A man answered, inquiring about the farmer's health. "He's fine. I just saw him yesterday."

The man instructed Roche to get some rest and asked how he should address a package that would be delivered during the evening. The voice said that 'Mister Breen' would be contacted in the morning. After the arrangements were made, Roche got some food then went to bed.

———

Bob Steck worked into the early morning, preparing a report of what he had learned up until the man carrying the wire was killed. He now knew that Al Kafajy Trading Company was the recipient of the stolen goods. He had heard the presentation that established the provenance of *The Hand Of Mohammed*. He had heard that the cost just to become a bidder was one million euros. He knew that the presenter's name was Chris Taylor. Charlie had a team of people working to identify as many of the audience as possible and to get a dossier on Al Kafajy Trading Company and on the man named Chris Taylor. It had been quite a night.

What he didn't know was who killed their plant and whether the murderer had gained enough information to trace back to the CIA bureau in Amman. He reviewed his report with Charlie then sent it by secure wire to Ryall Morgan at

Langley. After sending it, he sat back in his office chair wondering how much of the information he had just learned was already known to Randy Pullin.

Steck poured a cup of coffee and went looking for Gunny Grundstrom.

Muhammed Al Kafajy was furious when an exhausted Chris Taylor told him that their prize had been stolen. He vowed revenge on everyone. He wept on hearing that Tariq was dead. He derided even Ahmed for killing the young snoop rather than capturing him so they could find out who had sent the man. His ranting scared his body guard, who in seventeen years of service had never seen the boss lose his cool. When the poor man suggested a sedative, Al Kafajy slapped his face.

At length the boss recovered his composure and paced the room for twenty minutes in silence. Finally walking deliberately to his desk he sat, as if in preparation to issue commands. "Please clear the room, except for Christian," he said too calmly.

When they were alone, he stared at Chris for a long time with a face curiously devoid of expression. Chris felt like a piece of rubbish. He wished he could disappear into the carpet.

Al Kafajy broke the silence with a small quiet voice. "So, Christian, we have encountered a piece of bad road. Are you still willing to pick up the challenge and complete the journey?"

Chris Taylor sat up straight in his chair. "Of course I am." He was inwardly proud that the boss had not killed him on the spot. He was also proud that for once he had not stammered at a moment of stress. He cleared his throat and with his best professional tone continued. "Will you have enough confidence to give me free rein?"

"Absolutely," Al Kafajy replied. The boss really had no alternative. He had always relied on Chris to do the dirty work and the work from here on would be very dirty indeed.

"I have good contacts among those who can help us with acquisitions and with security." Chris was speaking slowly, forming his thoughts carefully as he went. "However, I am not as well-versed in the world of spies and agents of governments. In last night's theft, we are dealing with international thieves who may have militia at their disposal. We are also dealing with American agents who are as close as Saudi Arabia, maybe closer."

"So, are you saying it is out of your reach?" Al Kafajy looked worried.

"I am saying that it requires a different type of agent than we customarily have at our disposal. It happens that I have such a man in mind, one whom I hired just yesterday to rid us of those U S agents." Chris was gaining confidence as he spoke. "The man is a former CIA agent. He is here in Amman. I will make it worth his while to help us recover the prize."

Muhammed Al Kafajy shrugged then smiled. "You know the stakes we are playing for, Christian. The budget will allow much, if success can be assured."

"How much will the budget allow?" Chris knew he was pushing.

"Ten million before you need to consult me, more if you can demonstrate the need." Al Kafajy held his palms up as if to say "what else?"

"One more thing, if you please," said Chris.

"Go on, Christian." Al Kafajy said.

"Keep Ahmed out of this unless I ask for him." Chris knew he was testing the old man. He wanted complete control of the operation.

Al Kafajy hesitated. Chris was asking a lot for the boss to withhold his most trusted confidant. "I will keep him at my side until this is over, or until you ask for his services."

Susan Deet and two junior agents waited in the ante room of Robert MacFergus' office in Ottawa. It was seven-thirty a.m. They had traveled overnight delayed by a nasty storm. Susan had grabbed a few hours of speed-napping in the Learjet. The task at hand was to formalize the presentation of the material that had been discussed in the earlier conference call.

MacFergus arrived at eight sharp. He seemed surprised to see them so early in the day. After hand shakes MacFergus shed his hat, coat, umbrella and galoshes, while ordering an aide to procure some coffee and sweet rolls.

Susan sized him up, having never met the man. He was about sixty years old grey at the temples and balding on top. A squat man with puffy cheeks, bushy grey eyebrows and ruddy complexion, he looked as if he would be more at home in a kilt than in the off-the-rack wrinkled brown wool suit he had obviously worn for weeks.

Settling in a secure conference room, they were soon joined by several CSIS agents and a secretary. Susan noted that the small secretary desk was equipped with several antiquated recording machines and a stenotype, similar to those used in a court of law. The young secretary sat briefly at the desk, opened a drawer and produced a small digital recorder, which she set up in the center of the conference table. Susan was relieved to see modern equipment that would interface with hers. She guessed that the CSIS probably never threw anything away.

MacFergus sat at the head of the conference table. From an old weathered tan leather valise, he selected several pads of paper, pens and pencils, a curved briar pipe and a pouch of tobacco. He raised his gaze to meet Susan's, waving the pipe in the air. She signaled acceptance. All waited while

MacFergus filled the thing, fished for a small pack of wooden matches and lit up, drawing several small puffs to get the thing properly alight. The secretary produced an ashtray which she placed at his side. Susan figured this was all part of a ritual the man employed to take charge of any conference. She got the message that they were on his turf.

MacFergus opened with some ground rules for the meeting. There would be one and only one recording device used. He pointed to the digital recorder at the center of the table. A transcript of the meeting would be provided after the meeting, reviewed and signed off by both sides as accurate. They would confine the discussion to the case at hand. The meeting would last exactly two hours, followed by the document review. If necessary, an additional half-hour session would be conducted to resolve any open issues. "This is a classified meeting." He announced.

The coffee and sweet cakes arrived. Each of the Americans dug in. The Canadians demurred. Finally, after the secretary had passed a tablet for each of the participants to write their name, title and contact information, the meeting was officially called to order.

Susan was amused to consider the formality of this meeting as opposed to the relative laxity of form that prevailed at the JUMP team meetings. She did appreciate the structure, but felt in a tactical sense it might hamper the free flow of ideas and information she was used to at Langley and the FBI. She decided that this more formal approach was appropriate between two governments. Susan had been carefully briefed by Mort Lindsley and Ryall Morgan about maintaining a cordial protocol with the Canadians while reminding them that they had overstepped their jurisdiction. She was pleased that her bosses trusted her to handle a new career step, a step into diplomacy.

Mac Fergus opened with a methodical presentation of the facts as known by CSIS and reported to the JUMP team on the previous conference call. After a long pause while he re-lit his pipe, he announced that they had new information. Susan straightened in her chair, her mind suddenly on alert. She had no expectation of new information.

Satisfied that he had provided the proper segue, MacFergus deferred to Jon Rudie his principal case officer. Rudie was a slight built man in his early thirties with oversized eyeglasses and a blond crew cut. He spoke in a high pitch indicative of nervousness, but soon settled in to a more normal drone.

"Yesterday, a CSIS investigative and forensic team checked out several sites along the route between Coeur d'Alene, Idaho and Billings, Montana, along United States Interstate Route 90. Its purpose was to follow through on a hypothesis that one of our agents, Carole Hinson, might have been abducted and/or murdered at Coeur d'Alene and taken toward a Para-military camp near Bighorn National Forest in Wyoming."

"Let's be clear that the Para-military group we are concerned with is self-named *Free Nation.*" Susan interjected. Her intention was to convey to MacFergus her interest in recording a clear record of the events. His nod confirmed she had succeeded.

Rudie shuffled his papers, caught the nod from MacFergus and resumed his delivery. "At approximately two pm, the team discovered remains of a female in her late twenties at a roadside park near Yegen, Montana. The remains were in a shallow grave, estimated by our forensic staff to be less than two weeks old, which coincides with the incident at Coeur d'Alene mentioned earlier. The team, some of whom had worked with Carole Hinson in the past, identified the remains as those of Hinson."

"Cause of death?" Susan felt queasy discussing any agent's death while on duty. It always reminded her of her own mortality. She steeled herself not to show it.

"I have a forensic report here." Rudie set a four page sleeve bound report on the table and pushed it toward Susan.

"Primary trauma was a knife wound to the gut," Rudie continued, "but immediate cause of death was a .45 caliber round to the head from moderate range."

Susan glared at the report for a moment. Her mind's image was of the size hole that a .45 would make in a woman's head. She caught herself, turning her gaze to Jon Rudie's. "Where is the body?" she said.

"We have it here in Ottawa." Rudie said this with some hesitation.

Susan looked at MacFergus. He purposely studied his pipe to avert eye contact. She resisted the desire to let her anger out. To buy time, she reviewed several photos that Jon Rudie had stacked on the table during his discourse. The shots of the body were gruesome. She forced herself to look, confirming the dialogue Rudie had just concluded. From the final photo it was clear that the team had thoroughly cleaned up the site. "Well, it seems you folks have tidied this up quite nicely." She was speaking slowly, making certain of her choice of words. "May I assume there was no contact with the local police or any other U.S. authority that would compromise the security of this report?"

"There was none." The voice was that of MacFergus himself.

Now in better control, Susan addressed the room. "I feel constrained to enter into the record of this meeting that the actions you have taken in the matter at hand do not follow the protocols long established between the United States government and Canada. Each government has pledged not to enter the other's sovereign territory without the knowledge and permission of the other." She paused, waiting for someone to speak. MacFergus was too smart to fill the silence. He had ample evidence of similar violations of protocol by the FBI and CIA in his valise. Discretion bade him wait.

"However," she continued, "we acknowledge your excellent work and ask for your co-operation as the United

States pursues this case to conclusion. Further action of any kind within the United States will be at our sole discretion, understood?"

"Understood," replied MacFergus. "Please understand in return that we have lost one of our own, and will prosecute the matter most vigorously from our side. We will ask your kind assistance as and if further action in the United States becomes necessary."

"I request a viewing of the body before returning to Washington," Susan stated. She hated the thought of it but it was necessary for her report.

The meeting was temporarily adjourned, while transcripts were generated for review. During the break, Susan called Lindsley, who patched Morgan onto the line. They commended her then gave her direction to add some more dialogue. At Morgan's insistence, she was to privately ask MacFergus for CSIS cooperation in pursuit of a related but top secret matter and arrange a meeting between Morgan and MacFergus for a briefing.

Susan delivered the message in MacFergus' private office. He accepted, offering to meet Morgan in New York City.

"He'd rather you come to Langley, if that's possible," said Susan. She reckoned that Ryall would rather not spend any time away from his operations center over the next few days.

"Tell him I'll be there tomorrow, first thing." MacFergus welcomed an opportunity to work with Morgan, especially since he could use the chance to mend fences.

"In that case, can we offer you a lift?" Susan's plane waited at the airport.

"Right-oh, I'll take an hour to gather some things while you have a look at Carole Hinson's body." MacFergus seemed warmly disposed toward Susan. She was keen to add Robert MacFergus to her network of contacts.

CHAPTER 23

As 'Jacob Breen' sipped coffee and read *The Herald Tribune* in the breakfast nook of the Intercontinental Hotel he became aware of a new patron entering the room. He could not see the face, but the manner of walk and the overall look of the man seemed familiar. A cat-like sense of one's surroundings promoted longevity in his business. Keeping the newspaper in front of his face, he shifted position to get a better look.

When the man turned towards him to sit at a nearby table, Roche recognized him. How ironic, he thought, that he should encounter Bob Steck in Amman. How incredibly ironic it would be if Steck turned out to be his assignment! He supposed that Steck had just arrived from outside since he looked as if he had been up all night.

Though never short on brass, Roche decided not to test his disguise by allowing Steck to see him. He left the area as soon as he could verify that Steck was absorbed in reading a stack of papers he carried. In his room, Roche set up the laptop computer and printer he had rented. He created a fax letterhead for his fictitious law firm in London. He wrote some legal-speak on it and signed it Jacob Breen, esq. He paused in front of the mirror to check his disguise. Carefully, he adjusted the beard then stood back to get a sense of his overall look. He worried that even with changed hair color and complexion, a full beard and moustache he would be recognized by his former compatriot. He tried a slight limp, parading before the mirror. That might work, he mused.

Steck presented himself at the front desk to retrieve his room key and check for messages. The clerk produced the key. There were no messages. Steck paid scant attention to the gentleman next to him, who spoke softly in a British accent, asking for transmission of a fax and retrieving a package left for Jacob Breen. As the man limped away, Steck noticed he had left the fax face-up on the counter rather than waiting for the clerk to send and stamp it. His spy's curiosity aroused, he surreptitiously scanned the page. Thinking no more of it, he filed the man with a limp in his mind as an ordinary British lawyer.

At nine o'clock sharp, Jacob Breen's room phone rang. The voice was that of Chris Taylor. "Shall we meet this morning?" the voice asked.

"If you wish," replied Roche. "I'm anxious to get started."

They agreed to meet at a small park near the Intercontinental Hotel.

Twenty minutes later, Roche was waiting on a park bench, admiring a flower bed of various colored roses.

"Mister Breen?" a faintly British voice inquired.

Roche looked up. "Mister Taylor?"

From Taylor's voice on the telephone in their past contacts Roche had imagined a much older and more portly man than the callow, smartly dressed businessman standing before him.

"Let's walk," beckoned Taylor, heading off toward the far corner of the park.

Roche joined him. They discussed trivialities while both men took time to determine if it was safe to talk. Finally satisfied, Roche opened. "First, I acknowledge, with thanks, the deposit you have put down for this transaction."

"Not at all Mister Breen," Said Taylor. "It is also a sign of respect for your past performance on our behalf."

"My contact informed me that you need to dispose of two obstacles. Does this involve our most recent association?"

"Yes, Mister Breen, it does." Chris replied.

"Then I believe I already know one of the obstacles. You see, there is a person staying at my hotel who tried to pay me a visit in Virginia shortly after our last transaction. His name is.."

"Wait!" Taylor raised a hand to Roche's line of sight and stopped in his tracks. "No names yet, Mister Breen. We can go to a place I know where it will be possible to talk freely if you are still interested in the assignment."

"I am, but with reservations." Roche scanned the area trying to discern the source of Taylor's concern but found none.

"Very well, follow me," said Taylor, walking briskly toward a side street.

From the top of a building adjacent to the park a man with headphones said something in Arabic to the one next to him who held a dish microphone. A third man snapped photos through a telephoto lens, hoping to get a good image of the man who walked beside Chris Taylor.

After a telephone debrief with Grundstrom, Randy Pullin put out a directive to all his operatives worldwide. He asked for all eyes and ears to be vigilant for any mention of *The Hand of Mohammed*, any movement of Islamists or the governments of Muslim countries that seemed inspired by it and especially for any info from Iran. He summoned Muhammed Saleem Rafiq, one of his operatives in Pakistan to the post. Saleem, himself a Sunni Moslem was an expert on the Muslim religion and its factions.

He decided that as Grundstrom fed information about the bidders to him, he would create a dossier on each. His plan was to use this information to gain traction with Morgan. He would need help from people like Morgan if there could be any chance of coming through the aftermath of Brandt's indiscretion.

Pullin called a meeting to organize the effort, and soon had twenty people working it full time. He then called Brandt to his office.

Brandt entered the office in fatigues, snapped a smart salute and said "Major Brandt reporting Colonel, sir!"

"Get your stuff together Major," Said Colonel Randy. Be prepared to move out at sixteen hundred hours today. Your destination is Amman, Jordan. You are assigned to support Gunny Grundstrom and will be reporting directly to him." Colonel Randy handed him a manila envelope. "Here are your orders and travel documents. Call me when you're on the ground in Jordan."

"Yes sir!" Brandt accepted the envelope.

"Give me reasons to feel better," Colonel Randy said tersely, "Dismissed!"

Two hours after Brandt had started his trip to Amman, Colonel Randy received a call from Grundstrom.

"Colonel," Grundstrom announced, "somebody murdered three guards and stole that damn trinket."

"Does Steck know about that?" Pullin asked.

"Yessir, he does. I was standing in the room when he found out."

"Hot dawg," Pullin blurted. This was just the kind of situation he had hoped for. "Brandt is on his way to join you, Gunny. When he gets there, I want the two of you to get that thing back from whoever took it. Use all the resources you have and report to me at every turn. I'll get every bit of intelligence we can muster to help you."

"Yes Sir, will do." Grundstrom was puzzled but ready to follow orders.

"If you get it without Steck around, hold it and let me know. If Steck's with you, give it to him then let me know right away. The important thing is to get to the thing before some unfriendlies do."

"Yes sir, anything else?"

"Yeah, there is. This is real important to *Free Nation*, Gunny. I know I can count on you."

"Colonel, this mission will be conducted along side the Feds, but for our sole benefit, am I right?" Grundstrom wanted to be clear about it.

"That's right, Gunny. Use them and their information. Don't disclose anymore than necessary about our interests. At the bottom line, just get the thing back."

Pullin spent the next two hours planning his approach to this most important mission. If all went well, he would come out the hero and be acknowledged for it at levels way above Steck. This was his shot to save *Free Nation*.

Ali bin Akram Ajir stood at a folding table in a shabby back street hotel room. He sorted through the photos of Chris Taylor walking in the company of a stranger who could not be identified from the picture they had.

He turned to the four men who waited for his direction. "We must shadow Chris Taylor every minute. He will try to take action against us as soon as he comes to understand who has his object. You will report to me every three hours, day and night."

CHAPTER 24

Greg Liss lay on his stomach in bed, trying to operate his computer via a voice recognition program he had loaded a year ago but never used before. With it he could leave the computer on the floor beside his bed without dealing with how to align his hands with the keyboard from a prone position. The frustration of being shut-in at his apartment and not being able to work was much worse than the pain in his butt. After two days of effort, the voice program had 'learned' his voice well enough to enable a few emails. His next task would be an expanded report of the operation in Yemen.

Greg's next door neighbor in the town house subdivision came around twice a day to look in on him. She had just left, after getting Greg some toast, juice and coffee. Off to her job, Lisa Raines promised to bring him take-out when she returned at seven pm.

Greg hated being dependant on anyone, especially Lisa Raines. Lisa had been sweet on Greg ever since he moved in two years ago, but the feeling was not mutual. She was pretty and caring and competent, but there was simply no chemistry on Greg's side. Now in his hour of need, he felt trapped yet grateful for her help. Lisa worked as a nurse at a local clinic, which made it worse since she had just the skills Greg needed. She was delighted to have him all to herself and took the opportunity to coddle him beyond reason.

Greg's phone rang. It was connected through his computer via voice over internet protocol. He voice commanded the computer to accept the call, but it didn't work. Frustrated, he reached for the laptop but it was just too far from the bed. He grunted, adjusting his body to reach further. The thing stopped ringing and went to voice mail. When he realized that the voice was Susan Deet's he thrust his arm again toward the computer and lost his balance falling awkwardly to the floor. As he fell, his flailing arm hit the computer and sent it skittering across the rug, now well out of range.

Susan's voice was distant, as if from a cell phone. She wanted to stop by to see Greg after her return from a meeting in Canada. She expected to be back in Washington in the early evening.

Greg crawled on his belly like a reptile. He finally reached the computer just as Susan clicked off. Cursing, he resisted the urge to throw the thing across the room. Instead, he rose on one elbow and redialed Susan. Her phone was off. He waited for the voice prompt then said he would be glad to see her anytime. He suggested that if it was in the early evening he was expecting Chinese take-out and offered pot luck.

Greg spent the rest of the morning wriggling around, getting everything back in place. By the time he was back in bed ready to dictate his report he had become so exhausted that he fell into a nice long nap.

In a small office that had only one door and no windows, Chris Taylor told Roche the details of events leading up to their meeting, except for the theft of *The Hand of Mohammed* last evening. He wanted to get more comfortable about the choice of Roche to take over the operation.

Roche told him that one of the American agents on the case was Bob Steck, whom he had seen earlier at the Intercontinental. He said that it would only be a matter of time until he could identify the other agent or agents on the case. He said he was willing to eliminate them all. He filled Taylor in on his former relationship with Steck and others including Randy Pullin.

"You are still willing to eliminate any of them if necessary?" Chris asked.

"It's just part of the job," Roche replied coldly, "it's what I do."

Chris shivered inwardly. These guys have no conscience, no feelings he thought.

Satisfied that he had the right assassin, Taylor decided to enlarge the task. "A strange turn of events happened last evening," he began.

"Does it involve me?" Roche asked.

"If you are willing it will involve you," Chris replied. "But it's a separate deal from the one we've just discussed and could involve a lot more money."

"Magic to my ears," said Roche with a slight smile.

"The prize that we obtained from that crate was stolen from me last night. I have no idea who has it, but I can quickly narrow it down to a short list. Your task will be to help us find and recover the article. It must be done quickly because we have obligations to potential buyers that must be satisfied during the next seven days. If we fail to produce the object, our reputation will be greatly damaged." Chris paused to let Roche absorb the new information.

"Why do you need me for this?" asked Roche. "Surely in your business you have many operatives around the world who move in the cultures and circles of society where the thief would be known."

"For two reasons," Chris replied. "One is that we dare not let the news of this theft out through the very channels where our customer base lies. The other is that the involvement of American agents with their vast network is simply out of our league. You're our chance to recover the object and our reputation and hopefully without leaving tracks that would lead to greater trouble for our company."

A discomfort grew within Roche as Chris Taylor spoke. His inclination was that this was far too risky an operation. He could project no positive outcome from the bit of information he had received. He didn't even have good contacts in some of the places that had already been visited in this charade. He decided to hear the man out.

"What resources do I have to work with?" he asked.

"Many resources," Chris replied. "My entire staff with offices around the world will be at our command. I can supply all the money you need. In addition, your personal compensation will be double our present deal."

Four million dollars, Roche pondered. "Not enough," he said at length. "If I understand the task, the risk to me is much more than you're offering."

"I am at a disadvantage, Roche." Chris was willing to haggle but he saw no alternative and knew Roche knew it. "Name your terms," he said tersely.

"Add four and a half million to the deposit," Roche said cautiously. "That makes the total five million. I keep it win, lose or draw. Finally, one more million if I deliver the object back to you in good condition within one week or sooner."

"That's a lot of money," Chris started, trying to look worried. Inwardly, he knew he could do the deal.

Roche shrugged. "It's a big task and a lot of risk." He looked away, as if losing interest. He was testing Taylor's mettle and probing to see if he had the authority and the means to do the deal.

"It's a deal," declared Taylor. "Let's set up contact and communication protocols. I'll give you my office here in Amman as your base of operations."

"Does it have a bedroom," asked Roche.

"It has a very nice apartment, yours to use."

"Good," Roche replied. "I'll be moving this afternoon. First, I need to visit an old friend."

Chris Taylor extended his hand. Roche took it and gave it a vigorous shake.

Roche walked directly to the business district, entering a butcher shop. "Rashid, old friend!" he greeted the man behind the counter. Realizing from Rashid's puzzled look that his disguise was working very well, he added, "It's me, Paul Roche!"

Bob Steck and Gunny Grundstrom had literally taken over Anwhar International, the front organization for the CIA bureau in Amman. Charlie West had placed all his resources at their disposal after a top secret secure call from Langley. It was the first time he had ever received a call from the director himself. The director made it clear that for the near term, Robert Steck would be calling all the shots. Now thirty agents plus their staff were all focused on the project, dubbed *Operation Retrieve*.

Steck really hated having a name for the operation. He much preferred the policy of the JUMP team not to bring attention to a covert action by giving it a name that might betray information to the enemy if leaked in some way, either purposeful or accidental. He accepted it in the name of tradition and policy at Langley.

In the first hours of *Operation Retrieve*, an incomplete list of attendees from last evening's presentation had been established and set on a spreadsheet grid. The grid was posted to the Amman bureau's secure local network so real time input could be received from any of the team. Some of the team worked to fill out the list by further review of the audio and visual tapes from last evening and from the registry of the Royal Amman Hotel obtained through a paid contact at the hotel. Information about each name on the list was being gathered from CIA files in Amman, from Langley and from other sources around the world. These facts were cataloged, edited and added to the information tree. It was a painstaking process, but one which would be invaluable as the operation proceeded.

Three hours into the operation, Charlie West returned from a short mission to collaborate with additional paid informants on the hotel staff. They were part of his network of local contacts recruited through years of consistent effort.

"I have astounding news," he told Steck. "There was a triple murder at the Royal Amman Hotel late last night. It occurred in the room registered to Chris Taylor."

"Whoa," breathed Steck. "Was Taylor a victim?"

"No he wasn't, not a murder victim at least." Charlie's complexion was even redder than usual. "The murders were incidental to a theft. The three men killed were all carrying heat and had been guarding the room. My informant says that Taylor was apoplectic about the loss of something extremely important from his room safe."

Steck took a moment to absorb what he had just heard. "Hey Gunny!" he shouted across the room. Grundstrom hustled to join the two men. "I think our objective has been stolen!"

———

Rashid the butcher stood vigil across the street from Anwhar International's office, just a block from his butcher shop. He spoke from time to time into a small voice recorder, dictating notes about the foot traffic coming and going through the street entrance of Anwhar International. He snapped stills of selected individuals using a button-hole camera tucked under his jacket. Others of his group of comrades kept similar watch at the Intercontinental Hotel and the Royal Amman hotel. He would be relieved at this post in the evening, to be replaced by another associate. He would contact Roche during the evening.

Roche checked out of the Intercontinental and set up shop at Al Kafajy Trading Company. He organized an information gathering effort quite similar to Steck's, using resources placed at his disposal by Chris Taylor. The use of an information tree was something he had learned years ago at Langley. He knew that somewhere in Amman, probably at the CIA bureau, Bob Steck was doing exactly the same thing. He reckoned that the CIA's contacts in Amman would soon uncover news of the theft. He figured that eventually he and Steck would both possess essentially the same information. The outcome would be determined by which of them made better use of it.

Chris Taylor spent midday at Aliyah's apartment. Being near her calmed him. After lunch and some relaxing chatter, he felt more himself. Leaving at two pm, he strolled along the busy streets of the Amman business district deep in thought about the events leading up to the theft of *The Hand*. His memories were less like a blurred nightmare now, so he went over the details carefully again and again. He was just turning toward the Al Kafajy Trading Company office when the thought struck him like a thunderbolt.

Ajir! It was Ajir who showed up out of the blue at just the time the theft would have taken place. It was Ajir who had uncharacteristically followed Chris even across the lobby of the Royal Amman Hotel. The man was obviously trying to forestall Chris' entry into the elevator. It had to be Ajir and his group that murdered three of his company's employees and took *The Hand of Mohammed*.

Taylor raced the last block to his office. Roche was busy analyzing some data when Chris burst into the room.

Out of breath, Chris grabbed Roche's elbow and gasped, "Ali bin Akram Ajir!"

"Ally ben who?" Roche thought for a moment that Taylor had lost it.

"Ajir," Taylor blurted. "Ali bin Akram Ajir. His trading groups are customers of mine. He is the thief!"

Roche almost laughed. He found it hard not to quip "All of us are thieves."

Instead he took a step back shaking Taylor's grip and replied, "Okay. What do we have on him? Where is he liable to be right now?"

Taylor tried to calm down enough to think about Roche's questions. He sat at an available desk and stared with furrowed brow at the desktop. Finally he looked at Roche. He may still be in Amman, or at least still in Jordan. His company, if that's what you would call it....I mean his reputation is ..." The thoughts were coming too fast for Chris to articulate.

Sensing Taylor's confusion, Roche suggested they go to a private office and get some coffee and a smoke. Taylor seemed grateful for the direction and marched off towards a short corridor. Roche followed him to a spacious office that was fitted with too many amenities to be Taylor's. He figured it was probably for the owner whenever he was in town.

The next hour was spent sorting information about Ajir. While they spoke, Roche had ordered several staff to fan out and try to track the whereabouts of Mister Ajir.

After Taylor regained composure, Roche methodically obtained from Chris Taylor a profile of Ali bin Akram Ajir.

Ajir was something of a social misfit because he had a Persian father and an Arab mother. Although both came from Iran and both were Shiite Muslims, his father was from ancient Persian stock while his mother's family were of Iraqi descent. His name betrayed this mixed background, so as a child growing up in Teheran he had been picked on by his purely Persian peers.

After frustrating years as an apprentice in his father's trading company, Ajir had struck out on his own. Sensing opportunity in the aftermath of the breakup of the Soviet empire, he founded a small trading company in Turkmenistan. Soon he had branches in Turkey, Azerbaijan, Iran and Kurdish northern Iraq. In these places his mixed cultural background de-fuzed the normal prejudice of heritage so common in that part of the world.

It was difficult to maintain a clean and lawful business in the region, unless one delighted in starvation, so gradually Ajir began trading in shady areas. At first, it was just household and business commodities that ran afoul of a given country's tariff laws. Eventually it extended to outright contraband and finally to arms and ammunition.

Anyone in the region who traded in contraband required well trained security. The change to arms and ammunition forced expansion of that security staff to resemble a small private militia.

For the past couple of years, Ajir was rumored to be providing vast amounts of armament to the Iraqi Kurds, the Azerbaijanis and even the Taliban.

Ajir was fluent in eight languages including Russian, Pashtun and Urdu. Chris regarded him as a brilliant tactician with few morals. He was also a good customer of Al Kafajy Trading Company with about five million per year turnover mostly in cotton, timber and petro-chemicals.

"What about his so called security department?" Roche asked. "How many are there? How well equipped are they?"

Taylor summoned one of Al Kafajy's senior security staff who spoke with apparent good knowledge of the subject. He reported that Ajir had several bodyguards with him at all times. They were extremely well trained and well equipped, not only with armament, but with electronic gadgetry. In addition, there was about a hundred staff, mostly thugs and mercenaries.

"Where do they train?" Roche wanted to size up their likely tactics.

"They train mostly in Iran and Yemen," was the reply, "lately mostly in Yemen."

"Terrorists, or at least terrorist trained," thought Roche.

Chris Taylor suddenly came alert. "Didn't they employ Nancy Kinnear?" he asked the man.

The man reflected for a moment. "Yes," he said "the Kinnear woman worked with them as recently as last year. I believe at that time she was involved in smuggling artifacts from Turkey."

"How stupid of me," mused Taylor "I missed the connection."

Roche asked, "Who in blazes is Nancy Kinnear?" His plan had been to peel the onion of this mystery to its core. New layers kept showing themselves as the conversation expanded.

"Kinnear was a mercenary Archaeologist originally from Canada. She works with an Archaeological team that is headed by a Dartmouth University professor. She dealt privately in stolen artifacts. Apparently she also worked for Ajir."

"You said she *was* a mercenary. Does that mean she's dead?" Roche asked.

"A few days ago, she was at a dig in Yemen with the Dartmouth team. Two American agents showed up with a photo of *The Hand of Mohammed*, asking questions. She reported this to some of her contacts at a terrorist training site near the dig. One of those contacts called one of the people who work for my company, in Paris. It's part of a system of information gathering that we always maintain in our business."

"Go on," said Roche, jotting notes as Chris spoke.

"Apparently, she came back to the dig and was killed. I think she may have been killed by one of the agents you will shortly eliminate."

At six o'clock, Taylor and Roche sent out for food. At midnight they were still working. Finally, Roche called it a day. He felt like he now knew enough to begin making plans.

CHAPTER 25

Ryall Morgan met the airplane to collect his friend and colleague Bob MacFergus. He invited Bob to stay at his home in Virginia for the night.

Paying Susan compliments, MacFergus invited her to join them for a drink. She accepted, relishing the opportunity to learn from these two senior spy masters. A suitable gin mill was found near the airfield and the three chatted for about an hour, talking shop, exchanging war stories and being careful not to discuss the present assignment in public.

As she bade the two gentlemen good night, Susan handed Ryall Morgan the written transcript from the Ottawa meeting. After Morgan and MacFergus drove away Susan made a courtesy phone call to her official boss Mort Lindsley. Doing this she wrapped up a very good day for her career.

One last task remained to complete the day. Susan threaded her way along the Potomac in thick traffic directing her Saturn coupe to Arlington. She arrived at Greg's town house at eight pm.

The door was answered by Lisa Raines who gave Susan a look that said 'Go Away!'

"Hi, I'm Susan Deet. I work with Greg." Susan fished in her purse for a business card.

"Greg's resting," Lisa declared coldly.

Susan observed the woman for a moment assessing the threat. She could smell Chinese food reheated in a microwave. She decided to blow by this person. "I have business that can't wait," she said in a slightly raised voice, staring into the hall beyond Lisa and placing a foot on the threshold.

Greg heard Susan's voice and called from the living room, "Hi Susan. Come on in."

Lisa gave her adversary a look universally understood between females. It said 'don't even think about moving in on me.' Then she smiled and stepped aside with a gesture of feigned welcome. Susan flipped one right back at her that said 'spare me, lady, I'm just a friend.'

Greg lay on the living room floor in khaki shorts and a tee shirt. He was propped up on two pillows under his chest. A small tray lay beside him on the floor. It held a dish of Chinese pork strips, red spare ribs and a glass of Coke. As Susan entered, shedding her jacket on a chair, Greg grinned, "Glad to see you Susie. Whazzup?"

"I decided to take you up on your invitation to pot luck," Susan said, emphasizing the word 'invitation' for the benefit of the gatekeeper.

"Great!" Greg said, missing the point. "Susie, this is Lisa Raines, my neighbor next door. She's been a great help for the last couple of days.

"I can see that," replied Susan. She smiled as warmly as possible as she shook Lisa's hand. It was time to offer a truce.

Lisa grinned as if to say, 'truce accepted.'

"I'll get you a plate," she said cheerily.

Soon, the three seemed as if old friends, chatting about superfluous things.

At nine-thirty, Lisa finally got the point that Greg and Susan needed to talk privately about some work related thing. She collected the remains of the Chinese food and packed it away in the fridge. Then she appeared with a glass of water and two pills. "Be a good boy and take your chemicals," she ordered.

Greg took the pills then giggled. "Hey Susie, this stuff would bring a lot of money on the street."

"Ill see you bright and early Greg," Lisa said, starting for the door. "Don't you mess with that bandage now, you hear?

"I can't thank you enough for all your caring Lisa," Greg said sincerely.

"Caring is what we nurses do," replied Lisa. "Good night Susan. Don't keep him up too late."

When they were alone, Greg gingerly rolled up on his side, wincing slightly at the pain. "Hey Susie, wanna see my wound?" he said, like a little boy with a prize booboo.

"No thanks," she said holding up her palm. "I'll leave that to the nurse."

"So where were you in Canada?" he said cheerily, "You know I have a great friend who lives in Canada. She works for CSIS."

Susan winced realizing that Greg had no clue what she was about to say.

"Carole Hinson," she said simply.

"That's her. Did I ever tell you about her?"

"Many times," Susan replied. "To answer your question I was at the CSIS office in Ottawa today."

"Wow. Did you see Carole? I mean, was she there?"

Susan sighed deeply. She dreaded the moment. "Greg, the reason I came to see you tonight is… well, I have bad news." She held up her hand as if to block him from saying anything. She gazed at the floor and said simply, "Carole Hinson is dead."

"Dead? Susie, how can that be?" Greg could not staunch the tears. His face became furrowed, staring at Susan in disbelief as the tears flowed.

Susan took his hand, sliding to the floor beside her colleague. Her empathy for Greg at this moment was so great she almost burst into tears herself. He sobbed uncontrollably. They lay together in a ball on the rug, Greg in a fetal position, Susan with her arm around him, her body pressed close in an effort to comfort him. Half an hour later, he finally just ran out of tears.

"I'm glad you could let it out," she finally said.

Greg made a noise, sort of half way between a grunt and a groan. He stared vacantly into mid-air. Finally he managed to speak. "How did it happen?"

"In the line of duty," she answered. "She gave all for her country, the same as you or I would like to think we would if faced with the choice."

Greg whimpered slightly. "Was it quick?"

"Yes, shot in the head. She never felt the bullet." Susan figured that was enough to tell him for now, purposely leaving out the gut wound or what might have led up to it.

Greg shifted and snuggled up closer to Susan. "Please don't go for a while." He closed his eyes and drifted off in thought.

Stroking his brow softly, she replied, "Don't worry, I'll stay as long as you like."

Ali bin Akram Ajir had come to realize that Amman was too hot a place for him to remain there any longer. A few of the paid informants used by the CIA also sold information to Ajir International Enterprises Ltd. on a regular basis. When he found out through one of them that the CIA in Amman was now involved, Ajir knew that he had to run. He shut down surveillance of Chris Taylor and made arrangements to be driven to Syria. From there, he could decide whether to go to Turkey or slip into Iraq, on the way to his final destination in Turkmenistan.

He put the little gold sack and its contents in his attaché and chained that to the wrist of his chief bodyguard. Together with a driver they set out on the road in an armored Range Rover. One hundred kilometers later near the Syrian border, six other Para-military vehicles joined the cortege. Soon, they had crossed discreetly and safely into Syria, thanks to good contacts and some well placed bribes. Ajir would spend the night at the home of an old friend near Damascus.

During the drive, he had time to reflect on the events of the past few days. Ajir himself had planned the 'acquisition' as he called it, just after receiving Nancy Kinnear's report. She had spoken with Al Kafajy Trading

Company before contacting Ajir. In that phone call, Ahmed had foolishly connected Al Kafajy's mysterious invitation only sale in Amman with *The Hand of Mohammed.* Nancy had passed the information to Ajir hours before her unfortunate death.

The irony was that Ahmed had arranged a nice payment to Ajir's group in return for the information. Nevertheless, Ajir now stood on the threshold of the biggest deal of his lifetime. He had identified three potential customers and had already received a positive reply from two. His plan was to complete the deal, close his trading company forever and vanish from the scene before Mohammed Al Kafajy could exact revenge. It was a bold and dangerous plan, but one that he could not resist trying. Every one of his peers in the international arms trade dreamed of becoming wealthiest and a hero of Islam at the same time. His would be the ultimate score.

Charlie West got more frustrated by the minute. Steck had ordered a majority of the resources for *Operation Retrieve* to be used to identify the thieves who now had possession of *The Hand of Mohammed.* He had promised Steck a quick answer, confident in his ability to obtain information on the street in Amman. Now of a sudden the street had fallen silent.

Steck built an impressive information tree with the inputs received during the long afternoon. He and two analysts now stared at a large flat panel display in the main conference area. Each of them made quiet comments, as they moved the puzzle pieces into order. A factoid would be moved from one point on the timeline spreadsheet to another then after quiet consultation it would be moved back where it had been. Another would replace it, then be moved somewhere else. This part of the process was painfully slow and mentally exhausting to all concerned. However it usually yielded information that allowed great leaps forward in any operation.

When Charlie entered the room to express his frustration, Steck was finally becoming satisfied that they had established some paths to follow. He directed one of the analysts to take a digital snapshot of the tree and forward it to Langley and to eighteen other CIA offices across the Muslim world.

"In your cover memo, request feedback from everybody who sees this," he declared to the analyst. "We need every scrap of information we can get."

Charlie informed Steck about the sudden disconnect from the usual information sources in Amman. Steck could see the angst in Charlie's eyes. "Come on, Charlie, let's take a break," he said. "I could use some fresh air."

As they found and donned their jackets to wear against the cool night air, Steck remarked, "You know, Charlie, when the street goes cold it's usually because there is some player orchestrating things, probably someone with a hell of a lot more local influence than we have."

Charlie acknowledged that, while expressing his hopes that they would find and unseal someone's lips soon.

The two men stepped into the street. As they did, Charlie half-whispered "Got it!" He put his arm into Steck's back and steered him straight ahead. Steck got the message. It meant 'keep walking straight and don't look around.'

After they had walked a block in silence, Charlie felt secure enough to talk. "The office is under surveillance by one of the top operatives in Amman. It's a guy named Rashid. He was across the street from us when we came out of the building just now."

"What does that mean?" Steck asked.

"I don't know exactly," Charlie replied, "but it gives me a lead to follow."

They turned left onto a side street and gradually worked their way back towards the Anwhar Trading

Company office. They took another left and were less than a block from the office. The cool night air had refreshed both men, who were walking in silence, each of them now thinking fresh thoughts.

Steck sensed something out of place, as if there might be someone observing them, someone other than the guy across the street. As they came closer to Charlie's office it became apparent that Rashid had disappeared.

"I don't like this." Steck declared.

Charlie had noticed Rashid's absence as well. The street was deserted, except for one car that sat with engine running two buildings away. Charlie fished in his pocket for the small electronic sender that could be used to unlock the door. No sense wasting time fumbling with a door key, he thought.

Safe inside, they looked at one another. "That was creepy," Steck offered.

Charlie nodded assent. Steck returned to the conference room. Charlie hustled up a stairway to the third floor and peered out the window from a darkened room. The source of their shared feeling stepped out of a doorway a hundred yards up the street and walked slowly down the sidewalk towards the car. Reaching it, the figure stepped in and the car sped away.

Charlie West was a resourceful man. He trotted down the hall to a closet, opened the door and checked to see if the surveillance camera had been tampered with. It was functioning normally, scanning the street up and down as ever. He took the elevator to the basement, where he quickly made a copy of the street surveillance from the past half-hour.

Steck had just begun to read the first replies to the memo he had directed. It was from the CIA bureau in Islamabad, just an acknowledgement of receipt. Charlie walked into the room, placing a memory stick at Steck's side.

"Bob, I've got the stalker we both sensed on video. Let's have a look."

Smiling broadly Steck replied, "Charlie, you're the best!"

CHAPTER 26

Randy Pullin personally met Muhammed Saleem Rafiq at the Denver airport, whisking him into a car to be driven about sixty miles to the heliport at a ranch just outside Fort Collins, Colorado. He had financed the heliport for his friend's ranch to have a secure remote site for *Free Nation's* comings and goings in Colorado. They boarded a Robinson R44 helicopter with white and yellow markings. The side doors were marked in big letters MARTIN RANCH, but the machine really belonged to *Free Nation*. They were soon airborne, heading toward eastern Wyoming.

On the way the two old friends spoke through their headset link, the only way to communicate over the noise of the machine. The pilot flew east, picking up Interstate 25 which he kept to his left as they sped north. He vectored around Warren Air Force Base to the east and north then picked up I-25 again, following it past Buffalo, where he picked up I-90.

A stop was made in Sheridan to take on fuel and pick up some supplies for the post. They arrived at *Free Nation* about dusk, the setting sun painting the hills around with its peculiar and beautiful Wyoming sunset glow.

"This is a most beautiful place," remarked Saleem as they settled in to Colonel Randy's office. "It is impractical though, so far away from everything."

"Part of the plan to keep us out of harm's way," joked Randy. "It provides the kind of seclusion you guys can only find hundreds of klics into the mountains of Peshawar."

"Hmm," Saleem said absently, reaching for a big red apple. "These days that area is not suitable either." He started to tuck the apple into his bag but Randy interjected.

"You don't need that apple, Saleem. There's plenty of fresh fruit in your quarters and I've instructed one of our cooks, who is your countryman, to provide you with proper Pakistani Muslim meals."

"Thanks so much!" Saleem replied. "When traveling, you just don't know what will be available."

"I'll join you for some of that good food, if you don't mind," offered Randy. "That way we can get down to business say, in about an hour?"

"That would be fine," said Saleem, standing up.

Randy summoned an orderly who took Saleem's baggage and bade him follow. Saleem settled in to the guest house just across the way from Randy's office. He grabbed a quick nap. He would need it as he expected to work well into the night.

After dinner at the dining table set before a crackling fire, Randy summoned eighteen hand-picked men and officers. They arranged themselves in various sofas and chairs around the guest cottage's living room.

"We have a new and most important mission to perform, gentlemen," Colonel Randy began. "A priceless piece of antiquity and relic of utmost significance to the Muslim religion was abducted by an unknown thief or group of thieves just a few days ago in Amman, Jordan. Unwittingly, we were involved in its disappearance from the United States and its transport to Amman. Now we have learned that in the wrong hands this item could ignite at the very least a bitter struggle among bad guys in the Islamic world and at worst a worldwide conflict of some unimaginable sort."

Some of the men shuffled in their seats. They heard Colonel Randy's words but also saw the concern on his face. One mumbled to the man next to him, "I've never seen the old man this worried."

"I heard that, Barry," Pullin remarked, staring at the man. "You're right. I've never been this worried. Since we were unfortunately involved in its disappearance, we have a duty to the principles of *Free Nation* and to the preservation of peace in the world to find and retrieve it. This will be job one for all until we accomplish the mission. You are our best men. Each of you is relieved of all other responsibilities and will concentrate on this mission until further notice, under my personal direction."

"What is this thing, Colonel? What are we looking for?" asked one of the officers.

"The object is called *The Hand of Mohammed*," replied Colonel Randy. He turned to Saleem. "This is Muhammed Saleem Rafiq, our colleague and friend. Some of you know him from past operations. He is a good guy. He will brief you on the object, its history, its significance and symbolism in the Muslim world. He is also developing ideas as to where to look for it. He will work side by side with me for the duration of this mission. You will all understand my concern from what you are about to hear. Take it to heart. We must not fail this mission. Saleem thinks that if we do fail, the word 'Armageddon' may not be inappropriate for the result. I don't fully understand that, but I trust Saleem."

Saleem stood and arranged some papers prepared for the briefing. He handed out some material to each man while addressing them.

"Colonel Randy has asked me to give you all an overview and opinion about *The Hand of Mohammed*. Since most of you are not of my faith, I will begin with an explanation of Islam and tell of the life of the prophet. To do that we will begin with the story of...."

While Saleem spoke, Pullin slipped out of the cottage and double-timed the short distance to his office. He rang up Grundstrom, pacing impatiently while the secure link beeped and squawked its way to Amman. Finally the connection was made. "Gunny, I need a report." He demanded.

"Brandt's here and we are both still allowed access to Steck's operations center, Colonel. He considers us members of his team." Grundstrom sounded confident and in charge.

"Any progress, any leads thus far?" Pullin sounded all business.

Grundstrom outlined *Operation Retrieve*. "This guy Steck is impressive, Colonel. He has gathered a lot of information and analyzed it well. We have some hypotheses but we have not yet identified who has the item. Whoever it is knows who and where we are, though. Steck and the local director have been followed. They think an attempt was made to take both of them out last evening but the guy got away."

"Listen carefully, Gunny. I want you and Brandt to locate a guy named Chris Taylor. He will probably be at the office of Al Kafajy Trading Company in Amman. If you can confirm he's there, put him under surveillance and let me know you found him."

"Colonel," answered Grundstrom, "Taylor's the guy who gave the presentation about the item to all those potential buyers. He's here, in Amman, staying at the Royal Amman Hotel."

"Is he under surveillance by Steck's team?"

"Yes sir. One of Charlie West's agents has him."

Pullin paused. He remembered Charlie West from years back. "Gunny, I want you to get a photo of Taylor and anybody with him. Do it without Charlie or Steck's knowledge. Send it to me as soon as you can." Pullin had a hunch Taylor was smart enough to hire some big gun to help him retrieve the object. He was keen to know who that might be.

"Understood Colonel, I'll get it."

When Colonel Randy returned to the briefing, Saleem was explaining the difference between Sunni and Shiite Muslims.

"First, Sunnis are in the vast majority in the world. Shiites are generally poorer but extremely zealous. Their fundamental difference in belief is a dispute over succession to the Prophet," he declared. "Succession and inheritance of position is very important in the world of Islam. If you recall, I told you of the twelve imams and their place in Islamic history. Now the Shia maintain the belief that Ali......"

As he spoke, the men were each taking notes. Saleem was frequently interrupted with questions, which he patiently took the time to answer. In the end, the men understood that Islamic scholars became world leaders in math, science, philosophy and the arts for many hundreds of years, while European Christians bickered, repressed advances in learning and spent most of their resources killing one another. When the Europeans finally united against Islam, the Muslims gradually lost power and in the long run became 'second-class' in the very areas where they had once excelled. The Industrial revolution in the west left Islamic countries even further behind. This, in turn has produced a mentality of underachievement that rankles Muslims. They feel disenfranchised in the modern world, even though they helped to create its knowledge base. Disenfranchised people can easily become terrorists and revolutionaries in their desire to change what they perceive as the oppressive status quo.

History tells us that such a status quo will only change when an overwhelming majority unites under a single banner. Once united, they can exert massive influence for change in the world. History also shows us that Muslim religious factions, tribal self-interests and nationalism have inhibited the advance of Muslim culture for centuries.

"Here, gentlemen, is the crux of the present issue. In the short run, *The Hand of Mohammed* will offer its owner freedom from Islamic law and free passage anywhere in the Islamic world. Imagine what Al Qaeda or any other of the hundreds of terrorist organizations could do with that. In the long run, however, in the right hands this object could become the banner uniting the entire world of Islam into a single force for change that would certainly initiate world conflict. That is why Colonel Randy has used the word 'Armageddon' and why this mission is desperately important."

———————

Susan Deet woke at three am, still lying on the floor beside Greg Liss. She slowly focused her thoughts without moving. Greg breathed heavily, still sound asleep. She realized he was not touching her anywhere. It would be a good time to move. Susan quietly got up, found her shoes and jacket and tiptoed out Greg's front door without waking him. She stealthily got into her Saturn and released the brake. It rolled back, away from the first line of parked cars. After pointing it away from the building, she started the engine and rolled to the frontage road. There, she switched on the headlights and began the rest of her commute.

Arriving at her place, a small cottage buried in the suburban sprawl around Washington, she made a pot of coffee and settled in to review some emails. No sense trying to sleep now that four am was ringing in, she thought.

Among the emails was one from Mort Lindsley received about eleven pm. He wanted to talk with her before the scheduled meeting of the JUMP team with MacFergus. That meant she should be at his office no later than seven am. She changed into sweats. Trudging to the sparc bedroom which she had turned into a small gym, she worked out vigorously for about half an hour. Sipping the last of her second cup she yawned, stripped and headed for the shower.

At five fifty am, Susan stepped dripping out of the shower with a big towel wrapped around her body. As a reflex, she suddenly dropped to the floor aware of someone in her front room. Her mind raced, plotting to retrieve her service revolver.

The front door closed. She gave it a five count. Not hearing any other noises, she leapt up and ran to the window that faced the street. A small car pulled from the curb and fled into the pre-dawn. She double locked the door, cursing that she must have left it unlocked when she arrived. Throwing on all the lights, she took inventory. Nothing was missing, not even the laptop from her desk or the revolver from her bedroom. There was no sign of anything disturbed or out of place.

Susan stood for several minutes out of breath with her heart pounding, wondering who had just paid her a visit and why.

At Lindsley's office, Susan related the events of the previous night to her boss. Lindsley wanted a team to have a look at Susan's home, dust for prints and look for clues. Susan asked for that to happen after work. She wanted to spend her day with the JUMP team. Lindsley agreed.

"The reason I wanted to see you, Susie," Lindsley drawled, "is we got a definite on your man Roche."

"Wow, that's good news." Susan was upset that she had not found him herself. "So, where is he?"

"In Mexico, just like you figured. His new identity is as a Brit with a moustache name of Hugh Coles. We decided to take him last night, but he never came home. The caretaker at his house didn't know where he had gone or when he would return."

Bob Steck sat at Charlie West's desk, studying blow-ups of several photos printed from the surveillance tape at Anwhar Trading Company.

First, he had run the tape as a video many times, trying to learn the gait of the man as he had walked calmly to the waiting car. He studied his hands, arm movement, size and posture. Now the blow-up stills gave him more detail of head shape, girth and even a good look at the Beretta he was carrying.

Slowly thoughts converged on a singular memory from years past. "Damn his hide!" Steck shouted in astonishment to Charlie West. "It's Paul Roche!"

CHAPTER 27

Ajir's entourage, a small convoy of up-armored jet black Range Rovers and Suburbans rolled to a stop at a small general aviation airport just outside Damascus.

Ajir emerged from his vehicle in a silk business suit, open white shirt and Bally shoes. Clean shaven, his look was that of a wealthy executive. His fine leather brief case contained a copy of the Financial Times, two cell phones, a small laptop computer and *The Hand of Mohammed*.

Flanked by bodyguards, Ajir hustled across the tarmac to his gleaming Falcon 900EX jet. He hung his own jacket in the closet near the aircraft door then had to duck his head slightly, greeting the attendant as he maneuvered his skinny six foot-three frame into the wide red leather swivel chair behind his fine rosewood airborne desk. The floor of the cabin was covered with the finest silk Persian carpet. The sides of the cabin were covered with wool carpet of the same design up to the windows.

Two of the body guards slipped in behind him and went directly to the rear of the airplane, where there was a small cabin with standard airplane seats for them.

Settling the brief case beside his desk, Ajir accepted a cup of tea from the attendant, a young Muslim girl in a long dress with head covering. Her face was strictly Persian with dark eyes and hair, full red lips and cappuccino colored skin. She was the daughter of one of Ajir's cousins, well trained in flight safety, quiet and very discreet, a requirement for success of any employee at Ajir International Trading Company. She stepped briefly into the well equipped galley. Moments later she appeared at Ajir's desk with a small tray of middle-eastern food. Smiling, she asked if anything else would be needed before take-off.

Ajir smiled, nodding in the negative. "Thank you Dorri, nothing else at the moment. Please prepare my bed after take-off. I wish to sleep on the way to Mosul." He sat back and relaxed a bit. He was grateful to have this girl on his staff. Her name in Farsi, the Persian language meant shining star. She was certainly well named, he thought.

After securing the doors, the pilot rolled the Falcon smoothly to the end of the runway. There was a pause while the co-pilot received the last clearance information to land at a small airport in Turkey, near the town of Mut. This was only about a hundred air miles from Damascus, but a necessary stop. Flights originating from Syria are not allowed access to Iraq, but from Turkey to northern Iraq could be arranged though complicated. After receiving permission to land at Mut, the pilot applied full power to the three jet engines and the sprightly Falcon took off. During the short flight, the co-pilot kept up constant radio chatter, trying to gain permission for their next leg to Mosul.

Half an hour later, the jet landed at Mut. Ajir slept while the crew continued the endless trail of paperwork necessary to satisfy the Turks. A few well placed bribes finally secured all the necessary permissions about two hours later.

Ajir rose from his nap just before take-off. He dressed in street clothes to blend in with the locals in Mosul. Although predominantly peaceful and incredibly prosperous, Mosul could still be a dangerous city in which to be a stranger.

During the flight, Ajir used a satellite link to speak with a contact in Teheran. Arrangements were made for a business meeting the next day. He would be meeting with representatives of both the religious and governmental leaders. Ajir knew that behind the scenes of that meeting, none other than the supreme leader, the Ayatollah Khomeini himself would be consulted at every point of the negotiation.

After the meeting in Teheran the final stop on his three stop tour to sell *The Hand of Mohammed* would be much more complex and difficult to arrange, but could turn out to be the really big score he craved. Within 10 days, he thought, this deal would be over and my new life can begin.

At Mosul, Ajir was whisked in a B6 armored Suburban to the offices of the local government. On the way, they passed through streets that held more cranes than minarets. Buildings were going up everywhere. Shops brimmed with merchandise. Sidewalk cafes teemed with both locals and foreigners, even some non-military Americans. The place looked more like a prosperous Iranian city than part of a country emerging from years of war.

At the government offices, he was taken through long corridors to a separate building in the back. The door of this purposely obscure shabby looking building had writing engraved on the glass in Farsi that proclaimed "Dream of Kurdistan, it will come to pass." Ajir had to repress a chuckle as he read it.

Generations of Kurds dreamt that one day they would be an independent nation. The problem was that the rest of the countries in the region wouldn't allow that to happen. The ethnocentric Kurds occupied pieces of many countries including northwestern Iran, northern Iraq, Anatolia which is part of Turkey, regions of Armenia and part of Syria. On the map, you can draw a single boundary that includes all the Kurdish regions. The Kurds have had that map in mind under the name Kurdistan ever since the time of Alexander the Great.

Ajir regarded the nation of 'Kurdistan' as a pipe dream, but knew better than to tell that to any Kurd, unless he placed no value on his life. His own name, Ajir, was a common Kurdish name. He knew he had some Kurdish ancestors in his family, but it meant little to him.

The present leadership in northern Iraq actually maintained a Kurdish 'government' of sorts. They hold great economic power, spend much on maintaining shadow diplomacy around the world and truly believe in a future Kurdish state. They would certainly benefit from being the possessors of *The Hand of Mohammed*. Ajir was only interested in how much money they were willing to part with to accomplish that desire.

The man he met with was Asam Talibani, a relative of the most prominent political family in the region. After much ceremony and exchange of courtesy, Ajir informed them that he had the object in a safe place. He showed them a clip taken from a very badly shot video. One of his men had shot it during Taylor's presentation in Amman. It clearly showed *The Hand of Mohammed*. The audio was better. The voice was that of Chris Taylor describing the provenance of *The Hand*.

Talibani declared that one of his people had attended the meeting in Amman, so what he was shown was nothing new. He demanded to see the object.

"You will see it," replied Ajir, "upon deposit of the one million Euro non-refundable bidders' fee." He was taking a page out of Al Kafajy's book. "The advantage for you is that whereas there were to be at least twelve bidders before, I will only allow three."

Much haggling followed, but in the end the Kurd agreed to the arrangement. Ajir instructed him to be prepared to come to Ashgabat, Turkmenistan between ten days and two weeks time. There, the final bidders would assemble and the *Hand of Mohammed* would be sold. In the meantime, the one million Euro deposit would be cleared to a Swiss account of the Ajir International Trading Company, in payment of a bogus invoice for Cotton ostensibly purchased from Turkmenistan.

Hours later during the flight to Ashgabat and his home office, Ajir reflected on a successful day. He sipped Turkish coffee and chatted amiably with Dorri as she shared a cup of the acrid stuff. The pilot applied extra power as the jet climbed over rugged mountain territory. The big plane behaved more like a commercial airliner than a business jet. He was proud that he could afford the machine, which was the envy of his peers. Its four thousand five hundred mile range and massive power made travel in his part of the world easier, especially its ability to handle high altitude take-offs and landings.

"One arrangement made, two more to go," he told himself. Tomorrow would be Iran then a visit to Pakistan and the stage would be set for his final business deal.

Rashid the butcher huddled in a doorway, smoking a cigarette and talking with Paul Roche. Taylor stood at the curb, watching for any surveillance he could identify. Taylor strained to hear what the two men were saying, finally deciding to wait for Roche to give him the information.

Across the street on a door stoop two young girls in school uniforms carrying book bags chatted noisily. Up the street, a delivery truck blocked traffic. Several irate motorists shouted at the driver to no avail.

The conversation between Rashid and Roche ended. Roche and Chris Taylor went up the street, towards the traffic snarl while Rashid turned the other way, toward his butcher shop.

Chris Taylor and Paul Roche never saw the camera held by the westerner with chiseled features, bright blue eyes and a big facial scar. "Gotcha." Brandt quipped as the delivery truck rolled away.

"See you at school tomorrow!" called one girl as she tucked her tiny button-hole camera into her book bag. The other waved acknowledgement as she strolled away.

Amman was a city like all the others in the Middle East. Information could be obtained inexpensively and easily as long as one knew the rules of Baksheesh, the time-honored system of bribes.

Soon, Brandt had wired his photo to Randy Pullin, Charlie West found out that a man named Ali bin Akram Ajir had possession of *The Hand of Mohammed*, Steck had a photo confirming Roche's identity and Taylor knew where Ajir had taken *The Hand*.

CHAPTER 28

The JUMP team meeting at Mort Lindsley's office lasted most of the day. In the end, Robert MacFergus had been totally briefed on the operation thus far and had placed all available resources of the CSIS at the disposal of the JUMP Team.

This pleased Ryall Morgan greatly. The Canadians enjoyed better relations with many of the Muslim countries in the world than the Americans. They had ears on the ground in places the Americans could not approach. It was agreed that MacFergus would work out of his office in Ottawa, pooling information and planning in a daily secure teleconference with Ryall Morgan and Mort Lindsley. Susan Deet would be in the position of liaison in real time with MacFergus. She would coordinate mutual efforts and be available twenty-four-seven.

Greg Liss was patched-in via internet protocol for part of the meeting. In spite of the terrible personal burden he carried, he wanted to stay current. He told Lindsley that he would be available for work within three or four days, but his mobility might be a bit hampered. Susan thought that another week would be needed to get Greg's head back in the game but kept silent about it for the moment.

At midnight Amman time, six pm in Washington, Bob Steck called in. The meeting became extended in order to hear his report.

"I've got a lot of new information," Steck announced. He sounded almost breathless.

"Go Ahead, Bob." The voice was Ryall Morgan's.

"Some guy named Ali bin Akram Ajir has the object. Our people in Amman can't find him. They think he's gone to Syria. Get me all you can on this guy." Steck knew Morgan and his staff would be all over that.

"Have a look at this," Steck announced, holding up the photo of Paul Roche by his PC camera. The room buzzed as the various members of the JUMP team recognized Roche.

"Roche is running an operation to retrieve the stolen article for Al Kafajy Trading Company. I think his involvement with the caper ended after the heist at Charleston. Now I think he was asked to come back in after the theft in Amman."

"Son-of-a-gun," exclaimed Morgan, now we know why he's not in Mexico."

Steck continued, "I don't need to tell you folks, especially Ryall that Roche is a good agent and a formidable adversary for any thief."

"I'll give him that," stated Morgan. "What do you propose to do with this new information, Bob?"

"I propose to use the resources we have including Charlie's crew and the soldiers of fortune that got us into and out of Yemen last week to tail him. Of course we will continue our operation in parallel, but I believe Roche will lead us to the objective as quickly or even faster than we can find it alone."

"Then what?" asked Mort Lindsley.

"Then, we take the thing back and go home with it." Steck knew that was easier said than done.

"And if you can't get it back?" Lindsley had a way of posing all the right questions.

"Then we blow it to smithereens." Steck knew he was leading guys that did not like to be led.

"Whoa, Bob," said Morgan, we will need to get you some input from bigger fish on that."

"Sure, Ryall," Steck replied. "I was just posturing, but it needs to be considered and I do need direction."

"You will get it shortly, Bob." Morgan and Lindsley exchanged a look. They would be talking to The State Department and probably to *The Man* himself.

"Good work, Bob," declared Morgan. "Let's talk again tomorrow. Don't lose the bugger this time."

"Roche is mine," said Steck with a grin.

The rest of the call was spent reporting to Steck about the new Canadian connection and progress on other background issues. After it was over the team dispersed. Susan took MacFergus back to the airport for a free ride home courtesy of Uncle Sam. Greg was contacted with the news about Steck's discovery. Steck went to bed.

Mort Lindsley and Ryall Morgan stayed in Mort's office, working well into the night with folks at State and Langley. It was truly time to get *The Man* involved.

After that, they had a long talk about *Free Nation* and its involvement in this affair. It was decided that they needed to allow their continued assistance to Steck for a few more days. They agreed that in the end, *Free Nation's* involvement in the whole affair needed a full criminal investigation.

Ajir's airplane touched down in Ashgabat, Turkmenistan just before dawn. His personal car met the plane on the tarmac, a convenience that had cost him a lot of bribes when it was set up and lots more to maintain. It was far better than trying to get through airport security which was particularly egregious, probably a throwback to the old soviet days. An ordinary traveler would be stopped and searched at least four times and faced passport control from five to eight times in one pass through the facility. The process took three or four hours at best.

The ride from the airport to Ajir International Trading Company's office and warehouse was very short. The company's building was a show place. It was part of the new government's designated industrial expansion area around the airport. Ajir had built it with investment money passed from the UAE to the Turkmen government as part of Abu Dhabi's program to corner investment in industry. The UAE wanted to be the principal source of capital for

Turkmenistan's rise to economic power predicted for the first half of the twenty-first century.

Ajir spent the morning catching up on commercial correspondence. He summoned his chief body guard Arad Arbabi. They made plans for the upcoming bidder's visits. This included preferred parking for their airplanes, passage through security, ground transportation to the Presidential Hotel and accommodations in its penthouse area.

At noon, Ajir took his brief case and went to the elevator near the door that separated his offices from the warehouse. He entered the elevator alone and pressed the button for B3, a level 3 stories below the street. The car stopped half way between B2 and B3. A display next to the controls flashed the Russian words Аццесс рестрицтед! Restricted Access! Ajir fished a key from his pocket, inserted it into a slot then turned it clockwise. The car started moving again and stopped at B3 level. He entered a short hallway and passed through another key-access point. This led to a massive vault door with a keypad. He punched in the access code and the door unlatched. Pushing it open, he deposited the gold sack containing *The Hand of Mohammed in a small* drawer.

"Be safe," he said to the sack as he closed the drawer.

Late in the day Ajir summoned his car and driver. He called his wife, announcing that he would be home for dinner.

At dinner, he told his wife to begin packing for an extended trip to their luxury vacation home in Dubai. She and the children would have to leave within one week without fail. She gave him an incredulous look, then as a good Muslim wife, lowered her eyes and resigned herself to obey his command.

———

Susan Deet arrived home accompanied by a forensics team from the FBI. They carefully scrutinized every square inch of the front entrance and the living room of her house but found no evidence of an intruder.

Zach Bailey, the leader of the team finally declared the place clean. "Either the intruder was interrupted before having the time to find their objective, or was simply trying to scare you for some reason," he concluded.

"Well," said Susan, "the scaring part worked really well."

It was late at night in the *Free Nation* compound. Randy Pullin and Saleem enjoyed a cup of tea while chatting about the present state of the quest for *The Hand of Mohammed*.

Pullin studied the photo of Chris Taylor and Paul Roche he had received from Brandt and Grundstrom. Although he had worked for Taylor, he had never met the man. He made a mental note to get the photo reproduced and into the hands of his entire team next morning.

"Saleem," he said, "I don't understand the connections between these various factions very well. The Sunnis hate the Shiites. The Shiites hate the Sunnis. Iran is Shiite, yet they support the Taliban who are Sunnis. Al Qaeda is Sunni, yet they support Hezbollah which is Shiite. None of this makes any sense to me."

Saleem smiled faintly. "Colonel, there is an old Arab saying that goes like this; *When your enemy is the enemy of your enemy, he is your friend.*"

Pullin looked quizzical. "Explain, please."

"I do not wish to offend you in any way but I must give you the full truth of this matter," Saleem started. "What I'm about to tell you emanates from the distorted but firmly believed viewpoint of the modern Islamist. It's not my opinion, nor that of most Muslims."

"Go ahead Saleem," Pullin insisted.

"Okay," replied Saleem. He stood up and paced as he delivered his message. "There is a new and common enemy for Islamists, be they Shiite or Sunni. That enemy is the United States. The Islamists believe that the United States is the 'Great Satan', the evil one, opposed to God and all his laws. From their point of view, the 'Great Satan" has purposely torn down family values, has fostered immorality as a way of life, is dissolute in drunkenness and debauchery, has allowed the blasphemy of homosexuality to be accepted and even in some quarters exalted, and is vigorously engaged in exporting those fallen values to the world. From a moral standpoint, they believe that the United States is by its very existence, an affront to God."

"I guess they have never attended church in the Midwest," Pullin quipped.

"We are not talking about individual God-fearing people," Saleem responded. "These Islamists do not want their children infected by the perceived ills of the West. They feel constrained by their own laws to fight against such an attack on their values, even to death. And then there is the Jewish problem. There are those Islamists that see Israel as a client of the U.S. But there are also those that see the U.S. as a victim of Israel. They believe that Judaism is the root of all this evil and that it must be destroyed as the first step in resolving it."

Saleem paused for a moment. Randy was trying to form a counter-argument, but was having trouble putting it all together. Saleem continued, "Now please understand this is not my philosophy. I am just trying to explain the perceptions that exist and why the Islamists are so fanatical.

Next is the Christian problem. Radical Islam believes that they have an obligation to God to either convert infidels to Islam or to kill them off. Any Christian that thinks they can reason with Islamic extremists has only to look at how Christians fared under the yoke of the Turkish Ottoman Empire. The Eastern Christian Church venerates thousands of Christians slaughtered during those times as martyrs. It is saddened by the thousands that caved in and accepted Islam to save their necks.

"So what about this enemy of enemies stuff? Randy asked.

"The point I am trying to make Colonel is that the various factions in Islam are likely to put aside their differences for a time and unite against what they perceive the common and greater enemy. As I mentioned in my briefing, *The Hand of Mohammed* could provide the focal point or 'banner' to unite Islam against the West."

"Wait a minute," Pullin said, holding up a hand. "I thought you said that not all Muslims believe this stuff. Now you just said ALL of Islam, not just the radicals."

Saleem paused a moment. He wanted the next part of his discourse to be taken in the right context. "The Islamists extreme rhetoric strikes a chord in the heart of every Muslim who has read the Koran. They base their every action on direct quotes from the Koran. Of course I do not wish for some group dynamic to take hold, Colonel but I cannot rule it out completely."

Saleem paused as the full impact of this sunk in. Randy Pullin now understood it all. "Armageddon," He simply said.

"Maybe not Armageddon, Colonel but not far from it." Saleem sat back while a more philosophical look replaced the earnest of the speech he had just made. "Of course if this does not come to pass, then the old differences between Muslims will certainly return to the forefront. Let's hope they do. I think they have done a lot to keep the whole world from exploding in the past. Bickering amongst the factions may be just the thing that keeps Islam from ruling the whole world."

CHAPTER 29

Chris Taylor and Paul Roche rode together to the airport in Amman. Now that they knew it was Ajir who had *The Hand* they had formed a plan. Taylor would go to his office in Tajikistan where he could make arrangements to put agents on the ground in Turkmenistan at Roche's disposal. Roche would go directly to Ashgabat to survey the situation and form a plan to re-capture the prize.

Tailing them to the airport was a small car and driver. From the back seat Brandt kept an eye on the big Mercedes. It stopped at Gulf Air departures. Roche got out, collected his baggage at the curb and went into the terminal. Brandt was upset that they were apparently splitting up. There was only one of him and now there were two tracks to follow. He figured Roche would be the one heading for the prize itself, so he ordered the driver to wait while he checked inside the terminal. The big Mercedes sped away.

Inside the terminal Roche had lined up for first class check-in on the flight to Ashgabat, through Bucharest. Brandt turned immediately to put his back to Roche. He knew that if he was seen Roche would recognize him, so he trotted outside.

Brandt got in the car shouting to the driver, "Did you see where that black Mercedes went?"

"Yes sir," the driver replied, pointing. "It's right over there."

The Mercedes was stopped at Turkish Air departures. Taylor was standing beside the car, giving instructions to the driver. He took his baggage and strolled into the terminal.

Brandt hustled along the sidewalk to Turkish Air, slipped inside the terminal and watched while Taylor lined up. He was checking in for a flight to Istanbul. There was no telling from the marquee whether that would be his final destination so Brandt edged closer, trying to get within earshot as Taylor reached the agent's desk.

Brandt was running short of loitering maneuvers and had decided to circle back to the passenger waiting area, when he finally heard the agent say "Dushanbe will be your final destination sir?"

Brandt hustled out of the terminal, got into the car and called Steck on his cell phone. "Roche is heading to Turkmenistan. Taylor is going to Tajikistan. What do you make of that?"

"I don't know," was the reply. Steck was puzzled as to why they would split, except perhaps to lay false trails.

Charlie West was late for work, so Bob called to one of the assistant agents. "Hey George, what assets do we have on the ground in Tajikistan and Turkmenistan?"

"None that I know of Bob, those are tough areas. Try contacting our bureau in Kyrgyzstan. Maybe they have some ideas."

Steck needed help. 'Follow Roche,' he thought. Charlie West would know how to get some help in Turkmenistan. "George, could you ring Charlie and ask him when he can get here?" Steck was somewhat annoyed at Charlie's absence.

"I called his apartment a few minutes ago," George replied. "There was no answer. He's probably on his way here."

Steck acknowledged George with a wave then went back to work on his information tree. He sifted through the facts again and again for anything he might be missing.

Steck's secure email program beeped. There was a message from Ryall Morgan. In it there was new information for the tree. First, Ajir was a big shot in international trade, mostly in the region of Iran, Turkey, Turkmenistan, Northern Iraq and the surrounding states. The home office of Ajir's trading company was in Ashgabat, Turkmenistan. He had flown recently to Mosul, then to Ashgabat but would soon be going to Teheran, according to intercepted aircraft radio traffic. There would be a briefing with *The Man* tomorrow and a new email as soon as practical.

Steck went to his computer and began tapping-in the newly received information. "Where's Charlie?" he shouted to those in the room. "I really need him." When there was no response, he turned to the rest of the people in the room. "Somebody please go get Charlie, right away!"

Two men left Anwhar Trading Company and jogged the two blocks to Charlie West's apartment. As they arrived, Charlie's wife and children were just emerging from a hired car that brought them home from an overnight visit to some friends just outside Amman. She froze when she recognized two of Charlie's agents hustling towards her front door.

"Good day, Missus West," said one of them, "Where's Charlie?"

"At work," she replied. Fear spread over her face just as it had many times before. She had never become used to having an agent as a husband. She gathered the two children to her, hugging them tight. "I spoke with him on the telephone early this morning," she offered. "He said he was going to the office." Her voice was shaky.

The man stopped between the West family and the door. He reached out his hand. "May I have the key, ma'am?"

She fished it out of her pocketbook and handed it to him. "My God," she said, moving toward the door. Then remembering the children she stepped back and added, "Yes, would you please?"

The agent took the key and entered the building. He returned moments later.

"Missus West, I think you may want to take the children to the park." She flashed alarm. He turned to the other agent. "Ravi, please take the children to the park for a walk."

As soon as Ravi and the children were out of sight, the agent took Missus West's arm. "Is he alive?" she said shaking.

He took her other arm, holding her up. "No ma'am." She fainted into his arms.

Twenty minutes later Steck and others arrived. Ravi sat comforting Missus West in the sitting room off her kitchen. She was sobbing and disconsolate.

The CIA team had already concluded that Charlie had been leaving the apartment; probably just opening the door when he was attacked. There was little evidence of a struggle. His assailant had somehow gotten behind Charlie and simply snapped his neck. Death had come quickly.

Steck recognized the M.O. This was clearly the work of Paul Roche. He figured that Roche had paid Charlie this visit on his way to the airport this morning. He reckoned that given the chance, Roche would have done the same to him. Steck spent the rest of the afternoon helping out with arrangements and catering to the family. He felt terrible for them. He made arrangements for Charlie's wife and children to accompany his remains back to Virginia in a U.S. Government plane. It was the least the 'company' could do for a man who had given his life in service of America.

As crass as it seemed to Bob Steck at the moment, his primary job now was succession at the Amman bureau and continuation of *Operation Retrieve*. After contact with Langley, it was decided that Ravi Monsour, Charlie's former second in command would take over the Amman bureau on an interim basis until a successor was chosen. Ravi was a fine officer and patriot, a Yale grad with middle-eastern family background. He had served his country with distinction in the Gulf War then stayed on at Langley as a specialist on the Arab countries. He was well connected and the CIA's best hope for continuation of Charlie West's excellent work on the ground in Amman. Steck figured he would be the top candidate for an eventual permanent assignment as bureau chief.

By the end of the day Steck had arranged for three agents to slip into Turkmenistan from the U.S. base in Kyrgyzstan. They would pose as cotton merchants on a buying trip. "At least that gets us boots on the ground," he related to Ravi and the rest of the *Operation Retrieve* team.

A load of information, mostly records of commercial transactions had been assembled on Ajir and his trading company. The information tree was growing rapidly and becoming more focused. They knew who had the object. Now they needed to figure out his plan.

Gunny Grundstrom and Brandt had slipped out during the early evening to file a report with Colonel Randy. They returned with some food from a local restaurant, offering Steck his pick. He chose a sort of bean and rice mixture and a Pepsi. The three made small talk as the food dwindled.

"So guys, how's my buddy Randy Pullin doing today?" Steck suddenly said. His tone became all business.

Grundstrom smiled broadly. "Oh, he's fine, sends his best regards. He has lots of assets in this region. He told me to tell you it's all at your disposal." Grundstrom spoke nonchalantly as if they were all one family. Brandt just studied his food.

"Have you any assets in Turkmenistan?" Bob asked half seriously.

"No we don't but there's a plan." Grundstrom frowned, realizing he might have gone too far.

Steck wondered what to do with these two. His inclination would normally have been to cut them loose. They already knew too much about this operation and would only get deeper involved as it moved forward. On the one hand he needed their help and advice. On the other, he may have already violated national security.

"What plan?" Bob asked. "Don't you hold back on me Gunny, I have been right up front with you all along."

"I think it's time you and Colonel Randy had a chat," Grundstrom replied. "How 'bout I arrange that tomorrow?"

"You do that, Gunny. I've got to decide how much further to go with you guys."

About ten pm Gunny and Brandt left for their hotel. Steck decided to stay at Anwhar Trading Company for the night, sleeping on a cot in one of the back rooms. At three am, he stood in front of the digital displays in the operations room. He studied the information tree with intensity. His thoughts were mostly focused on Paul Roche. Finally he decided to get some rest. "Roche, you bugger, I'm gonna get you this time!" he shouted to the wall.

CHAPTER 30

Ryall Morgan and Mort Lindsley made their presentation to the director of the CIA early next morning. The director listened intently to what they had to say then fired questions at both of them for over an hour. Finally satisfied that they had a succinct and comprehensive briefing to present, the director arranged for their attendance at a meeting of the National Security Council with the President later in the morning.

The President and his advisors took in the briefing without much comment but a lively question and answer session followed. Finally, the President spoke.

"I would like to thank the director for this briefing. I especially thank these members of the JUMP team, Mister Morgan and Mister Lindsley and their associates for the exemplary work they are doing. As you know, I have been following this issue for some time, receiving updates at my daily security briefing. Your presentation today sheds new and disturbing light on the matter and leaves us with sobering choices to make. I'm sure you will agree ladies and gentlemen that we cannot allow this symbolic figurine to fall into the wrong hands. I am asking that members of this council be briefed in detail daily by the director of the CIA or his designate and I expect that some of you in this room will want to attend the meetings of the JUMP team. I will speak with the prime minister of Canada by telephone. The Secretary of State will join me on that call. We have a long history of cooperation between our two governments. I will commend them for stepping forward and offering assistance. Please accept it and use it wisely.

I'm directing each of to you provide all necessary support to this effort as and if requested by the director of the CIA. Mister Director, I don't need to remind you of the potential consequences of failed operations in the part of the world we are dealing with here. Do the job, but keep a lid on it."

The President rose. "This meeting is adjourned."

Bob Steck received a call from Randy Pullin early next morning Amman time. He shut himself in Charlie West's former office and locked the door. This would be a private conversation. He listened to the animated Pullin, who sounded all business. Pullin had a dossier on Ajir that far exceeded the information Langley had been able to come up with so far. Steck was impressed, and thanked him. Pullin also had three helicopters and twenty armed men enroute from the town of Masr E Sharif, in Afghanistan to the desert region in the southeastern part of Turkmenistan. They would be in place within an hours flying time of Ashgabat by day's end. He gushed on about other resources he was preparing for Steck's use. Finally, Bob interrupted him.

"Randy, listen to me!" Steck shouted. Pullin stopped in the middle of a sentence.

"Randy, I appreciate all you've done and all you're doing but you need to hear something."

"Go ahead, Bob." Randy said, "I'm listening."

"The Canadians have reported to us that one of their agents has turned up dead in Montana, a girl named Carole Hinson. They also believe that the death of a man named Ralph Baker in Idaho was connected to her disappearance. Do you know anything about that?"

"Why should I?" Randy's voice sounded cautious.

"Steck had hoped for candor from his old friend. "Because Carole Hinson's assignment was to get information about *Free Nation's* involvement in moving stolen antiquities through Canada."

"It's probably just some liberal jerks trying to discredit us, Bob. We get it all the time." Randy was trying to act nonchalant.

"For God's sake, Randy, she was traveling with young Brandt at the time of the incident." Steck was feeling disgusted with Randy Pullin's evasiveness.

Randy paused for too long. Steck watched the sweep hand on his Rolex tick off twenty seconds.

"So what does this mean?" Randy had a lot of guts asking.

"What it means is I don't think I can protect you once this operation is over. The FBI will mount a formal investigation and you guys will be up to your neck in trouble. It means if I were you I'd be concentrating on getting to know some real good lawyers rather than helping me chase some antique out in the backlands of central Asia. It means I should throw Grundstrom and Brandt out of my operation if I ever expect to collect a pension." Steck was more exasperated than he thought he would be.

"But you need me, Bob." Randy Pullin was the kind of guy to never, ever give up.

"Like a drowning man needs a drink of water, Randy."

"I can help you finish this mission successfully," Randy began. "You guys don't have any assets in Turkmenistan. I have men on the ground as we speak and I can get more. I can get you into the highest circles of Turkmen government if you need it. Don't you know what's at stake here? Bob? The world as we know it could radically change or pass away if this thing gets into the wrong hands. I love my country and I want to help. When it's over, I promise not to ask any favors. In the meantime, you have two of my best trained guys watching your personal butt. You would be eating sand in a Yemeni grave if it wasn't for my guys. They saved your sorry backside in Yemen and I hope they get to save it again. Just let us help."

Steck knew that Pullin was right. He had no way to get agents in or even to get intelligence out of Turkmenistan without going through the American Embassy. At the moment, that was far too public. The only assets he could bring to bear in the short run from outside the country were big, military and already busy fighting a war. He figured that Morgan was about to be told by the President to keep the operation undercover, so all those American machines and soldiers would be of no use at all. He needed undetected penetration in Ashgabat, and he needed it now.

"Okay, Randy. I'll accept your help. You must understand that the folks you are helping here will be your worst nightmare once this operation is over."

Pullin didn't hesitate. "What can I do for you?"

"I want you to get Grundstrom and Brandt into Turkmenistan without the authorities knowing they are in country. I'm going to contact our Embassy in Ashgabat. Depending on what I learn from that, I may want to join them in a few days, as soon as I'm sure we have a game there."

"I'll do it," said Randy enthusiastically, "Anything else?"

"Yes, there is plenty. Start thinking about how to assist us if we have to go in to Iran. We think the guy that's got the object may try to sell it there."

"I'm on it!" Randy Pullin was, if anything, unflappable.

Steck clicked off wondering how he could be stupid enough to risk his whole career on such a crazy plan. After a moment, he laughed out loud, thinking to himself, "Plan? What flippin' plan?"

Paul Roche sat in the restaurant of the Sheraton Hotel in Ashgabat, reading *Neutralny Turkmenistan* the government run newspaper. He could make out just enough Russian to catch the drift of the stories. One extolled the virtues of chicken farming, another talked about the prospects for a successful cotton crop. The rest of the paper was filled with stories about the pending capital infrastructure contracts to build the petro-chemical industry and a massive resort area on the Caspian Sea. Most of these contracts were let to firms in Saudi-Arabia and the UAE. Roche remembered that Osama Bin Laden's family had made their fortune in these kinds of building projects. He wondered whether the next big terrorist organization would be financed from Turkmen profits.

The waiter brought Roche his meal of roasted chicken, plov, which is a traditional central Asian rice dish and tea. A small tray of fruit and three small glasses of assorted fresh juices completed the meal. He longed for a good beer to wash it down, but there was none. He decided to go to a place called The British Pub later on. It was one of only two places in Ashgabat that was a hangout for émigrés. At least there he could have a pint before bedtime.

Two days in country and he already had made good progress, he thought. He had the addresses of Ajir International Trading Company and of Ajir at home. He had studied both locations and had photos of the entrances and exits, a map of the areas and a plan of attack, should that become necessary. He had photos of each of the family. He had followed Ajir and family to the home of his wife's only relatives in Turkmenistan, a place she would certainly go to if there was trouble. Chris Taylor had hired two native Turkmen agents, former KGB who now lived in Tajikistan. They were on their way to Ashgabat and would soon be at Roche's disposal. Finally, he had risked a visit to the Ajir International Trading Company. Presenting himself as Attorney Jacob Breen, he had proposed a deal to buy Cotton through Ajir to support needs in Britain. As Ajir himself was out of town, he was hosted by one of the junior members of the firm, a man named Suleiman, whose business card said he was an assistant to the managing director. He charmed the man into boasting of his position, his accomplishments as a trader and his future prospects in the company. He had finally managed a complete tour of the facilities.

Back at his hotel, Roche had sketched the interior layout of the building, including the elevator that seemed to go nowhere. He was certain that would lead him to The Hand of Mohammed. The only problems he had not solved yet were how to defeat the Russian security system and what sort of locks or vault lay at the exit of the elevator.

Back in his room, he thought of calling Taylor in Dushanbe, just to check-in. He decided to wait, giving Taylor the opportunity to originate the call at his convenience from an untraceable source. Sure enough, moments later the phone rang.

"It's Chris Taylor. How are things going?"

"Things are going just fine. I'm all set up and waiting for the gentlemen from your end to show up."

"You'll find them at the President Hotel," Taylor said. "If Ajir is going to hold an auction for visitors the President would be the likely spot for the meeting."

"I'll contact them tomorrow," said Roche. "Urgabat is the name, right?"

"Right, Mister Urgabat and his associate, Mister Gronakat will be waiting to meet you."

"I need some help with Russian electronics and security systems," Roche declared. "Are either of those men able to give it?"

"Urgabat is your man," Chris replied. "He has extensive experience with common types of installations in Turkmenistan and their operation."

"I'm all set then," Roche declared. "This should be easy."

Taylor certainly hoped that Roche was right. "I'll call tomorrow evening, your time. We will need to do this as soon as possible. The more days that go by, the better prepared Ajir will become."

"Tomorrow night, then," Roche said and clicked off.

———————

Ajir flew in to Teheran, arriving quite late in the day. He dispatched his plane back to Yemen, where it would pick-up a load of employees to shuttle back to Ashgabat. He planned to stay at his parents' home for the next few days until the plane returned.

The men that the plane would collect in Yemen were part of the small militia that he maintained for security. Trained in terrorist techniques as well as guerilla warfare and special operations, these men would be protectors of The Hand of Mohammed until after its sale.

Riding from the Airport to downtown Teheran, he marveled at the pace of development, the modern buildings and showcase atmosphere of Teheran built up since his last visit home two years ago. The place was teeming with the prosperity that only an oil-rich nation can enjoy.

As he rode along, he relaxed, shedding his usual businessman persona to enjoy the company of family and friends for the next few hours. Except for tomorrow's meeting, the next two days would be like being a kid again. This would be the first time he had spent away from business for more than a year. He hoped it would be a taste of what would come after his big score.

Teheran was built right up the side of a mountain. At the foot of the mountain urban sprawl crept out onto the desert. At the top of the mountain, snow fell for a good portion of the year. In the heights of the modern city, just below the entrance to the lift that took tourists and lovers to the top of the mountain, he arrived at his father's posh home. The Ajir family came out to meet him at the curb. Early to bed, he promised himself. Tomorrow would be a long day.

CHAPTER 31

After speaking with Ryall Morgan about the orders from *The Man*, Steck called the U.S. Embassy in Ashgabat. He had not realized that this embassy had become more than just a backwater over the past few years. Langley even had a couple of agents on the ground, but they had not been there long. At least not long enough in Steck's mind to commit to *Operation Retrieve* without vetting. Even so, he was glad to have whatever assistance they could offer.

Within minutes, they had located Mister Jacob Breen, esq. He was staying at the Sheraton. Steck now had to decide how to use that information and whether to ask these junior agents that he knew nothing about to get closer to Breen. He decided to wait until he had checked these guys out. There was no use risking the loss of those two agents to that fox Roche before the time.

Steck figured that Roche would move quickly, as he usually did. Roche knew better than to let the underground eyes of any strange city gain information about him. Better they should be left to do that after he was long gone and his mission accomplished.

Steck checked the agents out by calling an old and trusted friend at Langley. He was surprised to find that they were two of the best men the agency had in central Asia. He figured they were part of the agency's renewed efforts to get back in the game across this part of the world. Both of the men spoke fluent Russian and were also able to read and write several local dialects, including Turkmen, a most difficult language to master. The official Turkmen alphabet had gone from Arabic to Cyrillic to Latin in just the past hundred years. Able to speak the language, they were well connected among the locals and had done some excellent field work. Their experience in clandestine operations was sparse. Still, they were what he had to work with so Steck called back and asked them to tail Roche.

The great decision that faced Steck this day was whether to stay in Amman where he knew the communications to be much better than he could hope for in Ashgabat or to go to Turkmenistan. If he waited longer, Roche might make his play before Steck could counteract it. He wished that Charlie West was still at the helm in Amman. If that were the case, he would be better off on the scene of the action. After much consideration, he decided to spend the day thoroughly briefing Ravi then to leave for Masr E Sharif in Afghanistan. From there, he could be inserted into Turkmenistan by Randy Pullin's guys. That way he would not show up in the official records of those who came and went through the airport at Ashgabat. It would also give him time to re-route from Masr E Sharif if the action turned in some new direction. At the end of the day he typed a dispatch about his plans, sent it to Morgan, and caught a flight to Istanbul.

———————

Ajir emerged from his meeting in Teheran a happy man. It was a long day of very delicate negotiations with men he knew did not have the authority to make a deal. He knew from long experience that the fate of the deal rested with these underlings. Nothing would come of it unless he persuaded them to take it to the next level. He remained polite, taking care to stroke inflated egos and kowtow to idiocy. No less than eight detailed explanations of the deal and its terms had to be made before the buffoons began to understand it. The patience his father had taught him had paid off in the end, when the meeting was suddenly adjourned for three hours with no explanation. Ajir knew that the hiatus was for information to be presented to the Grand Ayatollah himself. He sat, drinking ice water and chatting affably in Farsi to those who had remained to keep watch over him.

In the end, the meeting was re-convened. The spokesman simply presented a receipt for a one million Euro deposit made to Ajir's account in Switzerland.

As he was driven back to his father's house Ajir reflected on the day's success. He allowed himself to entertain the thought that Allah might be guiding him to put the prophet's hand into the right place. The resulting personal wealth would certainly be his just reward. Nevertheless, he would not talk of it nor boast even to his father until all was accomplished.

That evening, the family gathered at a restaurant owned by one of Ajir's brothers-in-law. He had closed for the evening in order to make it a private party for the family. They would enjoy Chalu-kabob, a lamb and rice dish with yogurt sauce. They would laugh and listen to secular music and re-tell family stories that everyone knew by heart anyway.

Tomorrow the airplane would return to Teheran to collect Ajir for the final leg of his business trip, to the Peshawar region of Pakistan. There he would arrange for the third and final bidder.

Rashid the butcher constantly received feedback from his network of operatives all around Amman. He had gradually collected pieces of information about *The Hand of Mohammed* until the picture was quite clear to him. This was clearly the biggest deal in the entire Islamic world. Information about this would be valuable to many of his customers in the snoop business. He had been paid for the services performed for Roche and Taylor. In the customary unwritten rules of his business, that meant he was now a free agent.

After much thought, he decided that his most profitable next play would be with the Saudis. They had the most money to pay for good information and were usually ready to do so. He began by contacting a member of the Saudi security forces that he had dealt with in the past. He was careful not to disclose too much, but just enough to raise consciousness and interest in the rest of the story. By the time he had reached the third level of hierarchy, farther up in Saudi security than he had ever been, Rashid knew this would be a really big score.

Now the deal had progressed to the prepayment stage. Rashid had just confirmed that the down payment, fifty thousand dinari had been transferred to his wife's account. He was taking a chance, but it was worth the opportunity to earn ten times that amount if the information pleased the right people.

Rashid pulled up the collar of his overcoat, shielding his neck from the chill of the evening. He arrived at the appointed place and was met by two men he had never seen before. They exchanged a pre-arranged greeting and ducked into a small commercial building.

Two hours later Rashid was dead and six Saudi security agents in plain clothes were on their way to Ashgabat, Turkmenistan. There they would meet a member of the Royal family that was preparing to leave in all haste to join them. He would have the full negotiating authority to gain the prize. Their orders were clear. Regain possession of *The Hand of Mohammed* at all cost. Rashid had become the victim of the rest of the story.

The Kingdom of Saudi Arabia held the highest prestige among Islamic countries, simply because it contained Mecca, the birthplace of Mohammed and the holiest place in Islam as well as Medina, the second most holy place. It had actually been the repository of *The Hand of Mohammed* for hundreds of years until a safer place had to be found during the bitter war fought in 1818. During that war the Ottoman Turks occupied most of the country and cruelly put the leader, Abdullah bin Saud to death. *The hand* was lost to history for almost two hundred years. No one knew it had fallen into the hands of the Iraqi leader Saddam Hussein. Now the opportunity to regain it had come. For the sake of Saudi stature in the Islamic world, the security detail was told it simply must be found and brought "home."

CHAPTER 32

Steck took the opportunity to call his wife during his stopover in Istanbul. "Amy, I'm going into central Asia for a few days. I'll probably be out of touch, so don't worry if you don't hear from me. I should be back in Amman in about a week."

"Central Asia? Doesn't that include Afghanistan? Bob, are you going to Afghanistan?" She sounded worried.

He was not going to lie to her. "It's only a stopover in western Afghanistan, far away from the fighting. There is nothing to worry about."

"I always worry Bob, you know that. So is it Kyrgyzstan?"

"I can't tell you." He said simply.

"Take care of the farm and the horses, and take care of yourself. I'll be home soon." Bob felt lonely for Amy and for home.

"I feel lonely for you," she said softly.

"I know, so do I. Let's plan to have a few days in Florida when I return."

"Whatever you want, my love," she said thickly. "Take care and God bless."

She clicked off hoping the angst in her voice didn't upset him. He was grateful to have someone to worry about him.

A young Air Force officer approached him. "Are you Mister Steck?" the man asked.

"Yes, I am. Pleased to meet you lieutenant……?"

"Crutchley, sir, 101st Airborne. We need to get going, sir, it's a long way to Incirlik from here."

Bob followed the Lieutenant to the curb. They pulled away and headed for a heliport outside Istanbul. Within hours he was aboard a C-131 headed for Masr E Sharif and the next phase of *Operation Retrieve*.

Greg Liss was back to work. It still hurt to sit for more than twenty minutes at a time, but he was glad to be back at JUMP team headquarters and contributing again.

His task for the team was to follow up with Doctor Wigglesworth and get as much further information as possible. Reaching Wigglesworth at the Dartmounth campus by phone, he first offered his condolences over Nancy Kinnear's death. Greg could not share the details about the activities of the past week without violating security. He was able to tell the professor that the object was still in circulation. As the conversation went on, Wigglesworth asked if the Saudis had tried to take possession of *The Hand of Mohammed* yet.

"Why the Saudis?" asked Greg.

"Because if anybody has a legitimate claim to it, they do," the professor replied. He went on to explain the disappearance of *The Hand* in the early nineteenth century and that the Saudis felt like it belonged rightfully to them.

Greg received a promise of continued cooperation from Doctor Wigglesworth in return for the opportunity to see and handle the object after it had been secured by the U.S. Government.

At the daily meeting a few hours later, Greg presented the new information about the Saudis. Agents on the ground in Saudi-Arabia were notified and tasked with follow-up to see of there was any overt operation in progress by the Saudis to obtain *The Hand Of Mohammed.*

Greg asked if he could go to Saudi Arabia and take charge of the effort there. Lindsley returned a quizzical look. "Greg, we need you to manage Doctor Wigglesworth. I believe he'll be more important to us as this thing develops. Surely you understand that, don't you?" As he said this, Lindsley shot a look at Ryall Morgan that said "Don't worry, I'll handle this kid. He's worth having even if he asserts himself in immature ways."

Morgan smiled and looked away.

Ajir flew from Teheran to a small airstrip just outside Landi Kotal, thirty miles east of Peshawar, Pakistan. The pilot's instructions were to land west to east on a runway marked out for him by Ajir's host.

When the pilot flew in from the west he saw a dirt runway that had been marked out in the sand scrub by parking many pickup trucks in a parallel corridor. There were no lights and no buildings; just the pickups and what appeared to be tribesmen lining the landing area. He made a pass over the area then sent the co-pilot back to ask Ajir if this was for real. Ajir said it was okay to land.

The pilot objected. If he landed there, the aircraft might be damaged in the process. Furthermore, he saw no apparent means to re-fuel and worried that he would not be able to take-off again. He requested that Ajir consider flying in to Islamabad in accordance with his original flight plan filed in Teheran then hiring a helicopter to go back to Landi Kotal. He was also well aware that this aircraft's presence in Pakistani airspace was well known not only to the Pakistanis but also the U.S. led coalition forces in Afghanistan just miles away. Surely they had showed up on the American radars. He figured they had only minutes or hours before the Americans would try to locate them.

Ajir respected the pilot, but he had been given a thirty minute window to land. After that, any plane that approached the area would be counted an enemy and would be shot down.

"I take responsibility for the airplane," he announced to the pilot. "Please land now on the runway they have marked off and follow your instructions exactly."

The pilot obeyed. He made a second approach from the west and put the Falcon down onto the makeshift runway. The big plane rattled and bumped its way to a stop towards the end of the runway. The pilot shut down his engines right away, hoping they had not ingested too much dust.

Ajir stepped down from the front door of the Falcon. He was met at the foot of the stairs by several armed men who directed him to a white Toyota Land Cruiser parked by the edge of the runway. As he slid into the back seat of the vehicle, he was greeted by a slight built man with a sidearm in his hand. They exchanged the customary Muslim greeting. The man apologized for the rough runway, mumbling something about security. On a walkie-talkie, the man ordered that the jet be refueled. Two pickup trucks carrying tanks of JP fuel and small pumps driven off their drive train moved to the aircraft. With the help of the crew, they topped off the tanks. Then the aircraft was surrounded by armed militia. Ajir's host declared that the airplane would be guarded against any trouble while they conducted the appointed meeting. He then handed Ajir a blindfold. "Please put this on for your safety," he said in a quiet voice. Ajir obeyed. He knew that there would be such actions to endure on this trip, but still felt uneasy as the Toyota rumbled away.

Thirty minutes and many jostling miles later, the truck stopped abruptly. Ajir was led, still blindfolded into a large tent. There was the smell of sweat and wool and of tea brewing. After the flap had been secured, the blindfold was removed from his head. Several men with AK-47 assault rifles stood around the perimeter of the tent. Three men in traditional Lungee turbans and wool cloaks sat in a row in the middle of the tent. The man in the middle rose and greeted Ajir in Pashtun. Ajir returned the greeting in very broken Pashtun. The man smiled. He gestured to the two elder men who sat on either side of him then smiled and expanded the greeting in perfect Farsi. He was of medium build, with weathered looking hands and face. Above his bushy black beard, his eyes were hidden behind aviator type sunglasses.

"You are most welcome among us, Mister Ajir," the man said maintaining the Persian Farsi language. He indicated a large cushion lying on a large Tajik rug. "Please have a seat."

Ajir's host was the man known as Abu Daimb, third from the top in power of the Taliban. His outward demeanor was that of a well educated and genteel man. Ajir knew him by reputation as one who could be very unpleasant if he did not get his way.

Abu Daimb then dismissed the armed men, who filed dutifully outside. Ajir imagined they had taken up positions around the tent. Now there remained three Taliban. The identity of the other two was not offered.

After several rounds of tea and snacks, they got down to business. Ajir explained the provenance of the object that was for sale and gave the terms as already accepted by the other two bidders. He produced a photo that was passed around to "Oohs" and "Ahhhh's" from the men in the tent. They obviously knew the legend of *The Hand*.

"And who are these two bidders?" Abu Daimb said looking down at the rug. He wanted to know who his competition would be.

"They are worthy Muslim men." Ajir replied. Then he added, "I feel that for the sake of fairness, this should be a matter of confidence until the showing and sale of the object. Of course, neither will I reveal to them that you are one of the interested parties until the sale."

"I must know who they are," Declared Abu Daimb still speaking in a low voice, almost a whisper. "I cannot present this discussion to my friends or go forward in any way until I do."

Ajir sat in silence for a few moments, his face and his demeanor serene. Then he said "I cannot do that. Perhaps it is better for me to leave now."

Abu Daimb fixed his gaze on Ajir. "You are my guest, Ajir and I feel responsible for your safety. You will leave only when I decide you should leave."

A chill ran through Ajir. Had he come all this way just to die here in the wastes of Peshawar? Was this just a test to see if he would betray the confidence of the other bidders?

Ajir sorted these thoughts in his mind while showing no outward emotion. His gaze remained frozen on Abu Daimb's sunglasses. Finally, he spoke softly and deliberately.

"Your hospitality is most appreciated and your concern for my safety is certainly re-assuring," he said. Then shifting his gaze to each of the three, he continued. "It is unfortunate that you pay homage neither to the Prophet nor by inference to Allah by imposing your will against his."

The two elder men appeared shocked by this. Abu Daimb removed his glasses, revealing deep set angry brown eyes. "You fail to see your position, Sir," declared Abu Daimb, his voice rising.

"You fail to see your own," shot Ajir. "I am the one who possesses *The Hand of Mohammed*. As you are well aware, he who is the custodian of the Prophet's hand is accorded free passage anywhere in Islam. If you detain me, you violate this sacred tradition and as a consequence your whole cause will perish." Ajir studied their faces. When Ajir was sure his statement had sunk in, he added. "I cannot in conscience offer The Hand of Mohammed to those who neither honor his name nor obey his wishes."

The two elders seemed very troubled by Ajir's assertion.

"Abu Daimb," said Ajir raising his voice to the level of his adversary. "I will ask you one last time. Do you wish to be granted the opportunity to participate, or shall I inform the others that there will only be two prospective buyers?"

Abu Daimb was shaken. "I will speak with my friends." he said tersely. The three left the tent. Ajir remained seated on his cushion, eyes straight ahead, showing no emotion. He knew that eyes would be watching. Inwardly, he thought that he had either just sealed his fate or made the deal.

Ajir could hear animated discussion in Pashtun some distance from the tent but could not make out what they said. Then he heard the squawk of radio communications that lasted quite a while. At length, the three men returned, taking up their former positions. Abu Daimb had donned a fresh set of sunglasses. These had silver reflective lenses to assure Ajir could not possibly see his eyes.

Abu Daimb sat silently studying the carpet. After a minute one of the elders grunted almost imperceptibly.

The younger man then spoke softly in his studied even voice without raising his head. "Ali bin Akram Ajir, we accept your gracious offer to participate in the upcoming sale. Funds for your requested deposit will be wired to the required account by the end of the banking day today. Now please allow me to personally escort you to your airplane."

Ajir stood. The others stood. They exchanged manly embraces, invoked the name of Allah and the Prophet and adjourned. No blindfold was produced. They led Ajir back to the Toyota. Abu Daimb settled in to the back seat beside Ajir and commenced a stream of small talk that lasted until they had pulled up beside the airplane.

The pilot was relieved to see them. Before they had even stopped the Toyota, he was revving the engines, ready to leave.

As they made their farewells, Abu Daimb smiled. Looking over Ajir's shoulder to the doorway of the airplane, he remarked. "You are blessed with modest women."

Puzzled, Ajir turned to see Dorri in the doorway clad in a birka. Just her eyes showed through the screen of threads that covered the slit above nose level of the garment.

Ajir returned the smile. "She is my niece and she honors my house," he said.

Once Ajir was on board, the pilot used all the power of the three big engines on the Falcon to roar down the dirt trail of a runway. The plane leaped into the air after the shortest roll Ajir had ever experienced.

Once airborne, everybody seemed relieved. Dorri appeared with Turkish coffee, clad in her usual Persian scarf.

As she placed it on Ajir's desk, he remarked with a chuckle, "Where did you get that birka?"

"My mother prepared me well for the traveling life," She joked.

On the flight deck, the co-pilot received a call from the ground. "Aircraft over Landi Kotal please identify yourself!" The voice had a Texas accent.

The Co-pilot and Pilot exchanged looks. The Pilot switched on his COMM and replied. "This is Falcon two-eight-six-niner-hotel, enroute from Islamabad to Ashgabat."

The Texan consulted his flight log for the day to see if the aircraft was authorized to be in his airspace. "Gotcha, two-eight-six-niner-hotel. Please resume and maintain your exact flight plan sir with no further deviation. Otherwise, you *will* have company."

"Roger. Coming to heading two-niner-zero," the pilot snapped. "Have a nice day."

"Watch those mountaintops y'all," the ground controller quipped, "Out."

CHAPTER 33

Roche asked his driver to take him to the President Hotel. It was located on the outskirts of the city, a strange location, he thought for such a mainstream hotel.

The driver dropped him at the front lobby door, and drove to a limo waiting area in sight of the doorman. The hotel was finished in the finest white marble, a showplace, clean and orderly. Curious, Roche inquired about the rates and found them to be actually lower than his at the Sheraton. He guessed that was because the Sheraton is closer to the airport and much more useful to the commercial trade than this modern polished megalith.

Roche noticed a group of Saudis checking in at the main desk. He recognized a few of them as former associates and one of them as a prince. That signaled to him that the Saudis were definitely one of the parties interested in acquiring *The Hand of Mohammed*. It also told him that he was in the right place. Chris Taylor's assumption was correct. Negotiations for the sale of *The Hand* would probably take place here in the President Hotel, and soon.

His contacts Urgabat and Gronakat answered the first ring on their room phone. Presently, they appeared in the lobby, greeting Roche stiffly as "Mister Breen."

Over tea, Roche studied these two new members of his team carefully. They were certainly products of the KGB. He was worried that they would stand out like a sore thumb anywhere in public. He had to correct himself as he thought about it. After all, these men were Turkmen, while he was the one whose appearance did not fit the local mold.

Gronakat said he was familiar with the Ajir International Trading Company and its location near the airport. He had never been inside the building, but seemed familiar with its main outside features.

Roche described the lock on the elevator and explained that beyond that obstacle there would certainly be at least one unknown security feature. Urgabat seemed very confident that he could break any security code and gain entrance to any building or vault in Turkmenistan without exception. He said that most private vaults in the country were of Russian manufacture. If it was secured, it was only one of two possible types, both easily defeated with tools he already possessed. After a few more minutes of conversation Roche decided these two would do for his purposes.

The three men set a meeting in Roche's room at the Sheraton later in the day, at four pm. Roche told them that the operation would have to be carried out as soon as practical, even tonight if possible.

Gronakat offered to obtain an official government vehicle, one that would raise no concern running around the city after the eleven pm curfew. He would also arrange for 'hardware.'

When their discussion was over, the two agents went back upstairs to their room. Roche decided to stay in the lobby for a while to observe.

It paid off. The Saudis had gathered for tea in the coffee shop. He heard them chatting about their mission. His passing acquaintance with the Arabic language allowed Roche to pick up the gist of their conversation. Within minutes, he had learned that they were uninvited guests to the sale of the item, that they were prepared to pay whatever it took to get it and that they were somehow aware of his presence in Ashgabat. This last bit of information astounded Roche. How would these men know anything about him? Was Taylor pulling some sort of double cross with Roche as the fall guy? Or was someone else closer on his tail than he had reckoned, someone like Bob Steck, for instance?

After the Saudis had left the coffee shop and walked outside to take in the early winter noonday sun, Roche drifted toward the front door. He caught something familiar out of the corner of his eye. Suddenly turning to his left he stepped behind a wide marble pillar. Suleiman, the young man who had hosted him at Ajir Trading was walking straight across the lobby toward the main desk. The young man asked for the assistant manager, in English.

Roche strolled to the news kiosk and purchased a copy of *Neutralny Turkmenistan*. He walked back toward the main desk and sat with the chair back facing the desk. Suleiman approached the assistant manager, greeting him by name. "The boss is out of town. He called me today from his airplane, the showoff."

The assistant manager chuckled. "Well, I always say, if you have toys you should play with them. How can I help you Suleiman?"

Mister Ajir wants to make arrangements for a meeting here at the hotel next Monday. There will be three sets of guests with two or three in each party. He wants three of your best suites for his guests and also a meeting room, perhaps the board room?"

The assistant manager searched his book. "The board room is available, and for the meal?"

"Your best food, served in the board room," declared Suleiman. "I don't know who is coming yet, but by the sound of the boss's voice, they are very important."

The two men chatted for a while longer. Always trying to promote his hotel and in light of the fact that Suleiman had just booked thousands through him, the assistant offered Suleiman a room and meals for two nights anytime compliments of the hotel. "I will tell my wife," Suleiman answered enthusiastically. Then he smiled and added, "I should book all of our guests here."

"That's an excellent idea!" the assistant manager exclaimed. Both men laughed.

Roche had heard enough. The deal would come down next Monday. That gave him only four days at best. The Saudis, being uninvited, would make a play to trump everyone with a massive offer before Monday, he figured. He needed one last piece of information.

As Suleiman passed by Roche stood and called out to him.

"Oh, hello, Mister Breen," Suleiman replied affably, "I thought you were at the Sheraton."

"I am meeting a business acquaintance here," Roche replied. "I'm still interested in purchasing that cotton. When will Mister Ajir return?"

"He is on the way here today. He should be at our offices tomorrow. Shall I give you a call when he arrives?"

"Why, yes, please do." Roche had everything he needed.

"Until tomorrow, then," bade Suleiman as he walked toward the front door.

Roche waved his newspaper. "Cheers." He strolled slowly around the whole of the vast lobby to give Suleiman the time to drive away. When he was sure the man was gone, Roche hustled out and hailed his driver. Getting into the car, he told the driver "To the Sheraton, and quickly."

The big UH-60 helicopter landed in a cloud of sand and dust beside a tent in the middle of nowhere, Turkmenistan. As Steck waved to the pilot and moved quickly away from the prop wash, he had the feeling that the world was mostly wasteland, at least the parts he had trod lately.

He was greeted by Grundstrom, who invited him inside the large Yurta, a traditional Turkmen tent on a collapsible wooden frame covered with reeds and fel. This Yurta was rented from a local tribesman. Grundstrom chose it as a means of becoming invisible to satellites and aircraft.

Inside, Brandt and eighteen others were busy cleaning and checking weapons, loading clips and checking gear. They were packed tightly in the Yurta, but they seemed a cheerful and close-knit group. Steck wondered how they would be in combat then relaxed about it remembering the impressive training he had observed at *Free Nation's* post in Wyoming. Grundstrom set up a satellite phone for Steck, who was anxious to communicate with Langley.

An old Turkmen woman was busy laying out food and drink for the men including chicken, rice, vegetables, tea and even a few bottles of Turkmen beer. Her husband, the owner of the Yurta tended a herd of horses outside. The man was proud of his horses, a real sign of wealth in these parts. Steck chatted with the man for a few minutes, patting one of the horses on the flanks and snout. He appreciated good horseflesh and it was clear that the old Turkmen had done a good job of breeding. The man invited him to ride the steed. Steck was tempted but needed to get to business.

On the secure line, Steck received lots of new information. First, the Canadians had staged a team of specialists to the south-west of Steck's position. They were at the Afghan border, as close to Iran as possible. They were well trained in extraction of personnel from hot zones. Steck copied their co-ordinates and radio contact information. Ryall Morgan reported that the Saudis were one of the interested parties and could be a player. Tracking Ajir's airplane for the last three days, CENTCOM had reported known flights to Mosul, Teheran and Islamabad. "That would indicate," Morgan announced, "possibly the Kurds, the Iranians and the Pakistanis could be part of whatever deal Ajir was putting together."

"Great stuff," Steck acknowledged. "I'm concerned that we're late getting to Ashgabat. This thing might be over before we get there and I haven't got much for resources on the ground."

"I've got that covered, if you want to use it," Morgan replied. "Bob MacFergus has two agents on the ground in Ashgabat. They're tourists traveling on Canadian passports. They were inserted a few weeks ago, just a routine observation mission. MacFergus says they're well trained field agents and are available to you if you want them."

"Any combat experience? Steck asked.

"Yes. One of them was a Canadian army regular and has served in Iraq. The other has been under fire in a few incidents near Tora Bora."

"I'll take them," Steck replied. "How do I contact them?

"You can reach them at the President hotel in Ashgabat."

Steck was pleased to have others to work with, in case the *Free Nation* guys became unreliable. "What else do you have for me, Ryall? I would really like to have some more of our guys involved as well."

"Negative, Bob. We don't have much going on in that country and insertion now would be risky."

"I'll have to make do," Steck grumbled. "Have you got any direction what to do if I can't capture the item?"

Morgan paused. "Bob, as a last resort we have authorization to use the Predator system to conduct a strike directed by you alone. If that becomes necessary, you will notify me first. I will give you the means to initiate it. You must understand that this option is only to be used if there is no other way to keep the item from being used in the two specific scenarios we have discussed. Is that clear?"

"Clear," replied Steck.

"I think you better get to Ashgabat right away, Bob." Morgan sounded tense, but confident in his man.

"I'm on my way," Steck replied, "wish me luck."

Steck clicked off the satphone. He turned to Gunny and the others and said, "Hey guys, listen-up. We have work to do and we have our orders. We're going to Ashgabat tonight."

———————

Ajir pondered his plans for security as the Falcon flew over rugged mountains toward Dushanbe, Tajikistan. From there, the pilot would vector across the desert wastes to home base at Ashgabat.

244

The security forces ferried to Ashgabat from Yemen by Ajir's airplane were housed in a small hotel about five miles from Ajir's office. He would move them into place tomorrow, and they would keep 24 hour guard until after the sale. They would have to stay inside the building. The Government forces would get curious if armed guards appeared outside.

He wondered how soon Chris Taylor would figure out who had beaten him. Taylor was sure to try to regain his item. That's why the sale must be completed within days. Satisfied that he had it all arranged, Ajir decided to take a nap during the rest of the flight.

———

Steck communicated with his two agents at the American Embassy. They agreed to set up a room for him at the President Hotel under a name the embassy had cleared as an American tourist. They reported about their tail on Roche over the past two days. It was clear to Steck that Roche was ready to make the heist. He worried that it might already have happened.

Steck instructed the American agents to meet him at the President Hotel at seven-thirty pm sharp.

He contacted the senior Canadian agent, who was registered under the name Remick at the hotel. Steck was surprised when a woman answered. He found out they were traveling as a husband and wife, tourists from Toronto. He took their room number and told them to be available at seven-thirty pm.

Steck and Grundstrom briefed the men on the next phase of their mission. They would travel to Ashgabat in a bus acquired from a remote Turkmen army outpost two days ago. They would hold in an area near the President Hotel that was a parking area for military vehicles in transit. Steck would contact them after he had met with the two American and two Canadian agents at the hotel. A telephone call to the

American embassy arranged for lodging of Grundstrom's crew at the outskirts of the city in a hotel run by 'friendlies.'

"The rest," Steck said, "will unfold as we go along."

"What do we do after the mission is complete?" asked one of the men. "Like, how do we get out of the country?"

"There are two planned ways out, announced Steck. One is to come back here. In case that cannot be in the bus, each of you has the coordinates in your GPS. You all know how to call your friends in Masr E Sharif to come get you. The other is to make your way to a point where the Afghan, Iranian and Turkmen borders come together. I'll give you the coordinates to install as a waypoint in your GPS. They are monitoring secure channel eight sixty-six on your hand-held radios. At that location is a Canadian special services extraction team. They will get you out."

One of the men mounted a horse and rode, along with their Turkmen host to the place where the bus had been stashed. He returned in the bus with a full load of fuel, ready to travel.

As the men and equipment loaded onto the bus, Steck contemplated the final option discussed with Ryall Morgan. The Predator system was a unique tool that the CIA had used with great success for some years. It consisted of an unmanned aerial vehicle or UAV, a remotely piloted drone that carried a very special set of radar sensors and hellfire missiles mounted under the wings. The full system included a detachment of fifty support people, some at the basing point for the airplane, others in support roles elsewhere. The plane was piloted via remote control by a flight crew sitting at Langley.

Steck decided to confide in Grundstrom, but keep this final option from the men for the time being.

The bus finally rolled away from the Yurta, rumbling along a dirt road. The Turkmen horseman and his wife waved goodbye, as the man counted the cash he had earned for the past few days. It would buy a lot of horses.

A few kilometers later, they reached the M37 highway and struck out for the city of Ashgabat.

CHAPTER 34

Mohammed Al Kafajy could not remember ever feeling as anxious as he did at this moment. Several millions had been invested in hopes of making over a hundred million. Now any prospect of return was in the hands of Christian Taylor. If Taylor failed, Al Kafajy would have to fire him in order to save face. If so, he would lose the best manager he had and the only one he trusted to run the company for the benefit of the family after he died.

He had just returned from his weekly visit to the Parisian doctor who had followed his deteriorating health for several years. The news was not encouraging. A rare parasitic infection picked up as a child while swimming in the Nile had haunted him all his life. Weekly treatments with massive doses of expensive drugs kept him going for many years. Now even the latest super drugs were having less and less effect. Without some miracle, he would be dead within months, a year at best.

Al Kafajy kept the seriousness of his condition from his family and from his colleagues. His wife thought the disease was only a nuisance that her husband had to endure. Her children just thought daddy got sick every so often. Only he and his doctor knew the real story.

"A hundred million," he uttered staring at his visage in the mirror. It could provide for his family forever in one transaction. Then he would not need the Al Kafajy Trading Company.

Al Kafajy went to his study, unlocked a cabinet behind some books and withdrew a bottle of Napoleon brandy and a glass. He poured himself a stiff one, something he would never do in public being prominent in the Muslim community. He downed it in one gulp then poured another. After the third, he placed the bottle and glass back into the cabinet and locked it, replacing the books that covered the door.

He had promised Christian Taylor not to meddle in his operation, but now he felt driven by new and urgent circumstances to take every possible step to recover *The Hand of Mohammed*. He sat at his personal desk for half-an-hour lost in intense thought. Under the half-stupor induced by the brandy he finally picked up the phone and called Ahmed.

By the time Paul Roche met with his two accomplices at four pm, he had decided that they would act tonight. Certainly the Saudis would pay Ajir a visit early next morning. Their aim would be to offer him enough money to persuade him to cancel the sale. Then they could just leave town with the prize and the game would be over. Roche saw no choice but to go and recover *The Hand* before that could happen.

The two men arrived in a Turkmen government car, distinguished by symbols of the army painted on its side and the unique number plate that identified official vehicles.

Roche was impressed that Urgabat and Gronakat had also made an escape plan and that the arrangements had been completed by Chris Taylor during the day. After recovering the prize, they would drive to a spot about a hundred miles to the west. There they would be met by a small plane that would take them to Krasnovodsk on the Caspian Sea. From there, a Helicopter would ferry them two hundred miles across the Caspian to Baku, Azerbaijan where they could get a flight to Istanbul.

They spent two hours going over the details of the strike. Darkness fell over Ashgabat at about six-thirty pm this time of year. They would move at seven.

Steck and the others in the bus arrived at the vehicle parking lot about six pm. They decided to take a brief ride out to Ajir International Trading Company before dark to get a look at the place. Satellite photos already had been studied, but Steck felt that one good look would be better than a stack of pictures. When they got there, Grundstrom suggested that they leave one man to keep an eye on the place. They found a place of suitable cover and left the man with food, a warm coat, weapons and a hand-held radio.

Returning to the President Hotel, they dropped Steck then parked again at the military transfer lot just a block away.

Steck strode across the lobby in a slightly wrinkled business suit and open shirt. He looked like a businessman seeking lodging after a long day. The clock over the main desk rang seven o'clock. Steck went to the house phones and dialed the room number of the Canadians. The man who answered said he would come right down.

Steck took in the massive lobby. "Not bad," he thought.

The Canadian arrived greeting him with open arms. "So glad to see you, friend," he said, slipping Steck a passport. "One of your mates gave me this for you," he added in a whisper.

Steck returned the greeting then made small talk as he feigned fumbling in his pocket. He came up with the passport which proclaimed him as Mister George Doak. The picture was of himself as a younger man. He figured that the embassy had retrieved it from Langley out of some file shots. A visa card in the name of George Doak was tucked inside.

Steck presented the passport at the main desk and checked in. During the process, he noticed two men watching him from across the lobby. Those would be the two American agents, he reckoned. One of them came within ear shot as Steck announced to the Canadian, "Let's meet in my room seven two seven at seven-thirty." Alone in the elevator, Steck sighed relief. So far, so good, he thought.

In his room, he hurriedly ditched the suit and dressed in casual slacks, sweater and sneakers.

At seven-thirty, four people knocked at Steck's door. The introductions and briefing began immediately. The

Americans handed Steck a layout of the interior of the Ajir building. "Good work, guys," he offered. "How about security locks and the like?"

"Covered," one of the men, named Arnie said. The stuff is all pretty simple Russian made junk that I can break in seconds." He flashed a small electronic box. "You can buy these on the street in Moscow," he added.

At seven pm, Roche and his two companions left the Sheraton and drove the short distance to Ajir International Trading Company.

"Drive once around the block," ordered Roche. Gronakat took the car slowly around the four sides of the Ajir lot. Everything looked calm. Roche was surprised to see no guards or watchmen outside the place. Maybe they would be inside.

Behind a clump of decorative desert bushes, Grundstrom's man watched the government car circling the building. Since it was the only car he had seen since establishing his watch, he followed it with his small night vision scope. He figured it was some sort of government police patrol, common in Turkmenistan. The car pulled into the front parking area near the entrance of the building and parked. No one got out.

Inside the car, Roche and the men were going over their plan one last time. They had two small military-looking ABS cases to carry. One contained burglary tools, an electronic box of the type Steck had just seen and four fist sized plastique charges. The other was empty, except for the type of soft packing material normally used to protect sensitive electronic instruments for shipment. Each man carried a compact H&K assault rifle and a Beretta. Each man had pockets stuffed with extra clips for the weapons. Each man had a small arms protective vest.

When Roche was satisfied that their presence had not aroused any suspicion, he and Urgabat got out while

Gronakat drove the car clear of the entry gate and parked it along the west side of the building in a spot that would allow for a quick exit if necessary. By the time Gronakat rejoined the others, they had already gained access to the building and found to Roche's amazement and delight that it was empty. There were no guards and apparently no secondary alarms to deal with.

Roche led them to the elevator. At level B2 Urgabat jimmied the lock and the elevator kept going, stopping at B3. Roche felt better now that he saw Urgabat's expertise in action.

As the elevator door opened, Urgabat put out a hand to stop his companions. There was a group of photo cells casting laser beams across the short hallway leading to the vault. He lit a cigarette and blew smoke to show the beams more clearly. Digging in his case, he produced a small box and began pushing buttons in sequence. One by one, the laser beams disappeared.

Stepping into the hallway, Roche spied a staircase that he had not noticed during his recent tour of the facility. He reckoned it was an emergency escape in case of power failure. He cursed himself for not calculating that one would logically be there. He motioned Gronakat to check it out, go to the top and wait on the ground floor by the elevator, keeping an eye out to cover them.

Gronakat opened the door to the staircase, slipped inside using the small light strapped to his headband to illumine the stairs then gave a thumbs-up. He disappeared up the staircase.

Urgabat had already gone to work on the final obstacle. There was a keypad beside the big vault door. In seconds, he had set his box, triggered the tone pattern and smiled as they both heard the click from the relay in the lock.

Roche tried the handle. It moved easily and they were in!

Outside, the guard had clicked his transmit button three times just as the three men entered the building. Gunny recognized the signal, clicked back twice then called Steck.

"Somebody's inside the building," he said.

Steck's eyes widened. Turning to the others he asked, "You folks got a car?"

"Yes, the American agents nodded," looking puzzled.

Raising the phone to his ear, Steck shouted "Go, Gunny, we'll be right behind you!"

The Canadians were already hustling to their room down the hall. By the time Steck had grabbed the Beretta and clips from his flight bag and hustled out to the elevator with the two Americans, the Canadians came running down the hallway, loading and locking their P226 SIGs.

The elevator car indicator was still showing it to be at floor three. "Go down the stairs!" Steck shouted. The five agents hustled down eight flights of stairs, dashed out to the car and stuffed themselves in. Steck hated that he was the only one puffing short breaths.

The ungainly bus had only traveled half way to the industrial estate by the time Steck and the others caught up. He figured they were about ten minutes away. "Pass them," he ordered. The car sped around the bus and careened around a right turn accelerating down a boulevard that led straight to the site.

Gunny raised Steck on the radio. "We will come in from the east side."

"Good. We'll try to block the entrance gate," Steck replied.

"Negative," squawked the sentry. They parked on the west side of the building."

The American agent driving nodded understanding to Steck. "Gunny, fan your men to the North and south sides of the building. Leave three guys on the east with the sentry. Take cover and watch out for cross-fire! Maybe we can drive them to the east and trap them there."

"Got it," answered Gunny. He nodded to Brandt, who counted off the men and assigned them positions.

Inside, Roche had just finished packing *The Hand of Mohammed* into the transit case. He signaled to Urgabat, who started for the elevator.

Gronakat suddenly appeared in the doorway of the stairs. "Company coming!" he whispered, pointing up to the ground floor.

Deciding not to wait for the elevator the three bounded up the stairs, bursting into the office area at the front of the building. Roche called "West door!" He pointed to the exit closest to their car. Gronakat burst through the west door and took up a defensive position. Urgabat edged toward the doorway. Roche went towards the front door, trying to get a look out the widows to the parking lot.

Steck and the agents arrived, parking with their rear bumper snug against the government vehicle. Noting that it was an official vehicle, one of the American agents signaled Steck, who had taken up a position of cover behind it. "It's the Turkmen military police," he said in a stage-whisper.

Steck didn't trust that. "It could be stolen," he replied. Spying a figure on one knee near the west door, the Canadian female raised her SIG. "I've got a clear shot," she whispered.

"He's armored," called her friend.

"I see it," she signaled by pointing to her eyes.

"Take the shot," whispered Steck.

The SIG barked and the man went down immediately, blood gushing from his forehead.

"Impressive, thought Steck as suddenly fire broke out from the downed man's position and from the north door simultaneously. The two American agents skulked along the edge of the parking lot to get position on the north door. Steck signaled the driver to break off and return to the car. He circled back and lay on the ground near the cars. Steck and the Canadian girl stayed with the cars while the other Canadian headed toward the south door.

On the east side of the building were the loading doors. Urgabat saw that his companion was down. He fired twice toward the cars then hustled to the east side of the warehouse. He ran south to north pushing the electric openers of all the loading doors. The sentry on the east side panicked and began firing at the imaginary army that lay behind those doors. For effect, Urgabat set the charges from his kit, one at the south door and three at the loading doors. Roche saw it and they signaled. The bomb at the south door would provide cover for a run to the car.

Steck kept looking up the boulevard wondering where the bus was. It should be here by now, he thought as he saw the girl leave cover and race toward the west door. She dove behind a trash container about half way to the building. Shots were coming from the east and the north areas. Then two shots came from the south. Steck saw the Canadian guy fall into the light cast by a parking lot lamp post.

Steck figured there could be as many as half-a-dozen enemy inside the building, certainly no more men than could fit in the car he was using for cover. He had no way of knowing that it was just two, running from place to place setting up fire as deception.

Two shots rang out from the north doorway. There was no answering shot from the American agent. Steck feared the worst. He moved toward the man's position, keeping low. Automatic gunfire emanated from the whole east side of the building, but Steck could not tell whether it was his own guys.

A big explosion ripped off a piece of the east side of the building. Another explosion came from the south end then two more at the east side.

Suddenly a figure came running from the south side, down range of the girl. Steck tried to get a bead on him but was blocked by the cars. Two shots pinged to his right, coming from the north area. He hunkered down waiting for the chance to get the girl's attention. Her weapon and her gaze were fixed on the guy she had shot, waiting for the next one to try that doorway. The enemy that had come from the south side was now at the cars. Steck was aware of the agent that had stayed with the cars, but he could not let the enemy get either vehicle. He aimed for the gas tank of the government car and pulled off two shots.

The bus pulled in. As the men hustled out, automatic fire came from the north corner pinning them down momentarily.

Simultaneously, the car burst into flames. Out of the far side of the fireball the Americans' car sped up the street, turned right and then right again.

A figure came running out of the north door carrying a case of some sort. He ran towards the east side of the building in an effort to meet the speeding car. He went down in a hail of bullets fired from and all around the bus. Two shots thudded into the car as it sped out onto the entrance road and took off down the boulevard.

Steck made his way to the south side of the burning car. The American agent lay bleeding at the curb. "I'm okay," he said, "just a shoulder wound. The bugger got me with a knife. I'm sorry I lost the car."

After several minutes with no activity, Brandt and three men entered the building. They quickly returned signaling it was clear. In the distance sirens could be heard. Steck figured it would be the fire brigade and a lot of local police.

"Get our wounded. Everybody into the bus," He barked. Spying Grundstrom standing over the guy who had run with the case, he shouted, "Hey Gunny is he alive?"

"Affirmative, Gunny replied."

"Get the case and the guy into the bus," Steck shouted back to him. "I need two guys over here," Steck hollered standing over the dead guy by the west door. Two men hustled toward him.

"Get this body into the bus." Steck jogged to the spot where the Canadian guy went down. He was dead. He summoned men to load him and the other American agent into the bus.

The sirens sounded louder now. As they turned up the boulevard, the bus disappeared down the south road and left the industrial estate. The driver turned onto a highway and circled back to the President Hotel, stopping again in the military lot. Steck and the Canadian girl got their stuff, loaded it and re-boarded the bus, which hustled everyone out of town.

On the way, they stopped at the American embassy, where one dead American, one dead Canadian, one wounded American and the two thieves were dropped off. Steck left word that the live thief would need to be interrogated if he survived and to contact Ryall Morgan at Langley for instructions.

The bus slipped out of town, taking the M37 highway back toward the desert.

As they rode along, Gunny, Brandt and Steck tried to piece together a report about the night's activity. It certainly hadn't gone well. The thief that escaped with the embassy car must have *The Hand*, they figured. Brandt and Gunny had searched the vault and found nothing. The ABS case they had captured was just full of tools of the trade. The guy that got away must have *The Hand*. Steck knew in his heart it was Roche.

As they rode along the Canadian girl whose name was Marya sat alone, her head in her hands. Brandt came and sat beside her. "It's tough to lose a partner," he said, trying to make conversation. He was impressed with her. She was very physically fit, a well-trained agent and apparently a crack shot with a sidearm. She looked tough as nails but strangely feminine and petite. She was certainly the kind of girl that a guy like Brandt would find extremely attractive. "The skipper says you made a real good kill back there."

She looked up, catching his steel blue eyes and scarred face. The man seemed somehow attractive to her. Rubbing the back of her neck she said "It's the second friend I've lost in this operation."

"Second?" He asked.

She sighed. "One of my best friends was shot dead during the early part of this mess."

"Geez, that's tough," he responded. Where did it happen?

"In Idaho, she replied."

CHAPTER 35

Paul Roche was in desperate straits. He was driving a hot car in a part of the world he knew nothing about. He had been shot in the left wrist during his getaway. He had wrapped the wound with part of his shirt. It throbbed and hurt like blazes. He felt it was broken because he couldn't seem to move his hand.

Pulling in at the rear of the Sheraton, he covered his left side with a jacket and slipped in to get his stuff. He washed the wound and dressed it with some clean underwear and antibiotic cream from his travel kit. He could see bone and it looked shattered. With fresh clothes, his passports, credit cards and money, he slipped back to the car and sped away. A city road map of Ashgabat taken from his room was all he had to navigate.

Outside the city to the west, he pulled over and studied the map. He recalled that three hundred miles to the west was the Caspian Sea, four hundred miles to the east was Afghanistan and fifty miles to the south was Iran. He couldn't remember what was to the north but thought it might be Uzbekistan.

Roche knew that he would have only the rest of the night before ditching the car. Driving in an American embassy car in daylight would be suicide. Buying gas would probably lead to arrest also. The car had a full tank of gas, so he figured he would not run out before having to ditch the car. The question was which way to go? He had no idea how to make contact with the airplane that his former partners had arranged or its exact location. He did not know the way to drive to Krasnovdsk and had no idea where the helicopter would be waiting.

Roche wanted to call Taylor on his satphone, but was now wary of contact with Chris. Who were the guys that jumped him and more important who were they working for? If it was Taylor a call would only lead his henchmen to the prize and would be his death warrant. Were they Ajir's men? He would like to think they were Ajir's. Was it Steck and the CIA? Probably not, since Roche knew they had few or no assets in this backwater place. What he had just faced was a small army.

Roche drove another ten minutes, where he spotted a place to pull over shielded from the road by shrubs and bushes. He took a minute to open the case. By the glow of the interior lights he opened the gold mesh sack and studied the figurine. It was delicate, exquisitely cast and colored with layers of vibrant but semi-opaque color. "So," he thought, "this is what all the fuss is about." It didn't look too special to him and certainly had no weird aura or anything like that. Just a nice piece of ceramic kitsch, like the stuff they sell in Mexican bazaars. He carefully placed it back in the sack, then the transit case.

At that point he realized indecision would kill him just as surely as running in the wrong direction. He called Taylor.

"Taylor," a sleepy voice answered.

"It's Roche," the voice on the line declared.

Chris sat up in bed, trying to rub sleep from his eyes and clear his brain. "Roche is that you? Where are you?"

"Near Ashgabat," Roche replied. "I have the prize."

"That's wonderful!" Taylor sounded sincere. "Are you following the path we set up?"

"Negative," he answered. "The others are dead. I've been shot. I'm just west of the city in a hot car and I have no idea how to get out of this place."

Instantly awake, Taylor tried to take it all in. After a moment, he said, "Go south on Highway L34. It's a tough mountain road but it leads to the Iranian border station. I'll have someone meet you there."

Roche shivered. "Iran? Are you nuts?"

"No, Roche, I'm not nuts," declared Taylor. "We have a branch office in Teheran and one in Mashhad. My guys can get you through Iran to Turkey. It's the only way without traveling with someone who has Russian ties. That's why you were traveling with the two guys I sent you, right? You would not make it through Azerbaijan alone."

"Who the hell jumped me?" Roche asked.

"How should I know," replied Taylor, puzzled by the question. "Ajir has security people."

"There was a pretty big crowd of them. I don't know whether to trust you, friend."

"The way I see it Roche you have no choice. Now stop this hallucinating and get going south. Call me in three hours." Taylor clicked off.

Ajir woke to the telephone ringing. The clock by his bed said it was midnight. "This is the National Police in Ashgabat, the voice announced. Please come to your office right away."

Ajir tensed. "Is there a problem, sir?" he said.

"There has been a fire. Please come at once."

"Yes of course," Ajir said, holding the phone with one hand and reaching for his clothes with the other. "I'll be there in ten minutes."

As Ajir raced toward his office thoughts ran wild through his head. If it was just a fire, the vault was most likely safe. Insurance would cover the loss of merchandise and repairs to the building. But what if it was more than that?

When he swung the Mercedes coupe into the lot at Ajir International Trading Company, he was horrified. The majority of the building was gone. Police tape cordoned off several areas in the lot with pools of blood evident. It looked like a war zone.

His first thought was the security force he had brought in from Yemen. Had they double-crossed him? He was shaking as he went through the usual questions from the police. At one point in what seemed an unending array of bureaucratic fumbling by the police examiner, he slipped away and made his way down to level B3.

The color drained completely from Ajir's face. The vault door was open. The prize was gone.

It took an hour to feign patience and out-wait the leader of police. Finally Ajir was allowed to go home with the provision that they would continue in the morning at police headquarters.

Ajir raced to the hotel where his militia was housed. They were sound asleep and obviously had not left the place that night. He drove home slowly, running scenarios through his mind. He decided it was either Al Kafajy or the Americans but could not figure out which of them could have done it.

Too angry to sleep, Ajir spent the rest of the night on the telephone calling everyone he knew that might be able to help retrieve his property.

Chris Taylor called a friend and colleague in Mashhad, Iran. They talked in generalities, since the Iranians often eavesdropped telephone conversations. After exchanging innocent small talk that signaled the need to communicate, they hung up. A few minutes later, secure links opened and they spoke freely.

When they were through, Chris's friend Irad went to his car and started the fifty kilometer trip to the border.

Taylor called Mister Al Kafajy in Paris. "The item is no longer in the hands of our enemy," he announced.

"Do you have it?" Al Kafajy asked.

"N-not yet, sir, it's in transit. Our people will have it within a day."

"Very good, Christian," he declared. "Stay in touch."

Taylor then called Roche and told him that a man named Irad would find him at the Turkmen side of the border station.

Roche was half way to the border, high in the mountains. As he drove the winding road, only an occasional big truck passed by. He fought to stay awake, exhausted from the night's activity and weak from loss of blood. His wrist felt like it was going to explode. He checked the transit case. It was riding comfortably in the seat beside him.

Suddenly the car made a loud scraping noise. Realizing that he had just dozed off and the car was riding on the shoulder of the road next to a sheer drop of thousands of feet, he jerked the vehicle back onto the road and stopped. He got out and sucked in the cold night mountain air trying to force his senses to wake. Back in the car, he spied a turnout a few hundred meters ahead. He decided to pull off for a twenty minute nap.

Mohammed Al Kafajy summoned Ahmed. The mysterious man appeared at the door of the boss's study.

"Christian's men have recovered our prize from those who took it from us," the boss announced.

Ahmed extended his palms upward and rolled his eyes. "Allah willed it." He said.

"Perhaps we can cancel the small operation you have under way," Al Kafajy declared.

"I believe we should keep it in place for the moment," Ahmed replied. "When you hold the prize in your hand we can re-consider."

"I suppose you're right, Ahmed." Al Kafajy looked pensive.

"I am right, sir." Ahmed said simply. "We must always have a back up plan, in case of future lapses."

Back at the Yurta in the desert Steck and the others caught some sleep. They would be extracted back to Masr E Sharif in the morning. While the others slept, Steck couldn't help mulling where Roche might have gone with the item.

More than ever he wanted the chance to take out his adversary.

Steck decided he would go back to Amman and start again. He would have *The Hand of Mohammed* and would put Roche away once and for all or blow his career trying.

CHAPTER 36

Bob MacFergus and three of his agents spent the morning at the FBI in New York. They briefed Susan Deet, Greg Liss, Ryall Morgan and Mort Lindsley about the state of their relations in the Muslim community and ways that American agencies could carry out the generation-long job of penetration.

The Muslim community in Toronto is the largest and most dynamic in North America. Visitors to parts of the city would think they were in the Middle East if it were not for the obvious prosperity of the community as part of democratic Canada.

In Toronto Muslims, Christians and Jews work side by side and over time have become more mutually tolerant, even to the point of cautious friendship.

The rate of growth in Toronto's Muslim population is much greater than the other ethnic groups that make up this great melting pot of a city.

After 911 many Muslims actually emigrated from the United States to Canada. It offered them prosperity without the shameful persecution that ignorant Americans seem so ready to embrace.

Against this backdrop of Muslims as happy and prosperous ordinary citizens, those who would destroy the very freedom that feeds the Toronto community find it easy to fit in. Hundreds, if not thousands of wannabe or ex-terrorists live in the midst of the larger law-abiding community. They blend in if you look in from the outside, but they stick out like a sore thumb to those inside the community.

Robert MacFergus had wisely courted and mined the Toronto Muslim community for a generation. His organization boasted more Arabic speaking agents than any in the western world. Within his ranks Pakistanis held positions on the same team with Muslim Indians, Shiites with Sunnis, Yazeris with Uighers.

Ryall Morgan and Mort Lindsley envied their Canadian colleague MacFergus for these connections. They wished they could boast that same kind of structure, especially in the large Muslim communities of America like Detroit, Los Angeles, Chicago and New York.

Susan and Greg drank in all the CSIS people had to say. They had learned much today but the day was not over. They were scheduled to fly from New York up to Manchester later in the day. They had an appointment next morning with Doctor Wigglesworth and members of his staff to dig deeper into the history of *The Hand of Mohammed*.

It was noon before Morgan received the call from Steck. The four American agents huddled around the speaker phone in a small conference room. MacFergus joined them a few moments after the call began. By the time he joined them, Steck was just giving the bad news. MacFergus asked to speak with his agent, Marya Lukianov. She gave a terse account of the action ending with apologies for losing a partner.

Steck broke in. "I want you all to know that Marya was a hero last night. She took out one of the three enemy combatants we encountered and showed skill, cooperation and valor under fire."

"Thank you for that Bob," MacFergus responded. "I'll see that she gets full recognition at CSIS."

Morgan stepped in. "Bob, you are sure the guy that has the item is Paul Roche?"

"As sure as the sunrise," Replied Steck. "Our guys at the embassy in Ashgabat confirmed a few minutes ago that a certain Mister Jacob Breen has gone missing from the Sheraton. Jacob Breen is the alias that Roche was using in Amman. I'm certain he's our man."

"Where do you think he's headed, Mister Bob?" It was Lindsley.

"I wish I knew, Mort." Steck had no clue. "He could go west across the Caspian to Azerbaijan, East to Uzbekistan, even south to Iran for all I know."

"Do we have any contacts or any pull with the Turkmen border patrol?" asked MacFergus.

"I'll check with the embassy in Ashgabat on that," Morgan replied.

"They should feel a stake in this, since we got two of their agents shot last night, one of them killed. On top of that, the guy who did it stole one of their cars," said Steck.

"Roger that Bob," Morgan replied. "Let's talk again as soon as you get to Afghanistan. By the way, Randy Pullin has asked to meet me. I'm going to see him at Langley late this afternoon."

"Tell him that his men have been a great help, Ryall. I'm interested in why he wants to parley." Steck wondered what that rascal was up to.

"I'll let you know, Bob." Morgan clicked off.

Roche woke with a start as a big truck loaded with bleating sheep lumbered past. The wind wake of the speeding truck shook the small sedan. He checked his watch. He was alarmed to see he had slept for nearly two hours.

The dim light of pre-dawn cast an aura of grayish pink along the edges of the mountaintops to the east. Roche knew he was now late. He started the car to warm up the engine, set the brake and got out to pee before hitting the road. As he tried to reach across himself to pull the door latch open with his right hand the pain in his left wrist caused an involuntary scream. He wanted to look at the wound, but did not want to waste time trying to dress it again.

Soon Roche was racing toward the border. He had no idea how far he still had to drive. He hoped he would get there before Taylor's friend became sick of waiting. It startled him when he rounded a bend in the road to see the border station just a few hundred yards away.

The station was set up with two identical buildings separated by a parking area. The sign on the first building proclaimed it was "Government of Turkmenistan Passage Control," and the other "Islamic Republic of Iran."

The entire area was empty except for several government vehicles and one large truck with tape sealing the doors apparently confiscated by one government or the other.

In front of the Turkmen building sat a Volvo sedan with the engine running. A tall slim man stood in front of the Volvo smoking a cigarette. Roche slowed his car and initiated a turn toward the parking lot. The man stomped out his cigarette and waved, signaling Roche to pull up. Roche winced as he reached across to let down the passenger window.

"Are you Mister Breen?" the tall man asked.

"Yes, I am Jacob Breen," Roche replied.

The man squatted to bring his eyes to the level of the window. "I am pleased to meet you, Mister Breen. My name is Irad Arbani. Please take the car to the back of these buildings and park it. I will park next to you. We will transfer everything from your car."

Roche did as he was told. Irad opened the trunk of the Volvo and packed Roche's stuff including the ABS case.

"That's a bad looking wound you have there," he commented closing the trunk lid.

"Yes, I think the wrist may be smashed," Roche said truthfully, "it hurts like blazes."

"We will get some medical attention for you soon," Irad said almost absently. "Give me the keys for your car."

"How are we going to get through this place?" Roche asked as he handed them over.

"Just wait here." Irad went around to the front of the Turkmen building. Roche watched for him to re-appear. He was startled to see Irad emerge ten minutes later from the Iranian building. He carried a slip of yellow paper.

Irad came across the lot and got in the driver's side of the Volvo. He said softly, "Now we go."

Irad drove the Volvo around the building and back onto the road. As they passed the Iranian building, he waved. Roche could not see anyone behind the big front window but assumed Irad was waving to a border guard inside the building.

They drove in silence for ten minutes. Curiosity finally forced Roche to ask what had just happened back at the border station.

Irad showed the very slightest smile. "I traded the car for Turkmen silence. I traded money for Iranian silence. Mister Jacob Breen is unknown to the Islamic Republic of Iran. He was never here. Mister Jacob Breen never left Turkmenistan, at least not through this border crossing."

"Very impressive," said Roche sincerely.

"Do not worry about anything, Mister Breen. You are Mister Taylor's guest in Iran. That means you are also my guest in Iran. First, we will get medical attention for your arm. Then we will transport you safely to Turkey. There, you will be on your own."

Roche spent the time it took to drive to Mashhad thinking of what to do once he was in Turkey, if he ever got to Turkey. "One step at a time," he told himself.

Colonel Randy and Saleem arrived in Washington on a commercial flight from Denver. Pullin was out of uniform, his tall frame dressed in a western style suit that would blend-in around Denver but looked out of place in the east. The gray cloth was cut with wide lapels outlined in darker gray piping. The shirt boasted pearl snaps for buttons and white-on-white embroidered designs crowning dual vest pockets with big flaps. The pants accommodated a wide western belt and oversize silver buckle with a big piece of garnet in the middle. Tooled leather western boots rounded out the garb. He had discreetly left the Stetson at home. Saleem wore brown polyester, blue shirt and tie and his customary turban. They did not go unnoticed, even in Dulles International Airport.

They drove to Langley in a taxi via the parkway. At the main gate, they were detained while the guards performed their customary duties. At length, Steck's secretary, Mary appeared. She signed for them as their escort and led them through corridors with polished floors to a conference room. Mary then called Ryall Morgan's office.

"Hi Rachel, honey, please let Mister Morgan know that his guests are in Conference room three."

Mary stayed, making small talk with the two men until Ryall Morgan arrived. She signed the passes that the two visitors carried then Morgan signed as receiving them. Handing the passes back to them, Morgan quipped, "I am now your escort, gentlemen. Do not leave my sight please."

Morgan offered his hand which was vigorously shaken by each of the men. They all sat, while Morgan shuffled some files. The folder on top was titled 'Free Nation File / Morgan / Unclassified.' Pullin wondered what would be in such a file. He wondered even more what might be in the file marked 'Classified' if there was one.

Morgan began, "I spoke with Bob Steck this morning. He asked me to let you know how much he appreciates all your help."

"Thank you," answered Pullin. "I had a chat with my man Grundstrom this morning as well. He wants to see this thing through. He feels a personal stake in it since he and his guys took a lot of fire last night."

Morgan acknowledged Pullin with a nod. "So, Gentlemen, why have you come so far today to speak with me?" Morgan wanted them to lead.

Pullin sat up. "I came today to introduce you to my friend Saleem. He is an expert on the Muslim countries and has been of great service to me and to my organization in the present operation. I thought you might like to hear his take on the whole mess."

"Why sure I would," Morgan replied, "any information we can gather is appreciated."

Saleem gave a one hour dissertation on *The Hand of Mohammed*, its influence on Muslim thought through the ages, a history of the four groups that should be keenest to gain control of it and the reasons why. Morgan took notes. Pullin stayed quiet.

When the briefing was complete, Morgan summed up. "So, Saleem, you believe that the candidates to buy the item are the Kurds, the Saudis, the Iranians and the Taliban."

"That's correct, Mister Morgan. I believe you should concentrate on those organizations if you want to get *The Hand of Mohammed* back." Saleem was very confident of his conclusions.

"I want to thank you for coming here today and for the thoughtful information. I assure you we will act on it." Morgan was genuinely impressed.

"And now, I would like to present a theory as to where Paul Roche is right now and where he's heading," said Randy Pullin.

"Go ahead, Mister Pullin." Morgan shuffled the files again.

Pullin noticed that there was another file that was titled 'Muhammed Saleem Rafiq.' Pullin paused. He was amazed that Morgan had a file on Saleem. He recovered his composure after a moment. "I believe that Roche went to Iran. He didn't have any knowledge of the geography on the ground. He had a stolen car that had limited range without risking discovery. The shortest route out of Turkmenistan is straight to the Iranian border. His accomplices have offices in Iran and could arrange for his safe conduct."

Saleem nodded agreement with Pullin's theory as he spoke.

"That's an interesting theory," said Morgan, "we'll give it some thought."

Pullin was not used to anyone questioning his judgment. "Well where else would he go?" he asked.

Morgan was not going to share any theories with someone from outside the agency. "That's a good question," he said simply.

Pullin had hoped he could join the bandwagon and be allowed to participate. The reason for this trip was to test that. He was failing and he didn't like it. "That's the problem with you guys," he said, trying to smile. "You always suck information and never give any."

Morgan stood up. He elected not to respond to Pullin's complaint. He was not the one trying to gain influence. "Gentlemen," he announced, "it's time to call it a day. I'm grateful for your input and I will not forget where it came from." As he spoke he gestured toward the door.

Susan and Greg caught a flight to Manchester after the briefing with MacFergus in New York. On the drive from Manchester to Dartmouth College in Hanover, New Hampshire Susan asked Greg how "things" were going.

Greg wanted to appear okay. "Everything's okay Susie," he lied. Then he added, "I'm glad you're with me though. Carole and I were lovers on the Dartmouth campus. The place brings back a flood of memories that are painful."

At least he was being honest with himself she thought.

They rode in silence for a while. Susan sensed he could wallow in self-pity for the rest of the day. Better he should get it out now so tomorrow's meeting could be more productive. He's being maudlin, she thought, like a typical little boy. Still, she couldn't resist the opportunity to mother him.

Susan saw a turnout in the road ahead. She slowed the car, pulled off and stopped. Turning to Greg, she said softly,

"I'm here for you Greg." Looking into his eyes, she added, "Whatever it takes, I'm here to help you through this."

He kissed her. It was not just a peck on the cheek. She started to resist, then reminded herself what she had just said, so she decided to let it happen. Inside she felt a mixture of panic and satisfaction. The panic she understood. The satisfaction took her totally by surprise. She returned the kiss then after a moment broke it off.

After an awkward silence, they both spoke at once. "Whoa," she said. "Sorry," he said.

They finished the drive to Hanover in silence. They checked in at the Holiday Inn. About midnight, Susan's room phone rang. "Can we talk?" Greg asked.

"At breakfast," she mumbled through half-sleep. Greg hung up. Thirty minutes later, Susan sat sipping coffee and trying to sift her feelings. She wished the operation had remained just a domestic one to find Grayson's killer and track down a rogue agent.

CHAPTER 37

Irad took Roche to a public clinic in Mashhad in broad daylight. Roche felt very uneasy about this exposure and told him so.

"Please don't worry, Jacob. The doctor who runs this clinic is my brother. There will be no problem, believe me." Irad spoke softly with a kind of re-assuring tone.

"Okay," Roche replied, "I trust you, Irad," He lied.

The doctor showed no emotion, just went to work cleaning up the wound and trying to assess the damage to Roche's bones. He spoke in Farsi. Irad translated to English. After a couple of hours, images revealed that Roche was lucky. The bullet had chipped the radius bone just above the wrist. There was no sign of the bullet, so it must have skipped out of the wound. The doctor explained that the bone chip was causing most of the pain. Otherwise, the wound was superficial and would heal completely over time. He removed the chip, stitched and dressed the wound and wrapped it tightly with expandable cloth. He fitted a sling and gave Roche some pain killers. Roche offered to pay but the man smiled at his brother and declined.

It was noontime when they left the clinic. Irad stopped the car as the call to prayer blared from minarets all around them. "Just be patient for a while," counseled Irad, the prayers are mandatory."

"I'm familiar with this," replied Roche. "I worked in the middle east for many years."

After prayers, Irad drove straight to his own home outside the city where the sloping hills rose toward the mountains. His wife had prepared a meal of rice, lamb and Persian flat bread with yogurt, fruits and coffee. After a hearty meal and the medical attention Roche felt much better. He was gradually learning to trust Irad and was grateful for his help.

"You are a lucky man Jacob," remarked Irad during dinner. "My brother told me that if the bullet had hit just an inch below you would face serious reconstructive surgery."

Roche nodded but did not feel lucky yet. He would feel lucky when or if he ever got back to Mexico. For now, his plan was to accept the help he could get but always be ready to go it alone if that became necessary.

After dinner, Irad led Roche to a small room at the back of the house. It had two small windows that looked out at the mountains. There was a bed, a chair and a small table. Irad brought Roche's flight bag and the ABS case containing *The Hand of Mohammed*, placing them in the room. He collected Roche's soiled clothes and gave him a robe. He led Roche down a short hallway to a large bathroom. It boasted both Persian and European toilets, a bidet and a shower. Thirty minutes later, Roche was showered, clothed in clean underwear and sound asleep in his room.

At six pm, Irad knocked at the door. "Please get dressed, Jacob," he said. "Chris Taylor will call us at six-thirty."

Roche dressed quickly. Before leaving his room, he opened the ABS case to check on its contents. *The Hand* was whole and undamaged by the trip so far. He carefully replaced the packing material and closed the case.

The conversation with Taylor was short and to the point. He instructed them to take the prize to the Al Kafajy office in Teheran, where it would be placed in safe keeping. He asked Irad to take care of Mister Breen for at least a few weeks. The purpose of this was twofold. First, the trail to Mister Breen would have become quite cold for all those who sought him. Second, the last few miles to Turkey would have to be through the mountains on foot, so Breen would need the use of all his limbs. He would be met by friends who would help him carry the prize to Istanbul, where Taylor would meet him.

With their instructions clear, the two men spent an evening in lively chat about many subjects. They ate and slept. Next morning they set out for Teheran in Irad's Volvo.

Ajir spent the morning immersed in salvaging what he could of his company's headquarters. Whenever there was a break from Insurance business, Police business and concerns about contracts that would have to be shifted to the Mashhad office Ajir was on the phone with his contacts all around the country. His effort was to find the man who had made off with his most valued item of inventory.

A break came late in the day. One of his contacts had acquired knowledge of a car being broken up for salvage by a garage near the border with Iran. The contact was told to go there and find out what he could. Hours later, the man called. He had purchased the papers and some parts of the car from the thieves. The car was registered to the American Embassy in Ashgabat. There was blood on the inside driver's door panel. There were several bullet holes in the car.

Ajir was puzzled. Why would the Americans be interested in the item? Why would they even know about it? Did the Americans interrupt the thieves? Was that the reason for the fire fight in the parking lot? If it was the Americans, they would not have gone to Iran, the last place an American agent would go. That would mean that the thieves had stolen the embassy car, either at the scene or from the embassy.

Ajir finally concluded the real enemy had to be Al Kafajy. His best plan would be to go after Al Kafajy's offices in Iran, beginning with the one in Mashhad since it was closest to the border.

Late into the night Ajir worked his satphone, making arrangements to go after his prey. Finally, he called his pilot. "Get the crew together," he instructed, "we will fly to Teheran tomorrow."

Randy Pullin arrived at the post in Wyoming next morning by helicopter from The Martin Ranch in Boulder. Saleem had stayed east to keep an ear to the ground through his circle of contacts in the northeastern United States.

Back in uniform, Colonel Randy called a meeting of his task force and set the plan for the next few days. He was convinced that Roche and *The Hand of Mohammed* were in Iran. Over four decades *Free Nation* had established and maintained lots of contacts in Iran. He declared to his team that all resources were to be applied in Iran to find Roche and the item he carried. This would be the standing order until they found him or determined with certainty that he was not there.

Pullin spoke with Gunny Grundstrom and Brandt via satphone. "Where is Steck and where is he going next?" He asked.

"Steck's heading back to Amman tonight," Grundstrom replied. "He offered us a ride to Istanbul through Insurlik on a military hop."

"Go with him as far as Insurlik," Colonel Randy ordered, "then go to our friends in Van and check in with me."

"Van?" questioned Grundstrom, "that's one of the worst boondocks in Turkey."

"I believe that Roche is in Iran," said Pullin. "If I'm right, the best way to get him out of the country would be through the mountains in the north-west, beyond Tabriz. Just wait a few days in Van. I may want you to penetrate the area near Khoy. Brandt knows the area."

Grundstrom glanced at Brandt, who was nodding assent. He knew the area well from being part of three previous incursions by *Free Nation* operatives.

"Why not cover Maku as well?" Gunny asked. He was also familiar with the area.

"The highway at Maku is too busy," said Colonel Randy. "I think it would be Khoy, but I'll think about it. Maybe we need to cover both."

Grundstrom hesitated then said, "Colonel, are we after the guy or the goods?"

"Both the guy and the goods, declared Pullin. Do you think they will separate the guy and the goods?"

"Wouldn't you? Grundstrom asked. "Al Kafajy has at least three offices in Iran. If Roche is there wouldn't they separate the goods and ship them via normal channels?"

Pullin had to admit that was possible. "Maybe so Gunny," he said. "We'll try to cover that base if we can."

"A tough job," offered Grundstrom. "Brandt and I will hold up this end. If that snake tries to come our way, we'll have him."

Randy Pullin thought long and hard after his talk with Grundstrom. He concluded that Free Nation needed to raid Al Kafajy to get their hands on the prize. A plan began to form in his head.

At eight-thirty am Susan and Greg knocked at the door of Professor Wigglesworth. After several knocks, the professor himself finally came to the door. He looked confused and upset.

"I'm sorry Mister Liss and, er...."

"Susan Deet," she offered.

"Yes, of course, Deet," the professor seemed really distracted. "We cannot meet today. I'm awfully sorry to have you travel all this way but it's not possible today. Can I come to Washington, perhaps next week?"

Greg looked at Susan then at Wigglesworth. "Is something wrong, sir? Is your wife okay?"

"We're fine, Liss, just fine. Something's come up, something unavoidable. Please give me a call later." As he said this, Wigglesworth tried to close the door.

278

Greg felt Susan's hand poke his side. "Okay, professor," she said, "no problem. We'll try to call you later." She pushed Greg's thigh, a signal to withdraw.

"Very well then," the Professor said, "awfully sorry." The door closed.

"What's going on?" Greg asked in a low voice, as they walked back over the walk that led to the campus quadrangle.

"Just keep walking," Susan said. When they were out of earshot of the big house and in the midst of the campus, she added, "Something is badly out of place. All the shades are drawn at Wigglesworth's. That's not Missus Wigglesworth's style. I thought I saw a figure in the hall just behind the professor but to one side. I think they are being held by someone."

"If that's the case, we have to do something right away!" Greg's eyes showed his concern for the old professor.

They had reached their car. "Let's talk this through," Susan suggested. They got in and weighed their options. They decided to circle in the car to observe what could be seen from the vehicle. They found a vehicle behind the big house that was way out of place in the campus environment. It was a subtly up-armored Mercedes 450. On the next block, they observed two guys in a parked Chevy sedan. It had the look of a stakeout. All else seemed quiet.

Susan pulled the car to the curb out of sight of the Chevy. "Those guys look like cops," she said. Greg suggested they check with the local police. Susan thought better of it. They decided to call Lindsley.

Mort Lindsley answered at his desk. His secretary was off for the day so he was a bit grumpy at answering calls rather than getting work done.

"Mort, this is Susan." She quickly explained the situation.

"Hold on, Susie," Mort responded. "I'll be a minute."

Susan had parked along the north side of the quadrangle in a place where they could keep an eye on the professor's house.

"Hey Susie, have a look at that," Greg pointed toward the front door of the big house. There was a woman at the door. "Hand me the camera."

Susan reached in the back with one hand, holding the satphone to her ear with the other. She found and handed the camera to Greg, who zoomed the lens to focus on the front door. "It's Missus Wigglesworth," Greg said, "she's talking with a student."

Susan handed Greg the phone and took a look through the camera lens. "Hey, that's her housekeeper. I remember from my last visit." Susan snapped three quick frames.

The door closed and the housekeeper walked back to the quadrangle looking rather perplexed.

"Susie?" It was Mort Lindsley on the phone.

"No, this is Greg. Susie's right here." He handed her the phone.

"Hi," Susan said.

"Susie, we just checked with the Hanover Police. They do not know of any stakeout and no private detectives have filed with them today. I suggest you stay there and keep an eye on things. Do you think the Wigglesworths are in danger?"

"It's hard to tell," Susan answered. "The professor seemed rattled when he answered the door. We have just observed his wife at the door. She looks unharmed."

Mort gave Susan contact information for the local police along with the name of the officer he had contacted. "Call him, Susie and keep them in the loop. If there's trouble, they are the only ones in a position to help."

Susan and Greg watched for about an hour. The Hanover police sent a cruiser by to get and run identification on the registrations of the two vehicles. They reported to Susan that the Chevy was a rental from Manchester, but the

Mercedes was registered to a man named Ahmed Karabbi of New York City.

About noontime, three men left the Wigglesworth house and drove off in the Mercedes. They were followed by the Chevy. As they turned onto I-91 south, the Vermont State police put them under surveillance. When the Mercedes reached eighty miles-per-hour, Vermont troopers in two cruisers stopped them for a speeding violation then reported the identities of the three men. They were all citizens of Saudi Arabia. One was traveling on a diplomatic passport. They were issued a warning and released.

Susan and Greg decided to get some lunch then pay the professor another visit.

CHAPTER 38

Ajir was invited to dinner at the President Hotel by the Saudis who had hoped to visit his now destroyed office. He accepted because he wanted to find out what role they were playing in the events concerning *The Hand of Mohammed*. They expressed sorrow over his misfortune then asked if he still had a certain antiquity in his possession. He decided to see their offer. "It is still available," he answered.

The Prince spoke. "The item is the rightful property of the Kingdom," he asserted. "It was taken from us many years ago and to our knowledge had been lost until recently. If the item can be returned by you directly to the Kingdom, our gratefulness would be in the range of one billion dollars." The Prince paused to search Ajir's eyes. Ajir never broke his steady gaze. The Prince ended with, "If it is not returned to us, our wrath will amount to many times that value."

Ajir thanked them politely and said that their generous offer would be considered. Inside, he was seething. 'A billion!' he thought. If he only had the item, he would close the deal right now. After a pause, he said "There is a small problem, gentlemen. During the fire at my office last evening, the item went missing. I have men searching the remains of the building. As soon as the item is found, I will notify you and we can resume the transaction. Due to red tape with the authorities, this may take some time. It may be as long as three or four weeks. I assure you it will be found and that you will be the first considered."

The Prince's eyes narrowed. "We expect to be the *only* ones considered for which we will add an additional one-hundred million. That is the only offer and the best. Do you agree?"

Ajir swallowed hard. "I agree."

On his way home, Ajir rang the hotel where his militiamen were housed. "I expect to be flying to Teheran tomorrow morning," he announced to their leader, Hakim.

"Pick three of your best men. Send the rest to Mashhad by bus. Be sure they enter Iran as tourists. We can pack their weapons on my airplane. You and the three men will accompany me to Teheran as body guards."

Irad pulled his Volvo into the parking garage of Al Kafajy Trading Company in Teheran. It was just south east of the Doshan Tappei airbase.

Roche saw two fighter planes taking off from the air base as they passed by the end of the runway. They bore Iranian markings but they looked like Chinese F8's. Roche figured guys like Steck would love to know that. They probably did anyway.

Inside the building, Irad showed Roche to his home for the next few weeks. It was a small apartment that customers and visiting company brass used on occasion. It was comfortable enough, but lacked windows and only had one door. Roche thought it felt like house arrest. He was not naive enough to think that the place was for his security. It was more like an easy way for them to keep a lid on him. Still, it had a well stocked kitchen, fresh linen, plenty of books, satellite TV and even a bottle of scotch.

Once he was settled, Irad came and asked him for the ABS case. Roche knew that would happen but he still felt like a piece of his security had been taken away. Ostensibly the reason was to pack it away in a vault. Roche wondered if it would simply be shipped to some safe haven, which might render him superfluous.

Irad introduced Roche to the branch manager. His name was Khazeh, which Roche pronounced 'Casey.' He was a tall and dark Persian with genteel manners and believable eyes. Roche liked him. Khazeh gave Roche a list of services he could expect, including maid service twice a week, his choice of fresh cooked meals or self-made, a companion to walk with him if he wanted to go outside although they preferred he stay in as much as possible, and female companionship anytime he asked for it.

Roche decided it would be best if he took exercise just twice a week, in the evening when he could use darkness as a cover and that no female companionship would be required. He asked that one meal per day be furnished and that otherwise he would cook for himself as desired. Roche was tempted by all the perks, but knew he would be respected if he showed personal restraint.

The three men shared a meal together. Irad announced over coffee and a sweet desert pudding that he would be leaving to go back to Mashhad. They said their good-byes and Irad drove off. Khazeh went home for the day an hour later.

After Khazeh was gone, Roche tried his apartment door. It was unlocked. He stepped out into the hallway. There was an armed guard at the end of the hallway, where it opened into the office area. The guard smiled and waved. Roche tried to converse with the man in English. He seemed not to understand. He decided not to try other means yet. He smiled broadly to the man and said, "House arrest, eh?" The man smiled back, offering him a cigarette. Roche declined then re-entered the apartment and locked the door.

Susan and Greg dialed the professor's number. He answered. "Hello professor," said Greg. "Now that your guests are gone, will you see us?"

"I – I'd rather not right now," The professor still sounded shaky.

"I think you should," Greg asserted with a slightly raised voice, "or maybe we should ask a different FBI team to pay you a visit."

"When would they visit?" Wigglesworth sounded wary.

"It will be today sir, either the two of us whom you know, or a team of strangers who may decide to search your house. Have you ever had to clean up after one of our search teams, professor?"

"Okay, Liss," the professor sounded whipped. Come ahead whenever you are ready.

"We're right outside, sir." Greg clicked off and turned to Susan. "Let's pack our weapons, in case those visitors left a companion."

Missus Wigglesworth let them in without speaking. She led them to the study, invited them to sit and with a look close to contempt said, "The Professor will see you shortly."

"How are your orchids these days?" asked Greg, trying to act cheery.

Missus Wigglesworth fixed a stark gaze on Greg. "Today is not a good day for my orchids, Mister Liss. They are far too delicate to withstand for long the indignity of ill-bred men." The old woman assumed an air of purpose and strode out of the room.

"Well aren't we tense today," Susan said pointedly. Greg got her meaning.

"Fear not, Susie," he quipped, "she's only attacking the men."

Susan smirked.

Professor Wigglesworth entered the room dressed in Dockers, mocs and an open white shirt that sort of matched his beard. He looked strung-out.

"Good day, professor," Greg began.

The old man nodded. He sat in a plain wooden chair that faced them both. "What do you want to know?"

Susan nodded deference to Greg. He acknowledged it. "Let's start with your visitors this morning, sir. Who were they and what did they want?"

The old man answered in a low voice without his usual animated tone. "They were representatives of the Kingdom of Saudi-Arabia and their purpose was to acquire knowledge of *The Hand of Mohammed*, its whereabouts and suggestions as to how it might be returned to their country from which it was displaced a long time ago."

"And what did they learn from you, sir?" Greg asked.

"They learned that it had been lodged first in Iraq then America and that it is now in the hands of robbers in the Middle East."

"Did they know or did you tell them where in the Middle East it is now held?" Greg spoke simply and without emotion, as if he was mimicking the professor.

"They asked me and I told them truthfully that I don't know for sure but I thought it might be in Amman." Wigglesworth's studied monotone seemed to be infecting him. He looked as if he were about to doze-off.

"Professor," Susan interrupted, "did they pay you for your time this morning?"

"Yes they did," he replied.

"Did they offer more money for additional information if you should obtain it?

"Yes, they did."

"Did they harm you in any way, or did they threaten you or your wife?" Susan stared hard into the tired eyes of the old professor.

"No, they did not." Wigglesworth shifted uncomfortably. He tried to maintain eye contact too long then broke it awkwardly. He knew that she knew he was lying.

"Professor," Susan said softly, almost tenderly, "what did they threaten to do?"

He just stared without responding.

"Professor," she said in the same tone, "we want to help you. We can protect you. Let us help, please."

Missus Wigglesworth appeared at the door. "It's time to put things aright my dear," she said.

The professor shrugged. "Please, not yet. I have to get some things done first." He seemed to be pleading with his wife.

"It's time!" she replied emphatically. "This is too big for us now. If you will not tell the truth, I will."

"The truth," Susan asked, "the truth about what, Missus Wigglesworth?"

"The truth about our life and about our archaeological activities during the past forty years," she answered. The old woman pulled a chair from behind the professor's big desk and sat facing Susan and Greg.

Greg knew they were about to hear information that the professor's lawyer would never let them admit under oath. He fished for his mini recorder. Susan flashed him a look that said 'put that thing away!' She knew that what they were about to hear might not ever be heard if some interruption broke the mood.

Doctor Wigglesworth stared at his wife for a moment then he began. "Forty years ago I was a young un-tenured faculty member of this institution, a simple classics teacher with no particular future. I had stumbled across information about *The Hand of Mohammed* that at first fascinated me and eventually obsessed me. My obsession was all-consuming but I had no means to follow it, either financial or institutional."

He paused to gaze at his wife. She smiled encouragement. The Professor took a deep breath, sighed and continued. "At a conference, I was approached by a Saudi businessman who had heard of my obsession. He offered to fund an institute for the purpose of seeking *The Hand of Mohammed*. His offer included generous gifts to this college which, in turn gained me a prominent tenured professorship, use of this house and lots of other perks for my family. Blinded by my obsession, I failed to seek advice or to see through this offer to understand what would be required of me in return.

Susan put on her best compassionate manner. "So, professor what was required of you?"

Doctor Wigglesworth stared at the floor for a long while in silence. He seemed conflicted over what to say.

"We already know a lot about your trade in illegally acquired antiquities and about the channels you have used to move them through Canada into the United States," Susan announced, still using a soft voice and compassionate tone.

The old man took a long breath. "Then you know my shame," he replied. "My Saudi friends kept asking for more and more. Oh, they paid me well for the trinkets. Of course they re-sold them to private collectors at a vast profit. I put most of the money right back into funding expeditions. My goal was to keep digging in likely areas around the world until I could finally find *The Hand of Mohammed.* As you know, that never happened."

"And what if you had found it?" Susan asked. "They would certainly have taken it from you."

"Well of course they would. My reasoning was that justice would be served, since it belonged to the Saudis by tradition. But to have been the finder my place in history would be secured once and for all as well."

Greg felt bad for the old guy. 'Greed and pride will always win in this corrupt world,' he thought.

"So, what was the purpose of the visit today, I mean in light of what you have just told us?" asked Susan.

"Today they told me to use all my resources to find and take the precious thing for them. They believe I have more knowledge of its whereabouts than I let on." The old man's voice cracked as he said, "They will hurt my wife if I don't deliver it to them!"

Missus Wigglesworth calmly corrected him. "They said they will kill me if he fails," she said serenely. "Those people have a lot of nerve," she added. "I am not afraid to die. Neither would my dying be a burden except in my husband's eyes." Perceiving Susan's quizzical look, she added, "You see I've only a few months to live anyway. They would do me a favor if they cut my suffering short."

"Don't speak that way!" the professor shouted. Then in a small voice he gazed at her and added, "What would I do without my strength, my pillar, my hero?"

Greg looked at Missus Wigglesworth with a questioning gaze.

"It's an immune system thing, my dear," she said, "barely treatable."

Remembering how strong the lady had seemed just weeks ago, Susan said "But just a few weeks ago…"

"Diagnosed just a few days ago," the old woman replied, "we've only known since Saturday. The doctors think it may have something to do with long term exposure to rare plants. As you know they are my passion." Her voice trailed off as she said, "I will miss my *Orchidae*."

"I think that's quite enough for now," Susan announced. "We'll arrange for our agents to put this house under constant surveillance. We'll protect you both until this thing plays out."

They rose to leave. At the door, Missus Wigglesworth embraced both Greg and Susan. "I'm glad we have this off our mind," she said. The professor looked relieved as well.

In the car, Greg said "Wow that was intense."

"We have a long evening ahead," Susan observed. "Let's start with the local police and then the Vermont Troopers. The locals can begin surveillance until we can get a team here and the Troopers have the identities of those Saudis."

At seven pm Mort Lindsley called Ryall Morgan. "The young folks had a busy day, Ryall. Can you spend some time in video conference tonight?"

"Sure thing," Morgan replied. He sighed then turned off the NBA game he had been looking forward to watching and went to his computer console. This would be another long evening.

CHAPTER 39

After Paul Roche had been the guest of Al Kafajy Trading Company for three weeks he began to go out into the city, mostly at night, accompanied by his so called body guard. The man's name was Som. They walked for miles on each outing, part of Roche's plan to get in shape for his run to leave the country.

Som knew no English and Roche knew only a little Farsi, but each man learned from the other. Soon their walks were filled with lively conversation. By the fifth week Roche had developed a good friendship with Som and a better knowledge of conversational Farsi. He wondered if he could turn him but thought better of it. Roche was sure that Khazeh would not hesitate to have them killed if that became necessary to protect the company from embarrassment and he liked Som too much to expose him to that fate.

During one of their walks, Roche convinced Som to enter a shop that sold special Persian sweets. He had learned that Som loved the candies, but usually could not afford them. Roche gave him as much money as Som made in a week and asked to have some sweets that they could share.

Since Roche's presence in such a shop would certainly have raised questions, Som agreed that he should stay outside. By the time Som returned with the sweets, Roche had made a phone call to an old friend in Teheran and set up a contact arrangement. The two men dug in to the delectable candies and Som was none the wiser.

For the next two weeks Roche would pay for candies and Som would enter the shop for up to ten minutes at a time. Roche used a drop arrangement to converse with his friend and began to plan for an escape if that became necessary.

Roche's wrist was finally healed enough to use again. He strengthened it daily by playing table tennis with Khazeh.

Roche's plans were now ready. If his 'hosts' actually tried to get him out of the country, he would be ready and fit. If they refused, his friend would try a rescue.

Ali bin Akram Ajir had spent the month in Teheran at his father's guest house. His four body guards had trained daily sometimes as a group and sometimes together with Ajir. They were now ready to make their move on Al Kafajy.

Ajir had kept his ear to the ground but found no mention of any activity that would indicate anything other than regular business at Al Kafajy's Teheran location. The bidders from the Amman conference had been informed by Mohammed Al Kafajy himself that the sale would be re-opened within three months time at the Royal Amman Hotel. That meant he either had the prize or expected to receive it in Amman soon.

Ajir opened all channels of information but no sign of the prize was found. Ajir had paid a lot of bribes to get manifests of everything shipped by Al Kafajy from Iran. Nothing seemed out of place and nothing had been shipped by Al Kafajy from Iran to Jordan. He finally became convinced that *The Hand of Mohammed* must be stored at Al Kafajy's office in Mashhad.

Even after a month, Ajir's rage was barely controlled. His only desire was to regain the prize and collect his big score.

The rest of Ajir's little army had holed-up in an empty warehouse in Mashhad. The men were restless and eager to proceed with an operation.

Finally, all was ready. When Ajir and his four companions approached the Al Kafajy office, all the employees had gone for the day except Irad, who was just packing his laptop into the trunk of his Volvo. The five men waited until he drove off then moved in.

Two guards were quickly killed and the door was jimmied. One of Ajir's men disabled the alarm by electronically duping the keypad inside the entrance. Once inside, they searched every part of the facility.

After an hour they had found nothing, except a safe that the electronics expert was busy cracking. As he opened the door of this small safe, he heard a tell-tale click. It was a silent alarm, the kind that transmitted a millisecond code then went off the air. The safe cracker shouted, "Alarm, too late to disable it."

The team leader figured they had less than five minutes to clear the building before help arrived. "Get the contents of that safe and let's go!" shouted Ajir.

Irad was already on his way back to the building having sounded the alarm to armed men at his command in the neighborhood. He figured it was someone working for Ajir.

Four vehicles converged on the building. Ten men with pistols and assault rifles began firing at the five inside the building. Those inside returned the fire, but realized they were greatly outnumbered.

Ajir called the rest of his militia, who loaded into trucks and sped toward the scene.

Irad's Volvo screeched to a halt at the curb. He ran crouching to the leader of his men. "I know who they are," he shouted. "Keep them trapped inside. Wipe them out!"

As lively fire continued, the first of the trucks full of militia arrived. At first Irad thought they were more of his men. Then more trucks arrived and the men deployed with guns trained on his guys. Before he could react a fusillade erupted from all around the property. All ten of Irad's men were soon bogged down, a few were dead.

Bewildered, Irad tried to make it back to his car. Four bullets slammed into his chest and one directly into his throat. Irad was dead before he hit the ground.

It was all over within minutes. Three of Ajir's men had been wounded. All of their enemies were dead. As they drove away, Ajir realized that they had failed. They had failed to recover *The Hand of Mohammed* but even worse, they had alerted Al Kafajy to what would now have to be Ajir's next move, in Teheran.

Randy Pullin felt desperation. He had failed to get a warm response from Ryall Morgan. His men in Turkey had kept watch for weeks, but there was no sign of Roche at the border. For all he knew, Roche could have gone through Iraq or Afghanistan. He needed to recover the CIA's lost item to have any chance of getting the authorities to go easy on him and his group over Brandt's transgression. At the moment, he had no clue what to do next but to do nothing would certainly cost *Free Nation* severely.

The *Free Nation* post in Wyoming buzzed with activity. More than a hundred operatives were now reporting every move that could possibly involve the various parties to the hunt for *The Hand of Mohammed*.

Daily briefings went over every bit of the information gathered, whether or not it seemed relevant. Pullin pored over reports well into the night each day, frantic to find some lead that could be exploited.

It finally came as a message from his Persian friends. A raid had been pulled on Al Kafajy's office in Mashhad. The manager had been killed along with all his guards. The rumor was that Ajir had pulled the raid. Activity at Ajir's family's place in Tehran indicated that he was still looking for the prize. That meant it had to be at Al Kafajy's Teheran office. Pullin deduced that Roche had to be in Tehran, or at least *The Hand of Mohammed* had to be there.

Pullin spent hours communicating with everyone he knew in Iran. Finally, the big break he needed came. A former Iranian diplomat and agent named Kourosh Menzadah was working on a plan to extract an American and some precious cargo from Iran. Pullin knew he had a big break. He now had to figure the best way to profit from this information.

Kourosh Menzadah checked his appearance in the bathroom mirror of his room at the Parsian Esteghlal hotel in Tehran. He was of medium build with the chiseled features of his royal Persian ancestors.

The Menzadah family had enjoyed high status and much property in the days of the last Shah. Now the family had fallen on hard times. His father's fiery temper and secular habits had landed him in jail several times over the past twenty years. As a result there were retributions of the cruelest sort characteristic of the strict Islamists who now held power. Kourosh's excellent job in the security service had been taken away. Several members of the family had just disappeared, never to be heard from again.

One thing clear about agents and spies is that even if they lose their positions, they really never lose their training or their friends. In order to feed his family, Kourosh routinely took 'assignments' on the edge of society. He came to be known as a specialist at moving people with few or no credentials in or out of Iran. Taylor and Khaseh considered him the best choice to move Roche and the ABS case out of Iran.

Kourosh wiped some lint off the lapel of his business suit. He studied his teeth for specs of food then smoothed his close cut dark hair. He picked up his bag and took the stairs down three flights to the lobby. He cursed at having to wait in line for almost half-an-hour to check out. The hotel was clean but lacked the excellent service he remembered before the revolution when it was a Hilton.

Khazeh was anxious to see Kourosh. He paced his office floor waiting for nine am to come. He knew that Ajir's next target would be his facility and he knew about his friend Irad's death. He was afraid for his life. As long as Roche and the item he was carrying remained in Tehran he could be attacked at any minute. The eighteen Para-military troops that were guarding the property didn't make him feel any more secure. From all accounts Ajir had amassed a small army.

After a brief meeting with Kourosh, Khaseh fetched Roche. He introduced the men. He told Roche that he was to leave today with Kourosh for the Turkish border. They would stop briefly in Tabriz, where Kourosh had a safe house. From there, they would go on to a small town named Khoy, then to a place called Qotur. Just two miles from the Turkish border, they would leave the road and follow a mountain trail. That trail would be steep and treacherous, but passable. Then they would go through a valley and up and over a mountain of about six thousand feet. They would cross the border at a place called Glaad. After they crossed into Turkey they would go to a small settlement called Kapikoy.

Taylor and another man would meet them at Kapikoy and Roche would be driven to Van, where he could get a flight to Istanbul.

"That simple, Eh?" said Roche. "Where is the item I was supposed to carry?"

Khazeh sent one of his men, who returned presently with the small ABS case. Roche eyed it carefully. "I'll be right back," he said carrying the case out to the hallway. Khazeh said nothing nor did he try to stop him.

In the hallway, where Roche was alone, he opened the case. Inside carefully packed in soft material, he found the gold sack. In the gold sack was *The Hand of Mohammed*.

"I'll be damned," he whispered to himself.

It was the last thing he expected. Roche was sure that the thing had long since left the country without him. The fact that Taylor would personally meet him to receive the goods surprised Roche, so much for his theory that he had been written off.

By noontime Roche and Kourosh were on their way to Tabriz. The two former spies hit it off and soon were exchanging stories about 'the old days.'

Ajir's phone rang. He found it hard to believe that the man on the other end was who he said he was. After a few minutes of sparring, he became convinced that it really was Khazeh, the manager of Al Kafajy's Tehran office. The two men were acquainted having done business in the past.

"That was nasty business the other night in Mashhad," Khazeh said.

"What business?" Ajir feigned a lack of knowledge.

"You know what I mean," said Khazeh pointedly. "I want to tell you that the item you sought was not in Mashhad, but here in Tehran. I suppose you already figured that out."

Ajir let silent time go by then said, "Why are you telling me this?"

"I like my job. I like my life. I do not wish to lose my job, nor do I wish to wind up like my colleague Irad. I want you to know that the item is no longer here. It is in transit as we speak and far enough away so you cannot intercept it."

"So, what's next for each of us?" Ajir asked.

"Nothing is next. I hope you will consider the matter closed. You took our property. We took it back. Each of us has lost a piece of real estate. It's over."

"If you say so," Ajir sighed.

"I do say so. Call off your dogs, Ajir before everyone is destroyed over a trivial piece of crockery."

"Thanks for the call, Khazeh. I'll consider what you say, but I will make up my own mind about the future." Ajir clicked off.

So, he thought, the item is on the move. He spent a busy hour on the phone with many contacts. One of them had the information he wanted to hear. His billion dollar deal was on its way to Tabriz.

———————

Ryall Morgan and Mort Lindsley had just briefed Bob Steck about the Saudis and the Wigglesworths. There was serious discussion about whether they could find use for Doctor Wigglesworth to bait the holder of *The Hand of*

Mohammed into some sort of meeting. In effect, they would use him to gain access to whoever wound up with the thing after its whereabouts became known. They decided to table that notion until there was better knowledge of events.

Just as Steck was ready to end the call, Morgan broke in. "Bob, I've got Randy Pullin on the line. He says he's got credible information that *The Hand of Mohammed* has been in Tehran and that Roche is there with it. He says that a former Iranian agent has Roche under his wing and is planning to extract him to Turkey in the next few days. He thinks that Roche will be carrying *The Hand* with him."

"Patch him in and let's discuss this," urged Steck. While this was happening, Steck cursed his luck being stuck in Amman. Normal travel to extreme eastern Turkey would take at least two days.

Pullin's voice came on, joining the conference call. "Hey Steck, How are you?"

Morgan's voice answered, "Before you guys talk, please hear this: due to different encryption protocols, the patch to Randy Pullin is less secure than before. Be careful what you say."

"Right," answered Steck. "So Randy, my understanding is you are tracking the item and have the locale. The problem is what do we do with that information?"

"We act on it," answered Pullin confidently. I have people on the ground ready to intercept and take possession of the item. They know the territory. They have been into Iran before through that area." He was referring to Grundstrom and Brandt, along with others who had been waiting in eastern Turkey for weeks. "And," he added, "I can get you from Amman to the scene within twelve hours if you want to take charge of the ground operation."

"Randy, I'm going to put you on hold while we caucus," said Morgan.

The members of the JUMP team discussed Pullin's offer for a few minutes. Steck was concerned about following a single lead in case it turned out false. Lindsley asked why they should trust Pullin considering the Idaho affair. Morgan asked sardonically if they had any other leads to follow. Susan Deet offered that they could let Roche come back to the West but track him carefully. Then they would have more resources to bring to bear on the issue.

I think we should go with this deal," offered Morgan, "as long as we're sure Steck is in charge."

Steck's response was wary. "What if I get caught with pants down inside Iran with a bunch of armed Americans?" The last thing we need is another failed incursion." He spoke from experience since he had been part of the fateful rescue operation during the American embassy hostage crisis. The memory of that fateful night, his first real armed field operation had burned like a hot coal in Steck's heart for thirty years.

"Just stay on the Turkish side of the border," offered Lindsley.

"It's tough to tell where the border really is," offered Steck. "I can't be concerned about that if we are to be successful. Roche may have a local guide. If so, he's smart enough to suck us across the border and hope we get grabbed. I want to go wherever it takes to get the item." He didn't like what he heard himself saying. It sounded crazy.

They finally all agreed that they should get Presidential approval for the operation before committing to it.

Back on the line with Randy Pullin, Morgan said, "Randy, here's what we want to do: Please go ahead and move Bob Steck and whoever he wants to take with him to join your guys in Turkey. In the meantime, we need to get authorization from our superiors to proceed. It must be understood that nobody makes a move unless or until I authorize the plan directly through Bob Steck."

"Understood," was Pullin's reply. "This will work," he added, "I'm sure it will work."

Mort Lindsley clicked off the line to Pullin. "I wish I shared that fellow's optimism," he drawled.

CHAPTER 40

The Saudi Arabian delegation of six security agents and a Prince had not returned to the kingdom after their meeting in Ashgabat. Instead they had flown first to New York where they consulted with their colleagues who kept tabs on Doctor Wigglesworth then they flew on to Paris.

Mohammed Al Kafajy welcomed the Saudi Prince and his retinue with all the fanfare he could muster. They shared a sumptuous meal and lots of conversation after the Muslim custom of hospitality. After an appropriate time of sharing quotations from the Quran, Al Kafajy asked, "Why has Allah smiled on me today that I am blessed with your visit, Prince?"

"I have come to know recent events surrounding the Prophet's hand. I believe you do not have it at the moment but that you seek to regain it in time." The prince sipped his coffee.

"That is correct," Al Kafajy replied. "Some unfortunate events took place in Amman recently and we lost contact with the item briefly. I expect to bring it back under my control very soon."

Ahmed, who sat quietly at a side table with the six Saudi security agents added, "Perhaps as early as tomorrow, may it please Allah we will have the treasure." Al Kafajy gave Ahmed a stare that told him to be quiet.

"When you again become the custodian of this treasure, I wish to purchase it from you," the Prince declared.

"Forgive me Prince," said Al Kafajy, "but we have offered the item to be sold under a competitive bid. Many worthy men wish to acquire it and we felt that the only fair way would...."

The Prince cut him off in a raised but controlled voice. "The only fair transaction in this case would be to return it to its rightful owner which is The Kingdom. It was taken from us illegally by the Turks and must now be returned."

Al Kafajy worried that they might take it by force and he would be out of pocket. "But surely you must understand that we have incurred great expense to acquire it."

The Prince put his coffee down on the table in front of him. "It was the will of Allah for the hand of the Prophet to be among us as custodians and protectors for a thousand years. It must also be his will that it be returned to us. You will be paid out of our generosity a sum far greater than your reasonable expectations could be."

"And how did you determine my reasonable expectations?" Al Kafajy was getting hot.

"Given the opening bid you yourselves announced, I expect you were thinking about more than fifty millions," the Prince observed.

"Fifty?" Al Kafajy was red in the face. "My expenses are more than that!"

"In that case would two hundred million be fair?" The Prince was serene.

"It would be in the arena," Al Kafajy said. He knew he could not push too hard, lest the wrath of the Saudis be incurred.

"Very well, my friend," declared the Prince. A satisfied smile came across his face. "When we receive the Prophet's hand and after we judge it to be in perfect condition, we will transfer one billion dollars to your accounts."

Al Kafajy guffawed. "A billion?" he said almost in a whisper.

The Prince leaned across the table engaging Al Kafajy's eyes. "See how Allah smiles on those who do his will?"

"May he forever be praised," said Al Kafajy with a satisfied smile.

When the Saudis had taken their leave, Al Kafajy turned to Ahmed. "Our plans must be strengthened. Get Christian Taylor on the satellite phone right away."

Within an hour of their briefing with the JUMP team Steck, Marya Lukianov and two agents from Ravi's staff were on board a twin Cessna headed for eastern Turkey. Bob had chosen Lukianov as one with proven experience. He knew first hand how good she was in a fire fight. The other two were Jordanians trained by the Royal Jordanian Special Forces, a pet project of King Abdullah himself. They were among the best fighters in the Middle East. The small cargo area of the Cessna was packed tightly with body armor, weapons and ammo. This was a small but formidable force. When combined with Pullin's guys and whatever resources they had gathered in eastern Turkey they would be the best Steck could hope for.

Steck reflected on their situation. The Al Kafajy faction had possession of the object. Ajir's men would certainly be after it. Steck's coalition of Americans, Jordanians, Canadians and mercenaries must intercept it in Iranian territory and might have to fight both the Al Kafajy and Ajir people to get it. After getting possession of *The Hand* they would have to get out of Iran undetected. Then there was Roche. His cunning had somehow kept him alive through an incredible series of events against amazing odds. Maybe this time Steck would finally have an opportunity to deal with him once and for all.

Pondering these things that he knew, Steck worried what he did not know. He knew Ajir had been in contact with the Kurds. What about the Iranians? Certainly the Ayatollahs would have great interest in the item and the means to make a play for it, especially if they knew it was in their country. Now the Saudis seemed to be involved. How hot was the trail they were following? The prize had resided in Turkmenistan for a while. Would the Turkmen government believe they had rights to it? Would they be chasing it themselves?

In the end Steck came to realize that there could be dozens of factions after the figurine and he could never plan to counter them all. He would just have to adjust on the fly to whatever developed. Apprehension was the most positive feeling he could apply to his situation.

Abu Daimb, third in authority in the Taliban slipped undetected into Iran over the porous eastern border with Afghanistan under a false passport and identity. Making his way to Tehran where there are a million Sunnis living in repression by the Shiite Ayatollahs he met about two dozen militants trained at various times by the Taliban and planted as moles of sorts into the Tehran community. They were members of a secret Sunni political group with relations to Al Qaeda. Their agenda was to put political pressure on the Iranian government to improve the lot of Sunnis who are a clear minority in Iran.

Although at the beginning of the Iranian Islamic revolution Ayatollah Khomeini had proclaimed his desire for good relations with the Sunnis, his successors had routinely discriminated against them. This community of over a million in the capital of Iran was not allowed to even have one mosque.

Abu Daimb walked a political tightrope with the Ayatollahs because they represented a key and growing supply line to the Taliban, but were after all Shiites who repressed his Sunni brothers.

In the present case, he sought a prize that he believed had the potential to shift the balance of power in the Islamic world toward the Taliban's cause. After learning of the approximate whereabouts of *The Hand of Mohammed* Abu Daimb now organized these twenty-four fighters to pursue it. On the Turkish side of the border at the town of Ercis, three

Sunni sympathizers of the Taliban waited to extract the men after their operation was completed.

In the early morning of the day Roche arrived in Tabriz with Kourosh Menzadah, a bus left Tehran with the twenty-four Taliban on board. The driver dropped twelve of them at Qotur then headed north to drop the rest at

Maku. Satisfied that he had both probable routes to Turkey covered, Abu Daimb slipped back across the border into Afghanistan and raced back toward the eastern mountains where he could watch events unfold from the safety of his communications center.

Chris Taylor had lodged just outside of Van in eastern Turkey. He and one of the men who worked at the Al Kafajy office in Istanbul would wait for Roche to come across the border, if he ever made it. This part of Turkey was far more provincial than the western parts and the locals did not trust outsiders. Even if Roche made it across the border he would not be home free. Chris himself felt awfully conspicuous in a place where Brits were ill-treated at best and sometimes disappeared without a trace.

During the night, Taylor's satphone buzzed, waking him from fitful sleep. He sat up in bed, scratched his unruly hair, rubbed sleep from his eyes then answered the phone.

"Taylor." He said with a sleepy voice.

"Hello Christian!" It was the unmistakable voice of the boss. "Is everything set?

"Y-yes sir," Chris replied. "Our men are in place. They all know their roles. We should complete this part of the plan tomorrow."

"Good!" The boss sounded happy. "Call me as soon as you have everything accomplished."

"Of course sir, I will call you first." Who else would he call? Chris thought.

"I had a visit from a certain Prince today," the boss announced. "His group is very interested in the item. That presents a certain complication. We will talk about it when you reach Paris."

"Okay," Chris responded. He felt it strange that the boss would call him with such trivial news. "Don't worry," Chris added, "this is all going as planned."

Since he was now quite awake, Chris fumbled around and found his cigarettes. He lit up and took a deep draught. Blowing the smoke into the light from his bedside lamp, he pondered the conversation he had just completed with the boss. "He's just nervous," he said to himself.

The phone rang again. "Blazes," Chris thought, "What does he want now?"

He picked up the satphone. "Taylor." He announced.

It was Khazeh from Tehran. "Chris, there is a bad complication. The MOIS came here and took Som into custody a few hours ago. I called my friend at headquarters and he said Som is being interrogated at Evin prison. He has broken down and spilled the information about our guest. I took certain articles and papers and hid them in a safe place, but you know they will be back for me in the morning. They may even come to my house before morning, the way those jackals operate."

Chris had stood and was pacing as Khazeh spoke. The Ministry of Intelligence and Security (MOIS) was the Iranian secret police. "Be calm, Khazeh," he said, "You did the right thing by removing the sensitive items from the office. When they come try to discredit Som's story and invite them to search the office. Get your family out of the city now. Do they have a place to go?" He knew the MOIS had a habit of holding family members as a threat to obtain information from persons of interest to them.

"They are already in the car, going to a place I have reserved for such an occasion." Khaseh sounded in control.

"Good," Taylor replied. "After they complete a search and find nothing, contact our friends in the government and express outrage."

"I must tell you, Chris that Som knew Roche only as Jacob Breen. They had become friendly during his stay here. I have no way of knowing what other knowledge Som may have of this affair." Khazeh was being very thorough as usual.

"Thank you for that input," Chris answered. "Call me when you have more to tell me." Taylor clicked off. He lit another cigarette and sat on the edge of his bed to think.

The bus containing Ajir's militiamen stood outside a small Inn near Tabriz. The innkeeper, a friend of Ajir had closed the place for what the sign on his door proclaimed "a private party." The men had been fed and bedded down for the night.

The innkeeper became frightened when he saw all the weapons and equipment that the men carried. As soon as everything was quiet, he rang Ajir's paternal home in Tehran and asked to speak with his friend. After a long silence, Ajir came on the line. "Hello my friend how is everything?"

"What's going on?" the innkeeper began. "This inn is all I have in the world. If there's trouble I could lose it all!"

"Don't worry," Ajir replied. "My friends will only be there for one or two nights and they have strict orders to keep their weapons out of sight. I have a certain matter to resolve in the mountains. It's a matter that you would be better off not knowing about. They will go to do their duty and you will never see them again."

"I hope you are not involving me in anything illegal," the innkeeper asserted. "I have to live here after your deal is done, whatever it is."

"Have I not paid you enough?"

"No, please, you have been most generous Ajir. It's just that…."

"Don't worry. I will double it. Now please get off the line, it's expensive to call from Tabriz to Tehran." Ajir was worried that the ever present Islamic big brothers might be listening.

As Ajir turned off his phone, he smiled. Better the snoops think he is still in Tehran, rather than downtown in Tabriz on his cell phone. He dialed his father's number and thanked him for transferring the call.

After flying in from Tehran, Ajir had wasted no time confirming that Roche and Kourosh Menzadah were staying at a farm about five miles from the city on the road that led to Khoy. Now that he knew their intended route, he would follow with his men at a distance then close with them at Qotur. He was confident that he would soon recover his property, the property that would provide for his family in luxury the rest of his life.

Ajir went to bed. He had no way of knowing that the MOIS was just arriving at his father's house. In custody at Evin, the elder Ajir pulled all the rank he could. Finally he was informed by a superior officer who was an acquaintance that his son had offered a certain piece of merchandise to the government. They had been informed that it was no longer in his control and was in fact somewhere in Iran. The government had decided to claim it as their own since it was on Iranian territory. To assure that the item was turned over to them as or if it was regained by Ajir, the elder Ajir would be their guest for a few days.

———

Toward the end of the workday in Washington, Ryall Morgan received a call from Bob MacFergus.

"I understand that your man Steck has taken one of our agents with him into eastern Turkey." He began.

"That's right Bob," answered Morgan. "Marya was so much help in Ashgabat Steck wanted to have her on board the team that will wrap up this affair once and for all. That way you guys share the glory."

"I appreciate the opportunity to be of service," offered MacFergus. He continued, "The reason for this call, Ryall, is that my agents in Toronto picked up some intelligence today that will bear on the success of the mission."

"What information?" Morgan tensed. What could be important enough to prompt a personal call at this time of day?

"The Iranian government has become aware that the item is in their country," MacFergus told him. "Apparently Ajir had sought to sell it to them, but the fracas in Ashgabat fouled that up. Now they want to trap it before it leaves Iran and they're putting a lot of resources into the pursuit."

"This affair is getting more complicated by the minute," Morgan observed. "Thanks so much for the heads-up, Bob."

"Don't do anything rash, Ryall." MacFergus sounded concerned. "You've got one of my best field agents involved and I can't afford to lose her."

"Nothing will be done without full consultation, Bob. You know you can trust me on that."

"I trust you, Ryall," said MacFergus. "I don't trust our governments to avoid stupid moves."

"I hear you, Bob," offered Morgan. "I'll try to steer this toward a positive end result."

Immediately after hanging up, Morgan called his boss the Director. "We need to brief the President first thing in the morning," he said.

CHAPTER 41

Greg Liss and Susan Deet worked at a folding table set up in Susan's living room. They were preparing their part of the presentation that Lindsley and Morgan would make to the President next morning.

An FBI surveillance team from Boston had relieved the Hanover police and was now watching the Wigglesworth residence around the clock. A suspicious late model Ford sedan passed by now and then. The men inside were obviously working for the Saudis. The car neither stopped nor seemed threatening in any way. The FBI decided to let them alone, knowing they could either ask the Hanover police to pick them up or that as federal agents they could move on them anytime.

Missus Wigglesworth stayed in the house most of the time except for her weekly visit to Dartmouth-Hitchcock Hospital a mile or so away from the campus. The doctors there were fascinated by her rare condition and were trying all the known remedies along with a few experimental ones. It wasn't every day the doctors had the chance to treat conditions so rare that they inspired original study. She looked tired but was in good spirits.

For Doctor Wigglesworth it was back to class and his usual campus routine. He had arranged for an extra helper at the house, a student who waited on his wife while the student housekeeper-cook went about her regular duties.

While Greg compiled all of this information into a few paragraphs, Susan made dinner. She was not much of a cook but managed to turn out sautéed chicken, carrots and rice with a lemon sauce that came as powder in a foil envelope. She opened a bottle of cheap red wine and poured two generous glasses. They sat on her living room couch to eat the meal, watching the evening news on TV.

"Not a great supper," she said apologetically.

"Hey, it sure beats the pizza and Mcnuggets I usually live on," Greg replied. "It tastes great to me. What is that wonderful sauce?"

"I wish I could tell you it's an old family recipe," Susan smiled. "It's made from milk and a powder I bought at the superstore."

After packing the dishes in Susan's dishwasher they enjoyed a second glass of wine while editing the material Greg had written. They sent it to Mort Lindsley.

At her door, Greg thanked Susan for the dinner and announced he would see her in the morning at the office. After an awkward pause, she kissed him on the cheek. He gave her a hug. It was too long a hug to be 'just friends.' As she pulled back, he kissed her. She wanted to punch him and scold him like she had done with other guys but she didn't move. In fact she returned the kiss eagerly. He started escalating, pulling her body to his.

She broke the kiss and said breathlessly, "Whoa tiger, take it easy. There's something you should know about me."

"What's that?" he said absently while trying to renew the embrace.

"I'm an Orthodox Christian," she said, stepping back away from him.

"What does that mean?" asked Greg. "Like Greek Orthodox, you mean?"

"Yeah, like Greek Orthodox," she said.

He gave her a puzzled look. "What does that have to do with us? I mean here, now?"

"What it means is that I like you a lot but I'm a real conservative person and…"

"And what?" He didn't get this at all.

Susan had regained her composure. She looked him square in the eye. "And…I'm saving myself for my husband."

Greg seemed totally flustered. "You're *married*?" he blurted.

"No, silly," she giggled, "I'm saving myself for *when* I have a husband!"

Greg came back into the living room, closing the door behind him. He was having a hard time getting the concept. Perplexed, he said, "Isn't that a bit old fashioned Susie?"

Susan smiled. "Yeah, I guess these days it seems old-fashioned Greg, but it's what I am. I'm just an old fashioned girl who believes in traditional values." She took his hand and gave him a peck on the cheek. "You got a problem with that?"

Greg stepped back, absorbing what he had just heard. He gestured with both hands held out. "But you...you're an FBI agent, for Gawd's sake."

She frowned at him. "Does being an agent mean I have to be...promiscuous?"

"No, no," he said. "I mean, I guess not." He was totally thrown.

"I think we should try this conversation some other time," she said. "Greg, I want to continue this conversation so that... What I'm trying to say is I really want to give to you more than you know." She was on thin ice here and she knew it. Was this guy really her soul mate? Was she falling in love with him?

After a very awkward silence, Greg spoke. "I think I'm getting the gist of this, Susie. I respect you too greatly to go too fast with this, but I don't want to give it up. The fact is I've been hoping it would move ahead for quite a while now."

"Me too," she admitted. "Now I think you'd better go."

At the door again, they shared a new kind of long and tender kiss. "Good night," she said dreamily.

"G'nite," he mumbled.

Mort Lindsley and Ryall Morgan had briefed the President and his top security team three times in the past week. He was familiar with the operation and seemed to take a great interest in it. Today, he had asked the Secretary of State to invite State Department advisors on Iran to the briefing.

Lindsley's presentation spoke to the Saudi involvement. It was generally agreed that we should keep close tabs on them but not make any overt moves that might embarrass the Kingdom.

After Morgan had finished his presentation and it was clear that the Iranians were in the chase a lively discussion ensued. Some in the room maintained that we should not interfere in any way with the Iranians on their turf, nor should we even get close to their border. Protagonists reminded the group of the incidents in recent years involving military of both the US and Britain who had been taken by the Iranians outside their territorial waters but accused of invasion.

Another group, headed by the military members of the group insisted that possession of *The Hand of Mohammed* by the Ayatollahs would severely shift the balance of power in the region and the US would be a big loser.

"Well, if we don't get the thing then who do you think should wind up with it?" asked the President. What's the least evil here? Do we want to influence the outcome by steering it into the proper hands?

After lots of discussion in which each of the supposedly interested parties became eliminated, the only ones that remained were Saudi Arabia, the Emirates and Qatar. Further discussion left only the Saudis as the best choice for the interests of the United States.

"In the best interests of the United States *and* Canada," asserted Morgan. "Remember ladies and gentlemen Canada is our partner in this issue and has been a good one."

"I certainly acknowledge that your friends in Canada have been a great help, but this is our decision to make, correction: *my* decision to make as Commander in Chief," announced the President.

Morgan studied the floor.

Two of the military floated the possibility that US commandoes, such as the Navy Seals should just go in and take the thing then deliver it to the Saudis and proudly publish the result to the world.

The President discarded that idea right away. "That is not going to happen, gentlemen. The possibility of failure is too great."

In the end, the President ordered that the clandestine operation should continue, that if it went wrong the United States would deny it ever happened and that if successful, we would return the item to secure storage in the United States. "That way, its return to the Saudis could be made at any time we see the opportunity to gain favor and stature in the Islamic world."

The twin Cessna landed at Van in the glow of pre-dawn. The pilot had expended every bit of fuel the small plane could carry during their long flight, even every drop that could be carried in the plane's extra wing tanks. Beads of sweat ran down his face as he made his final approach. He fully expected a stall but it didn't happen. The plane set down smoothly on the tarmac. The pilot breathed a long sigh of relief.

Steck and the others deplaned and gathered their gear. His legs seemed made of rubber after the long cramped flight. By the time they reached the big Suburban and were greeted by Brandt, circulation had returned.

The pilot was given orders to re-fuel and wait for a maximum of three days. If no one showed by that time, he was to return to Amman.

Introductions and chatter broke out as Brandt drove sixty miles east towards the Iranian border. He stopped at a place where there was a turnout in the road. Shifting into four-wheel-drive, Brandt slowly ran the vehicle over a creek wash that he referred to as the 'local freeway.'

Two miles into the scrub, in a dry box canyon that ended at the entrance to a cave, he stopped the vehicle beside some equipment under camouflage. Grundstrom and some others emerged from the cave and greeted the entourage. Within minutes, they had stashed the equipment in two Suburbans and a pickup truck. The pickup was a full size Toyota, not the ordinary vehicle for these parts. Steck saw the barrel of a fifty caliber gun sticking out under a tarp that was draped over the back of the pickup. Gunny had amassed a bit of fire power.

They wasted no time. Gunny and Brandt gave a detailed briefing. For Steck and Marya it was review of stuff they had all studied thoroughly.

The area around Tabriz west to the border was mountainous and largely barren wilderness with just a few farms and ruins here and there. "Consider it like southern Arizona except colder," Gunny advised. The day time temperature during early winter would be around thirty-five to forty Fahrenheit. The nights would be in the teens or twenties, depending on your altitude. Foot paths through scrub vegetation with big rocky outcroppings and loose boulders were the way to get around.

"The border is eight miles that way," instructed Gunny pointing into the rising sun. "We have befriended some locals, who will help guide us around. There is a trail due east of here that the locals claim is the only way anyone gets here from Iran except by driving through at the border station on the road. I have two men watching the road and one Turkish border guard in my employ. He is the commander of the station and will screen every vehicle personally over the next four days. Until he sees the vehicle and its contents, his men will detain anyone crossing at the station." Gunny held up a small walkie-talkie. "He has a radio that can raise us anytime."

314

"So, where do we deploy?" asked Steck.

"I think we should deploy in a spot here on the map that I picked after several trips down that mountain trail," Gunny said, pointing to a spot on his map. "I have a couple of folks at the spot as we speak keeping an eye out for our targets."

Just to recap the targets, said Steck, "there is one male Iranian, five foot-eight with dark hair, brown eyes, clean-shaven. There is one male American, five-eleven, medium build, bearded or a moustache, reddish hair with gray streaks. The beard is a fake. He may speak with a British accent or in any of the following languages: English, Spanish, Russian, Farsi, German, Arabic or French. His name is Paul Roche but he has recently used the alias Jacob Breen. If you get close enough to this guy to hear him speak, it may be the last words you hear. He is a cold-blooded killer and very crafty. Don't let him bargain with you. If you can't be sure of his cooperation, kill him."

Grundstrom passed out maps to each of the team. "If you get separated from the group, find your way back to this place. If you are a sole survivor, contact the American attaché in Van, which is sixty miles down the road we came in on."

"Gunny, where will back-up ammo be stashed?" asked Steck.

"When we deploy, which may be at any time, you will armor up and stay that way. Carry all the ammo you can. We will move this pickup truck to the border over sheep paths which will take about two hours. It will be fully loaded with seven and nine millimeter ammo. If you hear a fifty cal, it will be firing from the mount on the back of this truck." He pointed to the Toyota.

One of the Jordanians raised his hand. Gunny recognized him by a nod. "Why do we have so much fire power to intercept just two guys?"

Steck answered. "The item we seek to recover is a small figurine shaped like a man's hand. It has archaeological and religious significance and is being sought after by many factions who may be in conflict with one another but certainly would consider us hostile. We do not know if any of those groups have personnel in this area, but we must assume there may be. If you receive fire, return it."

"Any more questions?" asked Gunny.

"When do we go?" one of the men asked.

Gunny looked at his watch. "We could go as early as two hours from now. It could be as long as two days before we go. We will get word when our targets enter the area. Get some sleep now and good luck."

CHAPTER 42

Kourosh Menzadah woke Roche at three am. "It's going to be a long day," he declared. "We move out in twenty minutes."

Roche dressed as warmly as he could by layering all the clothes he had. The hike today would carry them from ridge to gulch to mountainside ending with what Kourosh described as 'a thousand foot cliff to be scaled' within a few hundred yards of the border. The temperature would range from just below freezing to warm sun along some of the rocky ridges.

Roche felt fit and ready for a mountain hike. He also felt excited and apprehensive at the possibility of encountering hostility. Kourosh had described the locals as usually very friendly but fiercely Shiite in their world view. He was to keep his head down and use the Muslim greetings Kourosh had rehearsed with him. The locals had been known to kill unbelievers that offended their Shiite sensibilities. The local word for unbeliever was 'kiafir' Roche was told. If he heard that word, he should act accordingly. When he asked Kourosh what he meant by 'accordingly' Kourosh answered, "Run for your life."

The two men ate some food consisting of flat Persian bread, some fruits and coffee. The farmer's wife packed bread, fruit, cooked rice and some braised lamb for the men to take as a trail lunch. Two large goatskin canteens were filled with fresh water. Kourosh paid the farmer well and thanked him for the hospitality he could always expect from his old friend. Roche understood that the type of trip they were about to take was probably a regular source of income for both of these men.

They set out at three forty-five am in Kourosh's car. Skirting the city of Tabriz they set out on route four, the road to Khoy a hundred miles away. About half way to Khoy the two men were too involved in swapping endless 'war stories' to notice the small car that began to track them at a distance. Behind the car about three hundred yards, a bus joined the parade. The driver of the car kept in contact with the bus driver on a hand-held radio.

Kourosh finally noticed the car in his rear-view mirror as they passed the town of Marand. He let Roche know that they might have company. At a place called Evaghli, Kourosh suddenly turned off the main road and drove toward Maku. The car followed them. At a turn-out, Kourosh stopped and waited. The car passed them by. It looked innocent enough, just four men traveling a country road. When the car was out of sight, Kourosh retraced his path, speeding back southeast to rejoin route four. As they reached Khoy, they passed a bus that seemed to have engine trouble. The driver seemed to be struggling with something in the engine compartment.

Moments later, the car with four men passed the bus at high speed waving to the bus driver as they passed. The bus driver hastily drove back onto the road and followed.

They passed though Khoy in the nether-light of pre-dawn. Just outside Khoy was the only stopping point between that city of about a half-million and the Turkish border. Kourosh pulled in to get petrol and a snack. While Kourosh was inside, Roche went to the trunk of the car and dragged out his pack-frame, a gift from Khazeh. He carefully packed the food, the dis-assembled parts of an old H&K assault rifle, lots of nine millimeter ammo and the small case containing the prize. He hefted the pack and found it to be light enough. When Kourosh came out with bread, cheese and meat he told Roche plainly, "Get in the car."

Roche, who had just finished trying out the pack and adjusting straps for comfort did as he was told. In side the car, Kourosh admonished him. "This is the last place to show your American face, Roche. Every trucker and passer-by now knows for sure that someone is going to try the border today!"

Roche cursed himself for having been so stupid. His pride would not let him admit his folly so he protested. "Look at the turban on my head," he asserted. "I wasn't close enough to anyone to be recognized."

"You didn't have to be," replied Kourosh. "The back pack betrayed you loud and clear."

They drove away in silence heading down the rough back road that led to Qotur and the Turkish border.

Ajir and his body guards drove right by the petrol station and sped along the road to Qotur. They were followed by the bus which had fallen in between two large trucks carrying livestock. Ajir was pleased at the opportunity to slip past their quarry. Now they could set an ambush. West of Khoy was high farmland with big fields fallow for the winter. The trucks turned off to a farm where the hills rose into craggy mountain territory. At a place a mile from Qotur, the road became impassible for the bus. They pulled the big vehicle off the road, hiding it behind an outcropping of reddish gray rock. Within minutes, their trap was set. Ajir shouted last minute instructions to the men, including the admonition to take the men alive and not to destroy their belongings. After all this trouble a smashed figurine would be total disaster.

It was early evening in Washington. Ryall Morgan had finished his workday and was in the garage at Langley ready to begin his commute. He had started his car and was just about to head out when the red phone rang. "Morgan," he said tersely knowing no one would bother him this time of day unless it was an urgent matter.

"Hello Ryall." It was the voice of the Director.

"Hello, sir. What's up?" Morgan thought it might be news about Steck's operation.

"I've just come from the White House, Ryall," the director began. "The President has expressed grave misgivings about our ongoing operation. The Secretary of State is at a turning point in relations with Iran and the President does not want to endanger that in any way."

"Morgan's temperature was rising as the boss spoke. "Sir, we discussed that in detail and the President authorized the operation. We are in the midst of that operation as we speak. Do you mean to say we try to pull-back the operation now?"

"No Ryall, nothing of the sort. The President understands the importance of keeping that object out of the wrong hands."

"What then?" Morgan loathed politicians getting in the way of well planned operations, as somehow they always did.

"The President has ordered deployment of a Global Hawk drone to the area. Its high altitude surveillance capability will allow us to observe every move on the ground. The President has also tasked the Air Force to have air to ground attack capability maintaining high altitude over northeastern Iraq."

"What the hell for?" demanded Morgan. He knew perfectly well what for but he wanted to hear it from the boss.

"If anything happens that would embarrass the United States the Air Force may be asked to destroy the evidence." The Director waited for a moment then added, "The evidence is *The Hand of Mohammed*, Ryall."

"What about Steck and his team?" asked Morgan. Again, he knew what the Director's answer would be. He just wanted to force him to say it out loud.

"That's going to depend on which side of the border they're on."

"Are you still in your office, sir?" asked Morgan.

"Yes, I am still at my desk, Ryall."

"Stay there! I need to talk with you right away." Morgan clicked off without giving the boss time to say anything. He turned off the engine and locked the car.

Striding up the back stairs two by two, he reached the Director's office in minutes. The Director's secretary had left for the day, so he strode right through the office door. He tossed his coat and set his brief case down. He sat in the chair nearest the desk.

"Come in!" said the Director sarcastically.

Morgan's gaze was already fixed on the eyes of his boss. "I'm worried that those Air Force cowboys will just spread destruction everywhere if you let them go in there," he blurted. I understand the set up perfectly, but we can't allow the situation to become a flipping act of war in the eyes of the Iranians."

"Slow down, Ryall," the Director said holding his hands up.

"No!" declared Morgan, "Hear me out!"

The Director gestured as if to say 'go ahead.'

"I think we should get one of our Predator assets into the air flying from Mosul or Insurlik." He was referring to the CIA operated drone fleet that was routinely used to take out terrorists with its payload of Hellfire missiles.

"If this thing gets out of hand, we fire one round to take out Roche and the figurine. That rids us of two problems at once. Then we tell the Iranians that we took out a terrorist who was infiltrating from Turkey."

"It's probably too late to float your suggestion even though I think it has merit," the Director said. "This thing is already going down."

Morgan leapt to his feet. "Then let me talk to the President, if you won't." He was on real thin ice. The next few minutes might destroy his career.

"You need to follow the chain of command, mister." The Director was getting red in the face.

"I want to sir," Morgan nearly shouted, "but if you won't talk with the President about this I surely will try to get through." As he spoke this, Morgan picked up the secure phone on the Director's desk. He offered the receiver to the boss. "Which will it be?"

The Director stared at the phone for a moment. He realized that if he refused he would lose his best assistant Director and one of the CIA's best agents. "Okay Ryall, just cool down," He said reaching for the phone. "Let's give it a try."

High on a mountain ridge overlooking the road from Qotur to the Turkish border, twelve Taliban watched the deployment of the ambush. They stood less than a mile from the position Steck and his men had just assumed. Neither knew the other was there at the moment.

The commander gave orders to his men to take cover in the rocks. He positioned them so that they could fire directly down on the soldiers waiting in ambush. He did not know who these fighters might be, but he knew he would have to kill them all to get *The Hand of Mohammed*.

The men were all armed with AK-47 rifles. Extra magazines were tucked into their jackets. The men were quite familiar with the tactic of ambush but it was usually their job to initiate such an action. The commander was amused that he would now ambush an ambush.

He gave the signal to hold fire. They waited....

In Tehran the Ayatollahs were finishing their morning call to prayer. As they prepared for the government workday, a call came from Evin prison.

Hurried orders were given. Moments later, three fighter jets scrambled from Doshan Tappei air base. They flew west toward Tabriz at top speed. At Tabriz, two helicopters full of Quds guards trained in mountain warfare were ordered to prepare to get airborne as soon as practical. They would be joined by the jets in one hour.

CHAPTER 43

Susan Deet sat watching TV late into the night. She couldn't have described any of the programs she had watched. She was lost in thought about the events of the early evening. Was it love she felt for Greg? Was it just some physical attraction that would pass away?

Love wasn't something Susan knew a lot about, at least the kind that happened between a man and a woman.

She had experienced the love of her parents toward her. It was the kind that drove them to sacrifice for her sake and that of her only brother. They were working class people of modest means and always provided a secure but modest home for the family. Her father had worked two jobs, sometimes three and her mother had taken in work at home in order to afford the best college education for their children. Susan knew that kind of love.

There was the love between Susan and her brother. They had always 'been there' for one another even if it meant sacrifice. An example was the time when her brother lost focus and was about to leave school. Susan dropped her life for weeks to fly out to the west coast and help straighten his mind.

Susan had sometimes felt it odd that she had no inclination toward the dating scene that seemed to consume her friends. She thought it silly to be 'in love' one week and 'in hate' the next. She considered all of that to be a waste of time. She concentrated instead on her chosen career. First as a student then as an agent her drive was to be the very best she could possibly be. Love would have to wait until some 'mister right' came along.

Here she was in her thirties, still waiting for a relationship to last beyond a date or two. Susan figured part of it was her determination not to give her body to any guy who thought he wanted it at the moment. Most guys just walked away the first time she refused them. Even her girlfriends that gave in to those kinds of guys usually wound up losing them at the first sign of difficulty in a relationship. She knew that meant she had done the right thing to refuse them.

But tonight was different. Tonight she wanted to give so much, yet knew she had to refuse. Her religion told her to wait. She trusted its teachings and   traditions. For the first time in her life, she had wanted to ignore all of that and give herself to a man. Was this the real thing? Was she deluding herself? One side of Susan said to herself she had once again saved her integrity while the other screamed 'don't let this one get away!'

Early in the morning on her way to bed, Susan stopped by her hallway mirror and stared at her image. "Okay," she said, "what do you want to be for the rest of your life?" Her image just stared back at her not knowing whether to laugh or cry.

The President entered the private living area of the White House, tossed a jacket, picked up a tall glass of soda and exclaimed, "Whew, what a day."

The President's day had begun at five am with a pre-breakfast conference of advisors and had not stopped for even one minute. The pundits who call the job of President of the United States a man-killer were absolutely right, he thought. It sure was trying to kill him.

After greeting family and deciding 'what's for dinner,' the President sat in an easy chair to watch the evening news. As usual the media were criticizing the President's polices about everything. Just as the news about the State Department's recent success in opening talks with the Iranians was aired, the secure phone at the President's side rang. Realizing that it was the director of the CIA and remembering the actions that were in motion, the President turned off the TV and sat up straight to listen.

As the conversation progressed, the President put the call on hold then came back on with the Chairman of the Joint Chiefs and the Secretary of State on the line. Twenty minutes later a compromise had been reached. The Strike, if necessary, would be made by a CIA controlled Predator but the Air Force would still have ground attack assets in the area in case they were needed.

Ryall Morgan was relieved. He thanked the director profusely then trod the stairs back to the garage. His car was now the last one on its level. Inside the car, he dialed Mort Lindsley and brought him up to date on events.

Lindsley was not at all pleased by what he considered 'meddling' by politicians in the affairs of the security agencies. "Our best plans can be compromised in just minutes by those bumbling rascals," he complained. "It makes you want to just go silent and do the job, don't you know. Sometimes I think we should just let them know only when it's over. I always say it's easier to ask forgiveness than permission."

Morgan let him ramble. He knew Mort wouldn't do anything of the sort but had to admit there were times when the concept was attractive.

The airport at Tabriz was abruptly closed down. The few commercial and general aviation flights were told to hold their positions and prepare to circle for up to one hour. No other explanation was offered.

Minutes later the reason became clear to the pilots who were circling. Out of the sunrise three Sukkoi Su-25 jets came straight in at high speed and landed at Tabriz. Other Su-25's were sitting on the ground at Tabriz, but they were either non-operational due to maintenance issues or configured for a different mission than the three that had just landed. These three carried only rocket launchers and 'dumb' 500 Kg bombs in addition to the rapid fire 30 mm cannon carried by all Su-25's. No air to air missiles were present, as their weight and drag would slow the plane down and limit its fuel range. The aircraft, called "frogfoot" by NATO performs a close air support role similar to the American A-10 Warthog. These jets were perfect for today's mission: co-operate with sensor systems carried by helicopters to find and destroy a few people in the craggy mountains of eastern Iran.

The pilots remained in their cockpits as the ground crew topped off their fuel. Half an hour later the three aircraft had taxied to take off positions awaiting orders.

Kourosh Menzadah cursed his luck as he pulled the car off the road. The last thing he wanted was to change a tire in this open place but the sharp rock he had just struck in the middle of the road forced the delay. They had not come quite far enough to leave the car and get onto mountain trails yet. The spot where they could pick up the trail was still three miles away.

Paul Roche hustled equipment and Kourosh worked feverishly to get the tire changed. They wasted twenty minutes of precious low reflection dawn light to change the tire. Kourosh had wanted to use that particular time window to get free of the car and on the trail using the low reflective light to help cover them. Now they would have to make the transition to the trail in broad daylight.

The two men were just getting back into the car, when instinct froze Roche in his tracks. Moments later, Kourosh heard it too. The unmistakable crack of small arms fire emanated from a point just further along the road from their position. A few shots suddenly became a fusillade. Just ahead of them someone was engaging in a furious fire fight.

Kourosh looked around. He wanted to find a way around whatever was going on ahead. He spied a small path that seemed to drop out of sight of the road, but appeared again a bit further west as running parallel to the road. "I think we better leave the car here," he said. "It means a couple of miles more walking, but it's better than trying to get through that," he said motioning in the direction of the small arms fire.

"Let's do it!" Roche agreed. He had already spotted the path. "This way?" he gestured.

"Yes quickly!" Kourosh urged.

The two grabbed their gear and strapped it on. Roche slid a clip into his Beretta and stashed it in his belt. Kourosh produced a Glock 17 and shoulder holster from under the driver's seat. He clicked a clip into it and stuffed several more into his jacket pocket. They would have to wait for a sheltered spot somewhere down the path to take the time to assemble their assault rifles.

After the two were fully strapped up and ready to move out, Kourosh grabbed the car keys and they both dropped over the side of the mountain road to the path that ran ten feet below.

Minutes later they came on the scene of the fire fight. There were dead bodies strewn about the road. A couple of wounded made sounds like animals dying. A wide column of smoke rose from behind an outcropping of rock. No one was firing anymore.

Kourosh motioned up to the cliff above the scene. "I think these guys were ambushed from above," he whispered.

Roche nodded. "I think these dead and dying buggers had set an ambush for us," he whispered back.

Both men wondered who was on the ridge. Neither of them wanted to find out. Menzadah held his finger to his lips. Roche nodded. Silence would be necessary for a while.

Roche waited in the bushes while Menzadah flanked. Within moments he had moved to a spot where he could see the bus in flames. Two survivors were in cover behind a car. Their presence would be shielded from the view of anybody on the cliff. They were bogged down by the anticipation of more fire from the cliff.

Kourosh could not discern any other likely combatants. He counted twenty dead or dying. Circling back under cover of the roadway above, Menzadah slid beside Roche. He held up two fingers and pointed toward the turn-off. He made a signal that the two remaining unfriendlies were not a present threat. He motioned down the path toward the west. The two moved cautiously along the path keeping in cover from those on the cliff.

A few hundred yards away from the action, the two stopped, slid out of their packs and assembled their rifles. Fully loaded, they re-mounted the back packs. Kourosh decided to risk brief conversation.

"Those guys are not Iranians," he began in a half-whisper, motioning back toward the bus, "they're Arabs."

"Whoever they are, they were waiting to kill us." Roche declared. "They might be working for a guy I took something from, in Ashgabat."

"You think they're Turkmen?" Kourosh asked. "These guys look more like Yemenis to me, maybe Al Qaeda."

"That's possible," Roche allowed with a shrug. "Our more immediate problem is whoever's on that ridge."

"That's right," said Kourosh. "Once we get to the main trail we can be seen from that ridge for more than a mile."

Roche thought for a moment. "How 'bout we try to get a look at those unfriendlies on the cliff?"

"It would be nice to know who they are and how many," mused Menzadah. "Let's think about that a bit."

On the cliff, the Taliban commander was satisfied that he had neutralized the ambush but he was distressed that during the fight the bus had been set on fire. He had no choice but to let it burn out. The smoke would act like a magnet drawing in any other enemies in the area. It had probably also warned off the men he targeted.

He decided to post two men and a radio to keep an eye on the scene. He took the other nine men and scurried along the cliff toward the west. Eventually as the cliffs turned abruptly north he would have to give up the high ground and drop closer to the road. For now he wanted to get as far away from the smoke as possible without having to leave the cliff. He was lucky (or smart) that he had lost none of his men in the fight. He was worried that the men his adversaries waited for in ambush had not showed. They were his quarry too after all.

Finally he had no choice. If he did not cover the road itself, there would be no chance to stop a car, if one came. The Taliban commander confirmed by radio that no one had come along then detailed four men down to the road.

Kourosh and Roche had finally decided that it didn't matter who was on the ridge, they just needed to get as much distance as possible on them before they came down from the ridge. They also did not want to be anywhere near that column of smoke.

The two men hustled at double time down the small path that paralleled the road. About a mile from the smoke column, the path joined the main trail. This was the one that Kourosh had traveled so many times before. He knew this path like the back of his hand.

"Stay to the right," he instructed Roche.

Roche could see that the right side of the trail gave them the greatest cover from the cliff. "What about over there," Roche gestured. He was pointing toward the west, where there was a rocky topped mountain sticking up about two thousand feet from their position.

"That's our destination," Kourosh declared.

CHAPTER 44

From the position where they had moved the fifty caliber gun, Steck could easily see the column of smoke one and a half miles to the east.

"What do you make of that?" he asked Grundstrom, who had just seen it himself.

Gunny hopped onto the truck bed. "Let's have a look," he said. He swung the gun around to point it in the direction of the smoke and turned on the electronics. He bent to peer into the sight screen. After a moment, he let out a low whistle. "It's a bus, he said. Looks like it caught fire at a turnout in the road." Then he added, "I think there's been a fire fight."

Steck scrambled onto the truck bed. Grundstrom helped him figure how to use the gun site. "Got it," he acknowledged.

"Look beside it on the road," Gunny instructed.

"Casualties," Steck exclaimed, "lots of them."

"Where there are losers, there must be winners," Grundstrom remarked. "Look around the area."

"You're better with this thing than I am, Gunny. Here, you have a look around the area." Steck needed information, not control.

"I got a couple of guys on the cliff above the fire," Gunny said after a minute or two. "Two guys usually don't take out a couple of dozen. They probably have friends nearby."

"Is there a way we can find them?" Steck asked.

"Yup, there is." Gunny switched to the infra-red screen on the sight. "Hang on while I scan the area."

Within minutes Grundstrom had identified four additional figures near the road a bit west of the fire. Then he found five more on the cliffs above them. "I make it twelve," he announced.

"Is this thing good enough to get a good shot at the guys on the cliff, one good enough for identification?" Steck asked.

"Negative," said Gunny, "but I have a hi-resolution fine grain scope in the truck. Let's try that."

While Grundstrom dug out the intended piece of gear, Steck practiced using the infra-red optics on the gun. He watched as the four guys on the road disappeared. "Hey, I just lost the four at the road," he shouted to Grundstrom.

Grundstrom had the hi-res scope trained on the spot where the two guys above the fire were positioned. "Hey Steck, those buggers are Taliban," he exclaimed, "I can tell by the turbans." As he said this, the two in turbans scurried into a cave in the cliff.

"Something's messed up on this infra-red thing," Steck complained.

"Naw, the gear's good," declared Gunny. "I think they figured out we're watching them and they're taking cover to reduce their thermal signatures."

"Or that someone else is looking for them," Steck said, indicating a helicopter that had just appeared over the ridge behind the Taliban. "That's probably Iranian," he said. "I think this is getting too hot for us. Let's pull back across the border."

Gunny was already shouting orders. The team headed back to the border and Brandt hopped into the truck, started it up and turned around. In the scrubby rock trail, the truck had to move at a painfully slow pace. If the Iranians picked him up on their sensors, they would have company fast.

They seemed to be in luck. The helicopter was soon joined by a second one and both swung toward the burning bus. One set down and poured out several personnel while the other hovered nearby. From a spot dead on the border according to their GPS, Steck and his team watched. The Iranians seemed pre-occupied with the aftermath of the recent events on the road, not realizing that the source of all this killing was probably watching them.

Paul Roche and Kourosh Menzadah were still moving at a brisk pace now almost a mile away from the helicopters.

Kourosh realized there was no way he could go back across the trail as he had done so many times before. The Iranians would keep guards on that road for a month or more. His car was probably already sealed off by the army. It was only a matter of time before either prints or some forgotten personal item would connect him with the vehicle. He figured his best shot would be to ask the people waiting for Roche to get him out of the area. Maybe, he thought, he could make a new life in Turkey.

The trail made an abrupt transition to ascent, emerging from the dense brush to climb nearly straight up the rock face. They had about another mile and a quarter to go, but in the next half mile they would climb almost a thousand feet in altitude.

Roche was holding up well physically, but internally tension was high. There was no way that the burning bus had attracted two Iranian army helicopters. They were obviously looking for him. There were many groups chasing after the figurine and they all seemed to know where he was. He wondered whether to trust Menzadah. Was he aware of the value of the goods? Was he working with one of the groups that sought the figurine? Roche reached for Kourosh's hand to help him up and over the next rock. It was best to have a partner for the climb, but he made up his mind that as soon as he was at the Turkish border, he would kill Menzadah.

At an airbase in the United States, the information beamed back from the Global Hawk drone high over the mountains of north eastern Iran was streaming in. As it did, constant analysis of the data was processed and reduced to a description of action on the ground.

The road that led through Maku was quiet but the one through Khoy and Qotur was alive with action both on the ground and in the air. At least thirty combatants had been identified and they had fought against one another. Two Helicopters on the scene, also with combatants on board were now being joined by three close air support jet fighters in Iranian dressage. At the moment the fighters were standing off the scene but it was clear that they could swoop down and inflict damage very quickly if commanded to do so. The blue team near the border had withdrawn to a position inside Turkey.

As this information was shared in near real time with Langley a small group including Morgan, Lindsley and the Director were kept informed. It was decided that three sets of co-ordinates for a strike by the CIA predator hovering in Turkey over Kapikoy, near the border would be pre-loaded into its fire control system but not authorized until it became clear that any of them would be used. That would save seconds in case the situation on the ground demanded it. They changed the orbit of the predator to put it one minute from the helicopters on the ground near Qotur.

"I think our guys are in the soup," Morgan mused. "There's been a fire fight with lots of casualties on that road. I'm wondering why they went so far into Iran."

"Those helicopters are obviously Iranian and they are at the scene of the fight. I think it's safe to assume that they're taking our guys into custody," said the Director.

"That assumes that it was our guys who engaged whoever was in that bus," offered Lindsley. "Is there a way we can confirm that?"

"Let's try to raise Steck on a secure line," suggested Morgan. He knew the Director was already thinking about damage control, wondering if the Air Force could destroy three fighter planes and two helicopters full of prisoners then somehow make it like they were never there.

Morgan dialed the numbers and codes then pushed the speaker key. Everyone was startled to hear Steck's voice loud and clear.

"Steck Here," he said without the slightest indication of stress.

"Steck its Morgan," Ryall answered, "What's going on there?"

"Some kind of fracas between Yemenis and Taliban, if you can believe it," said Steck. Just in case Morgan didn't believe his ears, Steck repeated "That's Yemenis and Taliban, you heard it right. We're watching from the Border. We pulled back when we discovered the action. There's a couple of Iranian Helos in there at the moment cleaning up the mess. We think the Yemenis got ambushed. The Taliban are still watching from close by. Can you guys see any of that?" Steck knew that satellite and drone surveillance would certainly be part of a mission this important.

Morgan shot a look at the Director. "Yes we can but we couldn't see whether you were mixed up in it."

"Negative. We are in the catbird seat at the moment."

"What about the target?" Morgan was finished with diversion and wanted to get to the core issue.

"No sign of the target yet from our position. We figure that fight we just saw was over who gets a shot at the target first. They made a lot of noise fighting each other. Knowing the target, we think that probably scared him off."

Morgan was satisfied that they still had a game to play. "What are your plans?" He asked.

"We're going to sit tight under cover and watch the rest of this sideshow. I still think the target will try to come through our position eventually, if he wasn't scared back into the countryside by what just went down."

Morgan agreed and nodded ascent to the others in the room. "I don't think that target scares so easily," he said into the speaker.

"Roger that," said Steck.

"Do you have anything else to tell us?" Morgan inquired.

"Negative, but I have a question." Without waiting for a response, Steck continued, "What other assets do you have for us?"

Morgan looked around the room. No one made any moves. "There's a company bird nearby."

"Thank you kindly for that," Steck responded. That meant there was a Predator armed with precision strike capability in addition to whatever was the source of Morgan's intel. "Can we access that asset?"

"Through me and only me," Morgan said emphatically.

"Roger, Out!" barked Steck as he clicked off.

CHAPTER 45

Greg Liss pulled his car in to a space in the parking lot of his town house complex about one o'clock am. On the way from Susan Deet's house he had stopped for a beer. He wanted to think about her unexpected behavior when he tried to make a move to get physical.

Many beers later, he had worked it out. He loved Susan more than any woman he had ever met. He wanted her by his side every minute of every day. He did not understand her behavior but he respected her for being her own person. Maybe an old-fashioned girl is what he had been searching for all these lonely years. Carole Hinson certainly hadn't been an 'old-fashioned' girl. If anything Greg himself had been the 'old-fashioned' one in that relationship.

Greg had started several relationships since Carole. They were all based in physical attraction and seemed to follow a pattern of hot and heavy beginnings followed by disaster at the first disagreement.

He had thought Lisa Raines was different. She was kinder than the others and more patient with his intellectual ways. The problem was she bore lots of baggage from some past relationship that she refused to talk about. She became so possessive of Greg that he sometimes wondered if she was insane. He had tried to break it off with her but she was obsessed about keeping him as her own. He had finally just let her hang around to slake her passions. He was actually worried what she might do to herself if he dumped her.

Now everything had changed. He was in love. He was totally, hopelessly in love with Susan. He wanted her to be his wife, end of story. He hoped he could pull it off. This might be his last chance at happiness. He prayed not to screw it up.

Greg got out of his car. He staggered slightly on the way to his front door. As he fumbled for the key, the door opened.

"Where have you been, baby?" It was Lisa Raines.

Greg cursed at having given her a key. "Oh, Hi Lisa," he slurred.

"Out with the boys?" Lisa asked playfully. "That's okay, honey. You've got to have a night out once in a while." She kissed him open-mouthed.

After the kiss Greg faked a big yawn. "I've got to get some sleep. See you tomorrow?" He tried to go around her intending to head for his bedroom.

"Oh no you don't, big boy," she teased. "I'm going to put big baby to bed and keep him warm."

Greg was not up to a big hassle, especially in the fog of half-drunkenness. He would have to confront his new reality another time. He waved an arm at her and headed for the bed. "Whatever," he sighed.

Paul Roche and Kourosh Menzadah stopped about a hundred yards from the top of the mountain ridge where the trail was leading them. They needed to catch a breath and to eat a bit of food. The place was sheltered from the wind, but open to the scant winter sun. Though the temperature was just at the freezing line, they both felt warm from exertion. Long clouds drifted in from the north-west, a portent of rain or snow. Judging from the cold temperature, Roche figured it would be snow.

Above them lay a rock plateau about a quarter mile wide. At the western end of that plateau was the Turkish border. They did not have far to go, but it seemed the worst part of the journey. There was virtually no cover on the plateau except for a few rock-boulders strewn here and there by some ancient geological event. If they went now it would be in mid-afternoon daylight. If they waited until after the snow they would be awfully easy to track.

Kourosh extracted his binoculars from his back pack. He set the zoom to 24X. Using his knees as a stand to steady the instrument, he studied the spot where the bus had burned out. There was barely a wisp of smoke now and then rising on swirls of air as the cliffs to the north broke up the north-west breeze. No personnel could be seen. Down the road a few hundred yards he searched for any sign of his car. He sighed as he focused on the scene. His car was sealed with yellow material that denoted it as evidence not to be disturbed.

The Helicopters had both flown back towards Khoy an hour ago, carrying bodies and prisoners, if any. Kourosh knew that they would return soon to look for him and for Roche. The Iranians knew the path that Kourosh had used to get where they were. They ignored it most of the time during winter because they did not expect much traffic there. It would be the path they would search first given the present situation.

At a noise above, he swung the binoculars, swinging the zoom back to 8X in hopes of seeing what sort of aircraft was there. Three noisy Su-25s flew by in loose formation. They were flying at slow speed just traversing the area. He had heard them off and on all day, but had not taken time to have a look.

"Those are 'frogfoot' jets, Roche commented as he squinted to see what Kourosh was gazing at.

"Yes, I know that model," Kourosh declared. "They could be real trouble if they get any idea where we are."

"Right you are," said Roche. The thirty cal gun on those things can strafe a wide area and chew right through this brittle rock." He gestured to the stuff they sat on.

"I think we should wait for darkness to make the last leg of our hike," said Kourosh. "In darkness we could make it all the way to Kapikoy where Mister Taylor will be waiting."

Roche thought about it for a minute. If he agreed, they would remain exposed to Iranian fire for yet another two or three hours. If they crossed the border in darkness, he would need Kourosh as a guide for longer than he had anticipated.

Before he could answer, the rhythmic sound of a helicopter engine came from the east. The helo was flying NOE (Nap Of the Earth) bobbing up and down the rough terrain. The machine followed the trail that Roche and Menzadah had just traveled. In just a minutes or so it could cover the distance that took the hikers most of the day.

"Come!" shouted Kourosh, "I know a place!" The two men scurried down some loose rock to a small clearing. The clearing sat at the mouth of a small cave. They scrambled into the cave just as the helicopter passed nearby.

They lay quiet in the cave. Roche was afraid they might have been picked up on the helicopter's infra-red gear.

Moments later, one of the jets swooped down. Beginning at the end of the trail near the remains of the bus, the pilot strafed the trail with his rapid-fire cannon. Belching rounds at thousands per minute, the gunfire chewed up the trail. Vegetation and rock chips flew in all directions. The pilot soon spent all his ammo. He pulled up abruptly streaking skyward. Behind him came the second jet. He began his strafing pattern just behind the end of the first pilot's. By the time the second jet pulled up, the destruction had reached a point near the spot Roche and Menzadah had just abandoned.

Roche and Menzadah peered out of their haven wide-eyed as the third jet came diving in to begin his run. Suddenly a noise was heard from just beyond the plateau. Roche strained to identify the noise. It sounded sort of familiar.

The jet fighter suddenly burst into flames and came apart. Pieces of the airplane fell in all directions, dripping balls of fire. The plane was close enough that Roche saw the pilot eject from the titanium tub that surrounded him to protect against small arms fire from below. The ejection seat functioned perfectly driving the seat and pilot high into the air above the disintegrating aircraft but the parachute did not. Realizing he was going to die but powerless to do anything about it, the pilot screamed just as he slammed into the rock face.

Just across the border, Gunny Grundstrom did not know whether to laugh or cry.

The pilots had failed to see the gun, the trucks and Steck's team of fighters snug under their camouflage nets. Steck ordered everyone to stay down and stay still.

As the third pilot made his approach to strafe the trail, Gunny realized that the strafing path would chop right through their position before the gun ran out of ammo. That would destroy the fifty caliber gun on the truck, blowing their ammo reserves and probably killing most of the team. He leaped onto the truck, sighted the gun and fired right down the Frogfoot's snout. The pattern of his shots caught the engines on either side of the fuselage and the frogfoot ceased to be an airplane.

The action was close enough that chunks of flaming frogfoot fell within fifty yards of their position.

When Gunny regained his composure enough to speak, he just shouted "Oh crap!"

Steck shared his feeling. They had better get out of there fast before the Iranians figured out what had just happened. "Pull back," he ordered. "Get back to base on the double."

By the time they all reached their cave just off the highway and stashed their trucks and gear under camouflage, the helicopter crew had realized that their fighter plane had not malfunctioned but had been taken down.

They wasted precious minutes obtaining permission to have a look across the border.

Steck meanwhile rang up Morgan. "What the Blazes was that?" Morgan shouted.

"We had to take out an airplane," was Steck's reply. "There's an Iranian helicopter with attack capability standing off," he said. "The pilot's probably trying to get permission to cross the border. When he gets it, he'll kill us all."

Morgan looked around the room. Lindsley didn't know what to say. The director finally nodded. "Send in the bird." He said quietly.

"Give me your exact position," Morgan said anxiously.

Steck barked his position.

"Take cover, Bob and good luck." Morgan clicked off then contacted the pilot of the remote controlled Predator. The pilot was actually two floors away from them at Langley.

"Do you see the helicopter?" he asked the pilot.

"Lined-up and locked-on sir," the man replied.

"Take it out," ordered Morgan.

Morgan turned to the director. "Sir, I Think we better call the President."

Steck and his crew hunkered down in their cave. They could hear the helicopter coming toward them at high speed. The pilot saw infra-red signatures of the truck engines, still warm after their run to base. Figuring he was alone, he took his time, swinging the big bird around to take aim with his rockets.

Before the pilot could give the command to his gunner to fire, the machine exploded from a direct hit by a hellfire missile. They never knew what hit them.

Steck waited a few minutes to be sure the helicopter would not be joined by others.

"Let's get our butts out of here." He ordered. "Hey Brandt, I've got a job for you. Take Marya and make your way to the road just by the border crossing. You'll see where the trail rejoins the road. If you spot Roche and his companion, tail them and report what you see."

The two prepared for their detail. They packed night sights, side arms and ammo. They each chose H&K 500's as rifles. They moved out just as the team finished packing the trucks for their pullback to Van.

When everything was ready to go, Steck summoned their attention. "We all owe our lives to one man today. He gestured to his second in command, "Great job, Gunny!"

Roche and Menzadah stayed in their cave, waiting for darkness. An hour later in light snow they began the five mile trek to Kapikoy.

"We didn't even have to fire a shot," Remarked Roche as they walked along.

"We're not there yet," replied a stern faced Menzadah.

Roche was so pleased that he had made it alive that he forgot about killing Menzadah. He dismissed the whole idea as probably just paranoia anyway.

As they walked along, the relief of making it to Turkey in one piece set in and the two carried on a lively conversation. They never noticed the two figures tracking them from a few hundred yards behind.

CHAPTER 46

Ajir and one of his body guards had survived the attack on the bus, only to be taken into custody by the Iranian army then turned over to MOIS for questioning. His wife and children had to make a run for it so they would not be taken.

He was put in an unheated cell that stank of urine and death. After intense interrogation he had been allowed one visitor of his choice. His lawyer came to visit.

Ajir was a pitiful sight. He had two black eyes. Blood had dried on his forehead after oozing for hours from a head wound sustained during interrogation. "Are my children safe?" Ajir asked.

"Your children and you wife are safely in Ashgabat," the lawyer told him.

"Did they take my airplane to Ashgabat?" he asked.

"No, they took a commercial flight. The government has impounded your airplane." The lawyer waited for that to sink in. "I bribed the MOIS and your father was released twenty minutes ago." he said. "I cannot get you out until you confess to whatever it is they want you to confess."

"I don't know what they want me to confess!" complained Ajir. "They won't tell me."

After the lawyer left, Ajir put his head to the floor and thanked Allah that his children and his father had been spared. He got up and began to plot how he would get out of Evin prison.

Roche and Menzadah finally made it to the appointed pick up area just outside the village of Kapikoy in Turkey about eight o'clock pm. As promised, Taylor and one of the Turkish employees of Al Kafajy trading company met them.

"Well, we finally meet Mister Roche!" Taylor announced. "Did you bring my precious trinket?"

"Trinket indeed," muttered Roche. "The thing almost cost me my life."

"You were paid well to risk your life my friend," said Taylor, "the full amount we greed upon will be deposited to your account tomorrow morning."

Roche brightened. "So, you are a man of your word," he allowed.

"As always," Chris replied. He produced a pint of good Scot's whiskey and offered it to his companions. Roche took a long draught. The Muslims declined. Between Taylor and Roche the bottle was half empty by the time they had each recounted the day's activities.

Just yards away, hidden in some snow-coated brush Brandt and Lukianov recorded the conversations of their enemy on a small MP3 machine.

For safety's sake they did not try to communicate. Lukianov smiled when the bottle came out and held her hand up as if holding a glass. Brandt got the inference and held up his own. They made an imaginary toast. Brandt could almost taste the whiskey.

"So, where are you guys headed after Istanbul?" Taylor asked Roche and Menzadah.

"I'm going to stay in Turkey," Menzadah declared. "It will be too hot for me in Iran for quite a while."

"I'm going to hit the beach in Spain," said Roche, "How about you Taylor?"

"I'm heading for Paris." Chris held up the ABS case. "My boss is waiting to receive this."

When the last of the bottle had been consumed the men loaded into the car for the trip to Istanbul.

Brandt and Lukianov retreated. They had what they needed. Finding a small cave just off the road, they holed up and dialed up Steck, who had already reached Van. Steck sent Gunny with a car to extract them. Within hours Steck had relayed the pertinent information to Morgan.

Next morning after reaching Istanbul, the men split up.

344

Menzadah took his payment as a grub stake to establish a life for himself in Turkey.

Roche took a flight to Spain. He had decided to rent a villa on the Mediterranean near Marbella to settle in for a month's vacation as Jacob Breen. Eventually he would catch a flight back to Mexico. His bank account had been seriously enriched in the past weeks. He left it with Taylor that he might be available for future operations but only on a very selective basis. He had enough money to live the way he wanted to live for the rest of his life.

Chris Taylor caught Air France to Paris.

Morgan and Mort Lindsley consulted about how to proceed. They decided to contact Interpol to have Taylor picked up in Paris. They were told that Interpol's constitution prohibits 'any intervention or activities of a political, military, religious or racial character.' It would take three to five days for Interpol to study the request and make a determination whether the Americans were simply chasing thieves or if there were some political overtones that would violate Interpol protocol. Of course if they waited three days Taylor would be long gone.

Morgan fumed at what he perceived as "bureaucratic nonsense nearly equal to those NATO idiots."

They contacted one of Morgan's counterparts in French Intelligence and within hours had two agents; one Frenchman and one American waiting at the gate for Taylor's plane.

Greg Liss woke next morning in his own bed beside Lisa Raines. As consciousness spread Greg tried to remember what had happened last night.

Lisa's eyes opened. She snuggled up to Greg.

"Did we...uh did we do anything last night?" Greg asked.

"No, baby but I'm ready if you are," she said seductively.

"I'm not," he replied scrambling out of bed.

"What's wrong?" Lisa looked puzzled.

"Lisa, we have to talk," Greg began. "Look, I don't know where to begin but I can't go on like this." Greg reached for his pants. It would be a long morning.

Air France flight 2391 from Istanbul to Charles De Gaulle arrived on time at eleven-forty a.m. The crew had to wake Taylor, who had slept through the four hour flight in his comfortable first class seat. Chris was last off the plane.

Two men came along side him as he walked briefcase in hand down the long moving walkway towards passport control. Moments later he was in custody, riding in a vehicle run by French security to a place off the airport grounds where he would be searched and interrogated.

At eight pm Washington time, Morgan received a call. *The Hand of Mohammed* was in the possession of an American agent who would catch a flight to Dulles next morning. That meant the figurine would be in the JUMP team's hands within twenty-four hours.

"Gosh," Lindsley blurted at the news, "that was easy once the thing got to Europe."

The JUMP team spent all day writing reports and cleaning up paperwork in preparation for closing the operation.

Susan Deet suggested that Doctor Wigglesworth have a look at the item before it went into storage. She argued that it would be a kindness to the old man since he had spent his life searching for the thing.

Lindsley was against having Wigglesworth involved. "For goodness sake, Susie, we're going to open an investigation into his illegal trafficking in antiquities as soon as we wrap up this operation," he said. What use would it serve?"

"Hold on a minute Mort," Morgan said. "I think Susan's idea has merit. If we let old Wigglesworth see the thing with his own eyes we could send a message to the Saudis to back-off in a way that would allow them to 'save face' diplomatically."

Susan flashed a look of appreciation to Morgan. She wondered why Greg hadn't shown up yet this morning. She knew he would support any kindness toward his old professor. She wanted to have his support to add weight to her argument.

Lindsley finally came around. "I will support Susie's initiative," he said, but I still have misgivings."

Greg arrived in the early afternoon offering a lame excuse for being late. He and Susan exchanged longing glances then went to work on a joint report.

The glances did not go unnoticed by Mort Lindsley. He wondered what was going on between his two protégés. Young love was a thing he always favored, but not between two of his agents that had to work together every day. He decided to keep it to himself for now.

Lindsley got a message to Wigglesworth by having one of the agents watching his house meet him at his door and taking a walk with him across the Dartmouth campus. He did this because he knew the Saudis were still in the area. There was no telling what kind of electronic surveillance they might have in place beyond the rudimentary stuff the FBI had already detected.

Morgan and his boss the director contacted the President, who was happy that the item was back in American hands. He asked for a call when it arrived safely.

At the end of the day around nine pm, the JUMP team sat at their conference table staring at the item that had been their objective for months.

Greg Liss was ecstatic. Morgan was pleased at the outcome. Mort Lindsley drawled, "The thing looks like the ceramics my aunt used to make. She always gave us some ugly thing like that every Christmas."

"Now that we have the thing," Morgan announced, "let's all call the President on the speaker phone and share the glory."

CHAPTER 47

Brandt and Marya Lukianov bid farewell in Istanbul. Her next posting was to Paris, where she would check-in with the local CSIS bureau. She liked working in France because among the many Russian émigré families in Paris were some of her relatives. Her job required facility in the French language, so she felt at home in Paris. Steck thanked her for her exemplary service and sent a long email to MacFergus commending her as an able and professional agent.

Marya tried to keep a line out with Brandt. She was very attracted to him and thought about a relationship outside work. Until the operation they were working together was over, it would have to be professional. Now that it was ending she let him know that he could look her up anytime.

Brandt was wary of a personal relationship with Marya. She was a very beautiful woman and he was strongly attracted but there was the issue of Carole Hinson. If they ever became more than colleagues, he knew he would let it slip sooner or later. Brandt had no doubt that Marya would kill him without remorse if she knew what had happened.

Brandt and Grundstrom flew back to Amman, where Gunny had some business to tidy-up for *Free Nation*. When they checked-in at the Intercontinental there was a message from Colonel Randy. He wanted to meet Brandt in Frankfurt, Germany. When Brandt called him, Randy was already in New York visiting Saleem. They made arrangements to meet in Frankfurt two days later.

When Professor Wigglesworth heard that *The Hand of Mohammed* had been recovered, he asked right away if he could see it. The agent assigned to him reported that the old man was eager to view the item, but that he was reluctant to travel and leave his wife at home.

At JUMP team headquarters, Greg Liss suggested that he take *The Hand* to Dartmouth.

"No way, Greg," snapped Lindsley. "We can't risk losing this thing. Either the old man comes here or we just put it away."

Morgan had to agree with Mort. Careless handling or some accident could be a disaster right at the cusp of victory.

In the end it was decided that Susan and Greg would fly to Lebanon airport, just two miles from Dartmouth College in the team's Learjet. They would pick up Doctor and Missus Wigglesworth and would fly them directly to Washington. They would stay with the couple as escorts then fly them back home.

Mort Lindsley objected to wasting taxpayer money for such a junket. He was overridden by his colleagues.

The next day Susan and Greg flew to New Hampshire and collected the Wigglesworths. Missus Wigglesworth was feeling quite well and enjoyed the ride immensely. She and Susan chatted like old friends. At one point just before landing in Washington, she told Susan, "You know my dear you should latch on to young Mister Liss. He's a bright lad with a good future, I would imagine."

Susan blushed. Greg smirked.

At the JUMP team's office, the group assembled and a case holding the figurine was produced. Doctor Wigglesworth opened the case and studied the thing for some time.

"May I pick it up?" he asked.

Morgan nodded. The professor held it, turned it and studied it for some time. He smelled it, which Morgan thought strange.

The team looked at one another. They hadn't anticipated his strange behavior. The professor kept mumbling to himself. Then he stuck out his tongue and seemed to taste it.

Lindsley was about to intervene when the professor set it back into the case. He took a step back from the table and said. "It's a fake."

Lindsley came straight out of his chair. "It's a what?"

"A fake, a reproduction," the professor said with a blank expression. "This is not *The Hand of Mohammed.*

Lindsley turned on his projector and flashed the picture that had been taken after the Gulf War, the same as the one that had been shown to the professor in Yemen. "When you saw this photo, professor, you thought the thing was real enough. Can you explain what has changed about it?"

"Yes I can," the professor said as he sat down. "You see that picture shows the genuine and original item. The item you have here is a recent casting. The plaster still smells fresh, whereas the real item would have no smell at all except for must or dirt in which it had been stored. Furthermore, the paint on this item is of a type unknown to artists in the seventh century when the real item would have been painted. Whoever made this reproduction knew he could never reproduce the colors using the original paint formula because the pigments used for it are simply not available today. He used modern Acrylic paint, which allowed him to obtain the colors. The bluish tint that he employed is from a compound discernable by its taste, a pigment only found in eastern Iran."

Mort Lindsley seemed mesmerized by the professor's analysis. The others were just exchanging incredulous looks.

"Finally," the professor added as he studied the photo on the big screen, "If you see the tiny indentation at the base of the thumb in this photo of the original it's plain to see that it's simply not there in the copy. The reason for that is that it was lost in the mould transfer process when they made the fake. The artist who did this probably supposed that it would not be noticed. He also probably did not want to risk damaging the copy by trying to use a tool to re-create that indentation."

"I guess that changes our game," observed Morgan, "again!"

Ahmed left Mister Al Kafajy's suite in Paris in early afternoon. He went to his flat and packed his bag for a three day trip.

It was his custom to have coffee in the evening with the door man in his building, a modest apartment structure at eighteen Rue des Chappelets that housed many semi-itinerant people who had Paris as a base. Most of the residents were seldom there, so it was a good place to be anonymous.

The door man, whose name was Henri had a small espresso machine at his counter in the foyer. Seeing the small suitcase Ahmed carried from the elevator, he was curious. "So Ahmed, where will you go this time?" Henri asked, loading the machine with finely ground coffee.

"I'm off to Tehran, then to Jordan, Henri," Ahmed announced. "If Allah wills it, I will be home in three days."

The two drank coffee and chatted for about ten minutes until Ahmed's taxi arrived to take him to the station. As he drove away, Henri made a telephone call to a Paris number. "He's on his way to Tehran," monsieur. "He returns in three days."

Ahmed took the train to the airport then flew from Paris directly to Tehran. After spending a day with Khazeh reviewing the books of the company's Iranian trading activity, He departed on a flight to Amman.

After checking in at Al Kafajy Trading Company's Amman office where he deposited a package for safe keeping, Ahmed checked in to the Royal Amman hotel and called the boss.

"Do you have it?" the boss asked.

"Allah has allowed it," said Ahmed stiffly.

"Very well, old friend," the boss said. "Bring it to me tomorrow."

"How is our friend Christian doing?" asked Ahmed with an air of insensitivity.

"Our Lawyers will have him released possibly tomorrow." the boss answered, "but it will cost a lot of money."

"Allah provides," declared Ahmed. "I will see you tomorrow, if Allah wills it."

Brandt cut quite a figure in the new suit he had purchased in Amman for the trip to Frankfurt. His athletic six foot-two inch frame, chiseled features, bright blond brush cut hair, tanned skin and flashing blue eyes turned women's heads as he strode through the Frankfurt International airport. The scar on his face completed the picture. His look was that of some movie star that no one could quite place.

Colonel Randy met him at the customs exit dressed in the same sort of business suit. His was custom tailored, a necessity to fit his six foot-four broad shouldered frame.

The two men ducked into a Mercedes taxi for the ride to a small hotel near the airport.

"I'm proud of you son," said Randy. "Bob Steck says you did really well on this last mission." The smile was genuine, but turned immediately back to the stern countenance that was Colonel Randy's trademark expression.

"Our job is not done yet," he announced to Brandt as soon as they were in private. "I had a hunch about the operation you just finished before it even started. You see, I did not believe that a guy like Taylor would be stupid enough to send something as precious as that *Hand of Mohammed* thing through the mountains of western Iran on the back of some thief, especially an American."

Brandt gave him a quizzical look. "What do you mean? Do you think Roche didn't have the thing?"

"That's exactly what I mean. The chances of a guy like that making it out of the country alive were pretty slim from the beginning. A whole bunch of bad guys from different places were all after the object. It's bad enough that Roche had to elude the Iranians but much less likely he could elude all those others as well."

Brandt was getting interested. "So, you decoy all the enemies in one direction while you move the object in another, and if the guy they're chasing gets killed you don't care."

"That's precisely what I think was going on," said Randy. "That's why I had some of our friends in Paris keep an eye on Taylor's boss, the guy that owns the trading company. It took a while, but I began to see how the guy operates. He has a side kick, a guy named Ahmed who is somewhere between a body guard and friend. This Ahmed is a shadowy character that does most of the old man's dirty work. So I had him tailed while I checked Ahmed's reputation on the street." Randy handed Brandt a photo of Ahmed in full Arab dress. He looked quite sinister.

"What did you find out?" Brandt was fascinated.

"I found out that Ahmed is a cold-blooded killer, a schemer and some kind of religious fanatic. He has the sort of mentality that's a necessary trait in your garden variety Islamic terrorist."

"Do you think Ahmed is the real deal, the guy who has the real goods?" Brandt wondered inwardly if this was true and if so whether Steck knew he had bogus results.

Randy grinned. "I think Ahmed was ordered to wait until the diversion was played out, then to quietly move the thing from Iran to Paris."

"When will that come down?" Brandt could see that playing this out couldn't hurt.

"It's coming down right now," said Randy with a self-satisfied expression on his face. "Ahmed left Paris night-before-last to go to Tehran. He is due to return tomorrow after a stop in Amman which is just a standard practice to shift the trail, I figure."

"So why are we in flipping Frankfurt?" Brandt asked.

"Same deal, son," he replied, "to shift the trail."

Brandt got it. "Were not staying here, are we." He declared.

"Here's the plan," Randy announced. "We stay checked in here in Frankfurt. The flight records will show that we are both in Frankfurt and the hotel register will show us here for the next few nights. I have a car and two EU passports so we move freely. We drive to Paris now, snatch the goods from this Ahmed character tomorrow night and return to Frankfurt. Then we fly to Washington and give the thing to the FBI in return for their turning a blind eye towards *Free Nation* after the dust settles."

Brandt considered what he had just heard. If Colonel Randy was right, they would be heroes. If he wasn't, the world would have one less bad dude. "Let's get started." He declared.

CHAPTER 48

Susan and Greg completed their escort duty delivering the Wigglesworths back to Hanover and safely back to their home. They stayed for dinner at the insistence of Missus Wigglesworth.

At dinner Susan gave the professor and his wife clear instructions that were not to reveal anything about the day's activities. Their cover story would be that they had attended a conference in Baltimore.

As they flew back to Washington, Greg and Susan discussed the state of the JUMP team's operation. "This one has sure been a roller coaster ride," he commented.

"Yeah," Susan agreed, "kind of like our ride, eh?" She searched his eyes for a response.

Greg took her hand. "I hope our ride is just beginning," he said returning the gaze. "I think it won't be like a roller coaster, Susie. I hope it will be steady and strong like a rock."

"With a strong foundation," she added.

Greg squeezed her hand. "I broke it off with Lisa. That's why I was late the other day."

She wanted to say something like 'what did you see in Lisa anyway.' Instead she returned the squeeze. "That's what you wanted?" she asked.

"That's what I wanted."

They were both silent for a while.

Susan was encouraged but not cocky. "How much of what I said the other night made sense to you?' she asked.

"Most of it," he admitted. "I mean after I had time to think it through I understood the way you feel."

"How do *you* feel Greg," she asked it like a little girl.

"It's not what I expected, I mean from any woman these days. But I realize it's you and what you are and I respect you too much not to accept it."

Susan decided that was enough for now. She was so excited inside she wanted to shout and dance but she was afraid to let that out just yet. "Thanks for respecting me," She said simply.

Marya Lukianov returned to her new place, a small furnished apartment arranged for her use by CSIS. She had just finished a relaxing extended lunch in a local sidewalk café. She felt good about her new quarters and was settling in for some quality personal time, something she did not get as often as she liked. She carried a small volume of Voltaire, just the perfect book for wasting time in Paris.

She nodded to the door man and headed for the elevator.

"Oh, Mademoiselle," the door man called after her. "There is a message for you from the building manager."

She turned and pulled her dark glasses lower on her nose. Peering over them, she said "For me?"

"Yes, Mademoiselle, the manager wants to know if everything is all right with your flat. Is there anything else you will require?"

"Everything is fine. I don't need anything else at the moment. Thank you for asking, Monsieur."

"Henri," the man added, "My name is Henri, at your service Mademoiselle. "Would you like some Italian coffee? I have it here all the time for my friends in the building."

"No thank you, Henri. Thank you for the message." Marya stepped into the elevator. She hoped the man would not become too annoying.

She decided to spend the rest of the day reading Voltaire. This evening, she would take a long hot bath and be early to bed. Tomorrow she would have time to unpack and put her personal things away.

Marya had just finished drawing her bath and was ready to step in when her secure satphone rang. She grumbled at the thought of losing all that hot water. She wrapped a bathrobe around herself and reached for the phone.

"Marya, hello, it's Bob." She couldn't believe it was the boss. It had to be nearly midnight in Ottawa.

"Hello Bob," she answered, "you're up late."

"I have Ryall Morgan and Mort Lindsley on the line from Washington. We're all patched in together."

She sat down and opened her laptop in case she needed to take notes. "Well hello everybody," she said, "I guess this is important considering the hour."

"It is," MacFergus declared. "I'm going to let Ryall speak for the three of us."

Morgan nodded to Lindsley. "Marya, we have a problem with The Hand of Mohammed," he began.

"What kind of problem?" she wondered what the 'problem' could be.

"The one you and the team rescued from the thieves who took it has turned out to be a fake, a reproduction."

Marya sat up straighter. "It's a fake? Wow, I can't believe it. But how could that be?

"We think the chase in eastern Iran was a set up to decoy us away from the real scheme to move the thing out of Iran."

"Bummer," she mumbled. "So why the call so late in your day?" she asked.

"We think it may be headed for Paris."

Now she understood the reason for the call.

Morgan continued, "The trading company that set up the heist in the first place is run by a man named Mohammed Al Kafajy. He lives mostly in Paris and we know he's there now. We think he will want to handle the object's movement himself since his best guys lost it once already. We have no time to get a team put together, so we consulted Mister MacFergus and he suggested we contact you since you're already in Paris."

"I'm ready to help in any way I can," she offered. "Where does this guy Al Kafajy live?

"He is at the Hotel des Chaumes, near the Place de la Concorde. He has a permanent suite there." Morgan paused. "We'll send you a dossier first thing tomorrow your time. Please get some surveillance put together and find out what you can about Al Kafajy's comings and goings. We'll get Bob Steck and a team to Paris within a few days to assist you."

"And if I run across the famous hand?" she needed direction.

"If the opportunity presents itself, take it," MacFergus interjected.

Morgan frowned. "Above all, be careful, Marya. These guys are an accomplished group of international thieves. They are a formidable enemy."

Marya chuckled. "After what I have experienced the past few weeks, I think you're preaching to the choir." She cursed herself for letting her Russian abruptness show. It was a trait she was trying to deal with in relations with North Americans.

Lindsley wrote on his note pad "FEISTY, EH?" and passed it to Morgan, who just nodded.

"I'll get on this right away," She said. "I'll digest the dossier tomorrow, set up a surveillance using some of our CSIS assets in Paris and report to you tomorrow night Bob."

MacFergus cleared his throat. He hoped her tendency to take charge wouldn't upset the Americans. "Please report to Ryall Morgan, Marya. He's running this operation."

"Okay," she said, "Anything else?"

"Just be careful," Morgan said. "Good night."

Randy Pullin and Brandt had driven all the way to Paris from Frankfurt in what Brandt called "record time." They arrived on Rue des Chappelets at dusk, picking out a parking spot along the street and setting up a stake-out of sorts.

Their reward came only one hour later, as Ahmed arrived in a taxi from the air transfer station. He told the taxi driver to wait then headed for his apartment building with suitcase in hand. He would drop his clothes and return to the taxi to take the prize to Mister Al Kafajy personally.

Pullin recognized Ahmed from the picture he had posted to the sun visor of their car. "Let's go," he announced leaving the car. Brandt followed just steps behind.

Pullin approached Ahmed on the sidewalk just outside the door to number eighteen. "Ahmed," he called.

Surprised that some one on the street knew his name, the man turned toward Pullin. "Do I know you?" he asked, reaching for the knife in his belt, a move hidden from view by his ample trench coat.

"I want that suitcase then you can go," Pullin announced.

Brandt pulled his Beretta and flashed it so that Ahmed could see.

The taxi driver took in the scene and decided he was better off out of there. He put the car into gear and sped away.

Ahmed tried to run towards the taxi, which had enough speed that he never could have reached it.

Brandt clicked off the safety on his Beretta.

Pullin spun towards Brandt to instruct him not to shoot. Before he could raise his hand or speak the Beretta barked loudly, a warning shot that Brandt directed into some trash behind Ahmed.

Upstairs on the third floor having heard the shot Marya pulled aside a curtain to have a look at the scene. She saw three men on the street below. One of them was Brandt, the man she had just left in Istanbul. One looked as if he was working with Brandt. The third was their target, she reckoned. She watched with puzzlement and horror as the target hurled a knife at Brandt and caught him square in the chest.

She grabbed her SIG and slid the window open. Brandt slumped to the street. She took aim and put a single shot in the head of his assailant.

Marya left the window and bounded down the stairs in her bathrobe.

In the foyer, she shouted to Henri finding him cowering under his counter. She ran right by him out into the street. She held the SIG high with two hands out in front of her body, ready to shoot again if necessary.

Brandt and his companion were no where to be seen. The man she had shot lay in a heap, blood gushing from his head. She knelt to feel for a pulse. He was dead. Further down the block a car suddenly sprang from the side of the street and sped away. She decided not to fire after it since Brandt was obviously a passenger.

Trying to make sense of what had just happened Marya suddenly realized the scene the gendarmerie would find. They would find a murdered man and the murderess. They would find Henri, perhaps an eye witness or perhaps an ear witness but nevertheless a witness. Panicky, she ran back up the stairs, dressed, hastily packed her stuff and fled out the back of the building to fade into the Paris night.

In the speeding car, Pullin called to Brandt, "Hang on, son. For God's sake don't leave me." Tears ran down his face as he realized Brandt was dying.

Brandt mustered speech in a small distant sounding voice. "We got the real piece, didn't we?"

Pullin didn't know. He needed to put miles between them and Rue Des Chappelets before he would feel comfortable searching Ahmed's suitcase for *The Hand*. Knowing in his heart that Brandt was not going to make it, he replied with tears in his eyes, "Yes, son. We got the real piece this time."

CHAPTER 49

Marya Lukianov walked as calmly as possible a block away from the crime scene. Suitcase in hand, she paused at a street corner to study the street names. She would need to walk towards the Place de l'Opera. She spotted a taxi and hailed it. The driver pulled to the curb. She directed him to Rue Danou, number five. Her destination was a place called Harry's New York Bar.

On the way, she called a number on her cell phone. A pleasant voice answered, "The Embassy of Canada is closed for the day. Please stay on the line for the night operator."

"Night operator," came another voice this time a live one, "how may I direct your call?"

"To Mister Benjamin, please," Marya responded. There was no 'Mister Benjamin.' That was just a code requesting the CSIS officer in charge.

A moment later a man's voice answered, "Benjamin."

"Please have Mister Ganley meet me at Harry's in twenty minutes," Marya announced.

"Certainly, Miss." The man knew better than to ask who or why. He had an agent that wanted to come in.

Twenty minutes later, Marya sat at a small table in Harry's bar sipping a glass of wine. A man in jeans and a flight jacket approached. He recognized the woman at the table as Marya Lukianov. "Hi there," he said with a jovial smile sliding into a chair beside her, "long-time-no-see."

She forced a broad smile. "Care to join me for a drink?" she asked.

"Sure," he said waving to the bar tender. The bar tender knew Ganley well. He held up a beer glass with a questioning look. Ganley nodded.

They moved to a spot in the rear of the place. After a few minutes of chatter and the raising of glasses, Ganley said, "What's going on, Marya?"

"I just shot a man and I need to de-brief," she half whispered. "I need a place to stay as well."

His face showed no expression. "I take it that this happened at your new place?"

She nodded.

"Stay with us tonight," he said meaning in the building CSIS operated near the embassy.

"Okay," she said, "shall I meet you there?"

Ganley finished the last of his beer. "I think we should walk together," he declared.

Steck received a call from Langley at about midnight Amman time.

"We've opened a new chapter in *Operation Retrieve*, Bob." It was Morgan's voice.

Steck already knew that the thing he had risked everything to retrieve had turned out a fake and that the real one was probably being shipped to Paris. What could it be this time? "After all that's happened it's hard to be surprised anymore," He remarked.

"A man named Ahmed who worked for Al Kafajy was killed tonight in Paris. We think he might have had the prize in his possession when he was shot."

"So," Steck sighed, "we know where it is, at last. Did we wind up with it or do we have a new thief in the picture?"

"This is where it gets crazy, Bob. The thieves were Brandt and some other guy. The man named Ahmed seriously wounded Brandt in the fray. We don't know where Brandt is at the moment because he and his accomplice fled the scene with a suitcase they took from Ahmed. We checked the airlines and found that Ahmed had just flown in from Amman. He had been in Tehran just two days ago."

"So this Ahmed guy most likely had the real *Hand of Mohammed* in that suitcase?" Steck cursed his luck. He had probably been only a few blocks from the prize just last night.

"There's more, Bob." Morgan announced. "The shooter that killed Ahmed was Marya Lukianov."

"Blazes," Steck muttered. "What else?" he asked.

"From the description Marya gave in her de-briefing, we think Brandt's accomplice was Randy Pullin." Morgan paused then announced, "That's all we have at the moment."

"I think that's quite enough," said Steck. "I'll be leaving on the first flight to Paris."

"Why not just come home, Bob? The action's over in Paris. We have folks that can tail Pullin and every immigration officer in the United States will have Pullin's picture before dawn."

Steck started to say 'That doesn't mean they'll get the bugger,' but thought better of it. Besides, he really wanted to see his wife after months on the run. "Okay Ryall, I'll come in tomorrow night."

Three days later Steck showed up at the JUMP team headquarters at seven am. He was filled with that renewed energy that every agent feels after returning home from a long deployment. Spending the past evening and night with Amy had put a certain spring in his step as well.

The whole team was assembled and was already planning the next part of their job.

Mort Lindsley presented a plan to pick-up Paul Roche in Mexico. Agents were already watching Roche's place and would be ready when he finally returned.

Ryall Morgan delivered status on the search for Randy Pullin and Brandt. He was confident that they would finally retrieve *The Hand of Mohammed* within a few days.

They decided to take a break at ten o'clock before hearing from Steck. As the team prepared to make a dash for the cafeteria and mid-morning coffee, Greg Liss asked for the floor.

"I just wanted to announce," he said smiling broadly at Susan who was beaming, "that Susie and I have just become engaged."

Susan took her hand from her pocket, revealing a dazzling diamond ring. She held it up for all to see. The team gave a hearty cheer and general congratulations erupted around the room.

Mort Lindsley joined in congrats, but flashed a look at Morgan, who just smiled. Mort was about to lose a member of the FBI team.

Morgan sidled up to Lindsley. "I'd like your permission to recruit the bride-to be," he said.

Lindsley shrugged. "She'll make a great field agent someday," he said.

"Thanks to you my friend, she already is one," Morgan replied.

After break, Steck was just about to make his presentation. The phone rang.

"Morgan," Ryall answered pushing the speaker button. He supposed it was Bob MacFergus.

"Mister Morgan, there's a Mister Pullin in the lobby," the voice said. "He doesn't have an appointment but insisted you would see him. Shall I ask your secretary to escort him to your office?"

"No, thank you," Morgan replied, I'll be right there."

The silence in the room was palpable. Everyone was waiting for Morgan to speak. Steck broke the spell. "Every immigration agent in the United States had his picture."

Morgan knew that Steck wasn't mocking, rather was giving respect to Pullin's ability to move around at will.

"Take him into custody," urged Lindsley.

Morgan flashed a disdainful look. "I'll be right back," he said as he left the room.

They all waited in silence for about ten minutes until Morgan and Pullin walked in.

Randy Pullin was not his usual self. He spoke quietly and with considerable reserve. "Gentlemen," he paused to take in the faces around the room, "and ladies," he added.

Lindsley was agitated. Morgan put a hand up as if to say "Peace."

"For the past few weeks, my staff and I have been privileged to work side-by-side with some of you." Randy nodded to Steck. "We have worked with you in Saudi Arabia, Yemen, Jordan, Afghanistan, Turkmenistan Iran and Turkey. I'm proud that we had the opportunity to be of service and I acknowledge that we have been well compensated for our services."

"Your guys saved our bacon more than once," Steck asserted. "Thank you for that."

"No sweat," Pullin nodded to Steck. "A few days ago, I realized where the real *Hand of Mohammed* was and that it would be moved long before you guys could get to it."

Lindsley doubted that, but didn't interrupt.

"Three days ago, I went personally to Paris along with one of my officers to intercept the goods." Pullin paused as if what he was about to say was painful.

Steck said it for him. As a mark of respect, he decided to use the title Pullin would like to hear. "Colonel, we're aware of the action you took on Rue des Chappelets. We assume from the fact that you are here alone that Major Brandt has not recovered from that action as yet."

Pullin's face screwed up as if fighting tears. He took a moment to recover then said simply, "Major Brandt is dead." After a pained moment, he continued, "May I assume it was one of your agents that happened on the scene and saved me from the same fate?"

"You may," Morgan said.

"So, *Colonel* Pullin," drawled Mort Lindsley, "did you recover our figurine or not?"

"I did, sir." Pullin reached in his briefcase and removed a golden sack. He opened it and carefully removed the object, placing it on the table. "Here is *The Hand of Mohammed.*"

Greg Liss stared in awe at the thing. Mesmerized, he said "The professor will want to see this."

Lindsley picked it up and held it to the light. "Of course before we believe you we'll have to verify the authenticity of this thing."

"Whatever you wish, sir," Pullin said. Personally I wish I had never been associated with the thing. It has only brought grief to all involved." He closed his brief case and stood up. "I'll be leaving now."

Lindsley started to open his mouth. "I'll walk you out," said Morgan before Lindsley could speak.

Sensing where Lindsley's mind was going," Pullin added, "Don't worry, Steck knows where I'll be."

The two men left the room. Everyone knew exactly what had just gone down. Pullin had done what none of them had been able to do. Without Pullin's people, the operation never could have been mounted, never mind completed successfully. He had made his case for exoneration and was resigned to whatever action ensued.

Lindsley was already at the end point in the reasoning path. If they went after *Free Nation* a lot would be made public that the government could not afford to be made public.

When Morgan returned, He summed up.

"Well," he began, "we now have five actions on the table, in this order: One, we call Bob MacFergus and bring him into the information loop. Two, we go through the diligence of verification about the item through Professor Wigglesworth. Three, we call the President. Four, we find and arrest Paul Roche for the murder of Grayson. Five and last but not least, we find out from Greg and Susan; When's the big day?"

One week later, the President of the United States received an official state visit from The King of Saudi Arabia. They discussed mutual trade relations, the continuing struggle against terror in the world, and several political issues.

At the end of their meeting they posed for the media and gave the usual speeches.

Just prior to The King's departure, the President called him into the oval office for a private talk.

There was a small golden sack resting on the President's desk.

"I have something that belongs to you," the President announced. He reached for the sack. "On behalf of the people of the United States I present to you *The Hand of Mohammed*. Please return it to its rightful place among the national treasures of your country."
